An International Mission to the Moon

FROM THE SAME AUTHOR

The Adventures of Ethel King

An International Mission to the Moon
and Other Stories

by
Jean Petithuguenin

translated, annotated and introduced by
Brian Stableford

A Black Coat Press Book

English adaptation and introduction Copyright © 2016 by Brian Stableford.
Cover illustration Copyright © 2016 Jean-Pierre Normand.

Visit our website at www.blackcoatpress.com

ISBN 978-1-61227-466-9. First Printing. January 2016. Published by Black Coat Press, an imprint of Hollywood Comics.com, LLC, P.O. Box 17270, Encino, CA 91416. All rights reserved. Except for review purposes, no part of this book may be reproduced or transmitted in any form or by any means, electronic or mechanical, including photocopying, recording, or by any information storage and retrieval system, without permission in writing from the publisher. The stories and characters depicted in this novel are entirely fictional. Printed in the United States of America.

TABLE OF CONTENTS

Introduction 7
AN INTERNATIONAL MISSION TO THE MOON 15
THE GREAT CURRENT 119
THE SECRET OF THE INCAS 225

Introduction

Une Mission internationale dans la lune by Jean Petithuguenin, here translated as "An International Mission to the Moon," was originally published as a feuilleton serial under the title "Une Mission dans la lune" in the *Journal des Voyages* between July and September 1926. It was reprinted in book form under the fuller title by Jules Tallandier in 1933. With the exception of a few paragraphs of material additional to the book version—which were probably cut from the original to fit that section more accurately to the pagination of the *Journal des Voyages*—the two texts are identical, save for a few trivial alterations. Those include the introduction of extra chapter breaks in the book version and the alteration of some chapter titles; the correction of an arithmetical error; the addition of a more recent reference to a footnote; and the amendment of a series of annoying omissions in the feuilleton version inflicted by the magazine's editor, who decided to run a competition for readers, inviting them to deduce the omitted words, all of which were proper names or technical terms.

The second novella in the present volume, *Le Grand courant*, here translated as "The Great Current," was serialized in *Science et Voyages* in 1931 prior to being reprinted by Tallandier in 1932. The periodical in which it first appeared was a popular science magazine whose proprietor attempted to combine the long-standing appeal of the *Journal des Voyages* with much wider scientific interests, with the side-effect that the fiction it published in feuilleton form became far more imaginatively ambitious than the stodgier Vernian materials of its predecessor, including a good deal of futuristic and interplanetary fiction closely resembling the fiction that was currently being produced for the recently-born American science fiction magazines.

The third story completing the collection, *Le Secret des Incas*, here translated as "The Secret of the Incas" was reprinted by Tallandier in 1934 in the same format as the other two items, after a prior serialization in 1926-27. It could easily have appeared in the *Journal de Voyages*, and its didactic inclusions seem to have been designed for that periodical, but it is sufficiently conventional as an adventure story to have appeared in any one of several magazines of the period that routinely featured "geographical fiction" of the kind that Jules Verne had done so much to popularize and standardize.

Jean Petithuguenin (1878-1939) attempted to make a career writing for the theater, having two one-act plays produced in 1902, before switching media and becoming a prolific writer of popular fiction. Most of his early work consisted of feuilletons and part-works, including a long series featuring the adventures of *Stoerte-Becker, le roi de l'océan* [Stoerte-Becker, King of the Ocean] (1910-1913). He was one of many writers involved in chronicling the adventures of the detective Nick Carter, a character from American "dime novels" and pulp magazines, who took on an independent life in French popular fiction as a result of the popularity of imported silent movies featuring the character. In the same vein, Petithuguenin chronicled the adventures of *Ethel King: le Nick Carter féminin* [Ethel King, the female Nick Carter] (1913),[1] which is perhaps more interesting in its employment of a female detective in an era when they were still thin on the ground.

Inevitably, Petithuguenin's career was severely disrupted by the Great War, but he was one of many writers who turned their hands to writing propagandistic fiction for morale-building purposes in 1917, when he began the "*Patrie*" series of novelettes featuring heroic French exploits during key incidents of the war. He also published a considerable number of

---

[1] Available in a Black Coat Press edition, ISBN 978-1-61227-233-7.

love stories in booklet form in 1917-18, most of which had probably appeared previously in feuilleton form. When the war was over he continued to produce downmarket genre fiction on a lavish scale until the early 1930s, including numerous movie novelizations. As well as love stories and crime stories he made occasional ventures into adventure fiction, sometimes with a supernatural component, and occasionally attempted more respectable endeavors, most notably his account of *La Vie tragique de Marguerite d'Anjou, reine d'Angleterre* [The Tragic Life of Margaret of Anjou, Queen of England] (1928).

Within that overall pattern, Petithuguenin's two ventures into speculative fiction, undertaken relatively late in his career, are strikingly anomalous. Although produced as feuilletons for relatively downmarket publications, they are both highly distinctive and original. Although neither has any great literary merit, and in narrative terms they are spectacularly awkward by comparison with his usual fluency, but that awkwardness is a by-product of their remarkable imaginative ambition and earnest didactic intent. The author's interest in technological advancement and the possibility of space travel was obviously real, and also well-informed; he was, in consequence, one of the first experimenters in France with what would later come to be called in America "hard science fiction": fiction supposedly based on real technological possibilities, imagined and described with appropriate technical detail and discipline.

Une Mission internationale dans la lune is particularly interesting within the context of the evolution of speculative fiction because it is one of a group of novels produced in several different countries that attempted to produce realistic accounts of a voyage to the moon effected by means of rocket propulsion—or, as Petithuguenin puts it, "reaction engines." The notion that such devices were the only practical means of sending projectiles into space was initially popularized by the Russian Konstantin Tsiolkovsky, who published an essay advancing that argument in 1903, and then attempted to popularize it further in a novel, *Vne zemli* (serial version 1916; book version 1920; tr. as *Outside the Earth*). Tsiolkovsky's endeavors and those of experimenters such as the American Robert Goddard and the German Hermann Oberth—whose nonfictional *Die Rakete zu den Planetenräumen* [By Rocket into Interplanetary Space] (1923) was followed by the fictional popularization *Der Schuss ins All* (1925; tr. as *The Shot into Infinity*) by his friend Otto Willi Gail—resulted in the foundation in the mid-1920s of societies in Russia, America, Germany, France and England dedicated to propagandizing the possibility of space travel by means of rockets.

It is not surprising that the members of those societies routinely opted to use fiction as a means of propaganda because almost all of them had initially been inspired by works of fiction, most especially Jules Verne's *De la terre à la lune* (1865) and its sequel *Autour de la lune* (1870), initially translated into English in the omnibus *From the Earth to the Moon...and a Trip Around It*. Verne's archetypal novel had prompted previous imitations in France, most notably the first volume of *Aventures extraordinaires d'un savant russe* (1888)[2] by Georges Le Faure and Henri de Graffigny, the sequel by another hand *Un Monde inconnu* (1896 but written in the early 1880s)[3] by "Pierre de Sélènes" and *Les Allemands sur Vénus* (1913)[4] by "André Mas."

The pseudonymous Mas appears to have been a member of a propagandist group formed in advance of the 1920s rocket societies, and Petithuguenin might have known him; he certainly knew of his somewhat esoteric novelette, because he takes time out in the text of his own novella to explain why the

---

[2] Available in a Black Coat Press omnibus edition, *The Extraordinary Adventures of a Russian Scientist Across the Solar system,* ISBN 978-1-934543-81-8 and 978-1-934543-82-5.

[3] Available in a Black Coat Press edition, *An Unknown Word*, ISBN 978-1-61227-302-0.

[4] Available in a Black Coat Press edition, *The German on Venus*, ISBN 978-1-934543-56-6.

unusual method of space travel proposed therein would not work. Petithuguenin also explains why Verne's giant cannon, the *Columbiad*, would not be practical and why the modification to that method suggested by "Pierre de Sélènes" would not work either, although Verne is the only other author he mentions by name.

Although *Une Mission internationale dans la lune* was not the first quasi-documentary work of fiction popularizing the notion of traveling to the moon by rocket, therefore, it was the one with the most substantial literary pedigree, and it is also the most realistic. Although it seems naïve now that we have the actual mission to the moon with which to compare it, it is nevertheless far closer to that eventual reality than the even more primitive efforts of Tsiolkovsky and Gail. In spite of the Vernian precedent, however, it was something of a departure for the *Journal des Voyages*—which had previously steered clear of interplanetary fiction—to publish it, and its unusual nature prompted the periodical's editor to supplement the first episode with a justificatory note insisting on the story's rational plausibility and educational value, the competition to identify the missing words being a rather eccentric method of emphasizing the latter claim. Petithuguenin's work thus became an interesting experiment in "drama-documentary" format, perhaps too unusual to garner much approval in its own day, but now recognizable as a fascinating, if not entirely successful, literary experiment.

Le Grand courant is similarly experimental, and even less successful, although arguably all the more interesting for it. It illustrates very clearly the difficulties faced by writers eager to use fictional means of addressing questions of technical possibility and the philosophical issues surrounding the existential consequences of far-reaching technological progress. The first chapter includes a long speech on the necessity of developing new sources of energy to replace the fossil fuels that are inevitably in limited supply, and possible means of capturing solar radiation more directly—a topic that has only become far more urgent since 1932—whereas the third chapter is almost entirely taken up with scientific discourse. The attempt to frame these essays with a plot that is part love story and part "yellow peril" melodrama is extremely awkward, especially in the abrupt variations of its narrative pace and narrative distance, but such clumsiness is inevitable when writers move into new narrative territory for the first time, at least when they do not possess the exceptional brilliance that Jules Verne brought to that kind of thematic interweaving.

Many writers for the early American science fiction magazines were obliged to confront the same problems of narrative strategy that Petithuguenin did in constructing *Le Grand courant*, and many were equally maladroit in coping with them. Many would not have been able to publish that kind of work without the protective umbrella of the science fiction magazines' specific agenda, and the same is true of Petithuguenin, who would not have been able to publish *Le Grand courant* as a feuilleton anywhere other than *Science et Voyages*, and Tallandier would surely not have published the book version without the encouragement of that former publication. Writers of generic science fiction soon learned to develop the special narrative techniques required to make such endeavors more "reader-friendly," and modern readers now expect that particular kind of sophistication, but pioneering work like *Le Grand courant* still retains a certain primitive charm as well as deserving respect for its vaulting ambition, and it is a fascinating historical specimen.

Le Secret des Incas makes an interesting comparison precisely because it does not have to tackle the narrative difficulties that arose from the uniquely challenging aspects of the other two novellas, and is thus permitted a much smoother, faster-paced and coherent deployment of standard tropes. It is far more reader-friendly than its predecessors precisely because it is so amicably familiar, restricting its didactic intrusions to the kinds of "local color" necessary in adventure stories set in remote places, and drawing economically on history, ethnology and mythology by way of decoration. The story is a conventional Vernian potboiler—but it is worth bearing in mind that if such bland materials had not served to keep the Vernian pot boiling in such a lively manner for such a long period of time, the market space would not have existed for more ambitious and exotic ventures such as *Une mission internationale dans la lune* and *Le Grand courant*, each of which was unusually enterprising in its day, and can now be seen as significant stepping-stones in the progressive evolution of imaginative fiction.

The translation of *Une Mission internationale dans la lune* was made primarily from a photocopy of the Tallandier text made by Jean-Marc Lofficier, from an original supplied by Marc Madouraud; they also supplied a copy of the feuilleton version for the purposes of comparison, and I am greatly indebted to them for their efforts. The translations of *Le Grand courant* and *Le Secret des Incas* were made from the versions of the Tallandier editions reproduced on the Bibliothèque Nationale's *gallica* website.

Brian Stableford

AN INTERNATIONAL MISSION TO THE MOON

I. Wisdom or Madness?

There was a large crowd that day on the Delaware Quay in Philadelphia, on the edge of pier 49, alongside which a steamship, the *Montgomery*, was moored, with a strange object in tow.

About three miles wide at that point, between Philadelphia and Camden—the annex of the great American port—the river was covered with small boats laden with curiosity-seekers, which were hampering the maneuvers of the cargo-ships and ferries.

Everyone was pointing at the bizarre object that the *Montgomery*, whose engines were under pressure, was about to take out to sea. It was somewhat reminiscent of a powerful submarine about a hundred meters long, which, to judge by the superior part emerging from the water, affected the form of a long rectangular parallelepiped, tapered at the rear and terminated at the front by a rounded section like the head of a fish. The surface, entirely smooth, was coated with a kind of blue varnish on which seven capital letters were displayed comprising the word SELENIT. At the front, over about a fifth of the length of the machine, a number of small portholes could be seen, perfectly fitted, with neither hollows nor projections.

To the right and the left of the upper section, the rounded prow broadened out; it formed swellings over the rest of the side wall, which were prolonged at the rear by tubes some fifteen meters long, like large-caliber cannons, slightly oblique relative to the *Selenit*'s axis. The spectators who were close enough, and whose gaze pierced the surface of the river, were able to see other similar tubes disposed over the inferior surface. Those lateral cannons where welded along their entire length to the walls of the vessel by strong metal bulkheads that met the hull at an angle, in such a fashion that the entire apparatus resembled an enormous crossbow bolt.

The flanks of the *Selenit* were, moreover, partly masked by large pieces of wood fixed with cables, to which a series of large cylindrical floats were moored. It was easy to conclude that the machine was too heavy to float unaided and that it needed to be buoyed up to prevent it from sinking.

People endowed with good eyesight were also able to remark a thin circular line on the superior wall toward the front, and four solid handgrips that revealed the presence of a screw-hatch.

On the quay, and in the boats laden with sightseers, conversations were in full swing. Even the most sober individuals could not help feeling a considerable emotion at the thought that ten men would soon be enclosed in the metal monster, in order to attempt the most extraordinary adventure ever: a voyage to the moon.

For more than a year, that great project had occupied the minds of the entire world. Sufficient publicity had been generated by certain clauses in the will of Elie Spruce, the celebrated founder of the naval shipyard at Camden that bears his name.

Elie Spruce had been struck by the studies of certain scientists, which had indicated the possibility of sending a projectile to the moon in conditions such that humans could be enclosed within it without the risk of being killed by shocks either on departure or arrival. He had, in particular, retained the idea of Monsieur Esnault-Pelterie, who had advocated the employment of an apparatus propelled by the recoil of a fulminating powder.[5]

To tell the truth, Esnault-Pelterie concluded that in the present state of knowledge, the solution to the problem, although theoretically possible, could not yet be realized in practice. He observed that the most powerful modern explosives do not yield, for a given weight, the energy necessary for the propulsion of a vehicle designed to accomplish the journey from the Earth to the Moon.

Elie Spruce, however, did not accept the conclusions of the expert engineer without reservations. He made the observation that the latter limited the consumption of explosive arbitrarily, in admitting that a vehicle weighing one metric ton cannot burn more than three hundred kilograms of powder, less than one third of its weight, because, according to Esnault-Pelterie, at least seven hundred kilos has to be devoted to the construction of a habitable vehicle.

Now, the proportion is notoriously insufficient to oblige the projectile to quit the Earth.

Elie Spruce envisaged the problem in another fashion:

Given a mass of fulminating explosive capable of burning in its entirety and constituted in such a way that the energy disengaged by its deflagration propels it vertically as it draws away from the Earth, at what moment will it have acquired a velocity sufficient to escape the globe's attraction, and what will be, at that moment, the proportion of the mass that has not yet burned?

---

[5] Author's note: "*Considerations sur les résultats de l'allègement indéfini des moteurs. Journal de Physique*, mars 1913. See also *L'Astronautique*, 1930." The second reference, newly added to the book version, was Robert Esnault-Pelterie's first book on the subject of space travel; born in 1881, he was one of the most significant French pioneers of aeronautics and an experimenter with liquid-fueled rockets, his research in the latter field obtaining military funding aimed at the development of long-range ballistic missiles.

It is evident that that proportion could be replaced by incombustible materials, and it would be the latter that would constitute the useful weight of the vehicle. It is of little consequence that it is small, or even tiny; that would have no other consequence than obliging the constructors to employ an enormous quantity of explosive. For example, if it were necessary for them to consume nine hundred and ninety-nine kilos to launch a useful weight of one kilo, they would be far from the proportion of three hundred to seven hundred fixed by Monsieur Esnault-Pelterie, but they could nevertheless send a one-ton vehicle to the Moon by attaching it to nine hundred and ninety-nine tons of powder.

Elie Spruce's calculations, established on that basis, had, in fact, demonstrated to him the necessity of using a colossal mass of explosive in order to detach from the Earth a vehicle provided with all the indispensable resources, ensure its return from the moon, and procure, in addition, the energy necessary to decelerate during its descents on the Moon and the Earth.

The great American constructor drew up the plans of a machine capable of undertaking the voyage, but illness had not left him the time to put his project into execution. Feeling that he was nearing his end, he had instituted a legacy of six million dollars destined to finance a mission to the Moon.

That was what René Brifaut, a young French reporter for a major scientific periodical, explained to his wife, with whom he had obtained a passage aboard the *Montgomery*, among other rare privileges.

"Old Spruce had no children who might have complained about his generosity in favor of science. He made a grand gesture in the hope of immortalizing his name."

"You call that a grand gesture?" replied Madeleine Brifaut. "Personally, I think it's more like the act of a madman. After all, what's the purpose of such an enterprise?"

"It's necessary to think that it might be useful for something, since the scientists of the entire world, united in conference, have decided to profit from the Spruce legacy to organize an international mission to the moon. Believe me, it won't be uninteresting to go and see what's happening on our satellite."

"They're doubtless proposing to colonize it," retorted the young woman, ironically.

"It's easy to mock, Madeleine, but suppose they find an abundance of some very precious substance on the Moon, such as radium, which might help to ameliorate the conditions of life on our planet."

"It would be necessary to exploit it."

"It would doubtless be possible to bring back appreciable quantities. A hundred kilos of radium would metamorphose humanity."

"I'd rather leave the care of going to look for it to others."

"Naturally, it's no job for a woman, but I, for example, would be very glad to depart in the *Selenit*."

"It's got you too?"

"You didn't reproach me or my exploratory voyages in Africa and Tibet."

"Well, it's not the same thing."

"No…that was probably more dangerous."

"René, you're not being serious. I greatly admire the ten audacious men who are going to embark in the *Selenit*, but in much the same way that I admire Don Quixote when he charges at windmills."

"Seriously, Madeleine, I think those men, far from being mad, are giving proof of the greatest wisdom. They're going to accomplish a marvelous voyage, and for the price of their bravery, they'll receive a fortune, because Elie Spruce's legacy allows each of them a hundred thousand dollars. I sincerely regret not bring able to join them."

"That's all we need! I wouldn't let you go."

"There's no longer any question of me going, since there are only ten places and they're all taken. But you'll admit that if I'd been able to earn more than three million francs in a month, it wouldn't be a bad deal."

"You really believe, then, that those poor devils will arrive safe and sound on the Moon?"

"Certainly."

"And that, supposing they find the means of living there for a time, they'll succeed in coming back?"

"Yes."

"And that they won't be killed when they fall to Earth?"

"Everything has been anticipated in order to avoid accidents, either going or returning."

"Not everyone can be as convinced as you are, since it appears that they had considerable difficulty finding ten volunteers for the charming excursion in question."

"That only proves that the majority of men have a wife or a mother who doesn't want them to run the risk."

The young people had remained until then slightly isolated at the extremity of the deck of the *Montgomery*, from which, leaning on the bulwark side by side, they were watching the crowd, and the *Selenit*, moored to the flank of the cargo-vessel. There were a hundred people on board, delegates of scientific societies and correspondents of major newspapers. The government of the United States and the diplomatic corps were represented.

There was a movement in the crowd, and the members of the mission were seen arriving, accompanied by a few important people. They were all young and robust men. In spite of what Madeleine Brifaut thought, the number of candidates had been relatively large, but the commission charged with the recruitment of the lunar explorer had proceeded with a severe selection process. The candidates had to satisfy various demands: to possess a physical resistance proof against anything; to be experienced in sports and mountaineering; to have taken part in as many major missions of exploration as possible. They were also required to have superior intellectual faculties and advanced scientific knowledge. In fact, the members that the commission had designated had been nominated by the major scientific institutions of various nations.

The leader of the mission was a Dane named Scherrebek, who had been made famous by several expeditions to the North Pole.

As it had been necessary not to neglect practical details, only English speakers had been accepted, for it was indispensable that all the members of the crew understood one another.

Brifaut identified the explorers to his wife.

"The one marching directly behind Scherrebek is Dessoye, the Frenchman; to his right is the Englishman Galston, and to his left the German Lang.[6] Then comes the American, Garrick, between the Italian, Bojardo and the Spaniard, Espronceda. The dark fellow beside a naval officer in the Brazilian, Dr. Uberaba, Finally there's the smallest of the party, the Japanese Kito, beside the Belgian Goffoël, who is, by contrast, a giant."

Brifaut frayed a passage all the way to his compatriot, Dessoye, in order to congratulate him and introduce him to his young wife.

"I admire your valor, Monsieur," Madeleine declared, "and I have no doubt that you'll succeed in your audacious enterprise."

"Yes, Madame, we'll succeed. In a month, when we return to Earth, people will be able to say that humans have conquered the Moon."

---

[6] Although the present novella was serialized three years before the completion of Fritz Lang's film *Frau im Mond* (*The Girl in the Moon*) and a year before the foundation of the *Verein für Raumschiffart* [Society for Space Travel], which collaborated in the design of the rocket featured in the film, Willy Ley and Hermann Oberth had already been consulted as advisers for the projected movie, and it was known that it was planned as a follow-up to Lang's *Metropolis* (1926), so the fact that the German representative is named Lang is probably not a coincidence.

When he found himself alone with his wife again, Brifaut teased her ironically. "Rascal! You paid that fellow compliments of which you don't believe a word."

"Could I tell him that he won't come back? If only I still had some hope of preventing him from running to his death! But I know full well that I wouldn't be able to shake his confidence. Anyway, how could it be admissible that a Frenchman would pass for a coward by recoiling in circumstances where foreigners are marching without a tremor."

The young woman had pronounced the final words with a patriotic pride that brought a smile of satisfaction to her husband's lips.

The members of the mission had stopped, grouped around their leader. The delegate of the President of the Federal Republic, standing facing him with a piece of paper in his hand, was preparing to make a speech. The guests aboard the cargo ship formed a circle.

The officials had, at any rate, decided that the ceremony would be as brief and as simple as possible, for it was necessary to avoid weakening, and bidding the men departing for the Moon farewells like those of men condemned to death.

To tell the truth, apart from the members of the expedition and René Brifaut, no one aboard the *Montgomery* believed that the lunar explorers would ever come back. Even those who had participated in the organization of the mission, however, when they thought that they were sending ten men to their death, had calmed the revolts of their conscience by telling themselves that they were the faithful executors of the last will of Elie Spruce. If the expedition ended in catastrophe, the testator alone would bear the responsibility.

After the speech by the President's delegate, they heard a statement from the director of Mount Wilson Observatory, who had been charged, with two astronomers, to observe the departure of the *Selenit*.

Then, by virtue of a special derogation in favor of the ten heroes, who already no longer belonged to the Earth, bottles of champagne were uncorked and the fact that alcohol was banned in America was forgotten for a few minutes.

The important officials returned to the shore; all that remained aboard the *Montgomery*, with the members of the expedition, were a dozen newspaper correspondents, including Brifaut and his wife, and a small group of scientists.

The ship made ready to sail. The captain had displayed the flags of the ten nations represented in the mission.

The *Montgomery* moved off under the effort of her propellers, while the crowd cheered. Mariners climbing on to the *Selenit* busied themselves with putting it in a good position to be guided in the wake of the ship. A tug, which looked like a dwarf beside the *Montgomery*, had moored its prow to the rear end of the *Selenit*, and was also steering the machine, which, thus maintained at both ends, was running no risk of capsizing.

The banks of the Delaware began to file past before he eyes of the passengers.

"Where are we going, exactly?" Madeleine asked.

"Beyond the Bermudas to the mid-Atlantic Ocean, about the twenty-fifth degree of north latitude, in the abyssal zone were soundings reveal a depth of several thousand meters. It's there that the *Selenit* will be immersed. Copiously ballasted by masses of lead, the apparatus, constructed to withstand enormous pressures, externally and internally, will descend to a great depth. Deballasted, by means of an unhooking mechanism, it will take up a vertical position and rise upwards at an increasing velocity. The reaction engines will be engaged and when the *Selenit* reaches the surface of the water, it will emerge at a speed of about fifty meters a second."

"Is that all!" said Madeleine. "If it travels at that speed, it won't get anywhere near the Moon."

"So it will accelerate its velocity thereafter. But it can't go faster than the figure I've indicated in the water without having to overcome an enormous resistance, which would require an exaggerated expenditure of energy."

The *Montgomery* and the tug that was following her, with the *Selenit* between them, continued to excite the curiosity of the population. Groups of people were seen here and there, posted on the banks, and boats drew closer. Level with Greenwich Pier, at the point where the river broadens out to form Delaware Bay, a large dirigible of the Federal Army flew over the convoy and released banners that made a multicolored swarm in the sky. At the mouth of the estuary, when the *Montgomery* doubled Cape May, a cruiser saluted her departure with a twenty-one gun salvo.

Madeleine reflected on what her husband had said.

"The fashion in which the *Selenit* will be lifted into space is still an enigma to me," she observed. "I don't understand what force will impel it since it has no propellers and, in any case, won't be able to make use of the terrestrial atmosphere once it's outside it."

"I'll have the time to explain a great many things during the six-day cruise we'll have to accomplish before reaching the *Selenit*'s immersion point. But here's Dessoye coming toward us; we'll ask him to give us a little talk on reaction motors."

The French member of the expedition was, indeed, approaching, glad of the opportunity to talk to compatriots, and he had heard Brifaut's last reflection.

"It's with pleasure, Madame," he said, "that I'll satisfy your curiosity. I was able to remark just now that you're not as convinced as you'd like to be of the success of our enterprise. I don't despair of being able to communicate my confidence to you during the few days of the crossing....

"You were very young fifteen years ago. Perhaps, however you remember an acrobat who carried out some curious jumping exercises in that epoch. Equipped with two dumb-bells, he gathered himself, and leapt, for example, into the middle of a vat filled with water. The spectators had the impression that he was about to take a bath, but at the moment when his feet touched the surface, he threw the dumb-bells forcefully behind him, and was seen, animated by a new impetus, to rise up in order to come down further on, beyond the vat.

"That exploit, which seemed enigmatic to many people, was an application of an elementary principle of mechanics: action is equal to reaction."

"I know that."

"Good. Knowing, on the other hand, that the acceleration imparted by the same force on different masses is inversely proportional to the masses...."

"Wait—I'm no longer following."

"An example will illustrate it more clearly to your imagination. Let's suppose that by deploying a certain effort, I throw a weight of five kilos at a velocity of four meters a second. If, deploying exactly the same force, I then throw a weight of ten kilos, I can only impart a velocity of two meters per second to it. The force remaining the same, and the mass doubled, the initial velocity is reduced by half. Well, when our jumper threw behind him a weight of ten kilos, at a velocity of seven meters a second, for example, his body, which weighed seventy kilos, was, by reaction, propelled forwards with a speed of one meter per second, which permitted him to lift himself up and overshoot the obstacle into which he had been on the point of falling."

"I understand that," said Madeleine, "but it doesn't appear to me to have any connection with your reaction engine."

"You'll see that it does. The recoil of a firearm is a phenomenon of exactly the same order as that of the acrobatic feat of which I've just reminded you. The rifle that launches a ten-gram bullet at an initial velocity of three hundred meters a second is impelled in the opposite direction at a speed that is reduced by as much as its weight is more considerable. If, for example, it weights fifteen kilos, a mass fifteen hundred times that of a ten-gram bullet, the initial velocity of the recoil will be the fifteen-hundredth part of three hundred meters a second—which is to say, twenty centimeters a second.

"Now imagine a vehicle stationary on a road or a railway track, on which a cannon has been mounted, pointing along the road or track. If the cannon is fired, the vehicle, obedient to the effect of the recoil, will be set in motion in a direction opposite to that of the projectiles."

"Is that how you intend to launch the *Selenit*?"

"Exactly."

"In that case, I think the condition of spectator will be singularly dangerous. You're going to bombard us copiously when you set off for the Moon."

"Don't worry! The tubes of our reaction engine—or, if you prefer, our cannons—don't launch solid projectiles. They only expel the gases of the explosions."

"There won't be any more recoil, then?"

"Yes there will, because it's only the mass of the material that's important. A hundred kilos of gas have exactly the same effect as a hundred kilos of cast iron. Thus, artificial rockets rise into space without ejecting any solid particles. The *Selenit* behaves like an enormous rocket."

"But why so many complications? Why not simply have the *Selenit* launched by a monstrous cannon, as Jules Verne imagined?"

"It's true that the construction of a cannon like Jules Verne's Columbiad, able to fire a projectile with an initial velocity between twelve and fifteen thousand meters a second, would be relatively easy to build with the means of modern industry, but Jules Verne had forgotten one thing, which is that the human organism isn't solid enough to resist an acceleration of more than ten meters a second. A man who was forced to pass abruptly from immobility to a velocity of twelve meters a second would be killed as surely as if a weight of a hundred tons were to be dropped on his head. In reality, Michel Ardan, Barbicane and Nicholl would have been flattened like pancakes on the bottom of their bullet."

"But couldn't one imagine a very long cannon, which would launch the projectile progressively by successive deflagrations?"[7]

"Impracticable, my dear Madame. Do you know how long such a cannon would have to be in order always to remain within that uncrossable limit of ten meters of acceleration per second?"

"Several kilometers no doubt."

"More than seven thousand kilometers[8]—about a sixtieth of the Earth's circumference."

"How has that been calculated?" asked Madeleine, amazed.

"The problem is extremely simple," Dessoye replied, taking a notebook from his pocket. He stated to set out figures in pencil.

"The projectile has to travel ten meters in the first second, twenty in the second, thirty in the third, and so on, increasing by ten meters a second every time until it reaches a velocity of twelve thousand meters a second. It must, therefore, travel in the cannon a number of meters represented by the following sum…."

Dessoye put his notebook before the eyes of the young woman, who read the formula:

$$10 + 20 + 30 + \text{etc.} \ldots + 12,000.$$

"I've only written the first three terms of the sum and the last," he continued, because there are twelve hundred of them. But you can easily imagine those that I've replaced by the dots, since it's sufficient to increased each on by ten in passing

---

[7] This is the modification imagined by "Pierre de Sélènes" for use in *Un Monde inconnu*.

[8] In the feuilleton version this figure is given as fourteen thousand, because of the arithmetical error in the calculation that follows, for which an erratum notice was subsequently issued, after a reader had pointed it out.

on to the next. Such a sum is what mathematicians call an arithmetical progression—or, at least, the sequence of terms without the plus signs constitutes such a progression. Now, nothing is easier than to calculate the sum of the terms of an arithmetical progression, and, in the particular case in point, the sum of our twelve hundred numbers is given by this formula...."

Dessoye had inscribed new figures, which he showed to Madeleine.

$$S + \frac{(10 + 12{,}000) \times 1{,}200}{2}$$

"That makes exactly 7,206,000 meters. And the circumference of the Earth is, as you know, forty million meters. You understand now why one has to renounce constructing a cannon or a launch-path."

"But hasn't it been proposed," said René Brifaut, "to launch a hollow projectile to the Moon by means of a huge wheels whose movement is gradually accelerated, and which will act in the fashion of a sling?[9] The projectile would be detached automatically when it had acquired sufficient velocity."

"The idea is ingenious, but it doesn't take account of centrifugal force, and it's sufficient to recall what becomes of substances subjected to the action of industrial centrifuges to anticipate the fate reserved for the passengers in such a projectile."

"I understand," said Madeleine. "All that remains, in fact, is the system of the rocket, which you've just described to me. But it's necessary, in that case, for the *Selenit* to carry a large quantity of explosive."

"An enormous quantity, my dear Madame, and that's what creates all the difficulty of the enterprise, for the *Selenit*,

---

[9] This is the method proposed and illustrated by "André Mas" in *Les Allemands sur Vénus*.

as you see it, is obliged, for a useful weight of about a hundred tons, passengers included, to carry ten thousand tons of explosive. To store such a formidable charge, the *Selenit* had to be given that length of a hundred meters, of which only a fifth is occupied by the accommodation and its dependencies, the control room and the engine room."

"Why that colossal mass of powder? I don't think that such a vast proportion is necessary to launch a shell."

"No—but the shell, which acquires its maximum velocity instantaneously, has no need to carry its explosive with it. The *Selenit*, on the contrary, whose velocity has to be augmented progressively, and which is constructed on the principle of the rocket, has to contain the charge whose progressive deflagration will draw it further on continuously.

"Now, if it requires in these conditions, for example, ten kilos of explosive to bring after twelve hundred seconds, a one-kilo projectile to a velocity of twelve thousand meters a second, one has to add a certain charge to propel those ten kilos of explosive in their turn—but that second charge requires a third, and so on. It's because of that that one is required to employ an enormous quantity of powder to launch a relative small useful weight.

"On the other hand, it's necessary to keep a reserve of explosive to slow down the fall on arrival on the Moon, and to avoid a brutal contact with our satellite. Finally—and this is the most important point of all—enough powder must remain on arrival to permit the projectile to depart again from the Moon and land without encumbrance on our globe, for there wouldn't be any point in going go the Moon if we weren't certain of being able to come back."

"Indeed. I admire you for having that certainty, in spite of the extraordinary difficulties of your expedition, and the risks to which you'll remain exposed, in spite of everything."

"I'll prove to you, Madame, before the departure of the *Selenit*, that we've anticipated the slightest details of our attempt too fully for there to be any shocks to fear."

At that moment Captain Scherrebek, the leader of the mission, approached. He had himself introduced to Madame Brifaut.

"We have superb weather," he said, "and a smooth sea. The conditions are ideal for our departure. I also intend to take advantage of it to allow the few friends who have consented to accompany us in the last week of our sojourn down here to visit the *Selenit*. As there isn't much free space in the *Selenit*, we'll organize several visits, only conducting ten people at a time. The first will be this afternoon after lunch. Would you care, Madame, to do us the honor of taking part, with your husband?"

"With the greatest pleasure, Captain."

II. A Farewell Banquet[10]

During lunch, at which Captain Murray, the commandant of the *Montgomery*, presided, the conversation, as one can imagine, revolved around the Moon, the *Selenit*, and the chances that the explorers had of reaching their target safe and sound and getting back again.

In spite of the optimism that the guests were required to affect, it would have been easy for a perspicacious observer to divine that, apart from the members of the mission, the individuals present did not, in general, sincerely believe in the success of the extraordinary endeavor.

Madeleine Brifaut, the only woman on board, occupied the place of honor beside the commandant, facing Captain Scherrebek. To her right she had Dr. Lang, the German member of the mission. He was a tall fellow with a short-cropped moustache and a shaven head, who paid a great deal of attention to his neighbor.

As they were discussing the possible existence of an atmosphere on the surface of the Moon, the director of Mount Wilson Observatory took it upon himself to summarize present thinking on the subject.

"One never observes clouds on the Moon," he said, "but that's not sufficient to demonstrate that our satellite is absolutely devoid of an atmosphere, for water might not exist either in liquid masses or in droplets suspended in the form of mist when the pressure falls below a certain limit, and if there are gases at the surface of the Moon their pressure can't exceed one or two thousandths of that of our atmosphere. However, the observation of the occultation of stars has demonstrated that the refraction at the edge of the Moon, weak as it

---

[10] In the feuilleton version this chapter bears the title given to the subsequent chapter in the book version and the next chapter-break is omitted.

is, isn't completely absent. The deviation of the star's radiance varies between one and two seconds of angle."

"What does occultation mean?" Madeleine whispered, leaning toward her neighbor.

"It is, Madame," Dr. Lang replied, "the phenomenon produced when the Moon passes between a star and the Earth and prevents us from seeing the star, before which it forms a screen."

"One is led to admit," the astronomer continued, "that a lunar atmosphere exists whose density is about nine hundred times weaker than that of the Earth. It remains improbable that it is composed like ours. It is supposed that carbon dioxide is dominant there, especially in the seas."

"Madeleine had recourse once again to her neighbor's science. "The seas?" she murmured, astonished. "Hasn't he just said that there can't be any water on the Moon?"

"The name of 'sea,' Madame, is thus improperly chosen. Ancient astronomers, who had observed dark patches on the surface of the Moon, mistook them for large expanses of water and gave them names that modern astronomers have conserved by virtue of a respect for tradition, but their error was recognized a long time ago. It is known today that the seas of the Moon are simply vast depressions, whose dark hue is nevertheless not easy to explain. There are great divergences of opinion on that subject."

"Isn't it just the color of the ground entering into play?"

"No, because it happens that some seas appear darker when they're more fully illuminated by the sun."

"That is, in fact, odd."

"There must be elements there that absorb light, more fully the more intense it is. We know of only one substance on Earth capable of producing that effect, at least on a large scale, and that's chlorophyll, the green substance of vegetation. As it has also been remarked that the lunar seas often have a greenish tint, some astronomers have concluded that they're covered in a kind of vegetation."

"There might be forests on the Moon, then?"

"Forests no—but perhaps something analogous to moss or lichen, which can live at the expense of the soil and the carbon dioxide contained in the almost imponderable atmosphere."

Meanwhile, at the other end of the table, people were also discussing the possibility of life on the surface of our satellite.

"So," asked Brifaut, "you don't believe, Professor, that there are animate beings up there?"

"Don't put words into my mouth," protested the director of the Observatory. "It's certain that none of our terrestrial animals could live on the Moon, but it's not scientifically demonstrated that living beings organized in a manner completely different from those we know couldn't adapt to the special conditions of our satellite. Why, for example, shouldn't particular organisms extract from elements in the soil the oxygen that terrestrial animals obtain from the atmosphere? Any why shouldn't there be animate creatures that are even capable of doing without oxygen and deriving their vital energy from some other substance?"

"But how will the members of the mission, who are created to live on the Earth, be able to subsist up there?" asked Madeleine.

"Our precautions have been taken," declared Scherrebek. "We're provided with all that we need."

"You can't, however, transport the conditions of Earth to the Moon."

"Pardon me, but that's almost exactly what we're doing. The problem isn't very different from the one that has to be resolved when one undertakes an expedition to the North Pole. The polar explorer is created to live at an average temperature far superior to that reigning on the ice-sheet. He needs food, which he can't obtain in the desert of ice. Well, he takes fuel, food and apparatus with him, and finds the means to subsist in the heart of the empire of death, thanks to supplies that come from the temperate regions of the globe. Do you want another example? There's that of the voyager traversing the desolate solitudes of the Sahara, carrying the food and water that the sea of sand is incapable of furnishing."

"At the Pole, as in the Sahara, it's only a matter of contending with an extreme temperature and alimenting oneself, but on the Moon it's also necessary for you to carry the air to breathe."

"That's true. Thus, we'll be in the circumstances of men who, in order to subsist for a time at the bottom of the sea, employ a submarine or a diving-suit. In interplanetary space or on the Moon—which is to say, in a more-or-less perfect vacuum—we possess, inside the hermetically sealed *Selenit*, the reserves of air that are indispensable to us. On the other hand, we'll have veritable state-of-the-art diving-suits, thanks to which it will be possible to leave our refuge and move individually on the surface of the Moon.

Lunch had finished and the commandant stood up.

Scherrebek assembled the people he had designated for the first visit to the *Selenit*, among whom were René and Madeleine Brifaut. A kind of gangway had been installed between the *Montgomery* and the vessel in tow consisting of a deep canvas gutter supported by two cables. One by one, ten passengers, conducted by Scherrebek, crossed that shaky bridge to the *Selenit*, whose catch had been unscrewed by a sailor. The sea was so calm that there was no danger of any accident for the people or the apparatus.

III. In the Flanks of the Selenit

The visitors descended by means of an aluminum ladder and found themselves in a large rectangular room, poorly lit by narrow portholes that were not very numerous.

"This room," said Scherrebek, is seven meters long, seven wide and as many high, forming a cube. It's dark at the moment because the portholes pierced in the two lateral faces and the floor are submerged in the sea. Our vessel is equipped with electric lamps powered by dry batteries, but I haven't turned them on because we ought not to squander the light.

"The *Selenit* is presently lying horizontally; that's the position that it will normally occupy on the surface of the Moon. At the moment of launch, however, when it's completely submerged in the ocean, and during the journey from the Earth the Moon, it will be orientated vertically relative to the Earth's radius. It follows that the back wall of the room, which is facing you now, and which measures seven meters by seven, will become the floor for a while."

"Damn!" said Brifaut. "That will upset all your equipment."

"No, for our precautions have been taken. Everything is carefully secured. The trajectory, in accordance with Esnault-Pelterie's calculations, will only last a little more than forty-eight hours. We'll be constrained to spend them on the rear wall, which offers the same surface area as the normal floor."

The Dane operated a mechanism in one of the interior walls and lowered a section of the paneling.

"This is a folding couchette, which can, as you can see, be lifted up to the wall again and secured there, after the fashion of a trap-door, when not in use. There are ten similar ones disposed in two superimposed groups of three and two of two. Aluminum ladders permit the upper bunks to be reached. That dormitory occupies about four-meters fifty of the length. In the remaining space, the walls of the room are filled with cupboards for clothing, crockery, instruments of every kind and folding chairs. Beneath the groups of two couchettes, which leave a free space at floor level against the forward all, two trunks have been placed, which can serve as benches and which contain various supplies, including medicines.

"By looking through one of the portholes you can see that it affects the form of a tube. The length of the tube is one meter fifty, because that's the thickness of the wall it traverses. As the diameter of its section is only fifty centimeters, however, you can appreciate that it only offers a rather limited field of vision. One has to be content with these very narrow windows is one wants to avoid accidents. It's necessary, in fact, to achieve a perfect isolation. With that objective, we've constructed a triple hull. An initial shell, which envelops this room and the other chambers of the *Selenit*, is composed of an agglomerate of cork, equipped with a network of aluminum beams and wires; it's twenty centimeters thick.

"Around that first shell, hundred-kilo cylinders of compressed air are arranged, and under the floor there is an abundant provision of oxygen tubes designed to supply the divingsuits. A trap-door of agglomerated cork, fitted into the middle of the floor, permits access to those tubes as and when needed.

"Another shell constructed like the first, of the same thickness and separated from it by a space of sixty centimeters, forms a second rigorously sealed envelope, It's covered with a thin sheet of aluminum.

"Finally, the external wall of the *Selenit* is constituted by armor plating, similarly lines with agglomerated cork. It's separated from the intermediary shell by an interval of fifteen centimeters, in which there's an absolute vacuum. In those conditions, exchanges of temperature with the exterior are extremely difficult and practically non-existent, which is indispensable for crossing the interplanetary void and enduring without inconvenience the formidable alterations in temperature produced on the surface of the Moon. Connections are naturally ensured in places by a network of aluminum beams.

"The portholes are equipped with three windows, each corresponding to a shell. Those that are enclosed at the level of the two exterior hulls are hermetically sealed and there is a vacuum between them. The third—the interior window—is movable; it can be unscrewed in order to slide an agglomerated cork plug into the hole in the event that the sun's ardor renders that precaution necessary.

"Each window is composed of an assembly of twenty-two crystal disks one centimeter thick, separated from one another by one-millimeter sheets of mica. One thus obtains transparent blocks perfectly proofed against variations of temperature and shocks. Finally, a mechanism that can be operated from inside permits sheet-metal shutters coated with heat-proof varnish to be slid over them externally.

"To remedy the insufficiency of the field of vision provided by the portholes, we possess several periscopes that can be maneuvered by sliding them in tubes through the hull."

Scherrebek opened a little door in the front wall, and the visitors were able to observe that on that side too, the partition was impressively thick. Like the others, it was composed of agglomerated cork, although it simple served as a separation between the crew's lodgings and the pilot's cabin.

The latter terminated in a point at the front, by virtue of the symmetrical narrowing of the walls, the ceiling and the floor. It was provided with four portholes and two periscopes.

"Like all the chambers of the *Selenit*," said Scherrebek, "this one is destined to be utilized in two orientations, one vertical and the other horizontal. You can see here the acoustical funnels by which the pilot remains constantly in communication with the mechanic in the engine room and can also make himself heard in the crew cabin. He has before his eyes optical instruments that permit him to measure the apparent diameter of the Moon or the Earth and to deduce therefrom the *Selenit*'s own velocity. An astronomical telescope mounted in one of the portholes and rigorously parallel to the axis of the vessel serves to study the sky and determine direction in accordance with the position of the stars."

Scherrebek took his guests back into the crew cabin and crossed it in order to open another door in the rear. He penetrated into a room only three meters long with a ceiling noticeably lower than that of the principal room. The free space was limited by cupboards aligned on the walls.

Pointing at the ceiling, Scherrebek declared: "There's a lined reservoir here containing five cubic meters of water, which is an amply sufficient supply for ten men for thirty days, and even permits domestic uses."

He opened one of the cupboards.

"These wardrobes contain ten diving-suits of a special type, capable of resisting an interior pressure of one atmosphere in an absolute vacuum. The various items of apparatus possess articulations of great suppleness, although perfectly sealed. All the parts have a double wall, lined with insulating substances. A receptacle pierced with numerous holes receives a dose of caustic soda designed to absorb the carbon dioxide and water vapor given off in respiration. Tubes of compressed oxygen regenerate the air contained within the diving-suit.

"The man is not narrowly imprisoned; only his legs are boxed in the diving-boots. His body and head retain a certain play, and in particular, he can withdraw his arms from the metallic sleeves if he has some manipulation to carry out inside the apparatus. He can carry food and drink inside the body of the suit. A special double-walled valve permits him to reject organic debris outside.

"The metallic head is fitted with an anterior window and two lateral windows of double thickness, separated by a void, on the same principle adopted for the *Selenit*'s portholes. Screens of smoked glass or lead can be slid behind the viewports—an indispensable precaution on the Moon, where no atmosphere attenuates the sun's ultra-violet radiations."

The *Montgomery*'s passengers also visited, on the same side as the suit-room, the food-stores, which contained, in particular, a large quantity of pemmican, the agglomeration of meat, vegetables and fat well known to polar explorers. The heating system was powered by means of a slow-burning powder whose gases were distributed into all the compartments of the *Selenit* by means of pipes and radiators; that apparatus provided protection, when necessary, against the extreme cold of the long lunar night. To protect against overheating, if the sun became too hot, compressed air could be released, which determined a considerable lowering of temperature.

In the flank of the *Selenit* adjacent to the suit-room was the exit cylinder. It communicated with the chamber by a heretically sealed hatch; it was just large enough to contain a suit. A system of double doors gave access to the exterior through the hull of the *Selenit*.

"The passage is presently under water," Scherrebek explained, "so we can't open it. But that's the way we'll normally come in and go out when we're on the Moon, instead of passing through the screw-hatch. In fact, the latter couldn't be unscrewed without losing the air contained in the *Selenit* and immediately causing the asphyxiation of the passengers.

"The exit cylinder functions in three circumstances. When a person in a suit wants to go out, the communicating door between the cylinder and the chamber is opened, the man in the suit climbs in, and the door is resealed. Then, from inside the chamber, a tap is turned that allows the air in the cylinder to escape outside. Once the vacuum is complete, it only remains to open the exterior doors to emerge on to the lunar surface. When the main in the suit wants to return, naturally, the maneuver is carried out in reverse order, Thus, one loses as little air as possible every time."

It only remained to visit the engine room. Before going in there, Captain Scherrebek explained that the batteries of electric piles that provided lighting for the rooms and heating of the small culinary stove were installed under the floor.

The engine room resembled an artillery turret aboard a battleship. Like the others chambers of the *Selenit* it was constructed so as to serve in two different orientations, vertical and horizontal. Cylinders similar to the breeches of cannon were fitted into the wall, and the similarity was further enhanced by the presence of chains mounted on castors designed to take the explosive cartridges into the cylinders. The breeches were fitted with double seals, which avoided the loss of air.

In addition to the four large cannons designed for the propulsion of the *Selenit* there were several small ones that could not be seen from outside because they terminated level with the wall; they were arranged at right angles to the axis of the *Selenit*, some perpendicular to the walls and others oblique. Those small tubes would serve to correct errors in direction or cancel any effects of rotation that might be produced in the course of the voyage and inconvenience the passengers severely.

"The functioning of these items of apparatus," Scherrebek concluded, as he finished his explanations, "is still based on the reaction principle. If you fire to the right, the recoil deflects the *Selenit* to the left; if you fire tangentially in one direction, you cause the machine to rotate on its axis in the other."

The visit was concluded, and they went back aboard the *Montgomery*. Brifaut was enthused, Madeleine struck by admiration.

"But when you fall on the Moon," Brifaut observed, "the *Selenit* will be forced to remain where it has landed, and it might be in a very poor situation."

"Our machine will be capable of moving, because it's necessary that we can travel on the Mon and reposition ourselves for the return to Earth. Thus, we've disposed wheels with caterpillar tracks beneath the hull, which you can't see because they're under water. They're activated by an explosion motor, fueled by powder, naturally. The rear of the vessel will be sustained by struts. By those means, we can travel several hundred kilometers aboard the *Selenit*."

"I really admire your diving-suits," said Madeleine, "but they must be terribly heavy."

"They weigh about two hundred kilos, fully equipped."

"How will you be able to walk when you have such a weight on your back?"

"You're forgetting, Madame, that the gravity is six times weaker on the Moon than on Earth, and that, in consequence, the suit weighs no more up there than thirty-three or thirty-five kilos. You'll tell me that that's still a lot when it's a matter of moving on very uneven terrain, but a man only weighs a dozen kilos himself instead of seventy, for example. He'll therefore only have to carry a total of twelve plus thirty-four, or forty-six, kilos in total. You can see that, in spite of the burden of the suit, he'll feel considerably lighter than on Earth."

"That's true. You've thought of everything."

The members of the expedition spent the afternoon taking all the *Montgomery*'s passengers to visit the *Selenit* by turns. In the evening, the screw-hatch was closed; it would not be reopened again before the embarkation of the explorers.

During dinner, everyone conceded that an expedition prepared with so much care could not fail. No one was incredulous any longer.

When night fell, the passengers sat in groups on the deck in order to meditate beneath the beautiful starry sky.

"It's a pity," said Madeleine, "that the Moon isn't visible, when everyone's thinking about it."

"It's already set," Dessoye observed, "because it's in its last quarter. We're going to leave shortly after the new moon, in order to arrive on our satellite at sunrise."

IV. Replacement

On the third day of the voyage there was a deplorable accident aboard the Montgomery. Dessoye, the French member of the mission, fell on one of the stairways so awkwardly that he broke his wrist.

He thought at first that he would get away with a simple sprain and would still be able to depart, but the ship's doctor dispelled that illusion.

"It will be at least two months before you recover the use of your hand."

In those conditions, Dessoye could only be a hindrance to his comrades if he was obstinate in going regardless. He understood that, but he was desolate. For one thing, he would lose the payment of a hundred thousand dollars that the voyage would have earned him; secondly, he would miss the opportunity for an exciting adventure; finally—and this affected him most deeply of all—he would leave vacant the place reserved in the mission for a representative of France.

When Brifaut came to express his sympathy, he said to him: "Why can't you replace me? You're young and vigorous; you've undertaken several voyages of exploration and you speak English as if it were your mother tongue. Go to the Moon. It's a beautiful opportunity to see the place and make yourself rich."

"I'd like nothing better, if it only depended on me," Brifaut replied, "but my wife would never consent to it."

"Who can tell? Let's go find her."

The two men joined Madeleine in the lounge of the *Montgomery*. Dessoye, whose arm was in a sling, explained his proposition.

Madeleine uttered loud protests. "No, no! My husband won't launch himself into this crazy adventure."

"But you've recognized yourself," René ventured, "that its success can't be put in doubt, so many precautions having been taken."

"That doesn't alter the fact that something unexpected might happen that would spoil everything. What if the *Selenit* breaks down on the Moon, for instance, and that's the end."

"Everything has been calculated, Madame," Dessoye observed. "There won't be any breakdown. Remember that France is no longer represented in the mission. What will people say if your husband doesn't step in? A Frenchman will have recoiled, where an Englishman, a German and an American have gone without fear."

That argument had considerable weight with the young woman, who nevertheless argued for a long time and shed many tears.

In the end, she declared: "Well, I'll consent to let René go, but only on one condition: that I go too."

"But that's not possible. A woman!"

"Ta ta ta! Give that there's no danger—that's what you said, isn't it?—I don't see why I can't take part in the expedition. Anyway, a woman might render considerable services aboard the *Selenit*, for housework, cooking and medical care. I can also fill the role of secretary."

"Yes, yes…I understand…but provision has only been made for ten passengers, and it would be necessary to reserve separate accommodation for you."

"Bah! In war as in war—I'll sleep in the food-store."

"In truth…perhaps it's not impossible. I'll go talk to Scherrebek."

"Point out to him," said Madeleine, "that my company will add some gaiety to an austere circle of ten men."

"Certainly," said Dessoye laughing, "and that argument has all the more force when it's a matter of a Frenchwoman."

An hour later, the members of the expedition, including Dessoye, who had to renounce taking part in it, met in council in the commandant's ward-room to consider the question. The replacement of Dessoye by Brifaut was admitted without difficulty; the admission of Madame Brifaut, by contrast, generated considerable argument. Some members, especially the American and the Japanese, raised objections. But Dessoye, supported by Scherrebek, pleaded Madeleine's cause with so much ardor that they ended up winning the unanimous consent of their comrades.

When, at dinner that evening, Commandant Murray announced officially that Madeleine would be joining the expedition, the guests gave the valiant Frenchwoman an ovation.

Madeleine felt proud and glad; she was no longer afraid of anything. Such is the character of our race, which sometimes trembles at danger when it is far away, and confronts it with a smile at close range.

V. En Route

Installed in the pilot's cabin, with his instruments before his eyes and the acoustic funnels that permitted him to communicate with the various compartments of the *Selenit* in front of him, Scherrebek leaned over the one to the crew's quarters and announced:

"Depth two hundred meters. We're no longer descending. In exactly three minutes, I'll release the lead weights."

Into the apparatus communicating with the engine-room, where the American Garrick and the Japanese Kito were in service, he said: "To your posts! We're departing in three minutes."

The *Selenit* was in a vertical position, and to circulate between the compartments, which were placed one beneath another like shelves, it was necessary to use ladders.

On the wall that was, for the moment, taking the place of the floor in the crew's quarters, René and Madeleine were sitting side by side on folding chairs in the company of Lang, Bojardo, Espronceda, Uberaba and Goffoël. The Englishman Galston was climbing the ladder that led to the pilot's cabin, going to install himself beside Scherrebek in order to assist him if necessary. The electric lights had been switched on because, at the depth at which the *Selenit* was immersed, no light could reach the portholes.

Madeleine scanned her companions with her gaze and saw them composed, but a trifle pale. Her heart was beating rapidly, and she leaned instinctively on René's shoulder. Silence reigned; everyone was mentally bidding adieu to the Earth, thinking that they might not come back from the prodigious voyage to the Moon.

A slight shock was produced; Scherrebek had released the weights. The *Selenit*, lightened and drawn toward the surface by a girdle of buoys, which it would abandon on arrival in the open air, began rising with increasing speed. During the first few seconds the acceleration was scarcely perceptible, but it gradually increased. The passengers had the sensation of being in an elevator. A dull rumble announced that the engine had been activated. In truth, the noise was scarcely appreciable, for it as only transmitted through the metallic framework through the insulating triple hull of the *Selenit*.

After thirty seconds or so, the Spaniard Espronceda, who was looking through a porthole, announced in English: "We're out!"

They could, indeed, see daylight through the windows, and could make out the blue of the sky. The *Selenit* was soaring through the atmosphere.

Striving to suppress the tremor that was agitating her and to appear perfectly calm, Madeleine asked: "At what speed are we traveling?"

"Between fifty and sixty meters a second," Lang replied. "We ought to have reached the acceleration compatible with the resistance of the human body already."

In fact, Madeleine could still feel in the hollow of her stomach the painful sensation that passengers in an elevator feel at the moment when it moves off.

"It's making my heart hurt," she murmured. "Is it going to last long?"

"Thirty or forty minutes, Madame," said Lang. "I advise you to lie down on that couch—you'll suffer less motion-sickness."

The advice was good. Madeleine took advantage of it, installed herself on a folding bunk and closed her eyes.

"I thought," said René Brifaut, "that a projectile can't escape the Earth's gravitation unless it's traveling at twelve thousand meters a second. How will we succeed in reaching such a velocity in only fifty minutes?"

"Naturally, if we weren't being driven upwards by our engines, we'd fall back to Earth, whose attraction tends to slow us down by nine meters eighty-one centimeters a second. But it's sufficient for the propulsion of our machines to compensate for that retardation for us to continue rising. In fact, we're so far in excess of it that our speed is accelerating at about ten meters a second."

"You'll notice," said Bojardo, the Italian, "that we have an interest in not moving too rapidly at the outset, so long as we're not out of the dense layer of the atmosphere, whose resistance would be considerable if we exceeded a velocity of two or three hundred meters a second. We'd risk being subjected to a dangerous heating."

"And how thick is that layer?" asked Brifaut, who was the least knowledgeable of the team.

"Between thirty and forty kilometers. We'll be through it in about two minutes. After that, we'll be in an atmosphere sufficiently rarefied for its resistance to become negligible. Scherrebek will be able to increase velocity, and seven or eight minutes later we'll reach the interplanetary void at the extreme limits of the atmosphere, at an altitude of five hundred kilometers.

At the Lycée Fénelon, where she had been educated, Madeleine had been taught what the Moon was and what its movements were, but she had forgotten some of the astronomical details and was not sorry to have them repeated by Goffoël, the giant Belgian.

Goffoël reminded her that the diameter of the Moon is 3,480 kilometers, whereas that of the Earth is 12,732 kilometers. In consequence, the volume of the Moon is about forty-nine times less than that of the Earth, and, as the density of our satellite scarcely surpasses six tenths of the mean density of the terrestrial globe, its mass is only equivalent to one eighty-oneth of that of the Earth. In sum, the Moon, as a whole, is composed of lighter substances. The mass being smaller, the action of gravity on the lunar surface is also reduced; the smallness of its radius, however, concentrates the force, so to speak, so that weight on the moon is not one eighty-oneth but a sixth of weight on the Earth.

The Moon rotates around the Earth, and if one considers the time between two identical phases—two full moons, for example—one finds that the revolution takes twenty-nine days, twelve hours, forty-four minutes, two seconds and six hundred and eighty-four thousandths of a second. But as the Earth is itself rotating around the sun, that revolution, known as synodic, is longer than the time elapsed between two passages of the Moon over the same point in the sky—before the same star, for example. The latter is only twenty-seven days seven hours, forty-three minutes, eleven seconds and five hundred and forty-five thousandths of a second, which is the duration of the sidereal revolution.

The curve that the Moon describes around the Earth, the former being deemed motionless, is not an exact circle but an ellipse, of which our globe occupies one of the focal points. It follows that the distance between the two heavenly bodies is not invariable. The point at which the Moon passes closest to the Earth is known as the perigee, the one at which it is most distant the apogee. The interval that elapses between two passage of the Moon through its perigee, which known as the anomalistic period, is twenty-seven days, thirteen hours, eighteen minutes, thirty-seven seconds and forty-four thousands of a second. The minimum distance, at perigee, in 356,577 kilometers; the maximum distance, at apogee, is 407,000 kilometers; the mean distance in 384,300 kilometers.

"So you can see," Goffoël observed, "that we're very close to our satellite. One could almost say that it's within arm's reach, when one compares it to the distance of the Sun, and above all that of the nearest stars. Light takes scarcely more than a second to reach us from the Moon, while it takes eight and a half minutes to reach us from the Sun, and about three years from the nearest star."

Madeleine also learned once again that the Moon always presents the same face to us, which proves that its center of gravity is closer to us than its symmetrical center. It rotates on its axis in exactly the same time as it accomplishes a revolution around the Earth. Nevertheless, as its orbit is not exactly circular, and its velocity is, in consequence, not absolutely constant, and the Earth is moving through space itself, so that the Moon is sometimes above the plane of the Earth's orbit and sometimes below it, our satellite is subject to a kind of apparent oscillation from north to south and east to west, which alternately conceals and reveals the regions close to its edge. That oscillation is known as libration.

There is, in consequence, a part of the Moon that we never see, which represents forty-one hundredths of its surface, a part that is visible only at times, and finally, one that is always visible. The latter parts form collectively fifty-nine hundredths of the surface.

The apparent diameter of the Moon—which is to say, at the angle from which it is seen from the Earth—measures a little more than half a degree. That is approximately how one sees a length of a centimeter at a distance of a meter.

"Good," said Madeleine. "I think I can keep those figures in my head. I'll become a veritable astronomer."

Meanwhile, the speed of the *Selenit* was still accelerating, at such a rhythm that Madeleine was not the only once rendered uncomfortable by it. All the passengers were beginning to go pale and experience nausea.

"Garrick and Kito are pushing the engine too heard," Lang observed. "They're exceeding the tolerable limit of acceleration

The passengers' malaise was all the more painful because the stability of the *Selenit* was far from perfect. The slight inequalities of the reactions of the various tubes of the engine were causing a kind of oscillation, which was becoming more intolerable by the minute. The walls were vibrating in spite of their insulation; the *Selenit* was filled by a dull growl that was transmitted by the steels of the tubes and the beams of the framework.

At one moment, the machine began to swivel like a top. That motion, which the passengers in the crew section could not appreciate by sight, nevertheless became sensible as soon as it acquired a certain rapidity. Scherrebek corrected it by means of the tangential tubes, and telephoned an instruction to Garrick and Kito to reduce the acceleration.

A few minutes later, he calculated that the velocity was great enough to compensate for the effects of gravitation, and gave the order to stop the engine. It was sufficient henceforth to allow the *Selenit* to travel by its own momentum to reach the limit of terrestrial attraction and pass into the influence of the Moon. The engine would not be activated again until the neutral zone between the two heavenly bodies was reached, when it would be necessary to correct any deviation of direction.

The passengers immediately felt liberated from their anguish. All noise, oscillation and libration had ceased. Noting any longer rendered the movement of the *Selenit* perceptible in any fashion, although it was prodigiously rapid.

Madeleine sat up abruptly "We've stopped," she said.

She rose up into the air, as a balloon launched by a child would have done, and went to collide gently with the ceiling; then she descended again, slowly.

"What's happening to me?" she asked, amazed.

The other passengers had got up in their turn, surprised, and were all rising up in the same fashion as Madeleine, some bumping into the ceiling and others into the walls. After a few moments they all found themselves reunited on the floor, crouching or lying down, no longer daring to budge.

"My friends," said Lang, "I advise you only to move with the greatest precaution. We're now subject to the effects of the diminution of weight, for which the accelerating action of the engine had compensated until now, drawing us away all the more rapidly as the Earth retained us less. Well, it's easy to calculate how that attraction is reduced, knowing that it's inversely proportional to the square of the distance. At the distance we've presently reached, approximately equal to the length of the terrestrial radius, what does a mass that weighs a kilo at the Earth's surface weigh now? Since the distance from the Earth's center has doubled, the weight has been reduced by two times two. A kilo only weighs a quarter of its former weight, which is to say, 250 grams.

"So, Madame, without wishing to offend you, what has happened to you is that you've become a very light woman, for if you weighed about sixty kilos on Earth, you now weigh no more than fifteen. In addition, when you allow yourself to fall through space, instead of increasing by ten meters a second, as it would on Earth, your velocity no longer increases by more than two meters fifty. That's why you came down so softly after having leapt up to the ceiling.

"That considerable diminution of weight will also explain to you why we've been able to switch off the engine when we were still far from obtaining the critical velocity of twelve thousand meters a second necessary to liberate us from the terrestrial attraction; at the altitude we've reached the critical velocity is no more than 8,200 meters a second."

"Forgive me, Doctor," said Bojardo, "but for once, your science is in default."

"What!"

"May I ask Madame Brifaut whether she has the sensation of still weighing anything, even fifteen kilos?"

"In truth, no," Madeleine replied. "I feel immaterialized."

"You're right, Bojardo," Lang exclaimed, "And I'm nothing but a fool. We're no longer experiencing even the effects of terrestrial attraction. I'll explain why, Madame. We're traveling by courtesy of our own momentum, and if we weren't subject to the gravitational field of the globe, our velocity would remain as invariable as that of any body not subject to any force. Not being in proximity to any heavenly body we wouldn't be attracted by any, and we would be devoid of any weight, as we are at this moment."

"But that's not the case for us," Madeleine objected, "since we're in the neighborhood of the Earth."

"Wait! The Earth, in attracting us, is slowing down our velocity. If we weren't moving, we'd begin falling toward it with the acceleration of two meters fifty per second that I mentioned to you just now. As we have our own momentum, we're continuing to draw away, except that our velocity is diminishing by two meters fifty per second; we're yielding to the force that is soliciting us toward the center of the Earth, and in yielding to it, we're ceasing to perceive it. To feel it, we'd have to be struggling against it—which is to say, propelling our vessel with a force equal to the terrestrial attraction and in the opposite direction, which would compensate exactly for the effects of gravity. At any rate, as we draw further away, that will become less intense and our deceleration will become less evident. That's why our friend Bojardo is right...."

"Not entirely, though," Lang added, with a triumphant smile. We're not absolutely deprived of weight, because our *Selenit*, which is a microcosm, possesses a certain mass and it is attracting us toward its center of gravity—oh, very feebly, no doubt, but sufficiently for us to be able to maintain ourselves on this floor, as we are."

In fact, the passengers always came back to pose on the floor—but the slightest gesture launched them to the other side of the room.

Moving cautiously, Madeleine went to look through a porthole, and saw a fragment of black sky strewn with stars. Her movement had produced a slight oscillation, as if the *Selenit* were floating on a liquid.

"That's odd," she said. "The floor moved."

"Which is to say that by moving, you displaced the *Selenit*'s center of gravity and changed its equilibrium position."

Goffoël had consulted his watch.

"We've been traveling for forty-five minutes."

"But we left at four o'clock in the afternoon and it's already night," said Madeleine, bewildered. "How did that happen?"

"What makes you think that it's night?" asked Lang.

Madeleine pointed at the porthole. "Look—the sky's black."

"That's simply because there's no air, and no luminous diffusion is being produced; in the interplanetary void the sky appears black, and one can always see the stars in spite of the sun's light."

He headed for another porthole and said: "Look—there's a violet reflection at the end of this tube. That's the sunlight striking the *Selenit* obliquely from the front. We can't perceive it from here, but Scherrebek and Galston must be blinded by its radiance."

Scherrebek came down from the pilot's cabin with Galston and let himself fall through the air like a soap bubble. At the same time, Kito and Garrick, who had received an order to come up, sprang like sylphs through the trapdoor in the floor. The entire mission was assembled.

"We have forty-eight hours of tranquility ahead of us," said Scherrebek, "during which all we have to do is relax. I think that we can take advantage of it first of all by having dinner."

"Sit down," said Madeline. "I'll serve you."

She let herself fall into the food-store. Brifaut and Lang volunteered to help her, and the table was soon laid.

The air inside the *Selenit* remained pure and perfectly breathable. It was regenerated by a continuous release of oxygen, while the carbon dioxide and water emitted by respiration were absorbed by the caustic soda. Everything had been scrupulously anticipated in the construction of the *Selenit*, and they also had the means of expelling debris and ordure of all kinds, as well as waste water, thanks to a system of trapdoors and explosive charges.

By means of a theodolite, Scherrebek determined the exact apparent diameter of the Moon, and deduced therefrom that the *Selenit* was ten thousand kilometers from the terrestrial globe.[11]

---

[11] The remaining wordage of this chapter does not appear in the serial version, probably having been cut in order to prevent the text overrun the page, and the feuilleton version of the following chapter bears the title of the subsequent one in the book version, the chapter break having been deleted.

The explorers affected a cheerful attitude that was sometimes a trifle forced. They sometimes allowed their enthusiasm to run out, and a silence fell abruptly; everyone wondered, with a secret anguish, whether they would ever return to the Earth they had just quit.

But that did not last. Scherrebek, or one of his comrades, resumed talking, and the conversation was reestablished, in a tone of perfect confidence.

VI. Regarding the Moon

In addition to the periscopes in the pilot's cabin, there were others in the crew section and the engine room. They were tubular devices of barrow width, which could be extended outside at will. Thus, the passengers were able to observe, in turn, the Sun, the Moon and the Earth.

With regard to the Sun, its glare was absolutely unsustainable; they were obliged to attenuate it by means of smoked glass and lead screens.

"I imagine," said Brifaut, "that in the void, solar radiation is much richer in ultra-violet rays."

"Indeed," said Lang. "the terrestrial atmosphere absorbs and diffuses the blue and violet rays of the solar spectrum, and that's the origin of the azure sky. Here, we wouldn't be able to look at the Sun with the naked eye without being instantly blinded."

Viewed from the *Selenit*, the Sun was displayed with much sharper contours, but also less regular, for its protuberances, which are merely enormous eruptions of incandescent gas, sometimes attain three or four hundred thousand kilometers in height, becoming visible. In spite of the screens, the star appeared intensely blue.

That hue was also that of the Moon, whose slender crescent was shining at about fifteen degrees from the Sun. They were seeing it at a greater angle than from the surface of the Earth, and as, in addition, no atmosphere interposed itself between the object and the gaze, the principal features of the part illuminated by the Sun were already very clearly distinguishable.

The strange sensation of lightness that the passengers experienced was not absolutely untroubled, for their hearts, accustomed to pumping a heavy fluid, were beating too forcefully and too precipitately; the explorers had congested faces. Nevertheless, the elasticity of the arteries reacted, and Uberaba, the company's doctor, estimated that there was no danger of any serious accident.

By adapting the periscopes to a weak magnification, they were able to recognize in the northern part of the lunar crescent the large crater Endymion alongside the Humboldt Sea, and then Messala, Herzelius, Geminus, Burkhardt and Cleomedes, all extended into ellipses by the perspective.

"Above Cleomedes," said Lang, "that large dark plain surrounded by mountains, which affects an oval form, like the craters, is the Sea of Crises. Beneath it, you can see the western edge of the Sea of Fecundity. The sun is rising over that plain, which is about six hundred kilometers wide. Note that when one refers to the western edge of the Moon one means the part facing the west of the Earth. It follows that if you took at the Moon with your head turned northwards, you have the west to your right and not to your left, as on Earth."

Lang continued to list the craters descending southwards: Langrenus, Vendelinus and Petavius, the last-named remarkable for the great crevasse connecting its rampart to its central massif. Then came the extraordinarily tormented region of the south, which resembles the rough skin of an enormous animal covered in pustules.

"All the mountains on the surface of the Moon, then, have craters?" asked Madeleine.

"Not all, but a large number. The craters constitute a feature extremely widespread on the surface of our satellite. You can represent them as a plain sensibly lower than the surrounding region, surrounded by a circular or polygonal rampart, which sometimes attains an altitude of more than five thousand meters, at the center of which an isolated mountain generally rises, or a group of mountains higher than the rampart. The interior slope of the latter is abrupt, whereas the exterior slope is relatively gentle, and often scarcely stands above the plateau that serves it as a pedestal. There are, however, more or less rectilinear chains, like those baptized with names borrowed from the geography of our globe: the Alps, Apennines, Caucasus, etc."

"The craters are those of volcanoes," declared Brifaut.

"No," said Bojardo, "we no longer believe that today, although one can't deny their volcanic character. For my part, I'm a partisan of the theory of fissures and outflows. The lunar crust, having cooled and contracted more rapidly than the central mass, split into a multitude of little pieces, which can be compared to the squares of a chessboard, or, more precisely, to the hexagonal tiles that are used to pave the floor of kitchens, between those fragments, lava emerged, and formed the approximately circular ramparts that we observe."

"You can't be unaware," said Uberaba, "that that theory encounters grave objections. How do you explain, for instance, if the phenomenon is due to the extension of the internal mass, that the interior plain of the crater is so profoundly sunk? And what is the origin of the central mountains?"

"As for the latter, they're merely small craters formed afterwards, and as for the sunken bottom, it results from the void caused in the fluid nucleus of the Moon by the expulsion of lava at the surface."

"That amounts to saying that you sometimes admit an expansion and sometimes a contraction of the lunar nucleus, according to which you need to justify a theory conceived *a priori*."

"Perhaps," said Bojardo, becoming irritated, "you hold to the implausible theory of bubbles?"

"Why is it implausible?" exclaimed Uberaba.

"Because bubbles a hundred kilometers in diameter can't exist."

"On Earth, undoubtedly; on the Moon, that's another matter. As the gases expelled by the fluid mass tended to fray a passage through the thin and still pasty crust; submitted to enormous pressures, they weren't incapable of rising above vast extents of denser matter, which the feeble lunar gravity didn't, in any case, maintain strongly bound together. After the cooling, when the gases had ceased to act, the vault collapsed, uncovering the subjacent cavity."

"Ingenious, but insufficient. You can't explain the formation of the central mountains."

"Debris of the vault."

"But why isn't that debris spread over the entire interior of the crater instead of accumulating at the center?"

"That can be explained," retorted Uberaba. "I'll prove it to you…"

"Personally," said Espronceda, "I'm in favor of the bombardment theory."

"Oh, yes—by aeroliths!" exclaimed Bojardo and Uberaba simultaneously and ironically.

"Can you deny that the surface of the Moon looks exactly like a bombarded terrain? If our satellite was formed at the expense of the terrestrial mass, one has to admit that all the matter of which it's composed hasn't always been assembled into a single globe, as it is today. At one time, the Earth had a myriad of tiny satellites, which circulated in much the same orbit, and which finished up agglomerating, falling upon one another. In the final period of that concentration, the Moon, already constituted and covered in a semi-solid crust, was exposed to a bombardment of aeroliths that hollowed out the cavities we observe. The central mountains of the craters are explained by matter splashing back after the impact."

"It would have been necessary, then, for the lunar surface, which you assume to be pasty for the purposes of the explanation, to have solidified suddenly at the point of the fall, immediately after the impact. Otherwise, the trace would have been effaced by the effect of reactions that are normally produced in the bosom of semi-fluid mater. Now, an impact might determine the liquefaction of solid matter by virtue of the resulting elevation of temperature, but never, so far as I know, the solidification of a fluid matter. You can see, therefore, that your theory is unsustainable."[12]

---

[12] The "bombardment thesis" is now so widely-accepted as to be taken for granted, but in 1926 the notion of bombardment by matter from the outer solar system—asteroids or cometary

Brifaut listened with amusement to these arguments, which proved, in sum, that none of the admitted theories regarding the formation of the lunar relief was secure from criticism.

"But is it impossible," he ventured, "that the lunar craters, which resemble one another closely, from the greatest to the smallest, and which are so difficult to explain by means of purely natural causes, were constructed by intelligent beings?"

That reflection was greeted with bursts of laughter from all the other members of the mission, except Madeleine.

"Is my husband's idea so ridiculous, then?" asked the young woman, vexed.

"Madame," said Lang, "Monsieur Brifaut is not an astronomer. It would be quite excusable for him to sustain a hypothesis that has been seriously envisaged by scientists like Kepler, Schroeter and Gruithuysen, to whom we owe the first detailed observations of the Moon. But those authors didn't possess the optical instruments or the photographic means of modern observatories. They didn't appreciate the true dimensions of the lunar craters, nor did they notice their irregularities."

"However," observed Brifaut, unconvinced, "if the craters were for the Selenites something analogous to our ancient cities that are in ruins today, that would explain the deformations and irregularities of which you speak. If the Moon was once inhabited, but, as is probable, has been a dead world for a long time, the vestiges that we discover on its surface are the last traces of edifices that commenced collapsing millions of centuries ago."

"Specious reasoning," said Galston. "It's simpler to invoke the action of natural forces. Volcanic phenomena have certainly played an enormous role on our satellite."

---

fragments—still seemed bizarre and highly improbable, which is why Espronceda substitutes local projectiles generated during the formation of the Earth/Moon system.

The time of the journey went by in that fashion, occupied with peaceful discussions. They only renounced the controversy in order to eat or sleep.

The crescent Moon that the passengers of the *Selenit* saw floating overhead increased in size rapidly. The part of the disk that was not directly illuminated by the Sun presented a milky aspect; that was the well-known phenomenon of the ashen Moon, which is due to the reflection of daylight by the Earth upon our satellite. And, indeed, opposite the Moon, almost directly underfoot, the voyagers distinguished the terrestrial globe, enormous and brilliant, but already eaten into by darkness on the oriental edge.

Scherrebek, assisted by Galston and Kito, endeavored to measure with exactitude the apparent diameter of the Moon and that of the Earth.

"We'll reach the lunar zone of attraction," he said, "when the apparent diameter of the star reaches five degrees twelve minutes—which is to say, when it appears to us to be ten times greater than from the surface of the Earth. On the other hand, we'll only see the latter under and angle of two degrees six minutes—which is to say that it will seem to us about four times larger than the Moon appears from the Earth. The neutral point will be found nine-tenths of the distance between the Earth and the Moon, about 346,000 kilometers from our globe.

He took his measurements and declared: "We'll arrive at the neutral point in a few minutes. Everyone to his post! It's necessary first of all to prevent any deviation, in order not to go past the Moon, as happened to the characters invented by Jules Verne."

Garrick and Kito, as light as the air they were breathing, let themselves down into the engine-room. Scherrebek, in the company of Galston, went back up into the pilot's cabin.

VII. The Arrival

"Well, what do you think of our voyage?" asked Brifaut, whispering in Madeleine's ear. "Do you regret taking part in it?"

"Sincerely, no. I find it exciting. And I assure you that I'm not afraid at all. People talk about honeymoons—ours won't be banal, and we really will spend it on the Moon."

"Which proves that it isn't wrong to ask for the Moon—which is to say, the impossible."

The axis of the *Selenit* was directed almost exactly at the eastern edge of the Moon; but as that latter continued to move in its course around the Earth, there was a risk of missing the target if they maintained exactly the same direction. Scherrebek, deflected it by means of a few discharges of the transversal tubes in order to steer slightly outside the disk, at the point that the Moon would have reached when the Selenit, entering its zone of attraction, would be, so to speak, captured by it.

"In what region of the Moon are we going to land?" asked Goffoël.

"I think the captain has decided to select the Sea of Rains, in the vicinity of Archimedes," said Uberaba.

"Where's that?" asked Madeleine.

"Look at the map," said Lang.

He pointed on a world map of the Moon at a large almost-rectangular plain, which covered almost a quarter of the northern hemisphere, extending over a length of a thousand kilometers and a similar breadth: a surface area as large as France.

"That's the Sea of Rains. It's limited to the north by the massif of the Alps, which prolongs the Caucasus."

"But it's at the bottom of the map," said Madeleine. "You said it was in the north."

"Yes, on maps of the Moon the North Pole is usually placed at the bottom and the South Pole at the top, because that's the way the star is seen in astronomical telescopes, which invert images. To the south-west, the Sea of Rains is limited by the Apennines, an enormous chain whose culminating point reaches an altitude of 5,600 meters, while the Alps only rise up 3,660 meters.

"At the extremity of the Apennines, toward the east—and remember that on the Moon, east and west are the opposite way around to the earthly cardinal points—you see a deep crater some sixty kilometers in diameter, Eratosthenes, whose wall is 4,500 meters high. It's remarkable for its regularity and bright ring.

"Beyond Eratosthenes in the prolongation of the Apennines, still toward the east, on the tenth degree of north latitude, you can see a splendid crater, Copernicus, which measures ninety kilometers in diameter and whose encircling wall rises to 3,400 meters. In the period of the full moon, it seems to be surrounded by bright spokes that form an aureole of extraordinary brilliance. In that respect it's almost as remarkable as the famous crater Tycho, at the austral Pole, which radiates bright bands over the entire southern hemisphere.

"In the right angle formed by the direction of the Alps and that of the Apennines, facing the broad strait that connects the Sea of Rains with the Sea of Serenity, three craters stand out on the plain. Proceeding from the north, they're Aristillus, Autolycus and, to the east of the latter, Archimedes. The last-named measures seventy-eight kilometers in diameter; its rim, relatively low, only rises to an altitude of 2,457 meters.

"Such is the region that Scherrebek intends to explore, at least in part. It's well enough defined by maps and photographs for us to find our way round there without difficulty, and it has the advantage of concentrating within a relatively small area the characteristic types of lunar geological formations. Naturally, it will be necessary for the *Selenit* to transport us from one place to another, because, even on the surface of the Moon, where weight is feeble, we won't be able to cover a considerable distance on foot in our suits in a single stage. I think the *Selenit* will be able to cover five or six hundred kilometers without difficulty, though, on the plains of the Sea of Rains."

Sherrebek's voice resonated in the acoustic apparatus. "We're falling on the Moon."

In conformity with Monsieur Esnault-Pelterie's calculations, whose conclusions that constructors of the *Selenit* had accepted on that point, it would be sufficient to commence braking, but activating the engines to slow down the fall, when they were no more than a short distance from the lunar surface—approximately two hundred kilometers—but Scherrebek had to furnish a few blasts with the small tubes to make the *Selenit* turn around and place her posterior section downwards, with the prow turned toward the Earth.

The explorers now saw the lunar surface rising toward them, like a huge balloon, part of which, lit by the sun, was spreading a dazzling light, while the other, which was only receiving the reflection from the Earth, was gleaming feebly. The details of the dark part were nevertheless visible at that short distance in the "earthlight."

"How will we know when we're no more than 250 kilometers from the lunar surface?" asked Brifaut.

"Still by measuring the angle that the star presents to us—which is to say, the angle made by two visual rays tangential to the lunar surface, one at the North Pole and the other at the South. Trigonometry permits us to calculate what that angle will be when we're 250 kilometers from our satellite, the radius of the Mon being known. It's exactly 121° 5⊖4″, which is slightly more than a third of the celestial circumference.

From that moment on the passengers of the *Selenit* never ceased observing the progressive increase in size of the Moon. They could not help feeing a certain anxiety at the moment when they were about to make contact with the unknown world. In spite of the most exact previsions and the most scrupulous calculations, something unexpected might occur at the moment of landing, and the slightest accident might prove fatal. A delay of one second in the maneuver, or an engine breakdown, and the *Selenit* would crash into the ground instead of settling there softly. It was also necessary to take account of the inequalities of the terrain. Scherrebek might well have chosen a region of the plain that was relatively untormented, but they could still collide with an unsuspected projection or fall into one of the crevasses so frequent on the lunar surface.

"The sun's setting!" exclaimed Brifaut, who was observing through a periscope.

"What!" said Bojardo.

He looked too. The lunar crescent was diminishing, and the sun was gradually descending behind the prodigiously-magnified mass of our satellite.

"Of course," said Goffoël. "We're penetrating into the cone of shadow. In a few minutes, we'll no longer see either the Sun or the slightest illuminated zone on the Moon. We'll be in night, and we'll no longer be able to count on anything but the light reflected by the Earth, our fatherland."

"Would you believe how beautiful she is, our Earth, seen from here?" said Bojardo, with a lyrical enthusiasm. "Don't you think that one appreciates her better when one's separated from her, as we are, by a 350,000-kilometer desert? She's hospitable, fecund and generous. One can walk freely on her surface and breathe everywhere. One finds an abundance of water, plants, animals…oh, the Earth!"

"If you miss her so much," said Espronceda, "why did you leave her?"

"I didn't know that it was going to have such an effect on me. And then, in spite of everything, I have a keen desire to see what's happening on the Moon."

The Sun had completely disappeared. The *Selenit* was in night, but they could not have made out the contours of the Earth-lit Moon any more distinctly.

"Notice," observed Dr. Lang, "that because of the curvature of the surface, we can now only see a limited part of the lunar globe from the distance we've reached, close to the limit of 250 kilometers set by Scherrebek for the commencement of the braking maneuver. Seeing the Moon at an angle of about a hundred and twenty degrees, we can only embrace a sixth of its surface with the gaze—which is to say that we can discover a horizon whose diameter in approximately equal to the radius of the moon, which is 1,740 kilometers. That horizon is 5,463 kilometers in circumference, whereas a lunar meridian measures nearly 11,000 kilometers. If we were above the Earth, at the same distance, we'd see a much more extensive horizon because, the globe being larger, its curvature is less pronounced—and we'd also have to take account of the atmospheric refraction, which heightens images at the horizon, whereas the effects of the lunar atmosphere are insensible."

The dull rumble transmitted to the interior of the *Selenit* by the vibrations of the engine tubes became audible again. Scherrebek had just given the order to brake by activating the engines.

At the same time the passengers—who had lost all sensation of weight many hours before—had the impression of suddenly becoming material beings again. The deceleration that the engines brought to the fall by making an effort in the inverse direction was, in fact, equivalent to an augmentation of the lunar attraction, rendering it almost equal to eight at the surface of the Earth. Until that moment, by contrast, since the *Selenit* had entered the Moon's gravitational field, as it had been passively obedient to the force that solicited it, and escaping, so to speak, beneath the feet of its passengers, animated by the same movement, the latter had had no more weight than any other objects contained within the interplanetary vehicle.

"Well," exclaimed Dr. Uberaba, "we've ceased to be pure spirits!"

Fortunately, Scherrebek had instructed Garrick and Kito only to apply a progressive deceleration to begin with. If they had recovered their normal weight abruptly, the passengers, taken by surprise, would have fallen over and might have experienced serious accidents, such as syncope or congestion.

"Look out—the train's coming into the station!" said Goffoël.

"In how long?" asked Brifaut.

"We're reaching the end of our voyage. In three and a half minutes, we'll be at rest on the lunar surface."

Care had already been taken to secure all the objects inside the *Selenit*, in anticipation of the change of position that the machine, previously vertical, was about to undergo, in order to land on the Moon horizontally. The passengers installed themselves in such a manner as to suffer the impact without any accident.

Scherrebek steered in such a way as to land in the north of the Sea of Rains, not far from the rim of Plato, a large crater ninety-six kilometers in diameter, whose rampart rises up 2,417 meters, and which marks the north-eastern extremity of the Alpine chain. The great somber cavity was clearly distinguishable by earthlight, surrounded by a pale wall, to the south-west of which the numerous peaks of the Alps extended, while the little group of the Tenerife Mountains was also visible to the south. The massif of the Alps was cut through the middle by a large black band, orientated north-westwards, which indicated the position of the Great Valley.

Although the light cast upon the Moon by the Earth at that time was at least ten times more vivid than the brightest moonlight on the Earth's surface, it was nevertheless insufficiently powerful to permit all the details of the terrain to be distinguished. The chaotic, tormented surface of the Moon took on a fantastic and terrifying aspect under that illumination.

The horizon was shrinking rapidly as the *Selenit* drew nearer to the ground. The diameter of the lunar horizon, for a man standing in the middle of a plain, is less than five kilometers, while on Earth it surpasses nine. If the ground is perfectly flat, the gaze only extends 2,430 meters.

Dr. Lang. whose memory as a storehouse of numbers, was in the process of giving these precisions to Madeleine when the acoustic funnel caused the captain's warning to resonate:

"Look out! We're touching down!"

"Cut the power!" roared Scherrebek then into the acoustic channel to the engine room.

At the same instant, an impact—not very violent—shook the *Selenit* from top to bottom. The projectile vehicle had touched down at its inferior extremity. It remained in equilibrium momentarily, and then tilted slowly sideways.

"Gas to the right!" shouted Scherrebek.

As soon as the engine had stopped, the passengers had felt an abrupt lightening, as at the moment when they had escaped the terrestrial attraction. They no longer weighed more than a sixth of their normal weight.

In the engine room, Garrick and Kito were attentive to the maneuver. They knew that the fate of the *Selenit* depended on the rapidity and precisions of their actions. They brought one of the lateral tubes into play, in the direction in which the apparatus was tilting, in order to slow and deaden its fall.

For a moment, the *Selenit* seemed to float in mid-air, but it pivoted on itself, and leaned over in the other direction. Immediately, the engineers applied reaction in that new direction.

That struggle against weight lasted twenty seconds. Finally, the *Selenit* was lying on the ground. If the engines had not intervened to slow the fall, that would have happened in ten or twelve seconds, and the upper extremity of the vessel would have made contact with the ground at a velocity of sixteen or twenty meters a second, which might have been sufficient to cause a disaster. As it was, the velocity of contact was no more than two meters a second; that was still a rude shock, given the mass of the *Selenit*, but the vessel was solidly constructed; its envelope and all its organs resisted the impact.

As for the passengers, in spite of the precautions they had taken, they were forcefully jolted and thrown into one another.

Nor were they at the end of their ordeal. Scherrebek had not succeeded in landing exactly where he had intended, between the crater Plato and the little group of the Tenerife Mountains.

In the final seconds of the fall, the *Selenit* had been carried a little toward the north-west by its acquired momentum, and It had not landed on the plain but on the ultimate buttress of the southern slope of Plato. Scarcely had it touched down than it lurched sideways, and while the passengers let out a cry of anguish, it began to roll down the slope of the mountain.

The crew members tried to hold on to whatever came to hand. Garrick and Kito, were attached to their maneuvering station, but they had not had time to stand up, in order to assume a new posture, when the *Selenit* was lying on the ground, and they found themselves sprawling on the floor again, which the machine had already dragged along the declivity. Garrick bumped his head rather rudely against the wall, and, half-stunned, only just retained enough strength to cling on to the straps retaining him.

Kito found himself upside-down momentarily, but he was an energetic fellow endowed with great presence of mind. He succeeded in delivering gas to the tangential tubes whose reaction would oppose the rotation that had gripped the vessel. His initiative did not stop the fall, but it slowed it down.

For half a minute, the enormous mass of the *Selenit* tumbled down the slope, rebounding from rocky projections. If the misadventure had occurred on Earth, the hull would not have resisted, and the machine would have been torn apart, but thanks to the reduction in weight, the expedition escaped catastrophe on this occasion.

Having reached the bottom of the slope, the *Selenit* covered a further two hundred meters rolling over the plain, and stopped. Instead of resting normally on its caterpillar tracks and struts, however, it had ended up lying on its left side.

In the crew section, Madeleine and her companions came to their feet, standing on the lateral wall of the *Selenit*.

Scherrebek and Galston appeared in the doorway to the command post.

"Anyone injured?" asked the captain.

"Roll call!" shouted Brifaut.

Uberaba had lit three electric lamps a few seconds after the fall. Two were still shining, and permitted the members of the expedition to examine one another.

"Roll call!" Brifaut repeated. "Madeleine Brifaut!"

"Present!" replied the young woman, albeit in a tremulous voice.

"Bojardo!"

"Present!"

The Frenchman named each of the crew members who were in the main section successively. All of them responded. None had any injury, or even a serious bruise. Scherrebek and Galston were unharmed. Kito and Garrick made their appearance, They too were safe and sound.

"Everyone's in good health," said Bojardo. "It's only a minor problem, then."

But Scherrebek remained anxious.

"Let's make sure now that the *Selenit* hasn't suffered any damage. If the hull is beached, we'll need to repair it immediately.

They set out to examine every inch of the interior wall of the *Selenit*. It was intact. But the exterior hull might have been cracked, which would have put the crew in serious danger.

The manometers, however, indicated no diminution in the pressure of the air contained within the vessel. As the output of the oxygen tubes had not been affected either, they could deduce that there had not been any loss.

"I'll go out with Goffoël and Brifaut to examine the hull and reconnoiter our situation," said Scherrebek. "In the meantime, Uberaba and Lang will mount guard here. The rest can install themselves as best they can to try to sleep. We're all going to have to make great efforts; we mustn't get overly fatigued unnecessarily."

VIII. On Lunar Soil

They took the mattresses from the couchettes in order to lay them out on the lateral wall that would serve as a floor until further notice, and the members of the crew had not been designated to keep watch with Scherrebek lay down fully dressed. They were mostly very tired, for they had only slept poorly since the departure from Earth.

Scherrebek and his companions went into the suit-room, where, with the aid of Lang and Uberaba, they each enclosed themselves in an apparatus. The abnormal position of the *Selenit* made it awkward for them to get the suits and put them on, but they succeeded without too much difficulty, their movements being facilitated by the lack of weight. With his gigantic stature, Goffoël, who weighed a hundred kilos on Earth, weighed no more than seventeen on the Moon; he lifted up his suit like a feather, its weight having diminished from two hundred kilos to thirty-four.

"Aren't you afraid of being affected by the cold?" Dr. Lang asked. "If, as is generally believed, the surface of our satellite reaches two hundred and seventy degrees below zero during the long lunar nights, you're risking being frozen as soon as you step outside."

"The double envelope of the suit constitutes a perfect thermic insulation," Brifaut observed.

"Yes," said Scherrebek, "and the temperature of a body in a vacuum can only be lowered by radiation; because we won't be radiating heat, thanks to our insulating carapace, we won't cool down. At any rate, the loss of heat will be very slow, and we'll have all the time we need to examine the hull of the *Selenit*."

It only remained to screw on the enormous helmets of the suits, provided with portholes. As the explorers were only illuminated by the Earth's light, Scherrebek removed the screens of leaded glass garnishing the portholes, intended for excursions in sunlight.

The three suited men carried cables by means of which they could attach themselves to one another if necessary. They were able to establish electrical connections between them with flexible wires and plugs, which fitted into sockets mounted on the side of the helmet. That would permit them to talk to one another, a telephone powered by dry batteries being within reach inside the apparatus. They each had an electric lamp at the belt, protected by a metal tube and a network of iron wire, attached to a supple wire.

They equipped themselves with a few tools: picks, levers and irons bars, which would have been too heavy on Earth to be manageable, but whose weight on the surface of the Moon was barely sufficient to make them useful implements.

It was now necessary to accomplish the exit maneuver, passing through the release chamber. The explorers would be obliged to indulge in veritable acrobatics, the chamber being horizontal and the exterior hatch being located at the top like a trap-door.

"It's still lucky," Brifaut observed, "that the *Selenit* fell on its left side. If it were lying on its right side, the exit hatch would be applied to the ground and we'd have been imprisoned irredeemably."

"Perhaps not irredeemably," said Scherrebek. "Energetic men always end up triumphing over ill fortune."

That was, for the time being, the final word. Uberaba placed his helmet on his shoulders and sealed it hermetically.

The apparatus had an abundant supply of oxygen.

The exit maneuver was executed perfectly. Scherrebek, Goffoël and Brifaut met up again on the hull of the *Selenit*.

Standing side by side in the earthlight, in their rigid and monstrous carapaces, they offered a fantastic sight. An astronomer who had not been alerted to the presence of the explorers and who had been able to perceive them at that moment with the aid of a giant telescope would have taken them for inhabitants of the Moon; he would have proclaimed that our satellite is populated by strange creatures with bodies armored like those of crustaceans or coleoptera.

The gauntlets that terminated the sleeves of the suits, into which the explorers had to slide their hands, had been the object of particular care, for it was necessary both to retain a certain flexibility and to render them sufficiently insulated to avoid frostbite in the fingers. It would have been possible to replace them with pincers maneuverable from inside the sleeves, but it had been deemed that that mechanism would limit the action of the suit-wearers too severely. The gauntlets had been all the more difficult to design because, in order to render them capable of resisting the internal pressure of the suit, it had been necessary to fit them with a metallic framework made of steel plates and wires. In those conditions, their usage was rather awkward, and the suit-wearers inevitably became a little clumsy.

The explorers had before them a mountainous massif in which a profound gorge opened directly facing the *Selenit*, between irregular, sinuous and chaotic cliffs. Rocks, which appeared to be white in the earthlight and whose shadows, by contrast, were impenetrably black, rose up behind one another like the steps of a gigantic stairway.

An accumulation of summits barred the horizon, their white points cutting into the black sky. The mountains seemed to be leaning backwards; as they extended further into the distance, one might have thought that their last peaks were about to collapse behind the horizon. That was an effect of the curvature of the lunar surface.

To their left—which is to say, toward the north-east—the explorers discovered another gorge, of which the flat, inclined bottom resembled the dry bed of a broad torrent, which might perhaps have been a flow of lava.

The three men linked themselves together by their telephonic wires in order to be able to exchange their reflections.

"It's obviously down there that we rolled," said Brifaut, indicating the slope.

"Yes," said Scherrebek. "It's a miracle that we weren't shattered."

Behind them, toward the east and the south, the explorers had nothing but the plain, which remained somber in spite of the earthlight, but was nevertheless sufficiently distinct for them to see the line of the horizon distinctly, rigorously circular in that direction. The brevity of the line of sight, which only extended for two and a half kilometers—a brevity to which the three men were not yet accustomed—procured them the strange sensation of being suspended in the void over a narrow platform.

In that direction, they could not perceive any trace of mountains. In spite of their proximity, the Tenerife Mountains, which are of relatively low altitude, were below the horizon.

The sky was splendid. Not only was the Earth, considerably indented in the east, shining with a magnificent blue-tinted glare, but the constellations had a purity and vivacity that the inhabitants of our globe do not know. The light of the stars was not attenuated by the thick atmosphere; it no longer had the scintillation that is due to the movement and variations in density of the layers of air at different altitudes. The Milky Way was almost dazzling. Their light being brighter, far more stars were distinguishable than can be seen with the naked eye from the surface of the Earth, and all the celestial gleams had a blue tint, to which the gaze gradually became accustomed, thus becoming less sensible.

The breadth of the *Selenit*, with its triple hull, being ten meters, it was at that height that the three men found themselves suspended above the ground.

"How are we going to get down?" asked Brifaut.

"We only have to jump," said Goffoël.

Without waiting for a reply, he detached the telephonic wires linking him to his companions, and launched himself into space.

Although aware of the effects of the diminution of weight on the Moon, Scherrebek and Brifaut were astonished to see their comrade take more than four seconds to reach the lunar soil, when it would have required less than two on Earth. Goffoël was reminiscent of one of those large man-shaped balloons with which one plays during country fairs.

And to prove that everything becomes singularly easy on the surface of the Moon, Goffoël suddenly rose up like a sylph, and landed beside his companions on the *Selenit*, with a single bound.

After that exploit, which demonstrated the power that muscles habituated to rude exercise gave to Terrans transported to the Moon, the three men leapt to the ground and set about inspecting the hull of the *Selenit* minutely.

It was only after two hours that they acquired the conviction that their interplanetary vehicle had not suffered any injury. The solidity of its construction and the weakness of the lunar gravity had protected it. Even the system of caterpillar tracks and struts was undamaged.

But one serious problem was posed. In its present position, the *Selenit* was immobilized. It could not move over the lunar surface, nor, more importantly, could it reset itself to lift off and return to the Earth. It was therefore indispensable to reposition it, but at first glance, that task seemed beyond the strength of ten men, even if the muscle-power were sextupled. Although deballasted of a considerable load of explosives, and relieved of five-sixths of its weight, the *Selenit* still weighed about five hundred tons.

How could they move such a mass and set it upright? The large tubes of the reaction engine, which would have been able to furnish the necessary energy, was not orientated in the right direction, and the small ones, which served for steering, were too weak.

Having concluded their inspection, the three men leapt on to the *Selenit* and went back into the release chamber in order to return to their lodgings.

As Lang and Uberaba came forward in order to rid him of him suit, Scherrebek recoiled, gesticulating, to make them understand that they ought not to touch him. Indeed, the metallic carapace was covered with frost by the condensation of the water vapor contained in the *Selenit*'s atmosphere. The surface of the apparatus had been intensely chilled by the three explorers' sojourn outside. If it had been touched at that moment with a bare hand, it would have been cruelly burned. The suit-wearers had to help one another to unscrew their helmets with their gloved hands, which was not without difficulty at first, because of the thick layer of ice that had formed on their glazed viewports and prevented them from seeing.

Everyone had got up on hearing the little crew come back in, avid to know the news, on which their lives depended.

"No damage," Scherrebek announced. "Nevertheless, we're in a bad situation, and I can't see, at the moment, a means of improving it—but I confess that I'm very tired. If you wish, we'll have a small snack, after which we can sleep for a few hours."

IX. Plato

"Get up! Get up! It's time!"

Madeleine's voice resonated in the *Selenit*. The young woman, having woken up before anyone else, had got up without saying anything and had brought a pot of coffee, which she had found a means of heating up in the food-store, by setting up an electric stove.

The men sat up on the mattresses at the appeal of the gracious cup-bearer.

"Hip, hip, hurrah for Madame Brifaut!" exclaimed Garrick, with whom the other crew members joined in chorus.

In spite of their critical situation, the passengers of the *Selenit* had not lost their good humor.

Madeleine distributed buttered toast and everyone ate with a hearty appetite, while holding council.

Brifaut was the first to propose a practical solution.

"I can only see one means of turning the *Selenit* over," he said, "And that's to hollow out the ground on one side to lower the system of wheels until it finds a point of support."

"You can't think so!" exclaimed Bojardo. "A trench a hundred meters long and seven or eight broad would be a Herculean labor."

"I believe however," said Scherrebek, "that our comrade Brifaut is right. Let's not forget that we are, indeed, Hercules on the surface of the Moon. The effort required would be scarcely greater than that required to dig a trench fifteen meters long and three or four wide and deep on Earth. It's not a task beyond the strength of ten vigorous men. We'll share it, in two groups of five, who'll relieve one another every two hours.

A first crew was designated, and set to work immediately.

Nothing was stranger than the spectacle of the five suited men busy around the *Selenit* in the blue-tinted earthlight. In that motionless landscape, alongside the chaos of the mountains, the metal monsters struck the ground with forceful blows of their enormous picks, and tore away blocks that would have weighed a hundred kilos on Earth. They moved them out of the way as if they were masses of cork. When they hurled them into the distance the stones described an elongated curve and fell back solely and gently. And all of that was as silent as a cinematic vision, except that, sometimes, a slight vibration transmitted by the ground and the metallic envelopes of the suit reminded the workers that sound was not absolutely banished from the lunar surface. If there was an atmosphere—which the explorers, having other more urgent preoccupations, had not yet taken the trouble to ascertain—its pressure was too feeble to transmit sounds.

As Scherrebek had foreseen, the work progressed very rapidly. At the fourth change of shift—which is to say, after eight hours—the *Selenit* was only maintained in unstable equilibrium in its initial position; a relatively feeble effort would be sufficient to oblige it to turn over and bring it to rest on its wheels.

They decided to leave Madeleine alone inside the *Selenit*. The ten men combined their efforts to make the heavy machine swing into the trench they had hollowed out. The young woman had learned to carry out the maneuvers indispensable for the reentry of the suit-wearers. She did not even experience a painful impression when she found herself alone in the entrails of the vessel, all the more so given that it was impossible for her to look outside through the periscopes because she had to be on her guard against falling when the machine toppled over.

The ten men had placed themselves on the side opposite the trench. They braced themselves against the side of the *Selenit* and shoved together with a simultaneous movement. The apparatus began to rotate slowly, and descended into the ditch as if into a bed of cotton wool. The maneuver had been carried out without the slightest hitch.

If the explorers had been on Earth they would have saluted their success with three cheers, but in the empire of lunar silence they could only mark their triumph by gesticulating with the sleeves of their suits.

The *Selenit* was inspected again. They made sure that it could climb the slope of the ditch without difficulty, and Scherrebek gave the order, by means of signs, to return aboard.

Now that the *Selenit* was in the normal position, they hastened to make arrangements to enjoy all the comforts that the constructors had been ingenious in creating. In fact that vehicle of a new genre was at least as habitable as a submarine, and the care that had been taken to ensure the perfect regeneration of the air meant that they could breathe there without any difficulty.

The diminishing crescent of the Earth announced that the Sun would not take long to rise over the region into which the explorers had fallen. Consulting their astronomical ephemeris, Scherrebek and his companions ascertained that they had no more than twenty-four hours to wait to see the first rays of sunlight skimming the soil of the Sea of Rains south of Plato.

The experiment that the explorers had carried out during their first sortie in the suits had convinced them that the apparatus was adequately well-constructed to permit those occupying them to resist the action of cold almost indefinitely. The physiological heat disengaged by respiration and the oxidation of the tissues compensated amply for the loss by radiation into the void. It was therefore sufficient to be well-provided with reserves of oxygen and food to be able to undertake a long excursion.

The maps and photographs of the moon showed the exact position of breaches that existed to the south in the enclosure of Plato, the huge crater on the flank of which the *Selenit* had landed. Those breaches ought to resemble the rugged gorge of fantastic appearance that the explorers could see through the portholes, but the latter doubtless did not penetrate all the way to the center of the crater and it would not be prudent to venture into it.

Dr. Lang proposed the organization of an expedition in order to penetrate into Plato and study the interior plain, which is one of the enigmas of selenography.

"What's so extraordinary about it, then?" asked Madeleine.

"That the bottom of the crater becomes darker the more brightly it's illuminated. It will be interesting to discover whether it's covered with vegetation, as the abnormal phenomenon incites one to think."

"Personally," said Galston, who was a first-rate mountaineer, "I'd rather climb the 2,470-meter peak that dominates the east of Plato's rim, on the side of which one remarks, in photographs, the traces of a gigantic landslide. From that height, we'd see the sun rise over the other side of the crater and the Sea of Rains. It's a spectacle that we ought not to miss. Perhaps we could even see the summits of the Alps, whose long chain extends south-west of Plato."

"I doubt that," Kito observed.

For a few moments, the Japanese had been rapidly tracing figures on a piece of paper.

"Calculation shows," he said, "that from the top of a 2,470-meter peak, we wouldn't even be able to see the entire width of the crater. That's ninety-six kilometers, and our view would be limited by the horizon to ninety-three kilometers, so we wouldn't even be able to see the foot of the other edge of the rim. Only the summits would be visible, and in any case, they'd hide the massif of the Alps from us even if—and I'm not certain about that—their altitude is sufficient to allow them to appear over the horizon. Note that the bottom of the crater is below the level of the Sea of Rains, and that the altitude of 2,470 meters has been measured in relation to that. It follows that, on the side of the exterior plain, the horizon would be even closer.

"I think, nevertheless, that he ascent proposed by our comrade is worth the trouble of being attempted. From that height we'd doubtless be able to descend again inside the crater and make the anticipated observations. Then we could traverse the crater obliquely to emerge through the southern breach, outside which the *Selenit* could have come to meet us."

"Isn't that too long and too difficult an excursion? An ascent of at least 1,500 meters, a descent of 2,500, an eighty-kilometer walk across the floor of the crater and a new ascent to the breach in order to get out!"

"Divide all the figures by six," retorted Kito, "and you'll see that it's not beyond the strength of the giants we are on the lunar world."

That reply made Goffoël smile; in his eyes, Kito was a dwarf. Nevertheless, Kito was right; men could accomplish the journey that Galston had sketched out easily, even burdened by their suits.

Brifaut thought that he ought to raise an objection.

"The temperature of the Moon will rise considerably as soon as the Sun is irradiating its surface. Are you sure that we can stand up to thirty or forty hours of the increase that will occur after sunrise, if we don't have the resource of taking refuge in the *Selenit*?"

"Firstly," said Uberaba, "our apparatus is constructed so as to absorb as little heat as possible. Secondly, it's only at the end of thirty or forty hours that the Moon, extremely chilled by a long night of fifteen times twenty-four hours, will attain a high temperature under the action of the solar rays. Finally, don't forget that we're at a high altitude, not far from the North Pole, in a region that the sun's rays always strike obliquely, and remain, in consequence, incapable of brining about an enormous rise in temperature, as in the equatorial regions. Certainly, it's been calculated that in the latter, the sun warms up to about 184 degrees Centigrade; at our location, it ought not to exceed forty, which is still quite supportable by human beings, and that temperature will only be attained slowly as the Sun rises."

"In my opinion," said Lang, "those considerations are of no practical interest. We'd only suffer from the cold or heat of the ground if the boots of our suits were poorly insulated. Given that the apparatus is constructed to reflect or diffuse calorific rays into space rather than absorbing them, we could walk without inconvenience through a five-hundred-degree furnace."

"Well." concluded Scherrebek, "We've already proved the suits' resistance to cold; now we'll see whether they offer equally good protection against heat."

Five explorers were designated for the first excursion. They were Galston, the second in command, and leader of the party, Brifaut, Lang, Espronceda and Kito.

Madeleine would certainly have liked to accompany her husband, but it was thought prudent not to include a woman in that first expedition, when they did not know exactly what obstacles it might run into. In any case, the only suit that could be adapted for Madeleine's use was Kito's. The young woman was promised, in order to console her, that Kito would yield his place to her on another occasion.

Madeleine was anxious at the idea of being separated from her husband in such extraordinary circumstances, but Scherrebek had selected Brifaut because he judged him the most capable, in his capacity as a journalist, of describing the spectacles that the climbers were going to witness.

Two hours later, the little troop set out into the lunar night, while the rest of the crew got ready to move off in the *Selenit* in order to go around the rim of the crater and take up a position on the plain facing the great southern breach.

Scherrebek was counting on having his share of the spectacle of the sunrise. He would see it rising behind the buttresses of Plato, and would perhaps have, along with the members of the mission who had remained aboard the *Selenit*, a sight perhaps as beautiful as those who were undertaking the ascent.

Thanks to the marvelous photographic documents that we possess nowadays of our satellite, the explorers were able to orientate themselves reliably. It would have been impossible for them to set forth on such an adventure if they had not had a detailed map of the regions they intended to visit.

They would not have been able to risk themselves on the invisible face of the Moon; the country appeared to them to be an inextricable chaos, and they would also have lacked the infallible guide of the long lunar nights, always suspended at the same height for every point of the hemisphere facing it: the Earth, which the climbers could see shining in its final quarter, forty degrees above the horizon, almost due south. With a reference-point like hat, it was impossible to mistake their direction.

An experiment made with a compass placed flat on the ground had not given any practical result. The magnetic field lacked intensity, and its orientation remained dubious. Fortunately, as is evident, the magnetic needle, so precious on our globe, was superfluous for the explorers of the Moon.

They could make out quite clearly with the naked eye, on the blue disk of the Earth, the bright forms of continents and the dark surface of seas; in places, large bright irregular patches were spread out or disposed in bands, parallel to the equator; they were clouds masking the surface, but rendering the star all the more brilliant.

Linked to one another by a rope, like terrestrial mountain-climbers, equipped with alpenstocks and ice-axes, Galston and his four companions began to climb the slope of the mountain. From the outset they realized that the climb would be child's play for them, so agile did their lightness render them. They bounded from rock to rock like chamois. Thus, they did not take long to detach the rope that bound them together, and which was only impeding their movements. It took them no more than eight hours, including halts for rest, to effect an ascent that would have taken at least twenty-four hours in terrestrial conditions through such rugged terrain.

When they reached the summit, the great plain that formed the center of the crater appeared, partly-invaded by the impenetrable shadows projected by the mountains of the southern edge. To their right, still toward the south, profound gorges yawned, veritable gulfs into which the Earth's light did not insinuate itself, and which seemed to divide the rim into concentric rings.

They communicated their impressions to one another by means of their telephones.

"That great mass detached from the wall," Lang explained, "results from an enormous landslide. An entire section of the mountain has slid into the bottom of the crater."

"The Moon is definitely a dead world," said Brifaut. "All this is nothing but a desert of stone."

"Wait!" said Espronceda. "We'll see in a few hours whether or not the floor of Plato is carpeted with vegetation."

"Perhaps we'll find a forest with tall trees," said Galston.

"More like something analogous to mosses or lichens," Kito opined.

"The explorers had several hours to wait before sunrise, for they had climbed up more rapidly than they had anticipated. They installed themselves as comfortably as possible in order to try to get a little sleep while they waited for daybreak.

X. Sunrise

Standing up, facing westwards—which, for the Moon, in accordance with the conventions of astronomers, is where the sun rises—Gaston and his four companions watched. According to the calculations of Lang and Kito, the Sun was due to appear in a matter of minutes, but nothing—not the slightest glimmer—announced its approach.

"If zodiacal light were due, as some have sustained, to the persistence of a nebulous zone around the Sun, we would have seen it appear some time ago," said Espronceda. "It is, therefore, only a phenomenon of refraction in the upper layers of the terrestrial atmosphere.

"Twilight, such as we observe it on our globe, and which results from the diffusion of light by the atmosphere, doesn't exist in the Moon. That doesn't mean that there's no transition between night and broad daylight, because, given the slowness of the Moon's movement, rotating on its axis twenty-nine times slower than the Earth, sunrise last for a long time. Between the moment when the upper edge of the disk appears and the moment when the lower edge rises above the horizon in its turn, an hour goes by. It follows that for an hour, a point for which the sun is rising receives more light progressively, and passes gradually, in consequence, from absolute obscurity to full daylight."

The explorers were about to have the opportunity to observe that phenomenon.

A luminous dot appeared in the west, in a fissure in the mountainous crest that barred the horizon. It grew, like a violet flame of extraordinary intensity, which soon caused the bright earthlight to pale.

"Use your leaded screens!" advised Galston, over the telephone.

The climbers slid the glass plates designed to stop ultraviolet radiation into the grooves fitted behind the viewports of their helmets for that purpose, to avoid the risk of being blinded. They had withdrawn their arms from the sleeves of their suits and were able to manipulate the various objects freely that they had at their service inside the apparatus.

Brifaut had sat down on a rock to contemplate that sunrise, such as he had never seen.

"How deformed the sun appears!" he said.

The flame was projected in a plume against the black background of the sky.

"It's not deformed," Kito replied. "On the contrary, you're seeing it in its true aspect, when the radiance of its protuberances isn't absorbed by an atmospheric envelope. That plume that you perceive is one of the gigantic eruptions of incandescent gas with which the surface of the sun is constantly bristling, and which the air prevents us from distinguishing on Earth. Our astronomers have only been able to discover them during eclipses or by means of the spectroscope. Here, for us, the sun would have no rays; on the other hand, it won't appear to be round, but crowned with irregular flames."

The luminous patch slowly grew, and, while the bottom of the crater and the base of the mountain remained plunged in shadow, the explorers saw the rocks light up around them on the summit. Small as the part of the sun was that projected over the horizon, the objects struck by its light were already resplendent, in the bleak lunar desert, as if they belonged to another world.

Gradually, as the flame expanded, other tongues of fire sprang forth into the blackness of the firmament, underlined by a violet and fulgurant streak. On the flank of the mountain that served the voyagers as an observatory, the darkness slowly descended. Within the dominant blue tint, the Terrans distinguished steaks of brown and ocher on the rocks, which betrayed the presence of metallic oxides. In the ensemble, the aspect of those rocks was reminiscent of that of marble, but they were less compact in texture.

In spite of its glare, the sun did not extinguish the lights in the sky. The stars and he Earth were still perceptible, and the breaking day did not give birth to the azure so dear to the inhabitants of our world.

For an hour, the explorers watched the show scent of the star. In spite of the leaded screens, they were often obliged to turn their eyes away in order not to be dazzled. The daylight descended gradually over the eastern slopes of the enclosure and reached the bottom of the crater.

"Look," remarked Espronceda. "The edge of the circular plain at the foot of the rampart directly below us is still in shadow, although a luminous patch is forming some distance away on the floor. That proves that the central part is convex and that the edges are depressed, as in almost all the lunar craters. In sum, it's not a plain that the rim encloses but a sunken dome, something like one of the faces of an enormous lens."

"I don't agree," said Lang. "The marked curvature of the lunar surface is sufficient to explain the phenomenon you're pointing out, of which many astronomers, in my opinion, have made a false interpretation. For the crest behind which the sun is rising, the limit of the horizon on a perfectly horizontal plain would be precisely over the zone that's lighting up first; beyond it, the bottom is normally below the horizon, in the same way that the three-kilometer zone limiting the enclosure on the other side of the crater is for us."

XI. Lunar Vegetation[13]

The sun was now floating over the mountains, rising obliquely toward the south.

They could distinguish quite clearly, in the illuminated part of the crater, the pale streaks that all observers have noticed in the central plain of Plato at daybreak. It is only when the sun is already very high, toward the sixth day of the lunar cycle, that the floor begins to darken; it is almost black in the epoch of the full moon, to such an extent that ancient astronomers called it the Black Lake.

"Now we can try to go down," Galston proposed. "I think we'll find a route without too much difficulty."

The descent was more challenging than the climb, because on that side the slope was steeper, and if the landslipped section had not formed an immense bank against the cliff, the explorers would have had a great deal of difficulty reaching their goal. Thanks to that bank, however, although it was very uneven, they were able to make their way down from the top of the mountain, leaping from rock to rock, sometimes from a height of ten or twelve meters at a distance of twenty or twenty-five. They were intoxicated by the sensation of their lightness, and Galston, who retained his composure most fully, was obliged to remind his companions to be prudent.

Finally, they reached the plain at the foot of the cliff, pale and tinted like marble, which, except for the collapsed sections, rose up in fits and starts, forming a series of gigantic steps. And always, behind the dazzling crests, the starry black sky extended.

Brifaut bent down and scratched a dark patch with the tip of his gauntlet. He detached a gray fibrous mass from it, which had almost the same texture as German tinder.

---

[13] This extra chapter-break and title are absent from the feuilleton version.

The others drew nearer in order to look at it, and then the explorers put themselves in telephonic communication.

"Lunar vegetation!" said Lang.

"Some kind of fungus or lichen," said Brifaut.

"That piece must be a dead, or in a state of suspended animation," Galston declared.

Brifaut introduced it into his suit via the valves, in order to conserve it and study it at his leisure, an irrefutable witness of at least vegetable life on the surface of the Moon.

That felt-like substance was extended in many places on the ground, but it also left large areas uncovered. It presumably only proliferated at times of great warmth, then invading the pale-hued stony regions.

The explorers were delighted with their discovery.

Their horizon was so limited that they could no longer perceive the crater's rim except toward the east, at the place where they had descended and with which they were still, so to speak, in touch.

Orientating themselves by means of the Earth, they set forth in search of the breach by way of which they were to rejoin the *Selenit*. They found it and passed through it without overmuch difficulty. The found the vessel in the exact spot fixed for the rendezvous.

They had departed about thirty hours before, and throughout that time they had been obliged to eat, breathe and sleep without emerging from their suits, so they were glad finally to be able to liberate themselves from their carapaces.

Everything had gone well aboard the *Selenit* during their absence. Scherrebek and his companions had watched the sun rise over the Sea of Rains and had had time to carry out a few experiments. They had gone out in suits equipped with various measuring devices.

They had ascertained that there as a very tenuous atmosphere on the surface of the Moon, whose pressure was not even equivalent to a millimeter of mercury, whereas, on Earth, it requires a column of 760 millimeters of mercury to compensate for the pressure of the air. It appeared to be composed primarily of carbon dioxide, a substance at the expense of which vegetation can develop.

A thermometer exposed in the sunlight had risen to seventy-six degrees. Sheltered from the direct radiance and turned toward a fully-illuminated reflective surface at a distance of ten meters, it had marked a maximum of twelve degrees. Turned toward the shadow, it had fallen well below zero, and Scherrebek had been obliged to withdraw it to prevent it from freezing. As he had anticipated, the temperature of objects on the Moon was absolutely dependent on the intensity of the calorific radiation to which they were subject.

Scherrebek had calculated, with Garrick, that the *Selenit* could travel about six hundred kilometers over the lunar surface without using up too great a quantity of explosive. That almost represented a traversal of the Sea of Plains. They had established in consequence a program of exploration that permitted them to visit the Alps with their Great Valley northwest of the Sea of Rains; the three remarkable craters Aristillus, Autolycus and Archimedes, to the west; the chain of the Apennines, the largest on the Moon, to the south-west; then the crater Eratosthenes; and finally, if no accident disturbed the plan, Copernicus, the king of annular mountains, with its aureole of radiant bands.

XII. At the Foot of the Apennines[14]

It had already been five times twenty-four hours since the international mission had arrived safely on the Moon. That was a great deal, when one considered the precarious conditions of existence for eleven people in the immense desert. It was very little to explore regions as vast as those that Scherrebek had resolved to travel.

The members of the expedition had nevertheless found the time and energy to visit, after Plato, the Great Valley of the Alps and the group of three remarkable craters, Aristillus, Autolycus and Archimedes.

Madeleine, who had accompanied her husband during excursions to the Valley of the Alps and Archimedes, was enthused.

The massif of the Alps, impressive by virtue of the number of its peaks, which separates broad and profound depressions, offers nothing more grandiose than the valley in question, an immense breach a hundred and thirty kilometers long, which cut the mountain range into two stumps and connected like a dried-up canal the Sea of Rains and the Sea of Cold. It is a great rectilinear avenue bordered by sheer cliffs whose crests rise to an altitude of 3,600 meters. Narrow gorges open astonishing perspectives at intervals in its giant walls. Depending on the phase of the long lunar day, the abysms hollowed out between the rocks light up with intrinsic radiance, which alternates dazzling reflections with opaque shadows, or remain, by contrast, plunged in impenetrable darkness.

Archimedes is especially curious because of the regularity of its rim, formed by several stages of superimposed cliffs. In fact, to embrace its whole extent with the gaze, the explor-

---

[14] In the feuilleton version this chapter is entitled "Mountains and Precipices."

ers were obliged to make an ascent of its rampart, for the interior plain measures seventy kilometers in diameter.

Having reached that culminating point, at an altitude of 2,210 meters, Madeleine thought that she had been transported to the ruins of a colossal Roman circus.

"I find it hard to believe," she said to her husband, "that all those extraordinary formations, so regular, are only due to the hazard of natural processes. It seems simpler to me to imagine that intelligent beings once lived here, thousands of centuries ago, and that we're finding the vestiges of their civilization. What will have become of monuments like the pyramids of Egypt, cities like Paris, London and New York, when humankind has disappeared, after ten million years of abandonment? An animate being arrived from another world would no longer discover anything but effaced forms and heaps of rubble, and would believed that he was in the presence of natural piles of rocks.

"Remember what the ruins of Angkor Thom, the ancient Khmer city in Cambodia, were like only a few years ago, when our archeologists had not yet saved it from the invasions of the virgin forest. Nature, however, had only reclaimed them five hundred years before. Well, if intelligent beings had once raised constructions here, which had no reason to resemble our human edifices, or even to possess the rigidity of lines in which our architecture delights, they have been subjected to the insults of time. For want of wind and rain, the torrid heat of long days and the intense cold of long nights have taken charge of their disintegration.

"Who can tell what these vestiges represent? Perhaps they're the remains of immense shelters raised against the cold and the heat, whose roofs have disappeared. The weakness of gravity at the lunar surface renders the edification of immense vaults plausible, supported at intervals by pillars, which later collapsed, in the central plains of the craters."

"I'm inclined to think as you do about that subject," Brifaut replied, "but we'll do well not to sustain such opinions before our scholarly comrades if we don't want them to make fun of us."

The passage of the *Selenit* between Aristillus, Autolycus and Archimedes enabled the explorers to make the acquaintance of "grooves."[15] Having gone around Archimedes to reach its southern edge, they were, in fact, stopped by an abyss more than a kilometer in width, which opened abruptly in the plain and whose edges were level with the surrounding soil. That enormous ditch striped the Sea of Rains south of Archimedes for as far as the eye could see, in the region that selenographers have baptized the Marsh of Putrefaction.[16]

The explorers took turns to go out in suits to contemplate that fine specimen of a kind of accident characteristic of the lunar soil that depresses the rims and centers of craters. Discovered for the first time in 1786 by the astronomer Schroeter, grooves have since been discovered in numerous regions of the Moon. More than a thousand are counted today.

The one by which the explorers had been stopped was a gulf whose bottom was invisible. The sun only illuminated the top of the northern wall, causing it to appear as a bright white band, which descended almost vertically beneath the feet of the travelers. Here and there on the dazzling rocks, however, colored patches and streaks were discernible. Reflection from

---

[15] What the author calls *rainures* [grooves] are usually known in modern English astronomy as "rays," but that word already has more than sufficient meanings in the present translation and the term "grooves" is used by modern astronomers in connection with craters on other satellites in the solar system, so a literal translation did not seem unjustified, especially given that the text's (probably incorrect) explanation of the phenomenon is that they really are grooves.

[16] The Marsh of Putrefaction did make a brief appearance on lunar maps made in the 1880s (although Camille Flammarion called the feature the Sea of Putrefaction) but it disappeared some time before 1926, so in this instance the author seems a trifle behind the times.

the illuminated surface cast some light on the opposite all, which the sun could not reach, and its glimmer descended quite a long way into the abyss. Lower still, however, everything was drowned in darkness.

Scherrebek had packets of powder brought, of the kind used to make fireworks, which can burn in a vacuum. The *Selenit* had a small supply of them, for the circumstance had been anticipated in which it might be necessary to produce light or hat, or send a signal, when it was not possible to employ electricity. The cartridges were ignited by means of a fuse. Scherrebek ignited three of them, which were thrown successively into the gulf.

They were seen to fall with the slowness characteristic of the lunar world and descend to a depth so vertiginous that when they could no longer be perceived, no one could affirm that they had reached the bottom before going out. The explorers, standing on the edge of the cliff, shivered at the thought that one of them might fall into that unfathomable crevasse. Some astronomers estimate the depth of the fissures as ten thousand meters.

Having returned to the *Selenit*, the voyagers did not fail to exchange their reflections.

"When one thinks," said Bojardo, "that one false move or imprudence would have been sufficient to tip the *Selenit* into that abyss! Our bones would have remained on the Moon for all eternity, which, deserted and desolate as it is, already gives the impression of a cemetery."

"A grandiose cemetery!" retorted Scherrebek, smiling. "I'm convinced that we'll all get back safe and sound from this expedition, but if some misfortune were to overtake me before the return and I died here, it wouldn't displease me to be buried here. I can imagine myself quite serenely, beneath a crag, in a crater or in the middle of the plain, as a witness to the first journey of human beings to the Moon."

"That's not very cheerful, you know," said Uberaba. "Suppose we talk about something else."

After the visit to Archimedes, they studied the map and observed that the grooves parallel to the Apennines would prevent the *Selenit* reaching the mountain chain directly. The machine would be obliged to go southwards as far as the vicinity of Eratosthenes after having searched for a passage between the groove that departed south-westwards from Archimedes and another running parallel to the Apennines. There was a tongue of land there, it seemed, some five or six kilometers wide, which served as a bridge between the Marsh of Putrefaction and the southern region of the Sea of Rains.

They set forth again, therefore, going along the groove south of Archimedes. A few hours later, having covered about a hundred kilometers of rocky terrain, sometimes felted by the strange vegetation that the explorers had discovered in the crater Plato, they saw the majestic crests of the Apennines rising over the horizon. Then the *Selenit* veered southwards in order to travel along the transversal groove, and after a further journey of several hours, was finally able to reach the foot of the mountains. The stage, interrupted by rest periods and brief reconnaissance trips in suits, had lasted for twenty-four hours. Now the explorers were confronted by an enormous irregular cliff pitted by innumerable fissures, which the Apennine chain formed in dipping abruptly toward the Sea of Rains.

Since leaving Plato they had drawn closer to the equator, and, as it was nearly half way through the lunar day, the sun was floating in the vicinity of the zenith. The lunar terrain was therefore overheated. By means of a specially-graduated mercury thermometer, Lang was able to establish that the temperature rose to a hundred and twenty degrees in the parts that the sun's rays struck vertically. Although the *Selenit*'s insulation had shown itself to be perfect thus far, Scherrebek judged it prudent to keep the machine in the shade of the cliff, where a thermometer exposed to the reflection of nearby surfaces did not indicate more than twenty degrees.

The discussed the formation of the Apennines.

"The chains of the lunar mountains," said Uberaba, "are the traces of great fractures that have split the crust. One of the lips of the fracture has sunk; the other has remained in projection, constituting a cliff whose thickness might reach that of the crust itself at the moment of its formation. Although the depth of the fault was considerable, the internal mass of the liquid nucleus of the Moon expanded over the inferior fragment and covered it with a layer of lava. That is what gave rise to the great plains that are designated by the name of Seas."

"Some astronomers," said Lang, "even think that the seesaw movement must have been powerful enough, aided by lateral pressures, to make the superior fragment slide over the inferior one, bringing it to rest in a cantilever fashion, while the inferior fragment itself, thus overloaded, sank down into the liquid nucleus. That hypothesis explains why the edges of the plains are at a shallower depth than the center, as the measurement of shadows permits the observation.

"The great lunar mountain chains, therefore, always have one abrupt slope, the one that represents the upper lip of the fracture, and one gentle slope, which corresponds to the surface of the uplifted fragment. Cliffs are frequent all over the Moon. Some of them have edges that are almost intact, having not been disaggregated by time, and which present themselves like perfectly straight and regular terraces—such as, for instance, the famous Straight Wall, which is observed in the southern hemisphere and extends over a length of a hundred and fifty kilometers. One doesn't see anything on the Moon comparable to the phenomena of large-scale wrinkling that had contributed so much to the formation of the terrestrial relief."

After this short lecture on selenography, primarily improvised for René and Madeleine Brifaut, the explorers studied the details of the project they had conceived of climbing one of the highs summits in the Apennines. The culminating point of that chain attains and altitude of 5,600 meters and there is a series of crests, extending over the whole of the range, that rose to five thousand meters or more.

The mission selected a peak that overlooks the last buttresses of the chain between the Sea of Rains and the Torrid

Gulf,[17] Mount Wolff, from which the view ought to extend over a radius of about a hundred and thirty kilometers. That summit is certainly not the highest, but its relative isolation, its situation in the corner of the massif, over the line of separation of two vast plains, and its proximity to the crater Eratosthenes, a hundred kilometers to the south-east, ought to render the ascent particularly interesting.

Madeleine was in the process of observing a part of the mountain through the narrow frame of a porthole when she uttered an exclamation and stepped back instinctively

"An avalanche!" she said.

Garrick leapt forward to replace her at the porthole. He saw a section of the mountain, the orientation of which exposed it fully to the sun, and enormous rocks detached from the summit falling down its near-vertical wall, sometimes rebounding from asperities.

The *Selenit* was not a hundred meters from the place on which the avalanche was about to fall!

One last leap, and the blocks shattered on the plain, bursting like bombs and hurling their debris in all directions.

No noise had reached the ears of the explorers, but when the blocks hit the ground, the later transmitted a feeble vibration to the *Selenit*.

Garrick and Madeleine reported to the other members of the expedition what they had just seen.

"It's not astonishing," said Scherrebek, "that the mountain is disintegrating under the action of the burning sun after having been subjected during the lunar night to a cold more than two hundred degrees below zero."

---

[17] *Golfe Torride* is translated as "Torrid Gulf" in some English editions of Jules Verne's account of a journey around the moon, but does not appear on English lunar maps, where the feature usually has the Latin name Sinus Aestuum, whose literal English translation would be "Bay of Billows." As I have not been employing Latin names, in keeping with the spirit of the French text, it seemed best to translate this one literally.

"Do you think," Madeleine said, "that it would be prudent to venture into the mountains, at the risk of being surprised by an avalanche like that one?"

"Our route isn't orientated toward the sun," declared Scherrebek. "We can't postpone the ascent, for we still have a considerable program to complete and the lunar day will soon begin to decline."

The expedition was to comprise Scherrebek, Goffoël, Garrick, Bojardo and Uberaba. The captain thought it prudent never to expose more than half the crew at a time, in order that the other could organize a rescue if necessary, and remain capable of maneuvering the *Selenit*.

The ascent was demanding. The explorers were obliged to search for a route on a mountain whose form they only knew approximately, and which was terribly steep. In addition, they were inconvenienced by the ardor of the sun, to which they avoided exposing themselves for long as much as was possible, all the more so as the exercise they were undertaking was already contributing to making them very hot. Thus, having got half way, they were obliged to take a few hours rest. It was not until twenty-four hours after leaving the *Selenit* that they reached the summit.

The summit in question formed a narrow plateau on to which the sun was darting its rays vertically. The view extended in one direction over the Sea of Rains to the north, and in the other over the Torrid Gulf to the south. The two plains were traversed by numerous white streaks, which glittered as if they had been strewn with diamond dust. Those shiny zones all seemed to be radiating from the same point, situated behind the crater Eratosthenes, whose western wall could be distinguished, very high and regular, barring the Torrid Gulf to the east.

"Those bands are coming from Copernicus," Goffoël telephoned to Scherrebek. "It's four hundred kilometers away to the north-west. We can't see it, but we can see its aureole, whose glare is most vivid at this point in the lunar cycle."

The spectacle that the Terrans had before their eyes was truly extraordinary. The plain of the Torrid Gulf, which had become visible as they reached the summit, as resplendent with an almost unsustainable brightness; it would not have been brighter had it been made of white marble. The somber stripes that divided the bands diminished the intensity of the radiation slightly.

To the north, in the direction of the Sea of Rains, the bands were more widely spaced.

The white streaks, passing over Eratosthenes, were even prolonged over the massif dominated by Mount Wolff, which extended westwards, like tumultuous waves on a suddenly frozen sea. The mountainous barrier to the east, which separated the northern plain from the southern plain and extended to meet the northern edge of Eratosthenes, was no less chaotic.

The mountaineers did not weary of contemplating that marvelous panorama, over which the black star-strewn sky extended, dominated at the zenith by a violet-tinted Sun with edges bristling with flames. The Earth was no longer visible; it was new.

Suddenly, Scherrebek tottered. Goffoël, who was beside him, sustained him and asked, by telephone: "What's the matter?"

"The heat!" moaned Scherrebek.—and collapsed completely in Goffoël's arms.

The latter lifted him up like a feather, suit and all, and leapt ten meters downhill to a platform sheltered from the sun by a rock-face.

His comrades joined him, anxiously. Now that their attention was no longer absorbed by the spectacle of the fantastic lunar landscape, they all felt ill at ease. They had stayed exposed to the ardor of the sun for too long without precaution. Their suits had protected them at first, but once the insulating barrier was overheated it only cooled down slowly. They all had the impression of being in a steam-bath, threatened by congestion.

Their situation was distressing. It was impossible to free themselves from the carapace that was stifling them, but which was also their safeguard. It was impossible to relieve Scherrebek, who could be seen through the viewports of his helmet breathing convulsively.

Uberaba, who was a doctor of medicine, knew that he could have revived the captain had he been able to intervene, but he had to watch the man's agony, impotently. There could be no thought of opening the helmet of the suit even for an instant, to administer a drug to the sick man or to refresh him; a vacuum would have been created instantaneously in the apparatus, and Scherrebek would have burst like an overinflated blister.

They had to content themselves with setting the Dane down in the shade, in the hope that he would gradually recover a more supportable temperature. They did not even have the resource of increasing the oxygen supply within his suit in order to permit him to breathe more easily, for the controls could only be operated from inside.

However, the other climbers were not in much better condition than their leader, and were wondering anxiously whether they might not all be about to lose consciousness one after another. They, at least were still capable of struggling. On Uberaba's advice, they increased the oxygen level of the air in their suits and drew upon their ration of drinking water to moisten their head and face.

If they wanted to avoid a catastrophe, however, the surest way to do so was to get back to the *Selenit* as quickly as possible.

Garrick initially offered to help Goffoël to transport the invalid, but as it was difficult for two men to coordinate their movements on such uneven terrain, Goffoël preferred to take charge of the burden on his own. To carry fifteen kilos—what was that, for him, who was accustomed to weighing a hundred on Earth and who, on the Moon, even counting his suit, weighed no more than sixty? Scherrebek was attached solidly to his back with the aid of ropes, and the little troop set forth, trying always to remain shielded from the direct rays of the sun.

The explorers scarcely gave any thought any longer to contemplating the grandiose and desolate landscape that extended before their eyes. In the harsh light, unfiltered by any atmosphere, the most distant contours appeared as sharply as the nearest, and the effects of perspective were strangely modified by it. Even when the view extended in reality over a long distance, one had the impression that the scene lacked depth, while the black sky gave the lunar soil, by contrast, the appearance that an open air theater takes on by night; the stage can be illuminated with electric beams, but not the sky, and the artifice is apparent.

With great difficulty, the explorers regained the *Selenit*, where they were finally able to take refuge.

They hastened to get Scherrebek out of his suit, very anxious as to his fate. The members of the crew who had remained aboard were distressed when they heard what had happened.

The captain was laid on a couchette, and they tried to bring him round. It was in vain. He was still breathing, but did not recover consciousness.

The other climbers were in a poor condition and it was necessary to lavish cares upon them.

Madeleine multiplied her efforts around the invalids. She thought, with horror, that the excursion to Mount Wolff might have ended up even more disastrously. It would not have taken much for all five of the mountaineers to be afflicted with congestion. They might have died up there, and by the time anyone had decided to send help, it would have been too late.

Scherrebek was dying. Revulsives, and even bleeding, proved ineffective.

That catastrophe made all the members of the expedition feel the terrible dangers that they were running on the surface of the Moon much more keenly. Thus far, thanks to the resistance of the *Selenit*, its perfect organization and the excellence of the apparatus with which they were equipped, the explorers had not had a very clear consciousness of the extraordinary risks to which they were exposing themselves in undertaking such an adventure. Now they understood that their lives were hanging by a thread.

The most redoubtable threat of all had not come from the complications of a fantastic journey through interplanetary space, nor the immense fall of the projectile-vehicle on to the Moon—the perils that struck the imagination, and which the genius of the constructors had been able to ward off. But there were other, more insidious angers more difficult to avoid. There had been the formidable differences in temperature, which no human being was capable of resisting. There was the absence of atmosphere, which made the explorers perpetual prisoners, condemned to be hermetically sealed in the flanks of the *Selenit* or the diving-suits that isolated them from one another.

Certainly, the members of the mission would be able to take pride, if they ever returned to Earth, in not having had a wasted journey. They would have made many observations that resolved in a definitive fashion many enigmas of the lunar world, and collected specimens of rocks that would permit the nature of the soil to be studied. They would have brought back photographs taken with special apparatus, either from inside the *Selenit* or in the course of excursions in suits.

Except that, in order for all those results to be achieved, it was necessary to get back to Earth, and what had just happened to Scherrebek awakened the same thought in all of them:

Who can tell whether we might share the fate of our chief, and whether the Moon might be the cemetery in which we're destined to sleep our final slumber for all eternity?

XIII. Copernicus[18]

If there had been a colossal telescope on Earth powerful enough to permit an observer to perceive objects as small as the members of the mission on the surface of the Moon, a astronomer who had aimed his instrument at the Sea of Rains, in the region neighboring Mount Wolff, a few hours later, would have witnessed a scene worthy of the Apocalypse. He would have seen six monsters covered in carapaces emerge from the flank of the *Selenit*, dragging behind them a long inert mass enveloped in a cloth.

It was the members of the expedition rendering their final duties to their leader.

They had put Scherrebek's dead body back in his suit, which would serve as his coffin.

They carried him some distance away from the *Selenit*, dug a grave with picks in the rocky soil, and placed him in it. Gathered around, they remained motionless for a minute, meditatively, and bid a whispered adieu to the man who had guided them so valiantly. Tears ran down their faces behind the viewports of their helmets.

They filled in the grave and piled large stones on top of it to form a crude pyramid. At the summit, with three carefully selected locks, they constructed a cross.

The sepulcher completed, they returned sadly to the *Selenit*.

Thus Scherrebek was buried on the inhospitable Moon, in accordance with the wish he had expressed before the accident that had cost him his life, and his tomb would remain, in

---

[18] In the feuilleton version, this chapter is entitled "At Sunset." It could not have been entitled "Copernicus" there because the name of that crater is one of those removed from the text for the purposes of the competition.

that corner of the Sea of Rains, as a grandiose and tragic witness to the passage of the first explorers of the Moon.

The command of the mission reverted henceforth to Galston, who had previously been second-in-command.

"If we're fortunate enough to return to Earth," he said. "We'll propose changing the name of the Sea of Rains and baptizing it the Scherrebek Plain.

They held council.

After the sad adventure on Mount Wolff, they hesitated to undertake a further expedition while the sun was at the zenith.

Sheltered by a spur of the mountain, the *Selenit* was in the shade and was at no risk of overheating, but it was necessary not to think of exposing suit-wearers for long hours in uncovered terrain.

The mission had not completed all of its program. It still had to visit Copernicus, the most beautiful crater on the Moon, and the one that possesses, after Tycho, the most magnificent aureole. They wanted to try to determine the exact nature of that aureole and the cause of the brightness that the bottom of the crater taken on when the sun's rays strike it vertically.

From Mount Wolff to Copernicus is about three hundred and fifty kilometers in a straight line; with the obligatory detours, it was necessary to count on a journey of at least four hundred and fifty, not to mention the ascent of the rampart and he exploration of the crater. They could not, on the other hand, burn further quantities of explosive to move the *Selenit* and travel part of the distance inside it, because they had to keep more than enough in reserve to ensure the departure from the Moon and the deceleration of the fall on reaching the Earth. If they decided to attempt an expedition to Copernicus, they would have to accomplish it on foot. It was merely a matter of deciding whether such an endeavor as possible.

"Thanks to the weakness of the gravity, which, so to speak, gives us seven-league boots," said Galston, "We can cover twenty kilometers an hour, and ought to be able to make a journey of four hundred and fifty kilometers within twenty-four hours, to which it's necessary to add an equal time for rest. That gives us forty-eight hours to go, and as much to come back, or our terrestrial days. We're at the ninth day of the lunar cycle for the meridian of Mount Wolff, only the eighth for the meridian of Copernicus. The Sun will set for the *Selenit* in about five and a half days, and in a little more than six days for Copernicus.

"Our suits are constructed in such a way that we can enclose ourselves within hem without danger for five consecutive days. I propose to leave in three days, when the sun will already be too low to heat the ground on which we'll be marching. We'll follow its movement and we'll arrive at the rampart of Copernicus twenty-four hours before sunset. We'll have time to visit the crater, we'll see the sun set, and we'll come back by night, by the light of the Earth, whose eastern edge will already be designing its immense crescent in the sky."

Galston's plan was adopted. The chief designated Lang, Espronceda and Brifaut to take part in the expedition, but when Madeleine heard that her husband was about to leave for five days she could not contain her emotion.

"It's folly to attempt such a voyage of nearly a thousand kilometers," she groaned, weeping "You won't come back."

Brifaut tried to impose silence on her. "How can I refuse to march with the others?" he said to her, in a low voice. "Do you want me to pass for a coward?"

"Well then, take me! I don't want to be separated from you."

"You're not being reasonable. You don't have any pretention to be as resistant as a man. By taking you, we'd risk slowing down our progress, and your presence might be the cause of an accident that we'd avoid if we didn't have to sustain and watch over you."

"Didn't I do well during the excursion to Archimedes?"

"Yes, but after all…."

"Well then, I've proved myself; there's no reason to forbid me to accompany you on this expedition to Copernicus.

René, you can't imagine the torture of waiting here for you for five days, tormented by doubt, always wondering whether something had happened to you, if I'd ever see you again!"

The young woman found such arguments, and pleaded her cause so ardently, that she finally obtained permission to take part in the expedition, just as she had obtained permission to embark on the *Selenit* at the outset of the mission.

During the following seventy-two hours, the members of the crew completed the shipboard log, redrafted their notes and carried out a few experiments in the vicinity of the *Selenit*.

They also designed an immense cross on the dark soil of the Sea of Rains, with bocks of white rock collected from the foot of the mountain, of which Scherrebek's tomb formed the center. The principal branch of the cross measured two hundred meters, in order that the figure would be visible for the large terrestrial observatories equipped with powerful instruments. And, indeed, astronomers have since been able, with the aid of their telescopes, to make out its location at the foot of Mount Wolff, in the Scherrebek Plain.

The sun would only be shining over Copernicus for three more terrestrial days when Galston set out with Lang, Espronceda, René and Madeleine Brifaut.

They had decided to march at first, so far as possible, in a straight line, following the low chain of mountains that prolongs the Apennines toward the north-east as far as the crater Eratosthenes, and then the first foothills of the Carpathians, to the north of Copernicus. Then they would turn to march southwards, directly toward Copernicus, seeking a passage through one of the valleys of the Carpathians, a narrow and not very dense massif whose culminating point only rises to 1,600 meters. That route had one important advantage: it followed the shady fringe of the mountains and would permit the explorers to shelter easily from the ardor of the declining sun.

When the little troop had passed the crater Eratosthenes, with its high wall of more than four thousand meters, they penetrated into the zone of the aureole of Copernicus. The rocky soil was covered—or, rather impregnated—with a vitreous substance, as polished as ice, which reflected the rays of sunlight, and formed a dazzling surface whose glare the eyes could not sustain. The explorers were obliged to use smoked glass to reinforce the leaded screens with which they had lined their viewports to protect them from the ultra-violet rays of the sun.

Lang made the observation via the telephone that the discovery of that vitreous layer confirmed the hypothesis of the volcanic origin of aureoles like those of Copernicus, Kepler and Tycho.

"I don't believe however," he said, "that they're due to lava flows that have spread out in sheets in the vicinity of the crater. They're more likely, in my opinion to be matter exuded through the porous rock that constituted the original crust of the satellite."

Less than twenty-four hours after their departure from the *Selenit*, as they had foreseen, and not without having accorded themselves the necessary repose, the explorers reached the rampart of Copernicus. None of them felt fatigued; Madeleine was as valiant as the others, and Galston, who had initially been annoyed by her joining the expedition, no longer regretted having brought her.

The troop undertook the ascent of the mountain, which the shadow was beginning to invade on the western side. The Sun was no more than thirty degrees above the horizon.

From the top of the rim, the explorers could still see the reflections of the vitreous aureole when they turned toward the Sun, almost as they would have seen light reflected in the same conditions on a beach recently abandoned by the sea, which the persistence of a thin liquid layer transforms into a mirror. When they looked in another direction, however, they could no longer discover anything but somber ground similar to that of the Sea of Rains, for the Sun's rays were no longer reflected on that side.

Toward the interior of the crater, the slope, which might have been ten kilometers in extent, descended in successive terraces to a depth of three thousand meters. Without earthlight it would no longer have been discernible, because the Sun was too low and no longer illuminated it. The spectacle of the vitreous rocks, which seemed to have been heaped up by titans, and which, with a general movement, descended in steps to a prodigious extent, was gripping. The explorers saw them at their feet, under the soft light of the Earth. On the other side of the crater, in the middle of which a small isolated group of mountains rose up from the bottom, they could see the opposite edge, bathed in dazzling sunlight.

However much they desired to contemplate a fine spectacle, the climbers had to renounce waiting for sunset at the summit of the rampart; the subsequent descent would have been too perilous over a slope that the Earth no longer illuminated and which would have been plunged in complete darkness.

They went back down to the bottom of the mountain, where they arrived when the shadows of objects projected by the oblique rays of sunlight were elongating immeasurably. They too were accompanied by slender and gigantic silhouettes lying on the ground ahead of them.

Such effects of oblique light are produced on the Earth at sunset, but there the rays are attenuated; their color changes and becomes rosy; the contours of objects are softened and everything is impregnated with mildness. There was nothing similar here. The setting sun retained the same intensity and the same hue as when it floated at the zenith. Its light was as harsh and its heat as fierce for the surfaces as when its rays struck the vertically.

Finally, as it touched the horizon, the explorers climbed a small hill to contemplate it. Heights that depended on the outline of the Carpathians, whose summits could be distinguished in the distance, gave further extent to the perspective. The flanks of Copernicus were streaked with innumerable glittering wrinkles.

The edge of the Sun balanced on the summits marking the horizon, and the star slowly plunged, while the shadows continued to elongate, extinguishing the reflected gleams, drowning the lower ridges, which floated momentarily like sparks, crawling all the way to the hill where the members of the expedition were standing and gradually climbing the high rampart of Copernicus, whose cliff continued to shine like a streak of light against the black sky.

When the last ray of daylight had abandoned the lunar terrain and the desolate world was no longer illuminated except by the Earth in its first quarter, the explorers resumed the route to the *Selenit*.

It was not an entirely simple matter to orientate themselves by night in that desert, where the landscape always had the same appearance, where all the rocks, all the wrinkles and all the crevasses resembled one another and the brevity of the horizon prevented the gaze from discovering reference points. To be sure, they had the Earth, whose position permitted them to take a bearing, but it was still possible to stray a few kilometers to the north or south, which would then have obliged them to make a long detour—and they had no time to waste.

Thanks to the precision of their observations, however, and the care they took to send one of their number on reconnaissance from time to time, the explorers avoided that accident and succeeded in returning to the foot of Eratosthenes in the first stage of the journey, after which it was no longer possible for them to go astray, guided as they were by the Apennines.

They were extremely careful not to lose sight of one another because, in that world of silence where they did not have the resource of calling to one another, they might have searched for a long time without finding someone. When they were obliged to separate temporarily—in order to carry out a reconnaissance, for example—they signaled to one another from a distance with the electric lanterns that they carried externally, suspended from hooks on their suits.

Five times twenty-four hours after their departure, they arrived within sight of the *Selenit* and went past Scherrebek's tomb.

After being refortified by a good meal, taken under electric lights in the crew section, the varied menu of which seemed delicious after five days on a diet of chocolate and pemmican, the excursionists lay down on their couchettes and savored their flexibility voluptuously, because sleeping in a suit was definitely not the last word in comfort. Now, at least their bodies were free; they could stretch themselves out at their ease, and turn over without being impeded by an enormous metal carcass. They were soon all plunged into a profound slumber, including Madeleine, whose bunk was separately installed in the food-locker.

Eight hours later, when the members of the expedition gathered around the table to drink a milky coffee, which Madeleine had made using condensed milk, they began discussing the final phase of the expedition, that of the return.

XIV. The Return

The *Selenit* had been lightened by about seven thousand tons of explosive, which had been employed in drawing away from the Earth and slowing down its fall on to the surface of the Moon. On the other hand, the gravity on the Moon was much weaker, and it would be much easier to take off for the return journey than the outward one.

Thanks to those favorable circumstances, the explorers could envisage without anxiety the final act of their voyage, even though they were isolated, deprived of all help, on a hostile world.

First of all, it was necessary for the *Selenit* to depart in a direction close to the vertical, in order not to be brought back to the Moon by gravity after having followed a curved trajectory of some length. The explorers therefore set about searching for a mountain that offered a smooth slope ending in a crest as clear-cut as possible. The part of the Apennines at the foot of which the *Selenit* had stopped presented numerous near-flat surfaces orientated in the most various directions, but they had difficulty finding one that met all the requisite conditions.

When they had found it, it was necessary to make an ascent in order to examine it attentively and clear away any obstacles that might have caused the Selenit to slide or tip over. It was necessary to break up the inconvenient projections with pick-axes, flatten the wrinkles and fill in the crevices.

That labor lasted ten terrestrial days, during which they had to be content with the light of the Earth, whose disk was progressively enlarged, attaining a perfect circle, shining in its fullness, and then began gradually to decrease.

The lunar soil lost the enormous heat that it had accumulated during the day. Its temperature descended close to absolute cold, which, calculated on the centigrade scale, is 273° below zero. The explorers had, in consequence, to take the greatest precautions in order not to be gripped by the cold in spite of the insulating walls of their suits. They took care not to remain immobile for long and to stimulate organic combustion by providing a supplement of oxygen.

Espronceda and Bojardo were charged with monitoring the interior temperature of the *Selenit* and activating the heating system if it fell between eighteen degrees.

When suit-wearers returned home, the surface of their suits was immediately covered by a layer of ice formed by the condensation of the water vapor contained in the *Selenit*'s atmosphere, and they were obliged to wait until the exterior surface had warmed up again before being able to emerge.

Brifaut participated, like the others, in the labor of clearing the departure track, but he was also occupied in drawing up an exact and vivid account of the first voyage of exploration to the Moon. During rest periods he read what he had written to his comrades, and each of them made observations, rectifying any errors or adding forgotten details. They all agreed in saying that Brifaut's account was perfect as a whole.

Finally, everything was ready.

In spite of their reassuring calculations and all the precautions they had taken, the explorers could not help feeling a certain anguish at the moment of launching themselves through celestial space for a second time.

For one thing, if they failed in their departure, they would be running a great risk of being unable to make a further attempt; the Moon would become their tomb, as it was already Scherrebek's. When they thought that they had been on the Moon for twenty-five terrestrial days, and that they only had reserves of air for another five or six, they felt themselves shiver; of the *Selenit* suffered a malfunction, there might not be time to repair it.

When the preparation of the track was finished, the *Selenit* was taken to face the slope and carefully orientated in order to gain its initial impetus. Everyone went to his post, Galston and Goffoël in the pilot's cabin, Garrick and Kito in the engine room and the others in the crew section. They installed themselves in such a way as to avoid falls when the *Selenit* passed from the horizontal position to the vertical.

When Galston gave them the signal to be ready, the members of the mission felt a contraction of the heart. Madeleine pinched her lips and lowered her eyes, but she put on a brave face.

"Ignite!" cried Galston.

The machine moved off, began to roll, horizontally at first, and then climbing an increasingly steep slope.

The movement accelerated, and the men were thrown backwards.

The framework of the vessel transmitted the shocks that the landing gear experienced on the track, and the vibrations, communicated to the air of the *Selenit*, filled it with a hum.

All the vibration suddenly ceased.

"Hurrah!" cried Lang. "We're away!"

Scarcely had he pronounced those words however, than a shock more violent than the others was felt.

The machine had, in fact, left the ground for a few seconds, but its momentum had been insufficient as yet; it had fallen back, colliding forcefully with the rocky slope, and, as it had touched it at an angle, with only one side of the landing-gear, the wheels had broken under the impact. The *Selenit* tilted, its side began to scrape against the rock; a catastrophe was imminent.

The heavy mass was about to stop, and then, dragged by its own weight, slide down the slope like an avalanche, at the bottom of which it would be crushed.

Fortunately, at that critical instant, Galston retained all his composure and grave proof of his presence of mind.

"Increase the gas!" he shouted into the loud hailer. "Give it full power!"

Garrick and Kito were no less resolute than their chief. The engine rendered its full impulse. The *Selenit* dragged along a little further, and then detached itself again from the ground; this time, it did not fall back.

The voyage through space recommenced.

The Selenit was flying about six thousand kilometers above the terrestrial surface. From that altitude, the globe appeared as an enormous disk, as broad as a sixth of the celestial circumference. One part was sunlit, the other was dark, and its outline was only recognizable because it formed a screen in front of the stars. The crescent of the new Moon was still too slender and too close to the Sun to spread any light in the terrestrial night.

Some forty-eight hours had passed since the *Selenit* had quit the Moon, and it had arrived at the point at which its engines had to begin to brake in order to slow down its fall and prevent it from being crushed on the surface of the globe.

It was also important not to penetrate with too great a velocity into the atmospheric layer that extended to an altitude of more than five hundred kilometers if they were to avoid being subject to an intense overheating that would risk melting the walls of the machine and roasting its occupants.

Garrick and Kito restarted the engines and the braking had the immediate effect of returning the sensation of weight to the passengers, which they had lost since the moment they had entered into free fall toward the Earth.

That last phase of the voyage was due to last about forty minutes. They had discussed the best landing site at length. Ought they to come down over a continent or prefer the ocean?

At first they had inclined toward the latter opinion, contact with the sea being less brutal than with the land if the projectile still retained an appreciable velocity. As the *Selenit* was disburdened of its enormous cargo of explosive, it would float to the surface like a cork and would not take long to be picked up.

One disquieting observation had determined Galston to renounce that plan. Observing through a periscope, he had noticed that the surface of the *Selenit* had been badly damaged at the moment of departure from the Moon. The flank that had made contact with the rock had suffered a large rip. In those circumstances, if they had come down in the sea, the water would have rushed into the cavity between the double walls and they could not be certain that the *Selenit* would continue to float.

It was therefore necessary to resign themselves to coming down on land.

On landing, however, they would have one difficulty with which they had not had to cope when arriving on the Moon. As the Earth rotates on is axis in twenty-four hours, the points of its surface are animated by a velocity of rotation that increases from the pole to the equator. Very small in the vicinity of the pole, that velocity surpasses three hundred meters a second in the middle of France and four hundred and sixty at the equator.

It was therefore necessary to land in the direction of the Earth's rotation and with a velocity almost equal to that of the selected point of latitude. Without that precaution, they would be risking a mortal encounter.

Unfortunately, they did not have much time for reflection, and an immense expanse of cloud that was covering a large part of the Earth's surface hindered their observations.

They had penetrated the atmosphere. The air invaded the empty space that the breach in the hull had opened up, so the sound of the engine became much more distinct and the precipitate explosions that were almost confused rendered a loud hum.

On Galston's instructions, the engineers caused the auxiliary motors to imprint a lateral movement on the machine in the direction of the Earth's rotation.

Through gaps in the clouds, Galston had ascertained that the *Selenit* was going to fall somewhere in Western Europe. It was not without horror that he thought of what might happen if the machine came down in the middle of a city, but he no longer had the faculty of making considerable modifications in the trajectory. Given the difficulty of calculating a position at a great height and the complications caused by the Earth's own movement, Galston even doubted that it was still possible for him to choose between land and sea.

In a matter of seconds the *Selenit* traversed a layer of clouds and Galston saw the ground: fields, villages a forest, roads and railways, all minuscule and flattened by the distance.

"As long as we don't suffer any damage," he murmured, and shouted: "Gas to the right!"

He wanted to try to land in the forest. As well as there being less risk of injuring inhabitants, he calculated that the trees would provide a kind of mattress for the *Selenit*, which would deaden the fall. On the other hand, the hull of the machine was sufficiently resistant not to be staved in by the large branches.

There was no more time for reflection. The *Selenit* descended over the forest like a huge deflated balloon, and settled into the trees with an enormous din.

It had been seen falling in nearby villages. The local people came running, on foot, on bicycles or in vehicles. The gendarmes, having been alerted, also went into action.

The *Selenit* had landed in France, in the forest of Compiègne.

The machine was lying obliquely, and the members of the expedition ere ill at ease, obliged as they were to crawl over the sloping walls. They were exultant, however, at finding themselves alive after the extraordinary adventure into which they had launched themselves so audaciously.

"Well," said Goffoël, summarizing the general opinion, "now that we've come back to Earth safe and sound, I can confess that when we took off I wouldn't have given much for my skin. I thought we had ninety-nine chances out of a hundred of staying there."

"You might have made me that confidence sooner," said Madeleine. "But after all, you were right to let me believe that there was no risk Now that I've made contact with the Earth again, I'm very glad to have accomplished the voyage, far less banal than a trip to Morocco."

They unscrewed the hatch of the *Selenit*, which had not been touched since he explorers had descended into the machine shortly before departure.

Although the varnish was scorched, the local people had read the name *Selenit* painted on the hull. A schoolteacher had then declared that it was definitely the machine that had been constructed in Philadelphia to accomplish a voyage to the Moon, and which had come back after completing its mission.

Brifaut leap through the opening of the hatch. Repeating the words of Cyrano de Bergerac, he cried, triumphantly: "We've fallen from the Moon!"

Acclamations replied to him. The members of the crew were welcomed with delight, and a particular fuss was made of Madeleine, who had shown so much valor for a woman.

Cyclists immediately set off to telephone Compiègne.

Three-quarters of an hour later, automobiles began to arrive along the nearby road, bringing officials and curiosity-seekers.

A grandiose reception was organized in honor of the mission. Many speeches were made, and the future of interplanetary navigation was evoked.

Brifaut related the history of the mission and detailed the results acquired.

Scherrebek was not forgotten, and a religious service was held in his memory. It was decided that a commemorative monument would be erected in the forest of Compiègne at the place where the *Selenit* had come down; the names of the explorers, with Scherrebek's at the head, would be inscribed upon it.

A few weeks later, René and Madeleine Brifaut returned to America, to which the members of the expedition had been summoned to receive the prize of their exploit, in the midst of celebrations and scientific manifestations.

One evening, sitting on the deck of the liner that was taking them back to France, they were savoring the mildness of a beautiful summer night and watching the Moon rise among the stars, pouring a river of gleaming silver over the sea.

"Be grateful to her, Madeleine," Brifaut murmured. "She's made us rich."

"Yes," his young wife replied, "but I like her better from here; it's too inhospitable a world for me to have any desire to go back there."

THE GREAT CURRENT

I

In the year 2280, at the beginning of summer, Dr. Bormann of Zurich, the chief engineer of the Intercontinental Thermoelectrification Company, founded two years previously, judged that the enterprise was sufficiently far advanced to enter into its decisive phase, which was also the most audacious and the most difficult.

Except for the managing directors, who were habitually resident in Paris, from where they provided general stimulation, the senior staff of the company was divided into two main groups, one of which was based in Algiers under the orders of the Ponts-et-Chaussées engineer Hurtaut, of the École de Paris, and the other in Liverpool, presided over by Professor Gainsworth of Cambridge. The two groups had thus far had for their principal mission the preparations for works that were about to be undertaken on the one hand toward the equator and on the other in the vicinity of the North Pole.

The majority of their members, elite collaborators with the Intercontinental Thermoelectrification Company, were linked together by sentiments of amity or sympathy.

Paul Chartrain, of the École Supérieure d'Électricité de Paris, and Claire Nolleau, of the Algerian Institute of Science, the former attached to the Liverpool section and the latter to the African section, met that day for the first time in the large reception hall of the Company's building, to which Dr. Bormann had invited all his subordinates.

It would not, however, be correct to say that Paul Chartrain and Claire Nolleau did not know one another, because they had had frequent occasion to talk to one another via the televising telephone. As soon as they perceived one another, they came together and introduced themselves.

They were both young. The voice of the former was deep, that of the latter high-pitched and harmonious, and that difference revealed that the first interlocutor was a young man, the second a young woman, but they were wearing identical costumes: short trousers, stockings and shoes, a jacket and a white silk shirt retained at the neck by a gilded clasp.

The man, clean-shaven or depilated, had a face as fresh and skin as smooth, apparently, as the woman, while she had short back-combed hair exactly like the person who had just bowed to her.

To judge by their faces and the color of their hair they were between twenty and twenty-five years old, but Claire Nolleau of the Algerian Institute of Science, slimmer, with more delicate features, gave the impression, because of her boyish appearance, of being her companion's younger brother. If, like the women of the twentieth century, she had been wearing a dress and long undulating hair, that impression would have been attenuated, but she was living in the last quarter of the twenty-third century, and for a long time, fashions in feminine and masculine attire had been identical, except for evening wear. That is why Claire Nolleau, at first glance, resembled an ephebe.

Her costume however, had a few attributes that were the prerogative of her own sex. The lining of her sea-blue jacket was red silk, as were its decorations; the collar of her shirt was embroidered, and a brilliant stone ornamented the golden clasp that retained it. A red ribbon tightened the trouser-leg above the knee over stockings of the same color as the costume.

Those were significant details, which did not escape Claire Nolleau's contemporaries.

"Since we've been acquainted for some time at a distance," Paul Chartrain observed, "I'm glad, my dear comrade, finally be in your presence and to see you other than through a television screen."

"I have great pleasure myself in meeting you," replied the young woman. "I feel sympathetic toward you, and I'm sure that we'll end up becoming true friends. For my part, at any rate, I hope so."

"Thank you. I'm animated by the same sentiments in your regard—and I'm not saying that to flatter you, or for reasons of politeness."

"I regret, Chartrain, that we're not attached to the same center. Whereas you're about to leave for the Far North, I'm heading for the equator. We'll be forced to content ourselves as in the past, with the telephonic communications of our liaison service."

The young people were, in fact, responsible, one in the north and the other in the south, for maintaining a continuous correspondence between the various groups of engineers supervising the operations of the Intercontinental Thermoelectrification Company. In the present epoch, when material progress had been taken to its extreme, the televising telephone was constantly employed to overcome the inconveniences of the distance between the various collaborators in the same enterprise.

United under the presidency of Dr. Bormann, the assembly included, along with the Company's engineers, some twenty scientists, men and women in costumes almost identical to those of Paul Chartrain and Claire Nolleau, journalists from the world's major dailies, printed or spoken and televised, and representatives of the President, Secretaries of State and Parliament of the United States of Europe.

There was also a delegate of the Associated Republics of Asia, His Excellency Wang-Ti-Pou of Peking, who was there officially in the capacity of observer, with a mission to examine the question of whether the system of thermoelectrification adopted by the Europeans offered important advantages and could be applied to the Asiatic continent.

Wang-Ti-Pou was a phlegmatic individual with a closed physiognomy. His features were regular, his eyelids barely hooded, his complexion almost as rosy as that of his interlocutors. He was part of the elite of the yellow race that counts a high proportion of whites among its ancestors.

The reception, under Dr. Bormann's presidency, began with a speech of thanks addressed to all the artisans of the enterprise, which consisted of establishing a great electrical circuit between the North Pole and the equator, taking advantage of the enormous difference in temperature between those two extreme regions of the globe.

"Our work," Dr. Bormann concluded, "will revolutionize the European economy, because the construction of the thermoelectric sector, which we have acquired the habit, by virtue of the need for simplification, of calling the Great Current, will furnish Europe and Africa with enormous and unlimited electrical power."

After that speech, to which the representatives of the public powers responded by congratulating the directors of the Intercontinental Thermoelectrification Company and their collaborators, champagne was served, in order to drink a toast to the prosperity of the enterprise. Then the guests were at liberty to form groups to converse with one another.

Dr. Bormann had given Paul Chartrain the mission to attach himself particularly to the person of Wang-Ti-Pou, whom he suspected of being refractory to European civilization. The young man, assisted in that circumstance by Claire Nolleau, had therefore to gain the approval of the delegate from Peking, who was reputed to have a considerable influence on the Congress of the Asian Republics. Wang-Ti-Pou might be capable of bringing his people out of the routine that they had been obstinately following for centuries.

The dead weight formed by the enormous mass of several hundred million inhabitants spread over the Asiatic continent from the Urals to Kamchatka and from northern India to the Arctic Ocean was, in fact, a grave subject of anxiety for the Statesmen of Europe America, Africa and Australia. That considerable fraction of humankind, becalmed in outdated forms of civilization, which regarded the modern applications of science as a kind of insult to the divinity, represented a danger to the world. Poverty, famine, epidemics and the anarchy to which its stubbornness exposed it, determined reactions that had reverberations in the other continents.

Thus, the Europeans and the Americans, who were most directly affected by such perturbations, were striving to attract the Asiatic elite to their shores in order to inculcate its members with their concepts and methods. Philosophers, scientists and politicians came from India, Tibet, China, Mongolia and Siberia. They observed and admired what was shown to them, understood what was explained to them; their knowledge and intelligence could not be denied—but when they returned home, far from praising Euro-American civilization, they represented it to their people as the emanation of a diabolical mentality.

Dr. Bormann had been obedient to these preoccupations when he had confided to his young collaborator the care of informing Wang-Ti-Pou.

The latter was arguing with Paul Chartrain and Claire Nolleau, who had quickly become inseparable.

"The fate of humankind," he said, laughing, "becomes a veritable challenge to common sense in the midst of all your inventions. The fragile creatures that we are, incapable of resisting violent shocks or strong pressures, great heat and great cold, which trivial things are sufficient to destroy, are dancing a fantastic ballet today with the monsters created by their demented genius—monsters whose steel arms and jaws threaten to crush them at any moment, their fiery breath to volatilize them, and electrical discharges to blast them….

"I've come from Peking in a rocket-plane at a speed of two thousand kilometers an hour. During the journey, watching the ground fleeing beneath me, I couldn't help thinking about what would happen if we encountered another vehicle—or, rather, another projectile—of the same kind, or if we made brutal contact with the ground."

"There was no risk of that happening to you, Excellency," Chartrain protested. "The monsters we have created are docile slaves, not enemies."

The Asiatic made a gesture of indifference. "Oh," he said, "it's not that I fear death. In my country, you know, we still believe that a superior power presides over human destiny, and marks a term for each of us."

"We agree with you that the power in question exists," replied Chartrain, "but your fatalism is unjustified. We've proved in Europe and America that the famous laws of nature, supposedly inevitable, can be corrected by human intelligence. It's been more than two centuries since our physicians and physiologist found the means to slow down aging and prolong life. In the twentieth century, people began to get old at sixty, and often sooner; today, a centenarian is still at the peak of intellectual activity."

"Do you think that's a great advantage?" sniggered Wang-Ti-Pou. "The centenarians of which you speak bar the route to young people like you. In any case, that wouldn't be a good thing in the Asiatic Republics, where an excessively numerous population is stifling for lack of space."

"It would breathe more easily," Paul said, "if it didn't refuse obstinately to adopt our technology and methods, which have succeeded so well in other parts of the world."

"I'd like to think so."

"You'll have the opportunity to convince yourself of the immense advantages that humankind will procure, for example from the great polar-equatorial thermoelectric linkage."

Wang-Ti-Pou shook his head slowly. "Your marvelous inventions, your circuits, your machines, your trains that travel at three hundred kilometers an hour, your rocket-planes, your great ferry-gliders that go from Brest to New York in twenty-four hours, the miracles of your medicine and your surgery, all remain incapable of producing human happiness—for happiness results from internal contemplation and an equilibrium of the soul, which all the external advantages of your so-called progress can't give us."

"You're speaking as a philosopher, Excellency," Chartrain replied. "You'd be wrong to imagine that I don't share your opinion on that point. Happiness is, first and foremost, a matter of mental discipline."

"Certainly," Claire Nolleau approved. "However, I think that humans are aided to acquire that discipline when they're liberated from the scourges that torment them: disease, old age and poverty. That's the essence of the progress that you doubt, Excellency, and our technology contributes to it."

"Your faith is respectable," said Wang-Ti-Pou, laughing, "and based on imposing arguments."

Dr. Bormann, who had been conversing with a group on the far side of the room until then, came to join the trio. He suspected that the Asiatic delegate was in the process of expressing opinions unfavorable to European civilization, and feared that his young interlocutors might not have the strength to convert him.

His visage barely marked by a few slight wrinkles, the bright eyes, abundant brown hair and supple body of the chief engineer of the Intercontinental Thermoelectrification Company would have passed in the twentieth century for a man of forty, fit and in his prime, but he had celebrated his ninety-fifth birthday a few days earlier. He was not wearing spectacles; no one did any longer, except in refractory Asia, for opticians corrected visual defects by medical or surgical methods.

The doctor sat down beside Claire Nolleau, facing Wang-Ti-Pou.

"I was philosophizing with these young people," said the Asiatic. "You have in them two collaborators of whom you can be proud, and with whom it's a real pleasure to debate. But if you've come to take part in our discussion, I'm particularly honored and my pleasure is doubled. I'd be glad to have a few clarifications regarding the thermoelectric sector whose construction you're on the point of completing. Some people claim that humankind already disposes of sufficiently considerable energy sources not to need that excess of power."

"That's talking lightly," Dr, Bormann assured him. "The consumption of mechanical energy per head is increasing by the day in a geometric progression."

"Then you Europeans must really be squandering it."

"The energy we employ in powering our machines, heating, lighting, cooking our food, adding to the comfort and pleasure to our lives, increasing agricultural yields by electrification, propelling our trains, airplanes and airships, and replacing the muscular labor of the human creature everywhere, can't be considered as squandering. Remember that today, thanks to the utilization of waterfalls throughout the territory of Europe—only to speak of our own continent—and the numerous tidal power stations established on the coasts, every European represents an average mechanical power a hundred times superior to that which muscles alone confer upon him. The creation of the Great Current will double that proportion. Thus, by comparison with the humans of ancient times—the eighteenth or nineteenth century—the modern human being is a kind of giant."

"Assuming that that's an advantage!"

"It is one, for the physical power of the human body, such as nature has constituted it, is not in proportion to that of an intelligence capable of disciplining immense forces."

"Yes, but in addition to the mechanical energy that coal procures you...."

"Let's not talk about coal!" Dr. Bormann interrupted. "We no longer make use of it, except in the chemical industries."

"In Asia we extract a great deal, as much for industry as for domestic usage."

"I know that," said Dr. Bormann. "That's the real squandering! You're extracting without counting them the last reserves of coal that can still be exploited at moderate expense. It's been a long time since we adopted a more rational policy in Europe. As long ago as the nineteenth century our scientists were uttering cries of alarm. They calculated that by the year 3500, humankind would run out of coal. As for oil, which, has, in fact, become extremely scarce, they thought that the last wells would dry up toward the end of the twentieth century.

"Of course, they weren't taking account of deposits located at great depths, between a thousand and five thousand meters, which the people of their epoch were incapable of reaching, and, more, especially of exploiting economically with the poor means at their disposal. Improvements in telemechanics, and the complete substitution of automata for the labor of the human hand, now permit us to extract from the profound entrails of the Earth in Europe the treasures they still contain. But the fact that nowadays, almost all the deposits situated less than a thousand meters from the surface are exhausted, proves that the fears of our forebears were justified.

"You can, Excellency, criticize our civilization, which is characterized by the intense utilization of natural forces and the extraordinary development of technology, but we can scarcely imagine how it could revert, without catastrophe, to the form of ancient civilizations, in which human beings scarcely had at their disposal anything but the energy of their own muscles and those of domestic animals.

"It's necessary to admit that we've made mistakes. As soon as human beings sensed that they were the masters of their planet and capable of exploiting its resources, they hastened to profit from those that were the most accessible, such as coal and oil. They had found a treasure; they were in haste to enjoy it; but in their precipitation, they used up indiscriminately reserves that nature had constituted for them. For a long time they burned coal to extract only a tenth—and often less—of the energy it contains. Oil and its derivatives were no better employed. Humankind indulged in a wastage that only the illusion of possessing inexhaustible resources prevented them from deeming insane.

"Thinkers perceived the danger, and they predicted that the exhaustion of coal and oil would sound the death-knell of the great civilizations. Consumption increased year by year; from fifteen million tons per annum in 1800 it surpassed one thousand five hundred million—which is to say, a hundred times as much—at the beginning of the twentieth century. Then it rose to four and finally to five billion tons a year.

"At that rate, if our modern civilization had only depended on coal, it would have passed into history like a brilliant meteor. Fortunately, nature offers us other sources of energy, for example those of waterfalls, the tides, wind and solar heat. Hydraulic power, throughout the world, amounts to about seven hundred million horsepower, equivalent to two billion eight hundred million tons of coal per year. Today, we employ more than half of it. We've also learned to make use of the force of the tides, which is colossal. Just think that in the bay of Mont Saint-Michel alone, it represents about six million horsepower, the equivalent of all the hydraulic power of France.

"But by far the most important source of energy, which is also the great motive force of wind and waterfalls, is solar heat, from which everything that lives, plant or animal, obtains, directly or indirectly, its substance and its activity.

"The quantity of solar heat received per year and per hectare corresponds, according to the region, to an energy of between five and twelve million kilowatt-hours. That's enormous. The production of one kilowatt-hour consumes 1.3 kilograms of coal. Five million kilowatt-hours is therefore equivalent to six thousand five hundred tons of coal, or one thousand six hundred and twenty-five horsepower. It would suffice to absorb and transform integrally the quantity of that received by a surface area of twenty-five thousand hectares—which is to say, two hundred square kilometers, to replace all the coal consumed by a country like France, whose surface area surpasses five hundred and forty thousand square kilometers.

"Even if, in practice, one could only transform a tiny fraction of that heat, it's evident that one could still count on the sun to furnish the energy needs of the civilized world. Our Great Current is merely one means of utilizing solar heat. We intend to construct immense thermoelectric piles between the North Pole and he tropics. Perhaps you know about those that already exist in the Alps, the most important of which is the Mont-Blanc-Mediterranean Generator…."

"No," said Wang-Ti-Pou. "I haven't had the opportunity to visit them."

"One of the electrodes is plunged into the eternal snows of the mountain, the other exposed on the coast to the rays of an ardent sun. Everyone learns in school that if the ends of a copper wire and a bismuth wire are welded together, in such a way as to constitute a closed circuit, and then one of the junctions is exposed to cold and the other to heat, an electric current is produced, which passes from the bismuth to the copper across the heated junction.

"The invention isn't new; it dates from the nineteenth century[19] and has had numerous applications since that epoch. But it's only in our day that we've had the audacity to utilize it for the direct capture of solar heat, the source of all terrestrial energies except for that of the tides.

"The thermoelectric organization in our North Africa is the most important endeavor of this kind. It comprises a thousand generators, utilizing as a cold source, the great marine depths, where a constant temperature of four degrees is maintained, and as a heat source, either the sunlit coast or even, for some highly developed sectors, the desert regions of the interior."

"Yes, I know that the electrification of North Africa has contributed greatly to the economic development of the entire continent."

"Thanks to that, we can now send great express trains at three hundred kilometers an hour from the Cape to Cairo, Pointe-Noire in Algeria and Tangiers, and transversally from Dakar via Timbuktu and Chad to Zanzibar."

---

[19] This particular version of the thermoelectric effect is the one discovered by the French physicist Jean Peltier (1785-1845) in 1834; its principal application is in refrigerator cooling systems, in which electricity is used to produce differences in temperature rather than *vice versa*.

"Why not develop instead," Wang-Ti-Pou asked, "hydrothermic factories of the Georges Claude[20] and Paul Boucherot type, which utilize differences in temperature between the bottom and the surface of the sea?"

"Many of them have been established on the tropical coasts of Africa and America. Since the twentieth century, Georges Claude's invention has been greatly improved, but it doesn't provide a general solution of the problem of capturing solar heat, whereas thermoelectric generators permit the direct absorption of the solar radiation that animates everything on earth."

Dr. Bormann, excited by the grandeur of his subject, was speaking in an increasingly vibrant tone. He was eager to win over the Asiatic, whose suspicion reflected that of his people, to the cause of progress.

Wang-Ti-Pou was intelligent, to be sure, but he rejected Euro-American civilization, which seemed to him to be impotent to provide human happiness. What was the point, he asked himself, of so many inventions, which only ended up making people more demanding and always creating new needs for them? What was the point even of prolonging youth and life, since human beings could only achieve happiness by abolishing all desire in their hearts?

Beneath his cold gaze, Dr. Bormann continued to expound the thesis of progress enthusiastically.

---

[20] The inventor Georges Claude (1870-1960), once known as "the Edison of France" built the first practical Ocean Thermal Energy Converter in Cuba, in collaboration with the engineer Paul Boucherot (1869-1943), which became operational in 1930, shortly before the publication of the present story. They constructed another on a cargo ship in 1935; Petithuguenin had no way of knowing that the technology would be abandoned after both plants were destroyed by bad weather, nor that Claude would join the right-wing Action Française movement and collaborate actively with the Nazis in World War II.

"The sources of energy that civilized human beings have been able to capture in the last three centuries permit them to look to the future with confidence. Even so, all the installations created thus far have been, one might say, of local interest. They don't respond to a plan for the general organization of the globe. The Great Current proceeds from a much higher conception: we want to make the entire Earth into a vast generator of energy.

"The regime of marine currents, and that of winds and rains, and, in consequence that if the condensation of snow and the formation of glaciers on high mountains, are the consequence of the large difference in temperature that exists between the poles and the equator. Whereas the polar ice caps freeze in winter to nearly fifty degrees Centigrade below zero, the tropical soil causes the temperature to rise to fifty degrees above zero, and more. That hundred-degree difference makes the Earth resemble an enormous alembic whose cucurbit is at the equator and its refrigerant at the poles.

"Here the loss of heat by radiation isn't compensated by the action of the sub and cold precipitates atmospheric humidity. The resulting void summons new humid masses from the equator, where the seas are subject to intense evaporation. All the water on the globe would end up condensing thus, in the form of snow and ice, if the seasons didn't transport the coldest surface alternately from one pole to the other; winter is rife at the South Pole when summer prevails at the North Pole. Here the ice-cap melts and shrinks; it aliments the oceans, which the tropical evaporation tends to dry up, and the South Pole collects the condensations that the warmed North Pole no longer provokes. Then the seasons change; summer is transported to the South Pole and winter to the North Pole; the phenomena are reversed.

"There is, in sum, always one polar cap that is increasing at the expense of the other, the oceans and the atmosphere serving as vehicles for that back-and-forth movement. It's immediately evident that the forces brought into play to transport from the Arctic to the Antarctic, or vice versa, the masses of water that give rise to enormous accumulations of winter snow and ice are prodigious. Now, they simply represent a fraction of the energy that the sun pours on the earth in the form of heat, since it's precisely that solar heat which, in the final analysis, activates everything.

"Given that, the possibility arises of capturing by some artifice at least a part of that formidable energy, which goes to waste without any profit to human beings, lost at the poles by radiation into space. The solution of the problem consists of creating immense thermoelectric piles between the poles and the equator. The junctions playing the role of cold electrodes are installed in the glaciers of the Arctic seas; the hot electrodes are set up in the tropics.

"Those are the concepts that preside over the establishment of our project."

The explanations that Dr. Bormann gave Wang-Ti-Pou, whose heart he had to capture in order to conquer Asiatic opinion thereby, were potentially profitable to all those among the guests who were not scientists. Thus, while the chief engineer was speaking, journalists, officials and financiers had gradually come to join the little group. When he had finished his explanation, he was assailed by questions. Everyone wanted clarification on some particular point of the theory that had presided over the conception of the Great Current.

Dr. Bormann, completely surrounded and having to reply to several people at the same time, ceased to occupy himself with Wang-Ti-Pou, who soon found himself separated, with Paul Chartrain and Claire Nolleau.

An usher approached he delegate of the Asian Republics. "Monsieur Ta-Ho-Mai desires to make an urgent communication to Your Excellency."

Ta-Ho-Mai was Wang-Ti-Pou's private secretary.

"Bring Monsieur Ta-Ho-Mai in," instructed Chartrain.

The Asiatic delegate's secretary had darker skin, more hooded eyes, a short nose and thicker lips than his master. He had a wireless message from the Congress of Asian Republics to give to Wang Ti Pou.

Apologizing to the young engineers, the Asiatic delegate retreated with him to a corner of the room.

The dispatch was drafted in code, and as the translation required ten minutes, Wang-Ti-Pou, although he was impatient to know what it concerned, allowed his secretary to finish the task on his own and returned to Chartrain and Claire Nolleau.

"It's not bad news, I hope?" asked the young woman, who saw that he was looking worried.

"I don't think so. It's a communication from the Congress, which my secretary is in the process of deciphering."

The young people resumed debating the benefits of technology, which the Asiatic delegate contested.

"Let me give you an example, Excellency," said Claire, "of the advantages of mechanical progress, so often criticized by your compatriots. Have you not been struck by the atrocious conditions in which miners still work in China and Siberia while extracting coal? The seams that they exploit are relatively near the surface, of course. Nevertheless, as soon as their labor extends to five or six hundred meters underground, the workers, in spite of improvement in the ventilation of galleries, are subjected to almost intolerable temperatures. The manipulation of pneumatic borers and picks is exhausting, especially when it's carried out in narrow tunnels, where the miner doesn't have freedom of movement. The depressing sensation of being profoundly buried aggravates the physical fatigue. In addition, in spite of all the precautions, numerous accidents can't be avoided, due to collapses and firedamp explosions.

"Compare, Excellency, your outdated methods, which impose so many sacrifices on the proletariat, with those in use in our homeland."

"Your automata are marvelous," Wang-Ti-Pou approved.

"Then persuade your industrial leaders to employ them. As Dr. Bormann was saying a little while ago, it doesn't make sense to squander the power of a human brain by only giving it command of the weak body in which nature has enclosed it.

Thanks to the progress of telemechanics and the transmission of sensations at a distance, we now possess automata equipped with sensory organs, thanks to which the conductor, who maneuvers them from his control-box, can see, hear and feel whatever he would see, hear and feel if it were possible for him to put himself in the place of the automaton without dying of asphyxia, congestion or crushing.

"Thus, we have no more workers in the depths of our mines. We replace them everywhere by machines activated at a distance by electricity, which affect the most various forms, in accordance with the function for which they're destined. The human being is on the surface of the ground, while the machine he directs is at a depth of three or four thousand meters, and sometimes separated from him by a distance of seven or eight kilometers.

"Well, Excellency, can you deny that Europe and America, which are at the forefront of that industrial evolution, have worked for the good of humanity?"

Wang-Ti-Pou shook his head, and replied phlegmatically: "I'll ask you another question, Mademoiselle. Did the inventors of these marvels—which, take note, I don't refuse at all to admire as so many creations of human genius—really have the goal of liberating humans from the sad subjection of physical labor? Have they not rather been incited to the construction of their automated prodigies by the necessity of economizing on human labor and increasing profits? It's less a question of philanthropy than of financial prosperity."

The conversation was interrupted because Ta-Ho-Mai, Wang-Ti-Pou's secretary, was gazing at his master from a distance and inclining his head insistently to inform him that he had completed deciphering the telegram, The delegate of the Asiatic Republics, intrigued by the bizarre expression that his collaborator had adopted, moved away to rejoin him, even forgetting to apologize to the young people.

When he had gone, Claire Nolleau murmured: "He seems preoccupied." And she added, ironically: "Let's hope that he hasn't rendered himself suspect to his government by allowing himself to seem too sympathetic to the inventions of the European devils and is being recalled so that they can cut off his head."

"No," said Paul Chartrain, "it's surely not a matter of cutting off his head. See how his face is clearing—how happy he seems!"

Indeed, Wang-Ti-Pou, who had sat down beside his secretary at a small table, seemed excited, in spite of his phlegm and his fatalism. His eyes were shining. The piece of paper on which Ta-Ho-Mai had scribbled the translation of the telegram was trembling in his hand.

It was great news that he had just received.

Ta-Ho-Mai looked at him avidly. "Then…Excellency…you accept?" he asked.

Pride was reflected in Wang-Ti-Pou's expression. "Yes," he said, solemnly, his chin held high.

II

The reception had concluded. The guests were returning to their automobiles in the subterranean garage of the building, or their airplanes or helicopters on the terrace that crowned the edifice.

Paul Chartrain and Claire Nolleau intended to take the pneumatic tube: a kind of improved Metro that served greater Paris, and whose trains, propelled by compressed air, made a journey like that from Lagny to Saint-German-en-Laye in an hour, stopping at numerous stations.

As they were going through the large vestibule to emerge on to the Avenue des Nations, which, extending the old Avenue de la Défense Nationale, extended in a straight line in the direction of Saint-Germain, the great broadcaster, which proclaimed news from all over the world almost uninterruptedly, announced:

"Revolution had broken out in Asia, where the Evolutionist members of Congress have been arrested, the Conservative Party has taken possession of power. The President of the Associated Republics has fled. A provisional government has been constituted."

All those who were in the hall at that moment had stopped, surprised, in order to listen more carefully to the sensational news. As soon as the unreal voice of the radio had fallen silent, a hubbub of animated comments resonated under the vaults.

"Revolution in Asia!" exclaimed Claire Nolleau . "Well, Chartrain, that must be what the dispatch told Wang-Ti-Pou a little while ago, don't you think?"

"He seemed pleased," the young man observed.

"He might well be, for he's reckoned in Asia to be among the leaders of the Conservative Party. The victory of his friends is his own."

"In that case," said Paul Chartrain, laughing, "He'll certainly obtain some profit from the change of regime. Who knows? His Excellency Wang-Ti-Pou might be in command of all Asia tomorrow. Let's be diplomats, Nolleau, and make a friend of that individual, who's about to climb to the pinnacle."

Dr. Bormann, who emerged from the conference hall in company with Professor Gainsworth, seemed consternated.

"A revolution in our era is unexpected," he observed. "What barbarity! Asia is five centuries behind the times. It's a misfortune for the world. A misfortune!"

Professor Gainsworth of Cambridge, who was not only a remarkable engineer but also a philosopher, did not envisage the event with as much pessimism.

"Perhaps it's not a bad thing if a part of humankind remains close to its origins, and we thus retain, in the bosom of the civilized world, whose refinement doesn't always proceed without weakness, a reservoir of new forces capable of regenerating fatigued races."

"You like paradox, Professor," Dr. Bormann replied, irritated. "But those who reason like you and make light of the threat to civilized humanity represented by that immense nucleus of anarchy, will wake up from their bliss one day, I can assure you."

"Well, Doctor, an anarchic Asia isn't redoubtable. Disorganized hordes can't do anything against a solidly constituted Europe and America."

"If a leader of genius emerges—an Attila, a Genghis Khan or a Tamerlane, capable of assembling in his powerful hand the scattered forces of the Asiatic world—he'll have difficulty resisting the temptation to launch them in an assault on Occidental civilization. And if he succeeds in ruining Europe, America might well tremble."

Claire Nolleau, who usually lived in Algiers and had no family in Paris, agreed to accompany Paul Chartrain to the house of the young man's parents, who had a pretty villa near Versailles, and spend the evening there.

The two comrades talked enthusiastically about the work in which they were collaborating. They considered their time as an epoch of great progress, in which they were proud to live. They expressed that opinion to Monsieur and Madame Chartrain that evening, after dinner, in the garden of the villa.

For a long time Versailles, like Saint-Germain, had been no more than an eccentric quarter of the great Parisian city, but a development plan, well understood and rigorously respected, had preserved its villas, its shade and its superb views from the invasion of utilitarian constructions.

Thus, in the slowly-fading twilight, the calm of the Chartrains' garden was only troubled by the throb of aircraft, helicopters and dirigibles passing over, some at low altitude, resplendent with all their lights switched on, and others at high altitude, among the little pink clouds.

"When the people of 1950 proudly called their epoch the century of electricity," Claire Nolleau observed, "they had a very paltry idea of the role that that exceedingly flexible and manipulable form of mechanical energy would one day play in the world."

"Are you quite sure that they didn't foresee that role?" said Monsieur Chartrain, who occupied a chair in History at the Faculté de Paris. "The humanity of the nineteenth and twentieth centuries only lacked the means. It had imagined all that we have realized. Let's not be too proud, and let's remind ourselves that in spite of all the marvels of our modern civilization, we'll only seem to be humble precursors in the eyes of the people of the thirtieth century, who will play with the world like a child with a toy, and travel through sidereal space and fantastic speeds.

"You, who are undertaking the organization of the Pole, know in what season and in what manner the break-up of the ice is produced. You know how and in what direction the icebergs are detached from the sheet, and also how winter reestablishes the reign of cold over those immense extents. But remember that you owe your knowledge to the ancient heroes who were able to penetrate the secrets of nature, to the precursors, the mariners and scientists of the nineteenth and twentieth centuries who explored the icy solitudes of the Pole, often at the expense of their life, when the greater part of what people would one day clarify was still unknown. Those pioneers of past centuries, when they set out on the conquest of an unknown world, were perhaps ignorant of the purpose that their heroism would serve, but they had faith in the destiny of humankind; they felt sure that their disinterested efforts wouldn't be futile."

"We'll try," said Paul, "not to be inferior to those heroes of the past. The work that we're taking on will mark a new, particularly important stage in the electrical equipment of our planet. We're conscious of the fact that it won't be accomplished without effort, perseverance and sacrifices of all kinds."

Paul and Claire walked together for a few minutes along the garden paths, invaded by obscurity.

"I regret that we're not attached to the same section," the young man said. "I would have liked to have you as a colleague up there in the Far North, when we march to attack the ice."

"Well, perhaps I won't always remain in the tropical section," the young woman replied. "I confess that I'd have preferred to go to the Pole, where the struggle against the elements will be much more exciting."

"Yes, I'd like to hope that we'll see one another again, other than through the screen of the televising telephone."

They felt very close to one another in spirit and in heart, and they were saddened by the thought that they would be separated again in a matter of days.

"The world isn't so large," murmured Claire Nolleau, by way of consolation, as much for herself as for Paul. "A rocket-plane can travel from the center of Africa to Greenland in five hours. I don't despair of making the journey some day with Monsieur Hurlaut, when he needs to confer with Professor Gainsworth."

"Yes, that's right—ask to accompany him. The opportunity will certainly present itself. For my part, if I can come to see you…"

"Don't fail to do so!"

At nine o'clock, the Monsieur Chartrain senior switched on the loudspeaker to listen to the evening news.

The radio talked about the revolution in Asia. The governmental committee of the Congress had been overthrown, and those members that had not had time to flee had been arrested. But the big news was the election by the Revolutionary Assembly of His Excellency Wang-Ti-Pou as President of the Associated Asian Republics.

Having explained the situation succinctly, the speaker announced that His Excellency Wang-Ti-Pou, who was in Paris in the capacity of delegate of the Asian Republics when he had received the news of his election, had consented, in response to the request of World Radio, to make a statement.

"I am now handing over," the announcer continued, "to His Excellency Monsieur Wang-Ti-Pou, President of the Associated Asian Republics."

Claire and Paul instinctively drew closer to the loudspeaker in order not to miss a word of what the individual with whom they had had the opportunity to discuss the grave problem of human happiness was about to say.

After a few compliments addressed to Europe, whose hospitable virtues he praised, Wang-Ti-Pou expressed the diplomatic wish for a close collaboration, in all domains, between the two continents

"I do not know," he added, "Whether such a collaboration is presently possible, but I shall not neglect any possibility to bring it about. I shall be leaving you, for I need to be in Mukden[21] tomorrow, where the provisional Revolutionary Government has been established. A special rocket-plane will take me back to the bosom of my people, so different from

---

[21] Now Shenyang, in north-eastern China.

yours in some ways, but from whom you also, I think, have something to learn.

"We in Asia are deeply spiritual. Our civilization, founded on the culture of the soul and interior contemplation, perhaps seems too disdainful of bodily needs for your taste, but do not your philosophers and thinkers proclaim, like ours, that material progress is nothing if it does not serve as a pretext for spiritual progress, and does not contribute to the mental grandeur of humankind?

"You are working sincerely, I know, for the cause of that mental grandeur, and I shall always follow your efforts with a sympathetic gaze. I ask you in return not to judge the people of Asia severely if we do not adopt your methods with as much urgency as you would like, and if we try to attain the ideal by other ways than yours."

When Wang-Ti-Pou had finished his speech, Monsieur and Madame Chartrain, Paul and Claire, remained silent momentarily. They were emotional, for they were conscious of being witnesses to a great historic event.

Finally, Paul declared, thoughtfully: "I imagine that the new President of the Asian Republics will not be a friend for us."

"Bah! You think that he wants to make war on us?" said Claire Nolleau.

"Who can tell?"

"What could the Asian Republics do against us, with their wretched archaic armaments—their rifles, their machine-guns and cannons—against out automata, our gases, our ardent rays and our artificial lightning?"

"They have numbers. Suppose they succeeded, by means of a surprise attack, in putting the hydroelectric factories and industrial establishments of our frontiers out of action—or even took possession of them and used them against us. Nothing proves that we wouldn't witness an invasion of the civilized world comparable to that of the Goths and Visigoths in the days of the Roman Empire."

To put an end to a conversation that was threatening to become depressing, Paul proposed that he drive Claire back to the center of Paris, where she was staying for the duration of her sojourn.

He deliberately took the avenues planted with tall trees, with majestic perspectives, that descended from Versailles toward the old quarters of the capital, where the electric lighting was artistically filtered in order not to spoil the charm of a beautiful spring night.

The electric auto moved silently, like all those traveling along the avenue, seeming at times to submerge it like a flood, but the air was vibrant with confused sounds: the buzzing rumors of the street, fragments of orchestral harmonies or songs, confused speeches, a cacophony of innumerable loudspeakers that were resonating on all the floors of the houses, the purr of aircrafts and airships. That was a sonorous ambiance to which one became accustomed in all great cities, and which did not prevent the young people, brought together by an increasing sympathy, from experiencing a keen pleasure in their nocturnal excursion.

However, Paul and Claire, who had had the opportunity, while participating in the endeavor of the Great Current to penetrate, the former into the icy solitudes of the Pole and the latter into the sparsely populated regions of tropical Africa, were dreaming at that moment of a less encumbered world. They would have liked to be transported together to one of those distant locations where nature had not yet been tamed, where the rivers and streams, the waves of the sea, the snows of the mountains and the wind had not yet been disciplined and subjugated to human needs and pleasures. They had a nostalgia for virgin territory.

"You're not very cheerful, my children," Madame Chartrain put in. "The end of the world has been prophesied for you, or at least the end of civilization, but in the meantime, civilization is still triumphant and is doing quite well. Let's live tranquilly, if you please, and not give ourselves nightmares for tonight."

III

Consider a planisphere, in the Mercator projection. Everyone knows that the principal property and the great advantage of that mode of representation of the terrestrial surface is easily to furnish the shortest route from one point to another, by simply tracing a line between the two points.

Mark, to the north, on the eastern coast of Greenland, at the twenty-ninth degree of longitude west of Paris, Mount Petermann, which overlooks, from an altitude of 3,480 meters, the Franz-Josef fjord. The fjord is merely the mouth of a powerful glacier, which descends from the flanks of Mount Petermann and its satellites.

Mark, on the other hand, in the center of Africa, the point of intersection of the equator with the meridian of the twentieth degree longitude east of Paris.

Now connect the latter point, which is in the loop of the Congo, by means of a straight line, with Mount Petermann.

If you could displace yourself without meeting any obstacle over the surface of the Earth, that straight line would represent the shortest route that you would need to follow in order to go from the center of Africa to the depths of the Franz-Josef fjord.

Now, see where it passes over the planisphere. It chips the oriental extremity of Iceland and leaves the Faroe archipelago slightly to the east; insinuates itself between Ireland, on the one hand, and Scotland and England on the other; penetrates into France near Mont Saint-Michel; cuts through the Pyrenees east of the vale of Andorra and Spain near Barcelona' reaches Algeria level with Bougie[22] and traverses the Sahara.

If one wanted to build a bridge between Greenland and Africa, one would scarcely have to deviate from that line to

---

[22] Now Bejaia.

find the most advantageous conditions, because it is studded with lands that would serves as so many natural piles for that giant endeavor. One would scarcely have to make a detour via the Faroes to avoid too long a span between Iceland and the British Isles. For a stepping-stone over the Mediterranean one would use Minorca, the most easterly of the Balearics.

That approximate line is the most direct route and offers the fewest obstacles, from the Franz-Josef fjord, the reserve of cold, and tropical Sahara, the source of heat. Now, that is precisely the one chosen by the constructors of the Great Current to establish the first polar-equatorial thermoelectric circuit.

The laying of the cables only presented real difficulties in the coastal zone of Greenland, almost always locked by ice at the latitude in which the northern base was to be installed. Once the cold current of three or four hundred kilometers of sea hat flows along the east of the Greenland littoral has been crossed, however, one no longer encounters any but warm seas, and temperate or hot lands.

In addition, the Sahara, although its southern edge remains far above the equator, offers conditions in its tropical zone essentially favorable to the installation of the hot base of the immense thermoelectric pile that it was proposed to create.

In order better to comprehend the magnitude of the task that the people of the twenty-third century were in the process of accomplishing, it is always necessary to bear in mind that life on earth is maintained by solar radiation.

Whatever form of the energy of living beings one envisages, it is always obtained from the immense star around which we gravitate.

Vegetables assimilate the carbon contained in the atmosphere in the state of carbon dioxide, thanks to the action that daylight exercises on certain organs they possess, especially in the leaves; and the quantity of energy absorbed by the plant in the form of luminous radiation corresponds exactly to the quantity of carbon assimilated.

It is the same for all the other physico-chemical reactions that accompany the phenomena of vegetal life.

It follows that plants are nothing but transformers and condensers of solar energy.

Coal and oil, which result from the decomposition of large masses of fossil vegetables, are accumulated solar energy placed in reserve. When we burn combustibles, we are liberating the rays that the plants that provided them absorbed millions of years ago, in the same way that by burning wood we are liberating the heat that the tree has obtained from the sun in the course of the previous fifteen or twenty years.

Animals do not receive all the heat and light they need to move and constitute their own substance directly from the sun, but it is nevertheless from there that they extract their energy by an indirect route: herbivores obtain it from vegetables, which have received it from the sun; carnivores get it from other animals, which have themselves, in their turn, obtained it from vegetables.

One can see, therefore, that the existence of animals is narrowly linked to that of plants. Where there are no vegetables, animals can no longer live. But vegetables are self-sufficient, and one could easily imagine a world that would be exclusively populated by them.

Humans do not escape this general law. That is what determines the importance of agriculture, for, as soon as they begin to adapt the planet with a view to their particular needs, they must above all create provisions of energy in a utilizable and assimilable form, both for themselves and the other animals from which they obtain their substance. The simple picking of wild fruits, and the harvesting of uncultivated edible plants, which can, strictly speaking, content primitive populations already nourished by hunting and fishing, quickly become insufficient when human groups acquire some density.

Agriculture has, in consequence, long appeared to be an inevitable servitude for civilized peoples. Since the nineteenth century, however, scientists such as Berthelot and Fischer, or more recently Vernadsky,[23] have had no fear of affirming, more or less explicitly, that future humankind might be liberated from it.

What is necessary for that? That humans become capable of fabricating their aliments from minerals and with the aid of energy directly obtained from the sun. It is, in sum, a practical matter of effecting the synthesis of the organic compounds by which the human being is nourished.

Now, the research long pursued in this direction by the greatest chemists had finally concluded. Humans were capable of preparing their own aliments and those of the animals with which they thought it good to associate themselves industrially, collecting by new methods the solar energy that they had previously only obtained via the intermediary of plants.

Thus, the first step had been taken toward an evolution whose consequences were incalculable. Sources of energy other than the sun already entered into the equation; without mentioning waterfalls, the great motor of which is also the sun, humans captured the force of the tides to make them serve for the production of aliments.

But it was a matter, most importantly, of recovering the heat lost in vast desert spaces such as the Sahara. They set out to adapt great extents to collect and accumulate it. Transformed into electric currents, it would be transported to factories, some of which would have the mission of effecting the synthesis of aliments.

---

[23] The references are to Marcellin Berthelot (1827-1907), who popularized the idea of synthesizing organic compounds, including foodstuffs, from their elements; Hans Fischer (1881-1945), who won the Nobel Prize for Chemistry in 1930 for his research into the constitution of hemoglobin and chlorophyll; and Vladimir Vernadsky (1863-1945), who popularized the idea of the biosphere in a book published in Russian in 1926, and added to it the concept of the noösphere, or the sphere of thought.

The construction of the Great Current was a decisive phase in that evolution, which would eventually change the conditions of human life completely.

Certainly, one could ask the question, as Wang-Ti-Pou did, of whether the new order of things that would result from that transformation was capable of ensuring human happiness.

It is not easy to reply to such a question, for happiness depends on to many factors and is not synonymous with prosperity. However, when one thinks that in the twentieth century, the inhabitants of the Earth only employed a millionth of the energy that they received from the sun and foolishly squandered that which had been accumulated in the form of coal and oil, one is forced to recognize that the rational and complete utilization of all sources of energy attempted by the scientists of the twenty-third century would enrich humankind in enormous proportions and render life much easier.

The physical principle on which the engineers of the Great Current based their conception is simple. In figure 1, the equator is represented by E and the pole by P.[24] A thermoelectric element would be constituted by two wires of different elements, maintained in contact at E and free at their extremities at P. Between the extremities, (X and Y) there is a difference in potential that depends, in the one hand, on the nature of the metals of which the wires are composed, and on the other hand, on the temperatures at the point of contact (A) and the extremities X and Y.

---

[24] The "figure 1" to which text refers here is not present in the Tallandier edition, although it presumably appeared as an illustrative diagram in the serial version in *Science et Voyages*, and nor is the figure 2 to which subsequent reference is made. The explanation does not, however, depend on the pictorial representations, although it is admittedly rather clumsy. The symbols E and P are redundant, and the other symbols employed are a trifle confusing, but I thought it best to transpose them directly from the original rather than attempt any modification.

The thermoelectric couple has long remained difficult to exploit because of the small difference of potential that one obtains even with the best chosen metals. That difference does not exceed three-tenths of a volt for a temperature difference of a hundred degrees, and in practice, a tenth of a volt, when one renounces metals too costly for industrial usage.

The physicists of the twenty-third century, however, had invented complex alloys that permitted, thanks to phenomena of ionization unsuspected by their forebears, to realize a relatively considerable difference of fifty volts between the two conductors AX and AY for a difference in temperature of a hundred degrees.

At the equator, contact A would be plunged into a vat of heavy oil endowed with a great ability of calorific absorption, capable of being heated to some five hundred degrees without decomposing. An apparatus for concentrating solar radiation by means of transparent mirrors would permit the temperature of the bath of oil to rise during the day to the vicinity of five hundred degrees, whereas at the other extremity, at X and Y, the temperature is maintained lower than fifty degrees below zero. In those conditions, with a temperature difference of more than five hundred degrees, the difference in potential between X and Y would reach at least 150 volts.

By night, the condensers at the equator would naturally cease to function. But the mass of mineral oil, heated during the day and protected against nocturnal cooling by mirrors and shutters, retains a reserve of heat sufficient for the temperature not to drop by more than a hundred degrees between sunset and sunrise, with the result that the tension does not diminish significantly.

In order to utilize that source of electric energy it would be sufficient to link the points B and Bby a circuit (C) made of some conductive material. All the derivations of the users of the Great Current would branch from the circuit BCB The section of the wires of the element BAB and the circuit BCB' would be calculated to admit a current of 20,000 ampères.

Given the length of the cables from Greenland to the Sahara and from the Sahara to Greenland, however, which would have to cover a distance of between eight and nine thousand kilometers twice over, and the considerable losses that would result in spite of the excellence of the conductors and the perfection of the insulation, they would only have obtained an insignificant current with a single element. They had, therefore, anticipated that several elements would be mounted in series in accordance with the schema of figure 2, the first element BAB being in contact at B' with the second element B'A'B'', the second at B'' with the third B''A''B''', etc., and the utilization circuit BCB''' being installed between the extremity B''' and the latter. In those conditions, if the difference in potential between B and B, for instance, taking account of losses, fell to only fifty volts, there would be 150 volts between B and B''' for three elements and 500,000 volts if one assembled ten thousand elements in that fashion.

The conductors BA, AB, B'A' , A'B'', etc. having been suitably insulated in advance, were associated in a bundles and affected the appearance of an enormous cable. A thousand bundles of ten thousand elements had already extended between the Sahara and the Franz-Josef fjord, but it remained to construct the electrode bases where the bundles would spread out to their extremities in order to offer themselves, on the one hand, to the intense solar radiation, and on the other, to the influence of the cold.

The system would develop an enormous mechanical power obtained from the solar heat. The heat would be transported, in the form of electricity, from A, A, A'' to B, B', B'', where the production of the current would be accompanied by the melting of the ice in which the polar extremities would be plunged. The quantity of mechanical energy produced, taking account of the intermediate losses, would be exactly proportional to the number of calories captured at the equator and transmitted to the pole.

That transportation of heat, which nature operates by means of marine currents and winds, but at a pure loss, would thus be realized by humans, thanks to the instantaneous action of electricity, to the profit of civilization and all terrestrial life.

At the end of June 2280 a fleet of large cargo vessels, accompanied by a few ice-breakers, a flotilla of helicopters and a large dirigible, left the port of Liverpool, bound for Scoresby Sound, where a base had already been established.

The bay was free of ice in that season. It was only necessary to be wary, beyond Iceland, of collisions with icebergs liberated by the break-up of the ice-sheet or detached from glaciers in the coastal fjords. In places, they would have recourse to the ice-breakers to complete the disaggregation of the ice-field—which is to say, the fringe of ice still adhering to the coast and blocking its sinuosities—where the spring had not yet succeeded in doing so.

The fleet, which was transporting machines, provisions and a great deal of equipment, was well-protected against the particular dangers of navigation in Arctic waters. The aerial flotilla reconnoitered the route and signaled the presence of any icebergs that might have escaped the attention of the watchmen of the Greenland littoral.

For a long time, Greenland had no longer been a wilderness. The few wretched stations that had vegetated on the coast at the beginning of the twentieth century, which scarcely merited the name of villages, had become prosperous towns populated by the employees of shipwrights, large-scale fishing industries, and mining enterprises. They possessed comfortable hotels, which accommodated, in winter as well as summer, numerous tourists curious to see the Far North and experience the sensations of the long polar night or the strange spectacle of the midnight sun.

One of these agglomerations had developed on the shores of Scoresby Sound, about three hundred kilometers south of the Franz-Josef fjord but more than four hundred kilometers above the Arctic Circle—which is to say, in a region where humans could only subsist thanks to the powerful means furnished to them by the temperate lands.

Particular effort had been made in favor of Scoresby Sound when the works of the Great Current had commenced, for it was indispensable to possess a well-organized polar base capable of offering the resources of a refuge to the pioneers who proposed to exploit the ice of the Franz-Josef fjord.

The houses were surmounted by steep roofs whose slope was calculated to prevent the accumulation of snow. They were elevated on terraces in order not to be buried in winter, and mutually supported by stays.

In order to combat the cold and bad weather, the township possessed all the powerful means of civilization: dredgers, snow-plows, vehicles with caterpillar tracks, and a central power plant. Underground tunnels provided silent moving pathways, doubling all the roads and permitting circulation sheltered from the cold even when the roads on the surface were buried under four or five meters of snow. Electric lighting, conceived in accordance with the latest progress in the industry, permitted the endurance of the tenebrous winter.

As there was no waterfall or appreciable tide available for exploitation and coal had become far too scarce to be employed as mere fuel, the energy that Scoresby required to power its dynamos and ensure its heating was furnished in the form of hydrogen, which was sent in cylinders from the great ports of Europe. That hydrogen was extracted from water, decomposed by electrolysis in the factories of Europe. It could be burned either in contact with the air or, if very high temperatures were required, by mixing it with the oxygen obtained by the same process.

In essence, that form of latent energy, furnished by the factories of Great Britain and the continent, was a transformation of natural energies already captured by humans, such as those of waterfalls or tides.

When the Great Current began to function, there would be no further need for that expedient. Diversions would procure energy directly, in the form of electricity, for Scoresby and the other establishments on the Greenland coast.

Pushing through the floes—blocks of ice of small dimension—and avoiding icebergs, the fleet reached Scoresby Sound without any accidents.

It was not the first time that Paul Chartrain had disembarked in Greenland. The previous year, at the beginning of spring, before his trip to Paris, he had often shuttled between Liverpool and Scoresby, and had pushed on as far as the Franz-Josef fjord.

A great deal of work had already been done in that region, and also over the entire course of the Great Current. The thousand cables, each containing ten thousand elements, in which the electrical current would circulate between the North Pole and the tropics, had been laid. It was now necessary to take advantage of the eight or ten weeks during which the soil, laid bare by the melting of the snow between Scoresby and the Franz-Josef fjord would be sufficiently dry to permit the works to proceed.

The last section to the north of Scoresby was about two hundred and eighty kilometers, a distance that would have seemed enormous, in that ingrate latitude, to the people of the twentieth century, but did not frighten the engineers of the Great Current, equipped with the extraordinarily powerful means of the twenty-third.

The cables were constructed to admit a current of twenty thousand amps under half a million volts, equivalent to a power of ten million kilowatts. In order to carry such an amperage, the bundled conductors of each element had to measure about ten thousand square millimeters in section—which is to say, about 113 millimeters in diameter.

In order to make their manipulation easier, the groups of elements—called cables for the sake of brevity—were not disposed in cylinders but sheets of two hundred elements, fifty such sheets being arranged one of top of another. The breadth of an element, formed of two bundled conductors, being 226 millimeters and its height 113 millimeters, each cable measured, in its rectangular section, forty-six meters in breadth, taking account of the thickness of the insulating envelopes, and about five meters seventy in height.

A cable of that sort weighs more than 1,200 tons per meter, and it would have been a very difficult task to lay it completely assembled, but they proceeded in several steps. The elements were posed separately, in segments of a hundred meters, which were assembled in place one by one. At sea, they were sunk like simple telegraphic cables and then grouped into bundles under water, with the aid of submarines and diving automata.

In the terrestrial sections the sheets were assembled by simple ligatures, which it would be easy to undo in order to expose the successive layers if any repair became necessary.

In Greenland, from the Franz-Josef fjord to Scoresby, the cables were lodged in groups of ten in galleries of reinforced concrete, comprising eleven spans, with columns and arches to support the vaults. Those tunnels were very robust, in order to resist the enormous pressure of the winter snows.

On the eleven spans, ten, each measuring fifty meters in width, were occupied by the cables, or groups of elements, which rested in a basin between two sidewalks permitting easy access to all points of the line. Numerous mobile gangways, running on longitudinal rails, served for the inspection and maintenance of the cables.

The five spans to the right and the five to the left were equipped in that fashion on exactly the same plan. The central span, the presence of which brought the total number to eleven, was reserved for circulation. Twenty-five meters wide, it contained a railway with two parallel tracks separated by a twelve-meter platform. The electric energy that ensured the movement of the trains was to be extracted from the Great Current; until that was ready to function, the first vehicles used for transportation of materials in the tunnels were powered by energy from a large turbine factory installed at Scoresby, which employed hydrogen as a fuel.

Each gallery of eleven spans, including the thickness of the intermediate arches, the supporting walls and the external buttresses, was about five hundred and fifty meters wide. As it required a hundred similar galleries to lodge the thousand cables of the Great Current, and it was necessary to reserve spaces between them for the flow of water produced by melted snow in winter and summer, the ensemble occupied a width of sixty kilometers.

That sixty-kilometer-wide track continued southwards from Scoresby on the sea bed, where the cables were protected by a reinforced envelope. At the junction with the coast, they were conducted as far as a level to which the ice never extended, through completely watertight reinforced concrete channels.

All these works, which Chartrain had only followed at intervals, occupied as he was with the installation of cables between Iceland and Great Britain and on the territory of the latter country, were almost complete, thanks to the enormous apparatus, served by a considerable fleet, that had been put to work.

The young engineer had the opportunity to obtain a view of the ensemble when he went in a helicopter with Professor Gainsworth from Scoresby to the Franz-Josef fjord..

Entirely uncovered, under the summer sun, which never sets at the latitude of Scoresby at that time of year, the tunnels, some of which had only been completely closed for a few days, were lined up with impressive regularity at the foot of the snow-crowned coastal mountains, from which water was flowing in thousands of torrents

The flow of those waters in spring and summer had been one of the most difficult problems to solve. In many places it had been necessary to construct passages, either for artificial channels or for the natural beds of the streams. The hundred galleries had to cross as many bridges, many of which were extremely bold. In places, the galleries were staged on the sides of the mountain, and then took on, along with their viaducts, a grandiose appearance.

In truth, it was the work of titans that was displayed to the eyes. How many tons of metal had it been necessary to extract from the bowels of the earth? How many factories had worked incessantly, at full power, for years in order to fabricate the cables that were extended in thousands over the globe? How many quarries of stone and cement had been emptied to construct so many dykes, walls, tunnels and bridges?

Along the entire length of the Great Current, there had been no other region in which they had been forced to employ such prodigious efforts, but it was a matter of overcoming a nature more hostile than anywhere else.

The helicopter in which Chartrain had taken his place along with his chief and his colleagues flew for some time over the Franz-Josef fjord, because Professor Gainsworth wanted to take account for himself of the condition of the ice.

The fjord, which had been chosen for that reason, was the ultimate outlet of numerous glaciers that descended from the largest mountainous massif in Greenland. In that season, the speed of the glaciers' flow reached nearly twenty meters a day, which was relatively considerable. They came together in the immense valley constituted by the fjord, and collided, exerting formidable pressures on one another, which caused the ice to break up, lifted it up, bristling with seracs, hollowed out crevasses and dislocated it, while deafening detonations, mingled with the thunder of avalanches, rose from the chaos.

As the helicopter had to fly low because of the clouds rolling over the bay and masking the mountain-tops, the passengers could hear the din of the ice very clearly in spite of the hum of the propellers.

The vast and chaotic frozen surface of the fjord reacted intensely on the atmosphere above it, determining violent eddies into which the helicopter was drawn. In spite of the skill of its crew, the machine was subjected to abrupt ascents and descents, which the passengers found very disagreeable. The captain even thought that he ought to advise Professor Gainsworth that it would be dangerous to prolong the excursion; the overworked crew might make a false move that would end in catastrophe.

It was therefore decided to return to the base, going around the mountains at the extremity of the fjord. When the helicopter headed out to sea, the passengers were able to contemplate the front of the glacier, an enormous white, green and blue cliff that blocked the valley over a breadth of four or five leagues, and from which blocks dislocated by the pressure never ceased to detach themselves.

The captain, who was accustomed to flying in the region and had often witnessed the spectacle, drew the attention of the engineers to an immense vertical crevasse that split the ice-cliff.

"If I'm not mistaken," he said, "we're about to witness the birth of an iceberg.

He had the propulsion helices stopped, and the helicopter remained suspended five hundred meters in advance of the front of the glacier, two hundred meters above the level of its crest.

"It would be dangerous to hover any closer," he explained. "You'll understand why shortly, if what I anticipate actually occurs."

Professor Gainsworth and his colleagues armed themselves with binoculars in order to observe the phenomenon.

Formidable cracking sounds were heard, and they saw the crevasse slowly widening. Blocks ten or fifteen meters in height were detached all along the fissure, falling and colliding with one another, raising enormous waves and sprays of foam.

"Fantastic!" murmured Chartrain.

But the captain laughed and said: "You haven't seen anything yet."

A quarter of an hour passed during which the crevasse was further enlarged, while others formed, parallel to the first, and the fall of the blocks continued. Then the glacier trembled, an entire section twenty meters high and five hundred meters wide was detached from the cliff noisily. A veritable iceberg, a mountain of ice this time, perhaps a hundred cubic meters, fell obliquely into the sea, which splashed almost to the height of the cliff.

The captain had given an order. The suspension helices, giving full power, drew the helicopter upwards while the propulsive helices pushed it out to sea, because it was necessary to avoid being sucked in by the atmospheric disturbance that was inevitably about to be produced.

Indeed, in spite of the rapidity with which it had drawn away, the apparatus was forcefully tossed about, and for several seconds it followed a violent roller-coaster trajectory.

The iceberg and the front of the ice-sheet had disappeared behind an enormous veil of mist, but beneath the helicopter the sea was seething, white with foam between the blocks of ice that encumbered it, and which seemed to be prancing like a host of clumsy giants.

The helicopter circled at the entrance to the fjord until the mist had dissipated, and the floating mountain of ice could then be seen drawing slowly away from the cliff from which it had been detached. It only projected above the waves by a hundred meters, which was still very respectable and gave an idea of its enormous volume when one knew that the submerged part was five times as large as the part above the surface.

The passengers in the helicopter had not reached the end of their excitement, for they suddenly saw the iceberg oscillate. The inferior section below the surface must have split; its equilibrium had been modified and it was shifting in order to return its center of gravity to its normal position.

A four-hundred meter mountain performing a pirouette is not a banal sight.

A further revolt lifted up the howling sea; the floes began to prance again; a new veil of mist rose up, hiding the image of chaos from the spectators.

Accustomed as they were, by virtue of the progress of science and technology, to the domination of nature, the engineers of the Great Current who had just witnessed that grandiose manifestation were affected by it. Chartrain had a moment of doubt: was it not presumption on the part of humans, those pygmies, to attack such prodigious forces?

The passengers scarcely exchanged a few words before landing at the Franz-Jozef base.

There, they inspected the works in progress.

At that end of the line, the problem consisted of establishing, between the extremities of the elements and the ice that descended from the mountains and accumulated in the depths of the fjord, a contact sufficiently narrow to profit fully from the source of cold constituted by that immense natural reservoir.

They had thought of hollowing out approach conduits for each cable, the inferior extremity of which would terminate below the level of the ice, in such a way as to reach the frozen mass. Those conduits would be distributed along the entire length of the fjord. Thus, each cable could spread out, displaying its elements, in order better to capture the cold, over a conveniently-adapted broad surface.

To that effect, they had hollowed out a frontal tunnel parallel to the coast of the fjord, into which all the conduits opened. The materials produced by the excavation of the rock had served for the construction of the surface tunnels between Scoresby and the fjord.

It only remained now to establish a powerful framework in the frontal gallery, partly in iron and partly in reinforced concrete, the different traverses of which, disposed obliquely and terminated externally by enormous rostra, would be orientated contrary to the ice current, in much the same fashion as the prow of a ship is toward the waves when heading into a tempest.

Driven by the pressure against that skeletal system, the ice would be broken up by the spurs and slide between the traverses, which it would invade, gradually filling the tunnel. The extremities of the cables would have been divided up in the framework, the elements being lodged along iron beams in grooves designed for that purpose.

The whole of that construction would initially be carried out under ground, shielded by a wall of rock of sufficient thickness, which had been reserved and allowed to persist until the very end. When everything was complete, the wall would be demolished and there would be nothing more to do than await the invasion of the ice.

That plan had been adopted in spite of objections that had been opposed to it, the most serious of which was based on the irresistible force of the ice current. The project's detractors claimed, in fact, that the framework, no matter how solid it might be, would be carried away by the moving glaciers. The response made to them was that the pressure of the ice would be limited by the intense fusion that would be produced in contact with the cables under the action of the electric current, restoring at the polar extremity of the line the heat obtained at the other extremity in the tropics. For that was the entire secret of the gigantic enterprise: to melt the polar ice with heat obtained from the tropics.

It has been calculated that about twenty thousand cubic kilometers of ice is detached every year from the region of the North Pole in spring and summer. If one assumes that the figure is approximately the same for the South Pole, that is forty thousand cubic meters of ice that the Earth fabricates every year and then disperses in warm waters, where that enormous mass melts and disappears.

It is necessary to imagine the enormity of the loss of energy represented by that natural mechanism.

In order to liquefy without changing its temperature, a kilogram of ice, at zero degrees, absorbs a little more than seventy-nine kilocalories—which is to say, the quantity of heat required to raise the temperature of a liter of water by seventy-nine degrees. Now, that quantity of heat is equivalent to a considerable amount of work. It is theoretically sufficient to expend one kilocalorie to raise a weight of four hundred and twenty-five kilos to a height of one meter. The quantity of heat absorbed to melt a kilogram of ice is therefore equivalent to the effort required to raise a mass of thirty-three metric tons to the same height of one meter, or a weight of a hundred and ten kilos to the height of the Eiffel tower.

If one calculates on the same basis the quantity of energy absorbed by the melting of the forty thousand cubic kilometers of ice that the poles reject every year, also taking account of the heat absorbed in rising the temperature of the melt water, and that of the ice when it is older than zero degrees, one arrives at a figure of one thousand six hundred quintillion—sixteen followed by twenty zeroes—kilogram-meters.

The imagination cannot estimate such a number, but one can nevertheless form an idea of it if one thinks that that work is carried out over a year of three hundred and sixty-five days—which is to say, thirty-one million five hundred and thirty-six thousand seconds—which represents a little more than five trillion kilogram-meters per second, or nearly seven hundred billion horsepower: a thousand times the hydraulic pressure developed in the entire world by streams and rivers.

One can understand why the people of the twenty-third century were obsessed by the desire to utilize that enormous amount of wasted power—and after having envisaged the fantastic figures on which their ambition was founded, one can deem as modest their initial attempt, which was only a matter of making use of the ice rejected by the Franz-Jozef fjord, at a rate of eight or ten cubic kilometers a year. But the melting of ten cubic kilometers of ice is equivalent to a hundred and thirty-three million horsepower: twenty-two times the hydraulic power of France.

The game was worth the trouble of playing.

Certainly, they would only use in the beginning a tiny fraction of the total latent power that the great source of cold would draw from the equator, but if the first installation produced the results for which they hoped, they would hasten to construct others, which would rapidly multiply tenfold, and then a hundredfold, the energy resources obtained in that manner from the great animator of all life and all movement on the surface of the earth: the Sun.

IV

Paul Chartrain went into the special telephone and television cabin that had been installed at the Franz-Josef base for communication with Europe and Africa, particularly with the tropical section of the Great Current enterprise, which was working on the completion of the factories capturing the solar heat.

After extremely careful studies, the region of Timbuktu, in the vicinity of the seventeenth degree of north latitude, had been chosen for the installation of the hot base of the Great Current. The climate of that region is relatively constant; the temperature is maintained there between the narrow limits of twenty and forty degrees above zero, and rain is rare. The apparatus for the condensation of solar heat there could thus be designed to respond to a regular regime, which is an eminently favorable condition for an industrial installation.

In addition, the access routes were excellent; as well as the river route of the Niger, which had been continually ameliorated by major works during recent centuries, they had the Transsaharan and the Dakar-Timbuktu-Chad-Zanzibar railways at their disposal.

There would not have been any advantage in moving closer to the equator. The climate would have been less regular, communications more difficult, and what they would have gained in terms of the quantity of heat absorbed during the dry seasons would have been largely canceled out by reductions of yield in the major and minor rainy seasons.

Paul Chartrain thus intended to telephone Timbuktu, as he was accustomed to do almost every day, by virtue of his functions as a liaison officer.

The cabin did not resemble the booths employed for telephones in the twentieth century; it as a pleasant little room illuminated by a soft pink light. It had no window but one of the walls was coated from floor to ceiling with a milky substance reminiscent of porcelain.

The young engineer sat down in a comfortable armchair facing that screen, and waited.

A woman's voice—that of the telephone operator—became audible.

"May I connect you?"

"Yes, please do."

There was a slight crackle, and the milky wall in front of Chartrain was illuminated, seeming to vanish, allowing another small room similar to the first to appear, which prolonged it exactly, making the room seem twice as large.

A young woman was sitting there facing Chartrain. It was Claire Nolleau, dressed in white, as is appropriate in the tropics.

The engineer had the impression of really being in the presence of his colleague, who was speaking to him from Timbuktu. A novice having such a conversation for the first time would have been tempted to get up in order to go to meet the other, but he would have bumped into the wall that had apparently vanished.

In any case, Chartrain's gaze did not perceive the same illumination in the part of the room in which he was sitting and the one where his correspondent was seated. Whereas he was bathed in a pink half-light, Claire Nolleau was subject to an intense radiation, whose brightness was a trifle excessive.

Meanwhile, at the far end of the cable that put the station at the Franz-Josef fjord in communication with that Timbuktu station, the young woman had an inverse impression.

In fact, in order for the correspondents at the opposite ends of the line to have a clear view of their interlocutors, it was necessary not to be blinded by the light to which they were exposed themselves. The inventors of the television had had a difficult problem to solve in that regard; they had found an elegant solution.

The photoelectric cells that collected the image of each correspondent on departure were stimulated, not by white light, but by infra-red light, devoid of action on the retina. On arrival, the cells corresponding with those of the departure cabin, were illuminated by white light. The reflection of the screen nevertheless spread a certain brightness in the space where, before it was illuminated, only a soft pink light had reigned.

Since they had met in Paris, Paul and Claire had both looked forward impatiently to these conversations, which, limited as they were to matters of service, furnished them with the opportunity to talk to one another and see one another again. They had communicated once between Liverpool and Algiers, and a second time between Liverpool and Timbuktu; this conversation between the Franz-Josef fjord and Timbuktu was the third since their separation.

In spite of the pleasure they obtained from meeting like this, at a distance, they did not waste time in greetings and testaments of sympathy; that was not the custom of twenty-third century.

"I can confirm," the young woman declared, "that our tropical base will be completely equipped and ready to function one month from now."

"We hope to be ready ourselves by that date. The mounting of the ice-dividers in the sixty-kilometer frontal tunnel has begun."

"Don't you fear that a month might not be enough to complete such a task?"

"No. We already have two hundred and fifty machines in operation. In two days we'll have a thousand. The whole framework is in place. In a month, we'll have finished placing the wires and the sections of masonry, constructed with fast-drying cement, will be solid enough for the protective wall on the side of the glacier to be demolished. Let's hope that there isn't any mishap between now and then. If there were an error in the mounting of the line or a flaw in the cables, and the current didn't flow, the pressure of the ice in the frontal gallery might end up overcoming the resistance of the great divider."

"That won't happen. The cables have been checked too carefully. By the way, Chartrain, I have to notify you of an incident. You need to inform Professor Gainsworth in order that precautions can be taken in your sector.

"A few days ago, it was observed here that a cable had been sabotaged near its extremity, in a hall of the thermic base, at the point where it emerges from its sheath in order to spread out into the heating apparatus. A series of five elements had been cut with an oxyhydric torch, which naturally rendered the cable unusable. The gravest aspect is that an attempt had been made to conceal the damage with a coating of the same color as the insulating envelope protecting the wires.

"The attention of a watchman was attracted by a black streak that had dripped on to the floor from the cable when the saboteur had melted the elements and their enveloped with his torch.

"It was thought that it was a matter of an act of vengeance by a worker. The damage was repaired and the incident was considered as a warning to have surveillance increased. When I arrived here two days ago, precautionary measures had been taken so that no one could get near the bare cables without any reason of service. No further sabotage occurred.

"However, as the installation of the heat accumulators for the first cable had been completed, a trial was carried out yesterday. The hall had been evacuated the previous evening, as usual, but the ventilation panels were left open, because it was not yet known whether the trial would take place yesterday or today. The order to close the panels was given by Hurlaut only an hour later. The operation, as you know, is completely mechanized. The engineer installed in the control booth lowers a lever; the panels, activated by hooks, slide in their frames and block al the openings."

Chartrain was familiar with the disposition of the halls of solar heat concentration as they had been installed at the thermic base of the Great Current. It was a matter of vast glasshouses whose glazed surface received the sun's rays from sunrise to sunset. The extent of that surface was calculated to admit solar radiation equivalent to an average of about forty-five million kilowatts, which represented, in such a climate, about five hectares, a rectangle of five hundred meters by a hundred. There were a thousand similar glasshouses, one for each cable, and their ensemble covered a vast extent of desert sixty kilometers across and a kilometer and a half deep, comprising ten rows of a hundred glazed halls.

The anticipated power of forty-five million kilowatts per cable corresponded to a yield of ten million kilowatts, taking into account losses along the line and resistance, which gave for the thousand cables a total motive force of ten billion kilowatts or—given that one horsepower is equivalent to seven hundred and thirty-six watts—more than thirteen million horsepower, twice the hydraulic power of France.

The whole difficulty of the problem consisted of storing and retaining the heat that the sun transmitted through the glass by radiation. It is well-known that ordinary glass possesses the property of allowing luminous rays to pass through while being almost impermeable to the invisible rays that constitute so-called black heat. The light penetrates, is degraded on contact with objects, into calorific radiation that no longer reemerges. That is a phenomenon well-known to horticulturalists, who make use, in consequence, of greenhouses or, more simply, frames with glass tops.

In the twenty-third century, the engineers of the Great Current had special glass at their disposal whose diathermal power—which is to say, its permeability to heat—was very nearly zero. The windows of the halls of thermal concentration were made with that kind of glass and coated with a cellulose-derived layer of a substance analogous to collodion, perfectly transparent but elastic and unbreakable. Such armored windows were capable of resisting extremely violent impacts. If they were submitted to too strong a pressure, one could succeed in breaking the glass, but not the window; it cracked and was deformed, but the elastic material, almost impossible to break, continued to prevent it from fracturing.

The entire framework, the basal walls and the doors of the hall were perfectly insulated by antithermic coatings. Thus, when the ventilation panels were closed, all the calories transmitted by the sun remained enclosed within the glass and the temperature rose indefinitely.

In order further to ensure the accumulation of the heat, large vats containing a kind of mineral oil endowed with a great capacity for calorific absorption were disposed under the windows.

The ten thousand elements composing the cable ending in the hall spread out in groups of a thousand to their extremities in broad thin sheets, insulated with mica, a poor conductor of electricity but diathermal, which, some arranged on top of one another and others alongside one another, were plunged into the vats.

The absorbent liquid rose during the day to a temperature in the vicinity of five hundred degrees and its mass was calculated to retain such a reserve of heat that its temperature could not drop more than a hundred degrees during the night, even if the Great Current were functioning at full yield.

The ten groups of a thousand elements penetrated into their thermic hall on the long side of the rectangle, over a front of five hundred meters, with appropriately calculated intermediate distances. The thousand elements of each group were then separated from one another and divided between a series of vats aligned in a hundred-meter row. There were two hundred vats in all under the glass, each containing fifty elements. To avoid inequalities of temperature between one vast and another, communication pipes and a system of pumps maintained the continual circulation of the thermic liquid.

As it would be impossible, naturally for humans to live in such an environment, where the temperature of an oven reigned, and the hall could only be allowed to cool down, by interrupting the current, in very rare circumstances, the service of supervision, maintenance and repair, and the periodic renewal if the thermic baths, had to be assumed by automata endowed with organs of television and teleaudition, and powered by electricity, which were piloted from special cabins outside.

Now, Claire Nolleau related that a check had been carried out to verify the calorific absorption capacity of a completely-equipped hall, with full vats.

As it was simply a matter of measuring temperatures, indications of which were transmitted electrically to the post of the chief engineer of the group, it had not been thought necessary to employ the automata.

The gist of the young woman's story was that a man, a stranger to the personnel of the Great Current, had either found a means of introducing himself into the hall while work was still going on, and had remained hidden after the departure of the workers, or had got in via one of the ventilation panels while they were still open.

That unknown individual had not been aware of the experiment that was about to be carried out. He had, therefore, no suspicion of the danger to which he was exposing himself by allowing himself to be enclosed in a space that was about to undergo a rise in temperature to five hundred degrees.

He had repeated the act of sabotage that had been observed a few days earlier, but this time, making use of the time available to him during the night, he had put a large number of elements out of commission. He had not been disturbed; all the doors were closed, solidly sealed by electric bolts, and no one had suspected that there was a man in the hall.

Perhaps the saboteur had intended to get out again through one of the open panels, by repeating the acrobatic exercise that he had been obliged to execute to get in. He had been unable to do to because, an hour after the workers had left, the engineer on duty had activated the hooks of the glazed panels from his control both, which had engaged with their frames, hermetically sealed.

When he had observed that he was a prisoner, he had probably not been anxious to begin with. He had calmly finished his criminal work. Doubtless he hoped to pass unobserved among the workers in the morning when work resumed; he would then take advantage of the first opportunity to escape. But the sun had risen and its rays had immediately commenced pouring their heat into the immense glazed gallery.

The engineer who was observing the temperature indicators from his post, had recorded sixty degrees after only a hour. Twenty minutes later, the temperature surpassed eighty degrees. One can imagine the panic that gripped the malefactor when he felt the heat rise to that point. He could not have been very well informed regarding the conditions in which the Great Current functioned, and perhaps he thought at first that the temperature would not exceed a level compatible with life. He might have thought that the panels would be reopened, or that the workers would come to resume their work.

In the end, sensing congestion, he had tried desperately to escape from the oven in which he had imprudently allowed himself to be trapped. He had tried to force a door, and even tried to make use for that purpose of his oxyhydric torch; the traces of that attempt were discovered subsequently. But as the heat had risen rapidly and he must have lost hope of concluding the operation, he had tried to escape another way,. If he called for help, nobody heard him.

His strength must already have been abandoning him. He climbed up to the height of the first glazed panel at the top of the basal wall, and tried to break the glass. He only succeeded in cracking it and causing it to bulge externally. He fell before having broken it, overcome by the heat.

The experiment was not interrupted until the following morning at dawn. It had extended over twenty-four hours and it had been observed, with satisfaction, that the temperature of the hall, after having risen to five hundred degrees, as anticipated, had not fallen during the night, as the Great Current was not yet functioning, by more than five degrees. The absorption was excellent, the insulation perfect. The expectations of the constructors had been realized.

The panels were then reopened at sunrise in order to allow the temperature to fall, but as the vats retained a considerable degree of heat, it would probably have been necessary to wait until the following morning before being able to go into the hall.

"As I was about to telephone you," Claire Nolleau said, "the temperature between the vats, in the bright sunlight, was still more than a hundred and fifty degrees in spite of the air currents blowing through the open panels, but this morning, a watchman making an external tour of the hall noticed the deformation of the window that someone had tried to break from inside. He alerted his chief, who immediately decided to send an automaton to explore the hall."

The automaton to which the young woman was alluding was essentially comprised of a small vehicle mounted on pneumatic tires, slender enough to circulate easily through the walkways between the cable-beams. The body of the vehicle enclosed the engine and steering apparatus. A kind of chimney, able to tilt, elongate and retract at will, bore the artificial eye of a television apparatus at its extremity, capable of orientation in any direction. Microphones charged with transmitting sound were arranged along the four sides of the parallelepiped-shaped body. Two pairs of articulated arms of unequal length, the first pair measuring a meter and the second two meters, constituted its instruments of labor. Those arms were terminated by pincers or artificial hands with six branches or fingers, opposed in two groups of three. Such arms, equipped with flexible pincers, were adapted to all kinds of work and the usage of all kinds of instruments.

While waiting for the Great Current to become active, motive force was furnished, as for all the installations of the base, by the hydroelectric factories of the Niger. The current was transmitted by a cable, which markers guided from place to place, and which rolled up on a drum or unrolled, according to whether the machine was approaching or drawing away from its point of departure. The automaton could thus travel along the five-hundred meter transversal path reserved at the extremity of the cross-beams and, departing from that base, along any of the eleven hundred-meter longitudinal paths to the right and left of the hall between the cross-beams. Thus, by going back and forth eleven times across the entire length of the hall, moving successively along each of the longitudinal pathways, the machine could explore the entire hall and reach any point at which some maneuver or repair was necessary.

"Set in motion," Claire Nolleau went on, "the automaton discovered the cadaver of a man underneath the damaged window, literally cooked during his sojourn in the overheated atmosphere of the hall. The engineer realized what had happened. It's been decided to wait until tomorrow, when the hall will have cooled down sufficiently, to carry out more precise observations and carry out the repairs, which, at present, aren't urgent. The body has been left where it was found in order not to trouble the investigations of the police."

When he came out of the telephonic cabin, Paul Chartrain ran to see Professor Chartrain in order to inform him of Claire Nolleau's communication.

The chief of the Great Current's polar base was indignant. "Can it be that in our epoch there are still individuals both criminal enough and stupid enough to commit such acts of sabotage? The miscreant has been severely punished. Let's hope that his example will discourage those who might be tempted to imitate him."

"The repairs won't take long," Chartrain observed. "The saboteur might have been able to do much more harm if, for example, he'd attacked the line in the middle of the desert."

"But that would have been much more difficult," Gainsworth observed. "If he'd got off a train at one of the Transsaharan stations, his arrival wouldn't have escaped the vigilance of the guards of the line. He wouldn't have been able to operate alone, and the presence of several shady individuals carrying the equipment, necessarily bulky, that they'd need to attack the cables, would inevitably have awakened suspicion. If the malefactors had come by road in an automobile, their presence would similarly have been noticed. On the other hand, going a long way into the desert isn't without danger. Finally, surveillance is very active; it's carried out by patrols in the air and on the road, and by night, searchlights are employed.

"In any case, the cables are so well-protected in their envelope that one couldn't break them, even with explosives, without long and arduous toil. That explains why our saboteur operated at the extremity, at the most vulnerable point—but fortunately, the easiest to repair.

"It's sad to think that there are human beings who employ their intelligence and their energy in destroying rather that creating."

V

It was the end of July; the great day had arrived. Construction work on the Great Current had concluded everywhere. The tropical base was in a functional state. The cables had been carefully checked in all their sections: the African, the Mediterranean, the Hispano-French, the British and the Nordic.

The polar base was fully equipped. The extremities of the elements spread out beneath a simple mica envelope into the lodgings fitted out for that purpose. There was nothing more to do than demolish the exterior wall of the gallery to open the way to the ice of the fjord, which, under the effect of pressure, would quickly fill up the traverses of the Great Current.

The inauguration of one of the most grandiose endeavors of human genius was an event whose phases the entire world was ready to follow.

All the countries of Europe and Africa that were about to benefit from the energy of the Great Current, thanks to the numerous branches that had been established along the line had sent delegations to Scoresby. Tourism companies had chartered liners, large hydrogliders and aircraft to transport to Greenland the host of curiosity-seekers who wanted to be present to witness the prodigious opening of the great gallery and its invasion by the ice.

Powerful radiotelephone and radiotelevision transmitters would also permit all those who could not make the journey to Greenland to enjoy the spectacle that was in preparation. Everyone was checking their wireless receivers in order not to miss that truly sensational broadcast.

The countries that would not be served by the Great Current had also sent representatives, for the civilized world was following with a powerful interest the first large-scale attempt to be made the capture solar heat directly.

There was, nevertheless, one exception to the surge of enthusiasm. The Asian Republics, whose President Wang-Ti-Pou had been for some while, were not represented, and the troubles that had followed the revolution were not sufficient to explain that absence.

The fact had attracted much comment, and there was no shortage of pessimists to affirm that Asia resented the scientific and technological civilization of the other continents. Those prophets of woe claimed to know that Wang-Ti-Pou was secretly preparing massive armaments, and that he had been able to buy a large number to commercial aircraft since his accession to power in America and Europe, which would be easy to transform into bombers. He had, it was said, procured several thousand in less than a month. It could scarcely be denied; such purchases had not passed unperceived—but optimists affirmed that people were wrong to be alarmed. Had not Wang-Ti-Pou proclaimed that he wanted to direct his people along the path of progress, and was not large-scale commercial aviation the best rapid remedy for the insufficiency of communications between the immense territories of the Associated Republics?

Without believing in an aggression, the directors of the European Federation, in order to reassure opinion, had nevertheless taken a few precautions. A few hundred warplanes and military helicopters had been concentrated in the East; a few large submersible cruisers that were in reserve in naval bases had been rearmed; the checking had been ordered of a few thousand battle automata that would have to guard the frontiers in case of conflict, as well as the fixed and mobile command posts from which the defensive engineers would have to guide them.

The execution of these measures had hardly begun, though. Even those who admitted the danger did not think it was imminent, and the Ministry responsible for military forces, which had completely lost sight of its mission in a century and a half of peace, was not putting any haste into its preparations.

After the criminal attempts that had been perpetrated against the Great Current, and which had remained deeply enigmatic in some respects in spite of the efforts of the police, Dr. Bormann had reinforced the protection of the bases and the entire line of the Great Current. There was a military helicopter at Scoresby and a telemechanical apparatus at the Franz-Josef base, with its direction-post, for which a shelter had be constructed between the tunnels of the cables of the Great Current.

Paul Chartrain, who had done a period of military service as a pilot of telemechanical tanks and airplanes, had been designated to occupy that post in the case of an emergency. Professor Gainsworth had decided that the young man ought to train one of his colleagues in its operation, but he had not yet had time to do that.

Those were in any case, precautions that were taken as a matter of duty, but which were deemed to be entirely superfluous.

The opening of the frontal gallery was fixed for the first of August. At that time of year, when the sky was clear, the midnight sun could still be seen perched upon the mountains that limited the fjord to the north. The weather, which had been foggy on the previous days, cleared up, as if to participate in the glorification of the creators of the Great Current.

At six o'clock in the morning, the mines were exploded.

A swarm of aircraft, helicopters and dirigibles carrying official representatives and thousands of tourists were soaring over the fjord in order to permit their passengers to observe the effects of the explosion, which dislocated, with a rumble, the immense sixty-kilometer wall.

Blocks of rock flew away, mingled with blocks of ice. The chaotic surface of the fjord seemed to quiver, and when the debris had fallen back, the cavern in which the cables of the Great Current terminated appeared, open from one end to the other.

The coastline was not entirely straight, of course; it presented numerous sinuosities—capes and bays—and the gallery, which followed its contour, was occasionally hidden from view by a promontory, but in the clear weather, its general direction could nevertheless be followed all the way to the horizon by making use of a good pair of binoculars. The explosions had hollowed out a kind of ditch along its entire length, which allowed the gaze to plunge obliquely beneath the rock, even though there were numerous places where the ice cliffs surpassed the height of the gallery's vault.

Open water had appeared at the bottom of that cutting, and had absorbed the rocks thrown off by the explosion as well as collecting the disaggregated ice.

Immobility reigned for a few minutes over the ice-field; then the blocks that the mines had just dislocated began to stir; they swayed, sliding over one another and sometimes turning over with a loud crash. That agitation was transmitted further and further toward the open sea. The entire ice-sheet quivered, and, under an irresistible pressure, slowly drew closer to the gallery, which the debris of floating ice, pushed by the enormous mass, was beginning to invade.

The flank of the ice-sheet took about six hours to fill the space that separated it from the gallery, here a little more, there a little less. Then nothing was any longer visible but the rocky coast, the ice sheet dominated by immense bergs and, on the horizon, toward the west, the gigantic front of the glacier. It seemed that the titanic work of humans had been effaced by the still-formidable power of nature.

In the service chambers, however, the engineers were poring over their measuring instruments, watching for the slightest flicker of the voltmeters and ammeters, for they were impatient to catch the first signs of the electric current that was about to flow if all the anticipations of the constructors were verified.

At the other end of the line, in the desert to the north of Timbuktu, other engineers were observing other needles on other dials, whose immobility seemed to them to be an insult to human genius.

Everywhere, those who were waiting for the prodigy were profoundly emotional. They were accustomed to considering their anticipations as perfectly logical, in conformity with calculations, and necessary. And yet, at the present moment they were like neophytes who had been introduced into a mystical enclosure, having been told to expect a miraculous apparition. They were gripped by a kind of fear before the enormity of the work born of their genius, their audacity and their activity. The mathematical certainty that had sustained them thus far abandoned them. Might they not have made a mistake in solving their equations? Were those immense cables they had extended over the earth really capable of transmitting from one extremity to the other the instantaneous reactions of cold and heat?

Eight hours after the explosion, nothing had yet budged on the indicative apparatus.

"It's not going to work," someone said, in a loud voice.

Professor Gainsworth turned round angrily toward the incredulous individual.

"Everything has been anticipated; it has to work. It's necessary to give the ice time to expand into the tunnel and to make contact with the elements."

No one replied. And for another quarter of an hour, they waited for the miracle.

Then Paul Chartrain uttered an exclamation, which resembled the ancient cry of a triumphant Redskin removing the scalp of a fallen enemy.

A hundred voices joined his in chorus.

The voltmeter and ammeter of cable number one, the nearest to the depths of the fjord, had trembled, and their needles were moving slowly away from zero.

There was a minute of mad enthusiasm. The engineers the section chiefs and the official representatives who were there, many of whom were of a venerable age, were leaping madly and shouting without any concern for their dignity.

Other needles began to dance, announcing that cable 140, and then cable 326, had been touched by the ice in their turn.

Then it no longer ceased. Sometimes it was one and something another of the cables that entered into action—and in each one, the intensity of the current increased as the ice, obedient to the pressure of the sheet, penetrated more profoundly into the gallery and made closer contact with the wires.

They were able to proclaim the news of the victory through the loud-hailers, which the wireless broadcast. The telephone and the telegraph transmitted congratulations from all over the world to the general staff of the Great Current. They also had to communicate with the engineers at the Timbuktu base, who were demanding precisions and technical data. Chartrain thus had a new opportunity to correspond with Claire Nolleau, and their conversation was excited that day by the enthusiasm of success.

When each of them had obtained from the other the information that they needed, the young people expressed their joy.

"Let's be proud, Chartrain, of having collaborated in this great work. The incredulous and the prophets of woe have been confounded. We've just proved to them that none of their objections had any foundation."

"Well, Nolleau, you know how much faith I have in our work. Even if the victory escapes us today, we'll triumph in the end. We've demonstrated that the concept of the Great Current isn't absurd, that its realization is possible, and that's a vital point. But one danger still remains: in spite of all our calculations, we might have underestimated the enormous pressure of the ice and its power of traction. That's a doubt that has been haunting me since I've been working at the Franz-Josef base. I've witnessed the birth of icebergs and the quivering of the ice-sheet. When one sees the facility with which blocks of several million cubic meters are lifted up, one wonders whether such prodigious forces can really be tamed.

We'll have to wait for days and weeks before being sure that our ice-dividers won't be carried away, in spite of the solidity of their construction, with all the electric organs that they have to protect."

Chartrain was not the only one to experience such a dread. Professor Gainsworth also felt it, and it caused him to appear anxious at the banquet that was offered after the inauguration to the official representatives by the directors of the Great Current.

The engineers of Franz-Josef base had calculated that the gallery would not be completely invaded by the ice for three days, and the observations they never ceased to carry out confirmed that prediction. It was, in consequence, only toward the end of the third day that the pressure would have acquired its full power and they would know, one way or the other, whether the ice dividers were adequate to their task.

The phenomenon was tracked by the constant increase in the intensity of the current that was manifest in the cables as the terminal surfaces of the elements entered into closer contact with the source of cold.

As there was no surprise to be feared, either at the tropical base or, for even better reasons, by the sector heads in Liverpool and Algiers, the senior directors of the company, Dr. Bormann and Chief Engineer Hurtaut decided to travel to the Franz-Josef base to keep watch, with Professor Gainsworth, on the progress of the ice.

They too were anxious, and they told themselves that their collaboration would be useful is the mechanism they had adopted or the installation of the cold base of the Great Current proved to be incapable of the effort expected of it.

Sector Chief Hurtaut decided to take Claire Nolleau with him, in order to fulfill the role of his secretary. The young woman experienced great joy in consequence. Not only could she congratulate herself on being able to observe on location the phenomena that were in the process of giving birth to the Great Current, but she would be very happy to see Paul Chartrain again.

Thus on the third day, at the moment when it was anticipated that that the great cooling gallery would be entirely invaded by the ice, the principal heads of the general staff of the Great Current were assembled at Franz-Josef base.

Dr. Bormann and Sector Chief Hurtaut arrived at Scoresby by rocket-plane. That was the most rapid means of locomotion. Rocket-planes, which accomplish the greater part of their journey at an altitude of about twenty thousand meters, in regions where the rarefied atmosphere no longer opposes sensible resistance to forward motion, travel at a speed of two thousand kilometers an hour. It required four hours to make the journey from Timbuktu to Scoresby, including the maneuvers of take-off and landing.

By the end of the third day, the regime of the cables had attained the anticipated maximum of ten million kilowatts per cable, which, for the ensemble of a thousand cables, represented a total of ten billon kilowatts, or an approximate yield of thirteen million six hundred thousand horsepower. That was already a considerable source of energy, more than double the hydraulic power of a country like France, but which still only utilized a tiny part of the reserves of the ice. It could be rapidly quadrupled by means of new installations, if the first gave the expected results.

Now, the result had been attained. The ice-dividers were holding. The hopes of the constructors were becoming firmer by the hour.

On the fifth of August, however when everything was still functioning normally, and haste had already been made in all the countries served by the Great Current to make the numerous branches already constructed enter into function, alarming news regarding the international political situation was spread by the printed and spoken outlets.

First the wireless, and then the papers that came from Paris via rocket-plane to Scoresby and the Franz-Josef base, spread alarm regarding a possible general strike in the factories of North Africa.

In Cairo, Tunis, Tangiers, Tangier and Casablanca, individuals had been arrested, suspected of preaching anti-technological revolution.

Those agitators affirmed that the prodigious development of technology in Europe, Africa and America would end with the reestablishment of slavery and that the working masses would find themselves definitively enslaved by the machinery supposedly created to liberate them from constraint of labor, but in reality more tyrannical than the worst of despots. The theories of Wang-Ti-Pou and his Asiatic partisans were recognized. The interrogation of the suspects seemed to indicate, in fact, that they were more or less narrowly linked with the revolutionaries of Mukden and Peking.

The news from North Arica was not, however, the most disquieting, for the authorities were boasting that they had the situation well in hand; they affirmed that the general strike would be avoided.

There were more troubling events. All communications via wireless or cables with the Asian Republics had been cut off the day before at eight o'clock in the evening and all the frontiers closed; in ports, an embargo had been placed on departing ships. There had been no notification of those extraordinary measures prior to their application and no justification had yet been received in Europe.

A few travelers who had succeeded in crossing the frontier fraudulently and reaching Japanese or Indochinese posts during the night reported that the entire country was effervescent. A general mobilization had been decreed, and a huge concentration of aircraft was being organized on the coast of Canton.

There was no news from the embassies.

VI

The engineers of the Great Current were looking at one another with consternated expressions and discussing the great question of the day.

"Is it war?"

"They've gone mad," said Chartrain to Claire Nolleau. What do they want from us? If they demanded something from us, we'd have been able to discuss it."

"So you think they're going to launch a surprise attack on us, without any plausible motive?"

"How can their attitude be explained otherwise? They doubtless think that their only chance of victory is to strike a great blow to defeat us before we're able to mount a defense."

Paul was only too correct.

At nine o'clock in the morning on the Scoresby meridian—which corresponded to seven o'clock in the evening for the Mukden meridian—the latter city's radio broadcasting station, which had been silent since the day before, made its powerful voice resound in order to launch a proclamation from Wang-Ti-Pou across the world.

It was an ultimatum, in English, addressed to Europe and its allies.

Wang-Ti-Pou enjoined those tyrannical nations to "render independence to oppressed Africa," accused them of preparing for war and declared that he was forced to launch his armies to attack their territories in order to prevent them from putting their criminal plan into execution.

"Your accursed civilization, which is not concerned with souls but only with bodies," he added, "and which makes humans the slaves of machines, will be swept from the face of the world. You believe yourselves to be redoubtable with your fulgurant rays, your automata, your pocket-planes, your hydrogliders and all your diabolical inventions, and you are certainly capable of sowing death, of reducing cities to ashes, of ruining the peoples who resist you, but you will not triumph over the will of free men, whose countless multitudes will fall upon you like locusts on a field of wheat and exterminate you, along with your wives and children, in order that the servants of matter will disappear from the nations forever."

From that moment on, events succeeded one another rapidly, throwing the whole world into perturbation.

The radiograms that Paul Chartrain and Claire Nolleau gathered together, which completed the transmission of images animated by the reporters of the major news outlets, permitted the personnel of the Great Current to follow what was happening very precisely.

All the workers of North Africa were on strike, from Cairo and Alexandria to Tangiers and Casablanca. They had stopped work, claiming that they were "making common cause with their Asian brothers."

In Calcutta, the largest city in India, which had grown prodigiously in the last two centuries, multiplying buildings and skyscrapers, anxiety was at its peak. That great center sent the most alarming news.

The Associated Republics of Asia had mustered all their armies unexpectedly and were marching on the frontiers of Europe and Asia Minor. Large forces were signaled descending from Tibet toward India through the passes of the Himalayas.

All of Hindustan was in effervescence. Its government, affiliated to the Euro-African Federation, was hastening to organize resistance, but the authorities had been caught unawares. There was no plan of action. The considerable means at its disposal were, unfortunately, disseminated, difficult to assemble and to utilize.

Men were mobilized, automata requisitioned, along with machines of every sort, factories and railways. Aerial and maritime navigation were taken under the direct control of the Ministry of Defense—the name "Ministry of War" had long since disappeared from the official vocabulary. Even those women were enrolled who volunteered for services at the rear and as mechanics or pilots.

Wang-Ti-Pou's partisans unleashed their offensive with lightning rapidity.

The adherents of civilization, who, by contrast with their enemies, were called technologists, had not had time to organize their defenses before squadrons of aircraft, going around the Himalayas through Indochina, came to fly over the great cities of Burma and India and drop tons of explosives there.

It was believed that the machines at the disposal of Wang-Ti-Pou's armies were archaic in type and relatively slow, traveling at no more than four hundred kilometers an hour. They certainly did not have the improved engines of destruction that the technologists had invented long ago. Given that they did not encounter any serious aerial force before them, however, they were capable of carrying out frightful devastations.

At ten o'clock in the morning. Scoresby time, the radiophonic emissions that brought news from all parts of the world on different wavelengths became unintelligible. Disorderly emissions of great power on various wavelengths caused such perturbations that all communications became confused. It was assumed that the confusion was the work of antitechnologists who were sending out the disruptive waves deliberately.

At the Franz-Josef base, the engineers, and the official representatives, journalists and tourists who had not yet departed, were gripped by fear. Faces paled and gazes vacillated beneath contracted brows.

What did it mean? Were they about to lose contact with the civilized world?

To be deprived of communications with the great centers was a new and disconcerting sensation for people who were used to never losing contact with worldwide thought. The world had become an immense thinking organism in which all individuals, cells of the social body, required their ration of neural input.

The perturbations of the wireless did not prevent, to be sure, transmissions by wire; the telephone and telegraph lines continued to function; but, obliged to fill in for the immense traffic of the failing radio, they could not be sufficient. News only spread with a considerable delay, and its items were often contradictory.

Thanks to the privileged situation of the Great Current Company, an enterprise of public utility, Paul Chartrain, whom Claire Nolleau came to assist whenever she was not retained by Hurlaut, still received sufficient information to form a reasonably accurate idea of events.

It was known that the Great Current was threatened by the general strike in North Africa, which had turned into an insurrection and had cut communications between Timbuktu and Europe. It was felt to be necessary to maintain contact between the two bases at Timbuktu and Franz-Josef, and equally necessary to expedite, as a matter of priority, telegrams coming from the Orient destined for the Parisian centre, which were immediately retransmitted to Timbuktu, Scoresby and Franz-Josef.

At three o'clock in the afternoon at the latter base, which corresponds to about ten fifteen p.m. at the longitude of Calcutta, Chartrain received a retransmitted telegram from Hanoi announcing that large antitechnologist forces had just crossed the frontier north of Tonkin, flying at an approximate sped of four hundred kilometers an hour. They were expected to reach Hanoi in half an hour. Urgent measures were being taken for the protection of the inhabitants and all the aircraft that it had been possible to mobilize were being sent to intercept the enemy.

From that moment on, the dispatches succeeded one another without interruption, sometimes confirming and sometimes contradicting one another.

The authorities in Calcutta seemed to have lost their heads. It was necessary to ward off so many dangers at once that the administration was swamped.

To begin with, it had to be expected that the aerial attack launched by the antitechnologists would not stop at Indochina. It would fly over the peninsula, causing damage here and there on a more or less large scale, and try to reach Calcutta in order to destroy that great center, which was like the brain of India.

Now, by virtue of its extent, the city offered an excellent target, and its numerous skyscrapers were very vulnerable. In spite of the solidity of their construction, many of them would collapse under torpedoes,[25] burying the streets with their rubble.

The assailants would doubtless also have bombs loaded with asphyxiating gases, and, as war had not been anticipated, the authorities in Calcutta did not possess either reserves of antidotes or masks in sufficient number to protect a population of several million.

It was necessary to take account of the danger of false news, which had to be promptly denied in order to prevent panic, but in the end, in spite of all efforts, that panic could not be prevented from growing.

The terrible events only became known precisely in Europe, Africa and Greenland much later.

The government, meeting in Calcutta, had decided to evacuate the city. In order to escape two risks—the collapse of houses and asphyxiation in the cellars—there was no better mans than dispersing the population in the countryside, where the enemy could not drop enough bombs and torpedoes to ender a practically unlimited territory untenable.

The problem was, however, insoluble, the technologists' aerial army would be over Calcutta in less than five hours, and

---

[25] In 1931 the term *torpille* [torpedo] had not yet been restricted to missiles fired from submarines, and could still be used with respect to missiles dispatched from aircraft. Substituting the latter term would have been an inappropriate modernization in a story whose charm now largely rests on its curious patchwork of the obsolete and the prophetic.

they could not possibly evacuate four million people, prey to panic, in such a short time.

The evacuation had commenced of its own accord, but the crowds pressing to get out of the city in vehicles of every sort, overloaded with baggage, were moving with desperate slowness. The quays of the Hooghly, the great arm of the Ganges that irrigates Calcutta, were besieged. The police were unable to prevent the crowd from becoming dangerously turbulent, even though there already hardly any boats left to collect the fugitives. Many people fell into the water, where some drowned.

The last boats, laden with twice or three times as many passengers as they could normally take aboard, withdrew their gangplanks and cut their moorings, allowing clusters of desperate people who were clinging to the ropes in order to try to get aboard to fall; but people continued to pile up on the quays, which could no longer lead to anything but a soaking.

Half an hour after the first dispatch that announced the incursion of the antitechnologist aerial army, Hanoi telegraphed that a hundred helicopters assembled in haste to oppose the invasion had been destroyed to the very last, after a heroic but brief battle, not without having shot down, as far as could be judged, between two and three hundred antitechnologist planes. Many machines had fallen on Hanoi with their bombs, exploding as they fell, and causing frightful damage. Now the victorious antitechnologists were sprinkling the city with torpedoes.

The dispatch was interrupted. The telegraph and the telephone had been interrupted themselves by the rain of bombs. Perhaps, by now, all the inhabitants of Hanoi were dead, asphyxiated.

The President of the Republic of India, the mayor of Calcutta, the ministers, the commanders of the land, sea and air forces, had met in the governmental palace and were trying to imagine the efficacious defense and the stroke of genius thanks to which the capital of India might be preserved. In a short time-span of four or five hours it was necessary to com plete a defensive organization that had barely been sketched, and to do it while the terror of the population was paralyzing all services.

They had twenty fulgurant cannons at their disposal, which were hastily set up at the edges of the city. There were two on the Hooghly, carried by hydroplanes. Those machines were capable of working marvels in blasting the enemy on whom their rays succeeded in focusing. A contact of five or six seconds was sufficient to kill men and cause bombs to explode. The sole defect of the weapon was the enormous quantity of energy it absorbed, which it had to obtain, directly or indirectly, from power plants.

The helicopters that had been summoned from all parts of the country, initially by radio and then by telegraph and telephone, were arriving by the minute. They were gathering at the aerodrome of Serampour, between Calcutta and Chandernagor. It was hoped to assemble between two hundred and fifty and three hundred, which would remain a rather feeble force in confrontation with the three or four thousand aircraft that the antitechnologists had launched against the Indian metropolis, especially given that the majority of the machines had only been equipped with improvised armaments. Their number could not include more than fifty truly redoubtable cruisers. It was therefore necessary to expect that the air fleet in question, if it opposed the invasion, would suffer the same fate as Hanoi's.

As for telemechanical aircraft, which had no crew on board and were piloted from the ground by means of Hertzian waves, they would have rendered immense services if the government had had sufficient numbers at its disposal, but there were no more than a hundred distributed throughout India, in accordance with policing requirements, and there could be to question of assembling them rapidly enough to employ them collectively against the invaders.

There were three submersible cruisers in the Hooghly estuary, equipped with artillery sufficiently powerful to reach aircraft flying at five thousand meters, and which could, on the other hand, avoid bombs and serial torpedoes by diving. A fourth, which was at sea in the gulf of Bengal, was awaited. Unable to receive information via wireless, since the enemy was confusing messages, they had sent a helicopter to search for it and signal it to join the squadron as soon as possible.

Armored vehicles were also insufficient in numbers. The land, sea and air forces had not been designed for the large scale operations of war that now had to be envisaged, but simply to exercise policing functions, to maintain order within the country and stop bands of brigands at the frontier who attempted to penetrate Indian territory.

The military governor, who had the commanders of the three elements under his orders, proposed beating a retreat in order to allow time for help to arrive, which he had requested from all directions. The mayor of Calcutta protested, however, that they could not allow the inhabitants that had not had time to evacuate to be massacred without at least putting on a semblance of defense. If lives had to be sacrificed, at least they would be those of men who made a profession of fighting. His argument prevailed.

The President and Ministers of the Republic of India also considered that, even if the antitechnologists were victorious, they would pay so dearly that their momentum would be broken, and India would thus be the advance-guard of civilization. Thanks to their resistance, Europe and its satellites would gain sufficient respite to raise an insurmountable barrier before the barbarians.

Their point of view had been adopted when a rocket-plane coming from the east landed on the Hooghly. Its captain, having requested an audience, was immediately introduced into the council of war. He brought terrifying news. Hanoi had been destroyed and almost all of its population had perished. It was feared that other large cities had already suffered the same fate. The number of aircraft unfurled over Indochina and heading westwards was estimated at between four and five thousand.

At one o'clock in the morning, in the middle of the night, Calcutta was more animated and noisier than on major holidays of during great popular demonstrations. In streets bordered by skyscrapers, from which a sinister hubbub rose as if from the depths of a precipice, the crowds were jostling without making any progress. The police were impotent to maintain the flow of that excessive flood, and no longer dared try to forbid an exodus that appeared to be the sole means of salvation for a population condemned to extermination if it remained accumulated in the city.

Rocket-planes descending from a vertiginous altitude came to alight on the Hooghly in order to collect fugitives and departed again immediately, climbing toward the firmament. The electric lights shining through the windows of their cabins caused them to resemble fiery meteors. But a rocket-plane loaded to the extreme limit could not carry more than four hundred people, and that would only permit a tiny fraction of the population to be evacuated.

Helicopters were also seen, recognizable by their positional lights, landing at the aerodrome.

Soon, the watchmen at the military posts heard a hum coming from the air, scarcely distinguishable at first from the great rumor of the city. It announced the approach of the antitechnologists' aerial army. A nearer rumble drowned out the first, however; the three hundred helicopters that had been assembled with difficulty took to the air, in order to meet the enemy and make a desperate effort to bar their passage.

They rose up over Calcutta, and formed a double line in order to oppose a barrier to the invaders. They were flying slowly.

The council of war had decided that the air fleet would not go any further east than four or five hundred kilometers from the suburbs of the great city, in order to remain in liaison with the other defense forces—for without their support, it would be doomed to certain destruction, whereas by coordinating its action with that of the fulgurant artillery, telemechanical apparatus and all the other engines of war, it retained a chance of intimidating the enemy and inciting a retreat.

Showing their lights, without which they would be exposed to the danger of fire from the technologist artillery, the helicopters sowed the sky with hundreds of stars, which seemed to be performing an artistically regulated ballet.

The din composed of all the noises of the city, some near and others distant, some rising and others falling, became formidable.

The Hooghly was glittering with countless gleams.

A swarm of constellations rose above the horizon in the east, announcing the advance guard of the antitechnologist fleet. They surged over the horizon and soon gave the impression of a firework display, rising up like rockets, new ones appearing incessantly.

The aerial horde invaded the sky. The thunder of engines, all roaring simultaneously, now drowned out the sounds of the city.

Searchlights disseminated in the countryside extended their great luminous beams into space. Mounted on automobile trucks, they kept moving in order not to offer too easy a target to the gunners of the aerial cruisers.

The ordinary artillery and the fulgurant rays went into action; and the army of helicopters, which tried to climb above the antitechnologists, were still gaining altitude as the battle was joined.

Perhaps the invaders had not expected any serious resistance, because they seemed to hesitate. Some dived in order to pick up speed and thus avoid the helicopters that were confronting them. Others moved away laterally, and others turned round in order to avoid the rays and shells that were pursuing them. But a large number returned fire, and the battle immediately became terrifying.

The first victims were antitechnologist aircraft, which exploded under the effects of the fulgurant rays or were shot down by shells. Disabled machines exploded as they hit the ground. But the riposte also caused ravages in the technologist ranks. Helicopters were precipitated in their turn.

There as a gigantic and fantastic contest, but it was brief.

For a few minutes, the airborne machines whirled around one another. The fulgurant rays and the luminous beams of the searchlights striped the atmosphere. The noise of the cannonade was mingled with the throb of engines and helices. Airplanes tumbled in zigzags. Helicopters fell like stones.

Many more aircraft were shot down among the antitechnologists than among their adversaries, but as the latter were far less numerous, they were rapidly reduced to negligibility.

A few telemechanical aircraft, devoid of pilots, intervened as dawn broke, revealing the innumerable fleet of the antitechnologists. A certain disorder sown among the assailants had broken the neat order of their triangular formations. The telemechanical aircraft, plunging obliquely, blasting them with their shells and fulgurant rays, and the great birds of prey, mortally wounded, tilted, spun and crashed in splashes of flame with a thunderous din.

Thus, the antitechnologists paid dearly for their victory. Perhaps a thousand of their machines had perished in the battle, but it seemed that their number increased as they were destroyed. The sky was covered by them, like an immense flock of crows, and only a tiny number of technologist helicopters still remained airborne, which, having exhausted their munitions and the energy reserves required by their fulgurant cannons, had no alternative but to beat a retreat and rally to the army of support that was in the process of being aggregated far to the west.

Then the city and its suburbs were metamorphosed into volcanoes, while everything began to vacillate and crumble in a deafening racket. The skyscrapers were split open and collapsed, filing the streets with their rubble.

The crowd had disappeared; the streets were empty. During the battle, the inhabitants had rushed into the houses, piling into the cellars and subterranean roads in search of shelter from the bombardment—shelter that, for many, could be nothing other than that of the tomb.

The aerial army that had devastated Calcutta circled above the city for hours. The aircraft came to land one after another, at the aerodrome, which the defeated technologists were unable to think of defending; each of them disembarked dozens of men.

An army of more than a hundred thousand men, with artillery, was thus transported in twelve hours and assembled, as many at the aerodrome as at propitious landing-grounds in the environs of the city. They immediately occupied all the strategic positions, moved into the country requisitioning supplies, hastening to take advantage of the aerial victory that the antitechnologists had just won, which had completely paralyzed resistance by annihilating the great center of the nation.

Calcutta, in ruins, was no longer anything but a place of horror. More than half of the inhabitants were dead, asphyxiated or buried under the rubble, Many others were so dangerously afflicted that it would not have been possible to save them even if their collection had been organized and treatment given to them.

As for those who had escaped the scourge, they were nothing more than a disorganized rabble, deprived of reason, trying desperately to flee, yielding to all the excesses of panic.

Above the formless mass of collapsed houses, immense sections of wall, fragments of skyscrapers cut through the middle in the vertical dimension, loomed up like rocks. Opened apartments, overlooking the void, evoked the prehistoric dwellings of cave-men hollowed out in the walls of cliffs.

At midday, when considerable forces had already taken possession of the outskirts of Calcutta, an aircraft whose wings bore a cluster of golden stars landed at the aerodrome. It was immediately surrounded by officers and guards, because it was transporting, with his escort, a very important person: none other than President Wang-Ti-Pou, the supreme leader of the Asian Republics and their armies.

He descended into the midst of his officers and asked a few brief questions. He inclined his head deeply on learning that the victory had been bought by the loss of a thousand aircraft.

A hundred thousand antitechnologists had perished in the cause of liberating humankind from materialist civilization. Such, at least, was the interpretation that Wang-Ti-Pou and his general staff attributed to the circumstance.

VII

The news of the Calcutta disaster had scarcely reached Scoresby and the Franz-Josef fjord when one of the cables of the Great Current ceased functioning.

The chiefs of the enterprise demanded explanations telegraphically from the Timbuktu center, communicating via Dakar, which was linked to Europe by a direct cable. But nothing more was known at Timbuktu than at the Franz-Josef base. The abrupt arrest of the current had simply been observed; it had to originate from damage to the line. It was feared that the cable had been cut by the North African insurgents, who held four hundred kilometers of the line.

That opinion was, unfortunately, confirmed shortly thereafter, by the rupture of a second cable, followed by a third. The managerial staff of the Great Current witnessed with horror, during the hours that followed, the systematic destruction of the great work that they had had so much difficulty in completing, and of which they were so proud.

On the sixth of August, at eight o'clock in the evening, the thousand cables were no more than inert masses, which were not transmitting any electrical energy.

What a crime against civilization!

If, as it was necessary to hope, the insurgents were suppressed, the repair of the cables represented a small effort by comparison with those it had been necessary to furnish in labor and in capital for the construction of the line with all its bases. But the engineers knew that the Franz-Josef base was now menaced with a great danger. The current having ceased to circulate, the great frontal gallery, where the cold electrodes were installed, would be subjected on the part of the ice of the fjord to a pressure that was no longer attenuated by the melting provoked by the passage of the current. The sliding and the renewal of the ice no longer being ensured by that phenomenon, on which they had relied too much, the gallery would be entirely blocked by a mass that, when it was eventually displaced by the effect of further pressure, might perhaps sweep away the entire installation, established with great difficulty and at great expense.

They held council and decided to free the vicinity of the gallery by blowing up the ice with explosives, in order to suppress and reduce the pressure.

Helicopters succeeded in depositing large explosive charges on the chaotic surface of the fjord, which dislocated the ice-field—but the latter was reconstituted almost immediately, and it was necessary to start again. They realized that that means could scarcely slow down the catastrophe, when it was a matter of applying it over an extent of sixty kilometers.

They sent down cables via the adduction tubes to the automatic borers they had used to excavate the rock, and attempted to clear the gallery by extracting the ice from it.

That method gave better results than the first, but the work of the machines consumed a considerable amount of energy, which it was necessary to obtain from the power plant at Scoresby. That factory was fueled by hydrogen, which had to be shipped from Europe at considerable expense. Such an effort imposed further heavy expenses on the administration of the Great Current, which had not been anticipated.

In addition, in view of the troubled world situation, it was not certain that Europe, obliged to concentrate all its resources to defend itself against a criminal aggression, would be capable of satisfying the enormous demands of such an endeavor for very long.

Al the engineers were competing in zeal, multiplying observations, incessantly making and remaking calculations in order to try to answer the question of whether the framework of the ice-dividers could resist the pressure.

When the North African insurrection was announced, Hurtaut had thought at first of returning to Timbuktu, but he had changed his mind when the rupture of the cables had endangered the Franz-Josef base. It was there that all determination and competence had to collaborate in the attempt to save the part of the endeavor that had required the greatest effort and the most money.

On the eighth of August, while the alarming news from North Africa and India flowed incessantly, there was a further alarm.

The observation posts of Spitzbergen signaled that a suspect squadron, apparently coming from Siberia by an audacious flight through the polar mists, was heading toward the east coast of Greenland. Its strength and composition were difficult to evaluate. It comprised some twenty, or perhaps thirty aircraft, flying at a speed of between four and five hundred kilometers an hour.

Dr. Bormann and his colleagues were immediately convinced that it was a matter of a raid on Scoresby and the Franz-Josef base. They hastened to request help from Europe, which unfortunately risked arriving too late, and they got ready to defend themselves with the meager means at their disposal.

The military helicopter stationed at Scoresby received orders and took off. Chartrain was asked to check the telemechanical aircraft whose operation had been confided to him, in order to be ready to intervene if the enemy appeared above the fjord.

The young engineer had not yet had time to train the colleague who had been delegated to assist him; there had been too many other things to do since the inauguration of the Great Current, and events had unfolded too rapidly—but Claire Nolleau, who had naturally remained with Hurtaut, had done a training course in telemechanical piloting. She offered to be his auxiliary and his comrade.

VIII

The military helicopter stationed at Scoresby had taken off a quarter of an hour after the alarm had been raised by the observatory at Spitzbergen and had flown in the presumed direction of the suspect squadron.

Leaning over the shoulder of the operator of the listening-post, the commandant of the flying machine followed the indications given to him by his subordinate attentively.

He was flying through dense mist.

The sun was low on the horizon. The clouds that were descending the slopes of the mountain were also extending in height, for the humidity that had been distributed in the atmosphere during the relatively mild hours of the day, rising from the ground or transported by the sea breeze, was now condensing in an almost instantaneous fashion.

In the early days of aviation, it had been extremely dangerous to fly blind in that manner. The pilot lost the sense of equilibrium, diving or banking without realizing it, risking catastrophe because of loss of speed. But in the twenty-third century, the apparatus of automatic direction and stabilization had made such progress that flying in mist no longer involved any other risk that that of colliding with some unexpected obstacle. In order to detect their approach, there were also emitters and receivers of sonic waves whose echo was collected. If, for example, the flying machine had a cliff a kilometer ahead of it, the sound wave would take about three seconds to come back after reflection, six seconds in all to travel both ways, an interval that the apparatus' own speed reduced by one, two or even three seconds. The operator of the post was warned of the presence of the obstacle and its distance from the apparatus; even its direction was indicated by special goniometers.

The listening-post also permitted the detection of sounds too faint for the ear to perceive, or vibrations of too small or great a frequency to enter the scale of audibility, but propagated in accordance with the same laws.

The operator of the listening-post had detected the hum of the aircraft signaled by Spitzbergen, which would still have been imperceptible to the ear without the aid of the amplifiers.

Knowing that he was dealing with a force of several dozen aircraft, the commandant of the helicopter nevertheless did not think of fleeing from the battle. He was proud of the power of the armaments of his aerial vessel, which assured him, he thought, of a decisive superiority over his adversaries.

The apparatus consisted of a large hull, in the form of a ship, normally occupied by fifty crewmen: pilots, navigators, radio- and listening-post operators, gunners, bombardiers and operators of the fulgurant tubes, mechanics, helmsmen, a physician, a steward and various officers. It could land either on land or on water, the contact being made all the easier because its sustaining helices permitted it to land or alight on water by vertical descent without suffering any damage.

From Scoresby, the helicopter went along the coast as far as the entrance to the Franz-Josef fjord, because its principal mission was to protect the base of the Great Current. It circled above the fjord, on the lookout for the approach of the enemy.

The hum of the squadron soon became perceptible. For a few moments, the commandant of the helicopter, Captain Gefson, observed the dials of the various indicators that informed him of the operation of his flying vessel, and then tried to pierce the mist with his gaze through the windows of his post, which was forward of the main compartment.

The operator of the listening-post announced that the squadron was flying directly toward the Franz-Josef base, while gaining altitude.

"Climb!" Captain Gefson commanded. "Find clear air."

The pilot accelerated the suspension helices; the helicopter leapt upwards.

Gefson had had enough of flying blind. He wanted to get out of the fog in order to see his adversary.

The engine roared more loudly. As it rose up, the apparatus soon encountered a less opaque atmosphere.

When it was completely detached from the cloudy zone, the watchmen signaled the enemy flotilla about two miles ahead, still half-engaged in the ocean of mist, at an altitude slightly inferior to that of the helicopter.

Already, Captain Gefson, observing through the antimist windows of his post, had perceived the aircraft, which, flying at the level of the clouds, resembled ships besieged by the waves.

"Head straight for the enemy!" he commanded the pilot, via the acoustic apparatus. "Keep climbing in order to stay above them."

The entire crew was on alert, at their combat stations. The gunners and the operators of the fulgurant tubes were in their turrets beside their weapons.

A flash of light was emitted by one of the airplanes. A shell burst a few meters below the helicopter, peppering its hull with shrapnel.

"Fulgurant tubes, fire! Burn the planes!" Gefson's voice resonated via the telephone.

The order was immediately carried out.

A green-tinted ray, which contrasted with the ruddy reflections of the sun, floating on the horizon over the clouds, tinted crimson and russet-bronze, traversed space, oscillated momentarily, and fixed upon the airplane that had just fired.

The plane tried to dive in order to avoid the terrible burn, but it was too late; a great flame sprang from the hull and an explosion shattered the apparatus, whose debris spun as it fell, disappearing into the mist.

Already the ray was posing implacably on a second apparatus, which exploded like the first, not without having unleashed a cannon shot, too precipitate to be efficacious.

Then the squadron, warned by the destruction of the two machines, plunged as one into the sea of cloud, where it was not possible for the spotter to take aim with precision.

At an order from the commandant, powerful projectors of cold light began to search the mist in order to try to pinpoint the enemy craft, whose approximate position the listening-post operator continued to signal.

Captain Gefson was anxious, because, by carrying out their abrupt evasion, the enemy aircraft had succeeded in slipping underneath the helicopter and thus placing themselves between the latter and the Franz-Josef base.

"Descend at top speed!" the commandant ordered by telephone, which put him in simultaneous communication with all the chiefs of the different posts.

The suspension helices almost ceased to function. The cruiser fell like a stone—or, more precisely, like a raptor diving upon its prey.

Anxious but holding firm at their posts, the men waited.

When they arrived beneath the ceiling of clouds, the helicopter found itself almost confused with the enemy squadron, which was diving toward the grouped buildings of the Franz-Josef base, a veritable small village with steep roofs, designed to resist the pressure of the winter snows.

In five seconds, the helicopter's fulgurant tubes annihilated ten enemy aircraft. But those that remained had set about bombarding their adversary with cannon-fire. Two shells hit the target. One exploded in the commandant's post, killing him; the other exploded in the rear of the cruiser, killing several men, opening an enormous breach in the hull, and smashing the controls of the rudders.

In spite of the gravity of the damage, the helicopter was still flying, because its engines had not been hit.

The chief mechanic, taking account of the situation, gave the order to resume the descent, while the gunners and the operators of the fulgurant tubes, whose turrets had remained undamaged, hastened to riposte, causing further devastation in the enemy ranks.

The squadron did not try to finish off an adversary that remained so redoubtable. Satisfied to have disabled it, the enemy craft fled at top speed, in order not to be completely destroyed.

Incapable now of pursuing them, the helicopter completed its descent and landed.

The enemy flew directly toward the establishments of the Franz-Josef base.

IX

The control-panel of the telemechanical aircraft, the last hope of the defense, was sheltered in a bunker that seemed to be proof against torpedoes.

The aircraft itself was garaged under a concrete vault, from which it could emerge easily by rolling down an inclined plane.

It was relatively small, measuring no more than five meters in length, with a wingspan of six meters. It presented the appearance of a monoplane, like those constructed in the early days of aviation. It could not carry a passenger, but it possessed reaction engines, control mechanisms and television and teleaudition apparatus.

Mechanics had hastened to place cylinders of oxygen and hydrogen within the hull, which would furnish the engines with mechanical energy.

The machine carried three torpedoes, and was armed with a single cannon and a single fulgurant tube.

Chartrain and Claire Nolleau had taken their places at the control panel.

Slender beams of electric light illuminated the units of a keyboard and various instruments of which the conductor had at his service. But there was a series of screens, displays and dials that only lit up under the influence of waves emitted by the automaton when it took off. Aiming mechanisms, whose movements corresponded exactly with those of the aircraft's cannons and the launch-tubes permitted the latter to be directed remotely at the target whose image was on the television screen. A loudspeaker transmitted the sounds that a passenger aboard the aircraft would have heard.

Because of the mist, the young people, who were observing the images furnished by a periscope on a screen had not been able to see the phases of the combat whose consequence had opened a way to the base for the enemy squadron, albeit reduced in number by more than half.

When they perceived the antitechnologist aircraft, they thought that the helicopter had been completely destroyed. They were heartbroken not to have been able to intervene in the battle sooner; they swore at least to avenge the members of the crew who had just fallen victim to their duty.

Chartrain gave his mechanics the order to place the flying machine in its departure position. Electric winches immediately hoisted the apparatus to ground level. The reaction engines spat. The telemechanical aircraft took off, bounding into the air like a veritable rocket.

The engineer watched the approach of the enemy planes through the periscope. They were flying low because of the clouds. He shivered at the thought that the antitechnologists were doubtless about to drop bombs in an attempt to destroy the Great Current base from top to bottom.

"Increase the tension…five thousand volts!" he ordered Claire Nolleau, leaning over the control panel beside him.

He followed the rapid ascent of the flying automaton on the screen. But the units of the enemy squadron must have perceived their new enemy, and were taking aim at the place from which it had departed. Doubtless they also realized that they were dealing with a telemechanical apparatus commanded from the ground, because, while maneuvering to avoid it they began launching torpedoes at the point from which it had taken off, where the control system ought to be.

Chartrain had activated the flying automaton's television and teleaudition apparatus and now had the impression of seeing and hearing as if he were aboard the machine.

A screen placed directly in front of him offered the appearance of a window through which he sometimes saw the sky and sometimes a bird's eye view of the ground, in accordance with the evolutions of the automaton, launched in pursuit of the enemy. By virtue of a well-known phenomenon of illusion, although he was motionless in his seat and the images perceived through the window were moving. He had the impression of sometimes leaning to one side and sometimes the other, exactly as the automaton was doing up in the air, whose apparatus was transmitting its indications to him.

The torpedoes launched by the enemy made the ground tremble and imparted commotions so violent that the functioning of the equipment in the control room was disturbed. At times, the television image became less clear and, more seriously, the controls suffered faults.

The periscope and the television screen spread a half-light around the bunker, which added to the reflection of the disposed lamps of the lighting apparatus.

Chartrain observed his companion covertly while giving her brief orders. He was able to remark that she was pale and that her hands were trembling. He felt sorry for her, and regretted having accepted her aid in such circumstances.

While bombarding the ground with their torpedoes the antitechnologist planes tried to destroy the automaton itself with cannon fire. Being relatively small, however, the rocket-apparatus was a difficult target. It was also extremely mobile, making aiming even more awkward, while it circulated amid its adversaries. Finally, its essential organs were enclosed in armored containers, while its wings and fuselage were made of very light materials, which projectiles could go clean through without causing serious damage.

Chartrain had brought his artillery into action and his fulgurant tubes claimed three victims, one after another. But if the terrorists were criminals, they were no cowards. In spite of the losses they had suffered in their battle against the helicopter, they held firm against the new, almost ungraspable, enemy that threatened to exterminate every one of them.

In order to evade their fire, the telemechanical plane had to be swerving, rising or diving incessantly, but it returned constantly to the attack, maneuvering with a vertiginous rapidity.

"Nolleau," said the engineer. "Take over the cannon and the tube; I have enough to do piloting the machine."

No more than a minute had passed since the fantastic battle had begun, and five enemy aircraft had already been shot down.

The entire base was abuzz. In spite of the normal orders that had been given, people were risking themselves outside their shelters momentarily in order to catch glimpses of the combat.

Obedient to Chartrain's orders, Claire Nolleau set about aiming the tube and the cannon by means of the visors commanding the weapons by telemechanical correspondence.

Aiding and advising one another, the young couple were doing good work. The sky was being swept clean; the aggressors' aircraft were falling, one by one.

Claire suddenly had the impression of being projected backwards, while a formidable howl deafened her and a fulgurant light dazzled her. She was enveloped by dust and smoke, submerged by a rain of debris.

She experienced violent blows to the head, shoulders and back….

She reopened her eyes, and immediately took account of the fact that she had been unconscious for a time. She was lying against the wall at the back of the bunker, where the half-light furnished by the screens of the control panel and the lamps still reigned, augmented by sunlight that was penetrating through a gaping hole in the middle of the ceiling.

She sat up abruptly. She felt bruised all over, but the sentiment of danger caused her to overcome her discomfort. The dust that was still flying around the room convinced her that very little time had elapsed since the explosion—a torpedo launched by the enemy had doubtless hit the bunker.

Was Chartrain dead?

Still sitting in the pilot's seat, he had slumped forward on the control panel and was no longer moving.

Claire staggered across the room, tripping over debris. She looked at the television screen. The images were whirling and swaying. Earth and sky succeeded one another with vertiginous alternation.

Well, yes! The flying automaton, deprived of direction, was performing acrobatics that were the prelude to its fall and destruction.

A glance into the periscope told the young woman, on the other hand, that two aircraft—was that all that remained of the enemy?—rid of their adversary, were now circling over the buildings of the Franz-Josef base, about to rain down bombs.

One thought imposed itself upon her: *My duty is to take Chartrain's place, save the automaton, if there's still time, and continue the battle. I alone can prevent the total destruction of the base.*

She had seized Chartrain by the shoulders and was trying to pull him away from the controls.

She could not repress a sob. Now that she had raised her comrade's head, she saw blood on his face, and was devastated to find him inert in her arms.

Among the members of the mission, the young engineer was the person for whom she experienced by far the most sympathy, and the idea that he might be dead caused her a sharp anguish.

She succeeded in straightening him up and tilting him backwards in his seat, but she renounced trying to deposit him on the floor in order to take his place. He was too heavy and there was no time to lose. She slid between the engineer and the control panel and, in an uncomfortable position, began to operate the keyboard and the switches, in order to reestablish the automaton's equilibrium.

A loud bang announced that the enemy had just launched a torpedo, and through the periscope Claire saw a cloud of dust and smoke rising above the buildings.

The automaton was no more than a hundred meters from the ground when it ceased cavorting and, obedient once again to the direction of a pilot, resumed climbing with a precise trajectory.

The infernal racket was renewed. The enemy had launched another torpedo. The projectiles' effect was terrible.

The houses, although solidly built in reinforced concrete with iron frameworks, were being blown away like houses of cards.

If, as was to be feared, the enemy still had a dozen bombs of that kind to launch, the whole base would be reduced to dust.

The hope that had momentarily been born among the personnel of the Great Current, at the sight of the automaton precipitating its enemies out of the sky, had vanished at the spectacle of its fall,

In her caved-in bunker, Claire Nolleau, pale and clenching her teeth, hindered in her movements by Chartrain's inert body, stiffened her determination and guided the automaton straight at its two adversaries.

Fortunately, the controls were intact. The apparatus responded perfectly to the young woman's impulsions.

She aimed the fulgurant tube once again and succeeded in blowing up the nearer aircraft.

Then the pilot of the final enemy craft, understanding that it was about to succumb in its turn, began swerving and pirouetting in a disorderly fashion, in order to evade the attacks of its minuscule and ungraspable antagonist.

Claire renounced making use of the flying automaton's artillery. She assigned it the role of a projectile, which she attempted to hurl at its adversary.

While she was maneuvering it, she heard a grating sound above her head. Concrete debris fell in front of her on to the keyboard.

She swept it away with the back of her hand and, looking up, saw that a section of the vault, beside the breach, was buckling, threatening to collapse on top of her and crush her.

She made a movement as if to get out of the way, but changed her mind; if she abandoned her post she would leave the base defenseless, and the enemy craft would finish its work of destruction.

She brought her gaze back to the instruments and resumed piloting the automaton. She did not want to look at the vault again, because she was not sure that she would not give in to fear.

The enemy had just launched another torpedo. The bombardment was taking on cataclysmic proportions.

Those who still had the courage to look up at the sky saw the automaton rise up like an arrow, heading straight for its final adversary.

The latter avoided the impact by means of an abrupt swerve, and, renouncing the battle, beat a retreat toward the sea, descending in order to gain speed.

The automaton dived in its turn, and slipped into the wake of the enemy, swiftly gaining on it.

That final phase was so rapid that the crew of the aircraft did not even have time to open fire again, nor was the pilot able to repeat the maneuver that had permitted him to escape the mortal blow the first time. He tried to swerve, but only succeeded in offering his flank to the automaton, which crashed into it, ripping away the right wing completely and pulverizing the pilot's post as well as all the other forward compartments.

The two machines fell together, spinning, and sank in the fjord.

When she had seen the success of her maneuver, Claire had uttered a cry of triumph, which was also an exclamation of relief, even though there was no one to hear it.

At the moment that the automation had crashed into the airplane, the television apparatus had been destroyed, and the special screen to which it transmitted its impressions had ceased to reflect the images. It no longer offered anything but a dull and lifeless surface.

But Claire had seen the enemy's fall through the periscope.

Now that the victory was won, the sentiment of the danger to which she and the injured Paul Chartrain were exposed caused her to forget everything else.

She looked up at the vault and saw, to her horror, that the part that had already loosened was on the point of coming away.

She threw herself on Chartrain, seized him under the arms, and made a desperate effort to lift him from his seat and drag him away—but she lost her balance and fell to the ground with him, at the very moment that the roof collapsed.

X

When Chartrain and Claire Nolleau were pulled out of the rubble under which they were buried, bruised, broken and dying, their rescuers initially despaired of saving them.

In the hospital at Scoresby, however, to which they were immediately transported, life was successfully maintained in their mutilated bodies by injecting a special serum into their veins, charged with oxyhemoglobin, and the circulation of their blood was maintained by the impulsions of an artificial heart.

Their ribs broken, limbs crushed and skulls fractured, the young couple seemed condemned regardless, if they escaped the catastrophe, to be no longer anything but poor diminished creatures, infirm and incapable, to whom, in truth, it was not rendering a service to preserve their lives. Such, at least, would have been the opinion of a man of the twentieth century who had seen the two wounded individuals.

But the physicians of the twenty-third century knew their capability. They did not judge it impossible to heal those cruelly tested human beings and reconstitute them in their integrity.

The crushed limbs were placed in serum baths and carefully irrigated to maintain vital activity in the cells to which the vessels no longer furnished the necessary blood-flow. Improved apparatus substituted for the damaged central organs and maintained the conditions indispensable to life in the different parts of the body.

Meanwhile, a great surgeon was summoned from London and disembarked in Scoresby Sound by rocket-plane two hours after the catastrophe. He had given instructions telephonically before departing, and arrived with his aides, and the animals and preparations that he required to carry out grafts everywhere that it was necessary to repair destroyed organs.

Replacing a bone fragment here and a section of artery or vein there, elsewhere a tendon, muscle or nerve fibers, reconstituting the two injured individuals piece by piece, so to speak, he rendered them the form and figure that they had had before the battle with the antitechnologist squadron.

After that, there was nothing more to do than maintain their circulation and respiration artificially for a few days, in order to give their reconstructed organism time to readjust itself.

Meanwhile, the engineers of the Great Current, reunited at the Franz-Josef base, saw a new catastrophe approaching, which the sacrifice of their young colleagues had not been sufficient to prevent.

The great transformer of current at Franz-Josef, from which the machines occupied in clearing the ice from the frontal gallery received their motive power, had been destroyed by the bombardment. It was impossible to organize help promptly enough to put the machines back into action, or even to bring them back to a safe place. The Scoresby factory, which had been subjected for two days to exceptional demands on its hydrogen reserves, and had not yet received the new supplies requested from Liverpool, could not make available the quantities of fuel that would have been necessary to utilize the reaction engines that the Franz-Josef base possessed. It would have been necessary to make a huge effort to save the base, and they no longer had the means.

Liverpool, to which distress calls were sent, was short of materials itself, having been obliged to respond to too many demands since the beginning of the crisis.

The constructors of the Great Current were about to witness, despairingly, the ruination of their endeavor. The pressure of the ice began to increase again under the incessant descent from Mount Petermann, and ended up carrying away the entire framework of dividers installed at the price of so much hardship.

The engineers and their auxiliaries were overwhelmed by that fatal blow. They had thought themselves victorious, and fatality had reduced the magnificent result of their efforts to nothing. The blind violence of nature had found an ally: the stupid brutality of ignorance.

But Dr. Bormann, his features set hard, opposing his will to contrary destiny, simply declared:

"We'll start again."

XI

In Europe, the antitechnologists' war had exploded like a thunderbolt. Civilization had never been in such peril.

Measuring the power that the harnessing of the electrical power of the globe between the poles and the equator was about to give those he regarded as the vile servants of matter, Wang-Ti-Pou had wanted to prevent its accomplishment; he had gone to war before the realization of the Great Current was complete.

The African insurrection had been the first act of the drama. In spite of the principles they advocated, the antitechnologists hastened to get their hands on all the industrial installations of the tropical regions and the Mediterranean.

They knew full well that they could not fight with bare breasts against the formidable equipment and enormous resources of mechanical energy that Europe had at its disposal. By ensuring themselves of the possession of the thermoelectric factories of North Africa, however—which were, in that epoch, by far the largest in the world—they had procured a very considerable advantage.

Scarcely had they obtained that success than Asia went into action. The great onslaught, in the possibility of which people had refused to believe, was launched. Muscovy, the Ukraine and Finland were submerged by hordes that moved on foot or on horseback, only possessing rudimentary armaments scarcely superior those of the wars of the twentieth century.

The invaders were opposed with helicopters, rocket-planes, automata, asphyxiating gases and discharges of artificial lightning. The machines contrived a huge massacre, but the more people that were killed, the more arrived. They were fanaticized.

The new Attila, who was able to gather together their scattered forces and launch them forth to attack civilization, had materialized. Wang-Ti-Pou had imposed himself upon them and was guiding them as he wished.

The oriental barriers of Europe were broken down, one by one. Africa and Asia, in coalition, held it in a vice, which seemed to be on the point of crushing it.

The Asiatic antitechnologists were, however, stopped, thanks to improved weaponry that was brought to bear against them. The war might them have been concluded to the advantage of Europe if Africa, possessed of enormous mechanical means, had not made those advantages available to its allies.

As had happened in all great conflicts since the twentieth century, the antitechnologists' war quickly became a material struggle between two powerfully equipped groups, and it was obvious that the defeated party would be the one whose financial and industrial resources ran out first.

Europe's resources, certainly, were colossal. There were, throughout the territory of the United States of Europe, countless hydroelectric or thermoelectric power plants, which were immediately requisitioned. But they had the disadvantage of being scattered and thus escaping a general direction that would have been the only means of obtaining the maximum yield from them. The States did not agree with one another as to the best methods to employ in order to win the war, not the best manufactures. The unity of action of European armies not being assured, their enemies took advantage of that and obtained partial successes, the worst effect of which was to demoralize the population.

History is a perpetual recommencement. Humans can instruct themselves regarding faults and their deadly consequences, but they continue to commit them, as if their ancestors had never transmitted their experience to them.

The surprise of the invasion had caused the loss of many of the Europeans' factories in the eastern marches. They were weakened in consequence.

Meanwhile, their enemies were obedient to the firm authority of Wang-Ti-Pou, the leader who deployed so much genius in his will to destruction. An antitechnologist, advocating for humankind a return to a primitive state, which he represented as the essential condition for happiness, only one thing was important in his eyes: the contemplation of the ideal, from which, he claimed, modern technology turned humans away by driving them to seek material wellbeing.

One could reply to him, like Paul Chartrain, that material progress, far from loading humans with chains, liberated them from the oppression of nature. But he riposted with other arguments. And in any case, it was a waste of time trying to convince him. There were two opposed conceptions of human destiny, two irreconcilable deals that were at odds.

So, antitechnologist as he was, Wang-Ti-Pou understood very well that he needed machines to vanquish the industrial Occident, and he was able to profit, in that regard from the conquest of Africa, which he had achieved without firing a shot. He drew on the resources that it furnished him in order to fall upon Europe from the vast continent that it had enabled to develop—and the concentration of the factories of North Africa permitted him, in spite of the absence of a first-rate managerial personnel, to obtain a better yield from them that his adversaries were obtaining from theirs.

Equilibrium was established between the two human masses in conflict.

The attrition that was gradually destroying, on both sides, the accumulated endeavors and the reserves created by civilization, was bringing the world back toward barbarism.

If it had remained reliant on its own strength, Europe would have been exhausted, and, even victorious, would have been reduced for a long time to the primitive state to which Wang-Ti-Pou had been determined to diminish it.

It was then that America, sensing the danger posed to it by the ruination of Europe and its subjugation to a barbarian leader, set aside the sentiment of rivalry that had initially prevented it from intervening. Its economists had succeeded in demonstrating that the loss of enormous riches is always a catastrophe, even if the riches belong to one's neighbor.

From then on, the antitechnologists, overwhelmed by the formidable means that Europe and America combined could put to work, began to buckle. Their leader deployed all the resources of his malevolent genius in vain.

Africa was no longer sufficient to furnish the antitechnologists with enough mechanical power to stand up to two great civilized continents. Subject to the obligation to develop its own technological system in order to combat that of its adversaries, Africa wearied of having for allies people who were innumerable but disorganized. A day came when it decided to shrug off the yoke of the Asiatic dictator. The unity of command that had been the strength of the antitechnologists was compromised.

The technologists' diplomacy did the rest. Africa agreed to reenter into concert with civilization, rejected the alliance with Asia, and joined forces with Europe and America.

That defection decided the outcome of the war.

Left to rely on its own strength, only possessing feeble industrial means by comparison with those of the rest of the world, Asia was soon reduced to helplessness. Its armies broke up or metamorphosed into undisciplined hordes, as dangerous to the antitechnologists themselves as to their adversaries.

In his obstinacy, Wang-Ti-Pou rendered the tyranny that he exercised over his partisans increasingly harsh and intolerable. A frightful poverty was rife among the populations he had drawn into the adventure; famine and epidemics decimated them even more cruelly than the war. Revolts broke out, and Wang-Ti-Pou suppressed them pitilessly in vain; he ended up succumbing, and was massacred along with his principal partisans and his faithful guards.

The technologists had no more to do than enter as conquerors into an Asiatic world delivered to complete anarchy, in which humankind had almost reverted to a savage state.

The victory had been obtained after three years of a titanic struggle.

It had been very costly. The devastations of the war had annihilated a considerable part of the work of the previous hundred years.

After having squandered capital to sustain the struggle and save civilization, it was necessary to engage what remained in order to recover and complete the organization of the planet.

XII

While the war was unfolding, life went on, and after a sojourn of three months in Scoresby hospital, Paul Chartrain and Claire Nolleau had been able to get out of bed and walk. Transported to Nice, they had completed their recovery in a splendid hospital for convalescents.

The entire world had been fully informed of their adventure: the heroic combat that they had sustained against the terrorists, their injuries, and the care they had been given. In all the civilized countries the progress of their recovery had been followed passionately by the spoken or printed news outlets. And when the news of their marriage was announced, everyone applauded what they regarded as the natural epilogue to a stirring romance.

Together, they resumed their functions in the staff of the Great Current. It was deemed that they had already paid sufficiently with their persons not to be mobilized in the armies that sustained the struggle against the antitechnologists.

A new plan had been established under the direction of Dr. Bormann for the reconstruction of the northern base of the Great Current.

The system of ice-dividers that had been adopted initially appeared to be decidedly too fragile. An event such as the aggression of the antitechnologists, which had put the thousand cables of the line out of use at a stroke, along with the power plant at Scoresby, was doubtless extremely exceptional and one could hope that it would never be repeated, but it was imprudent nevertheless to leave an immense enterprise like that of the Great Current at the mercy of an accident of happenstance.

When, spring having returned, work was begun again in order to repair the disaster, a different conception had therefore been adopted.

The North African insurgents not having yet abandoned their Asian allies, they were naturally unable to think of reestablishing the Great Current immediately, but they could already begin the preparations for its reorganization, in order to limit the damage that winters would cause the installations if they were abandoned.

The plan consisted, firstly, of rectifying the frontal gallery, blowing up the promontories and filing in the fissures that their suppression left behind with masonry. That would obtain a kind of quay sixty kilometers long, over which the ice could slide without obstacles. The excessive pressure produced in the depths of sinuosities without issue would thus be avoided.

Secondly, the system of ice-dividers, which had the defect of making too close a contact with the ice-sheet, was abandoned completely. The new system selected by Dr. Bormann consisted of hollowing out a kind of channel in the rectilinear quay, in which the ice, driven by pressure, would travel freely throughout its extent, and in which it could also penetrate not only at its upper extremity but also along its entire external edge, limited by the rectilinear quay below sea level.

The walls of that channel would be hollow, composed of reinforced concrete vaults supporting an impermeable external cladding lined with a thick armor plating of chrome steel. In addition to their great resistance, they would possess the indispensable property of being excellent conductors of heat—and, in consequence, of cold.

The surface of the armor plating would be augmented by a series of grooves two or three meters deep, giving the whole the appearance of a gigantic sheet of corrugated iron, orientated longitudinally in order not to offer any obstacle to the advancement of the ice.

Underneath and on the sides of the armored cladding, in the empty pace maintained by the vaults, which would be carefully protected from any infiltration, galleries accessible at all times would receive the cables of the Great Current at the extremities, the elements of which would be insulated electrically by a simple mica envelope put in contact with the chrome steel wall.

The lateral and inferior passages, thus adapted between the rock and the steel channel, would be illuminated by electricity. Surveillance would be easy, and it would be possible to effect all the repairs therein eventually required by the wear and tear of the cables—which would have been very complicated with the old system.

The new plan had one inconvenience, however: its execution would be even more difficult and more costly than the original one.

In addition, as they could not work under the constant threat of the water and the ice, it was necessary not to think about using what remained of the original gallery after the work of rectification. Except for a few points where the general demands of the track obliged encroaching on the fjord, and where extraordinary means were put to work, it would be necessary to pierce a new gallery behind the first and to maintain it in shelter from the water and the ice until the conclusion of the work, by allowing a rocky wall to subsist externally, in accordance with the procedure employed during the first attempt, which would be demolished at the last moment, when everything was ready.

They would thus obtain a gallery about twice as deep as the first, containing the channel, doubled externally by a broad glacis.

So long as hostilities lasted, they could not work very actively on the execution of that grandiose plan. In spring and in summer, they brought into play the hundreds of machines that had not been requisitioned for the services of the army, and attacked the rock in order to rectify the littoral.

When the peace was signed, things took a different turn.

While they proceeded in Africa with the repair of the cables that the insurgents had severed, the piercing of the new gallery was begun at the Franz-Josef fjord.

Thanks to the considerable number of machines that then became available, the work was concluded in a single summer.

In the following season, they proceeded setting up the chrome steel sheets that were to form the walls of the channel, which were sent from Liverpool, Le Havre, Rotterdam and Hamburg. As soon as the sheets were in place, they hastened to install the cable elements underneath, which were to be put in contact with them in order to draw from the source of cold.

The second inauguration took place at the beginning of winter, when the sun had already ceased rising at the latitude of the Franz-Josef fjord some weeks before.

It was a triumph. However, the season did not permit the influx of tourists and official manifestations that had saluted the first. Nor could the engineers of the Great Current and the people who had collaborated with the great work, the delegates of the public powers and the representatives of the news outlets help mingling the joy of the success with the memory of the disaster that had so tragically reduced the efforts of the new pioneers of civilization to nothing.

Life recommenced.

The scourge of war, which had shaken the round machine once again, had at least procured humankind one benefit. The world was entirely conquered by civilization. Anarchy was vanquished everywhere. The rational utilization of all the forces of nature, subjugated by human intelligence, became possible in Asia as in the other continents.

New thermoelectric sectors between the poles and the equator were planned in Europe, Africa and America. The Great Current was already beginning to render the immense services expected of it to peoples who were henceforth narrowly bound together. Frontiers were definitively abolished, the ancient nations were no longer anything but the provinces of a great nation that covered the entire world.

As for Paul Chartrain, supported by the faithful collaboration of his wife Claire, he gradually climbed all the rungs of the hierarchy in the course of his long endeavors, until the day when he was appointed Chief Engineer of the European Thermoelectric Network of the Great Current.

Before reaching that elevated position, he had the honor of being selected to direct the study mission of the thermoelectric network of India, established between the glaciers of the Himalayas and the warm waters of the Indian Ocean.

In the course of that mission, which he accomplished with Claire, proud as he was of his long endeavors and convinced of the benefits that mechanical civilization was lavishing on the entirety of humankind, he was seduced by the charm of nature in the raw, and understood why certain mystics, like Wang-Ti-Pou and his partisans, had tried to stop the upward flight of humankind.

He felt a veritable intoxication in traveling in an autocaterpillar, sometimes even on a horse or mule, as his ancestors had done three centuries before, through a jungle populated by animals that humans had not yet domesticated or tamed. He experienced a poetic regret in imagining that it was the world of several thousand years before.

Then, nature had been stronger than humans, incessantly threatening to crush them—but how unexpected and picturesque the existence of primitive humankind had been! What heroism and ingenuity they had had to employ in order to defend their uncertain lives against so many hostile forces!

"Undoubtedly," Paul said, discussing with Claire the subject that impassioned her no less than him, "it would be puerile to claim that in our civilized country, where nature in its entirety is disciplined, where everything is adapted for comfort, hygiene and the wellbeing of the inhabitants and in order to extract the maximum yield from all forces, existence is devoid of the unexpected and does not involve either heroism or poetry. We can extend our knowledge and increase our power, but we shall always discover, whatever we do, a further domain that escapes our empire. The dangers that threaten civilized humans are no longer those that primitive humankind feared, but they're no less terrible.

"I believe, however," he went on, "that it would not be a bad idea to reserve, here and there, a few vast tracts of wilderness, that would be maintained in their present condition and would be, on a larger scale, like those national parks that it was fashionable to establish, three centuries ago, in America. Our young people, on leaving school, would be taken in groups to those parks, where they would stay for six months or a year, without any other means than those that our ancestors in past centuries possessed. That proof would not only have the advantage of completing their education and developing their strength, but also that of making them appreciate, by comparison, the benefits of modern civilization, which habit prevents them from sensing.

"Such an institution would respond to the criticisms of contemplators of progress, according to whom existence will end up becoming utterly tedious in a world too well organized."

"I'm not anxious in that regard," Claire replied. "Energetic humans endowed with the spirit of enterprise will always find exercise for their intelligence and activity, and undergoing adventures if they have a taste for it. There are still free spaces on the globe. We still have to explore the bed of the sea and the depths of the earth. Energies whose existence we scarcely suspect remain to be discovered and captured. And in the end, if there really were nothing more on earth to explore and conquer, we'd have the infinite heavens offered to our thirst for knowledge and our desire for dominion.

"Astronautics is still in its infancy, but soon it will be capable of taking us to the regions of the Moon, Mars and Venus, and we shall have to find means of descending on to those strange worlds, subsisting there and maintaining ourselves there in spite of their nature, so different from that of our globe and so contrary to our physical constitution.

"What interest we do have, some say, in doing that? That interest will be discovered as we go along. Perhaps an example can already be cited for the Moon. If an observatory were installed on its surface, astronomers would have an instrument of study of the highest order. Thanks to the absence of an atmosphere on the Moon, they would, in fact, be able to observe the stars with a clarity unknown on earth, and would discover a host of phenomena that are as yet hidden from us. As for meteorologists, they would be able to study with a perfect precision the formation and movement of clouds on the earth and would be able to predict the weather with certainty.

"That's only one example, among a hundred that one could imagine.

"The universe is infinite, and that's why the progress of humankind ought to be too."

THE SECRET OF THE INCAS

I

Jacques Lasserre sat up on his bunk. He had just opened his eyes and was astonished that it was so bright inside his tent, when he had given orders that he was to be woken up at first light.

He got up and shivered slightly, for the cold made itself felt at that early hour even under the alpaca-lined tent. He moved aside the curtain that served as a door and darted a glance around the camp.

Two small squat tents similar to his own were situated to the right. His two traveling companions, Paul Vauguyon and Pierre Estray, were sleeping in them.

On the natural platform that overlooked a precipice, however, which he expected to see occupied, as on the previous evening, by the mission's Indian servants and llamas, he saw nothing but a little detritus, the remains of the Redskins' meal and the ashes of a fire that had only just gone out, still smoking.

The roar of a torrent was audible at the bottom of the precipice.

On the other side of the gorge, above a crest of rugged rocks, the mighty summits of the Andean Cordilleras rose up vertiginously under the tropical sky. And there, between two mountains, the sunlight sprang forth, dazzling, forcing Jacques to turn his eyes away. The Indians, in accordance with their custom, had orientated the explorers' tents toward the east.

Jacques began to feel anxious. What did this mean? Had the porters and the llama-tenders deserted the mission? That was a frequent occurrence, which explorers must, unfortunately, always expect when they penetrated into difficult regions, or those rendered redoubtable by superstition.

In the fortnight since they had left Cuzco, the capital of the Incas, to penetrate into the heart of the mountainous region, not only had the voyagers had to overcome the most awkward obstacles, but they had also entered a region in which the legends of the Quichas, descendants of former subjects of the Incas placed the ruins of a holy city unknown to white men, and to which even the indigenes had forgotten the route.

The Vauguyon-Estray-Lasserre French mission, charged with searching for as-yet-unknown vestiges of the Empire of the Sun, had encountered the legend and had decided to investigate it, in spite of the incredulity of the Peruvian authorities and recommendations of prudence. Had not some authors affirmed that the Incas possessed, not far from their capital, Cuzco, a mysterious city, an inaccessible refuge whose secret had been jealously guarded and which the conquistadors had never discovered?

Jacques raised his voice. "Hey! Pierre, Robert! Get up!"

From the other two tents his companions replied:

"What! What is it?"

"Is it time to go?"

"Get up. There are complications."

Robert and Pierre appeared, very anxious. They had scarcely taken the time to put their boots on and throw ponchos over their shoulders.

"What's happened, then?" asked Robert, the leader of the mission.

"Look," said Jacques, indicating the deserted camp with a circular gesture.

Pierre uttered an oath. "Our men have run off!" he exclaimed.

"Yes, and I think we'd be wasting our time trying to catch up with them."

"We're in a fine mess now!" said Robert, consternated.

"Well," said Jacques, "I'm not overly surprised by what's happened. These Indians are stupidly superstitious. Haven't you noticed their anxious expressions and sly gazes since we left Cuzco?"

"The scoundrels!" Robert cursed. "If they'd only left us our llamas! But they've taken everything."

"Including our baggage," Jacques completed.

"Giving us a great deal of trouble, and causing us to fail when we're almost at the conclusion of our efforts!"

"If only," Pierre said, "the wretches had skipped out on us at the gates of Cuzco, we could have recruited more reliable companions. At any rate, we wouldn't have made this terrible journey for nothing."

"There's nothing else to do than go back, as quickly as possible," declared the leader of the mission.

After that exchange of bitter reflections, the three explorers fell silent momentarily. They could no longer find words to express their discontentment.

In the end, Jacques growled: "It's aggravating, all the same, to give up so close to the goal."

"Certainly—but what can we do? We'll already have to count ourselves lucky if, left to our own resources, all three of us succeed in getting back to Cuzco safe and sound."

After a further silence, Jacques observed: "I think, in spite of everything, that we ought not to panic. Damn it, we wouldn't be French if we couldn't shift for ourselves. We'll win through, provided that we give proof of energy and sang-froid. And we've no lack of those."

"You're right, Jacques. No point in recriminations. Let's think about means of getting out of it—and let's begin by taking stock of what the rascals have left us."

"That won't take long—they've taken everything."

"We've often been told that the Indians are cunning thieves," Pierre remarked.

"So all we have is what's in our tents."

"Meager luggage!"

"Let's console ourselves: if we had more, we couldn't carry it. The main thing is that we still have our weapons.

"Except that the crate of cartridges has gone."

While conversing in this fashion the explorers extracted from their tents the precious objects and those of constant usage that they habitually kept to hand.

Further exclamations of surprise and invective addressed to their treacherous servants announced that they had just made a disagreeable discovery.

With an infernal skill the auxiliaries of the mission, before fleeing had stolen everything, even from the tents, that had excited their covetousness. Without making any sound, they had slit the canvas with their knives and, slipping their arms through the opening, taken possession of weapons, watches and even their masters' toiletries. One carbine and two automatic pistols had escaped their cupidity and malevolence, but the cartridges with which the three weapons were loaded constituted all of the travelers' ammunition; that amounted to seven bullets for each pistol and five for the carbine. The hunting-rifle and cartridges had disappeared.

As for food supplies, they consisted purely and simply of three tins of corned beef that Robert and his companions kept in reserve in their knapsacks, as a precaution. The knapsacks themselves had been respected because the three friends used them as head-rests, and it would have been difficult to touch them without waking their owners.

"Let's sum up the situation," said Robert. "Fifteen bullets to defend ourselves against desperados or shoot game. No change of boots or clothing. Our watches and maps stolen. Three days' food if we ration ourselves, and it's at least ten days' march to reach the nearest village. Certainly, we're men to fight to the end, but I wouldn't give much for our chances."

"I propose," said Pierre, "that we set off immediately, abandoning our tents and our bunks and everything that isn't absolutely indispensable, in order not to slow us down. We ought to try to get back to Cuzco without losing an hour. Perhaps we'll be lucky enough to bring down a vicuna; then we won't be at risk of dying of hunger."

A vicuna, a kind of Peruvian wild llama, would indeed have procured the explorers an abundant supply of meat.

"We might also be able to find a few *tunas*," said Robert.

The tuna is the edible fruit of a kind of cactus.[26] It is perfumed and refreshing, but has little nutritional value.

Jacque, who had been immersed in silent meditation for a while, suddenly declared, with a tranquil gravity: "Well, personally, I don't want to return to Cuzco. I propose, on the contrary, that we continue our voyage."

His two companions looked at him with bewilderment.

"Are you mad?" said Pierre. "We're already in a desperate situation…"

"Precisely. It won't be any more so if we persevere boldly on the route to the holy city instead of beating a retreat. Whether we go in one direction or another, we'll have neither more or less difficulty getting out of trouble."

"You're joking!" Robert exclaimed. "The longer we remain *en route*, the more risk we're running."

"And isn't the discovery of the mysterious city of the Incas, in fact, worth our running those risks?"

"What prevents us once we're in Cuzco, from forming another caravan and undertaking another expedition?"

"And what kind of welcome would we receive in Cuzco? All those who called our expedition folly and advised us against going into the most deserted and dangerous region of the mountains will laugh at our failure. We'll be the butt of the sarcasm of the Peruvian authorities and journalists, and the Indians will regard us with ironic scorn because their brothers will have prevented us from reaching the sanctuary of the Incas.

"Do you even know whether the Corregidor will authorize us to recruit a troop? And even if he did authorize us to do

---

[26] *Opuntia humifusa*, commonly known as the prickly pear.

it, you can bet that our misadventure would be repeated, perhaps with even graver consequences than the first time. We've only had to deal with thieves; the next time, we might fall in with murderers.

"Anyway, my friends, need I remind you that we don't have much money left! We couldn't mount a second expedition like the first, and in consequence we'd have less chance of success. In the end, we'd be forced to return to France without having completed our program, and we'd be discredited in the eyes of the scientific community."

"But how, without weapons or means of any kind, can we continue our voyage into the wilderness?"

"We're in the heart of the mountains, and if the Indians chose today to abandon us, it's doubtless because they knew that we were on the point of reaching our goal. Believe me, we'll never have another opportunity like the one presented to us now to reach the holy city. We'll find the means to survive damn it! We'll nourish ourselves on fruits and game, and if we lack weapons, we'll make some. Are we less intelligent or less resolute than the half-savage Indians who live alone or in small groups on the high plateaux of the Andes?

"I say that we can't go back to France without having seen our mission through to the end. Thus far we've had great difficulties, but we haven't run any real dangers. Are we going to recoil at the first threat? No, let's get the better of misfortune."

Robert, who had listened to this reply with his head bowed, suddenly looked up and said: "Well, Jacques is right, we ought to risk everything to gain everything. We've talked too much to allow ourselves to go back with our tails between our legs. By recoiling before danger we'd be betraying those who had enough confidence in us go send us here. We're not taking a pleasure stroll, we have a duty to fulfill."

"A mission to carry out," Jacques insisted.

"Precisely. And we don't have the right to give up as long as we have the strength to fight."

II

The explorers had overcome the excusable discouragement that they had experienced on discovering the desertion of their auxiliaries; now they were no longer thinking about anything but stiffening their determination and deploying all their energy to see their archeological mission through to the end.

While avoiding overloading themselves with a burden that would have paralyzed them, they had collected everything that might facilitate a long sojourn in the wilderness, for it was not so much a matter of traveling rapidly as one of endurance. They had been forced to abandon their tents and bunks since they no longer had llamas to transport them. They would have to sleep on the bare ground, having no covers but their ponchos: large cloaks, primitive but practical, made of a single piece of red fabric pierced with a hole to allow the passage of the head. But Jacques had kept the pegs and strings that had served to stretch and fasten the sides of the tent.

"They might be useful. The pegs, fitted with iron spikes, can be used as weapons if necessary."

Pierre Estray was particularly sensible of the loss of his watch. "How can one travel comfortably without the time?" he grumbled.

But Jacques, who decidedly took all misadventures in his stride, observed that it was easy to do without a watch.

"It's necessary to resign ourselves," he said, "to living for two or three days like true savages, forgetting our civilized habits, which aren't all excellent. To regulate our time we have a great clock that we'll never lack, night or day: the splendid tropical sky."

Circling the environs of the camp, Jacques discovered a few tunas on cactus bushes. He collected them carefully, avoiding wounding himself on the sharp spines with which the tegument of the fruits was bristling. He brought them back triumphantly and stripped off the spines by rubbing them on a stone, as he had seen the Indians do.

"That will permit us to eke out our reserves of food somewhat. Let's content ourselves with a few tunas for our first meal.

It was with good humor that the voyagers consumed their frugal repast. To drink, they had to content themselves with the lukewarm water in their flasks, which the deserters had fortunately left them.

It was June, the autumn season in Peru, a country of the southern hemisphere. In that tropical region, however, the sun shines with a glare unveiled by the slightest mist, and its heat was only tempered by the high altitude that the explorers had reached.

They calculated that the Indians must have left the camp shortly after sunrise. The audacious thieves who had rifled everything they had been able to reach in the tents had certainly not been operating in total darkness.

On examining the tracks of the fugitives and their troop of llamas, Robert and his companions observed, with surprise, that they had continued up into the mountains along the path that the mission had been following until then, instead of going back down toad Cuzco, and would have seemed natural.

That was odd, to say the least, for there was apparently nothing to be found in that direction but ruins.

Was it prudent to take the same route, at the risk of falling into an ambush? The thieves might think that the Frenchmen were trying to catch up with them in order to punish them for their desertion—and perhaps, in that case, they would not hesitate to get rid of them by murder.

But the explorers had now decided that they would not recoil before any danger. They resumed their march toward the mysterious city.

They were wearing wide-brimmed hats of soft felt, of the kind known as *monteras*, which are the habitual headgear of Peruvian mountain-dwellers. When they had their red ponchos over their shoulders, outside their flannel costumes tailored in the sporting style, they could have been mistaken at a distance for simple Quichuas.

They followed the rocky crests alongside the profound ravine on the edge of which they had camped. Once, there had been one of the paved pathways there with which the Incas had furrowed their empire to the north, south, east and west, over trajectories of several thousands of kilometers. In the vicinity of Cuzco the paving stones had been ripped up by the conquistadors to serve for the construction of their edifices, and the causeway was entirely effaced, with the result that the voyagers had only discovered the vestiges of it after several days' march, following vague indications.

The Indians accompanying them had proved to be poor guides and had led them astray several times. What the Frenchmen had initially taken for ignorance was, they were now convinced, nothing but perfidy. When they had understood that they could neither discourage them not put them on a false route, the Indians had evidently decided to abandon them, at the risk of getting into trouble with the Peruvian authorities.

It was scarcely possible henceforth to be mistaken; the ancient paved path was too well preserved. Undoubtedly it had collapsed in places, and in others it had disappeared under vegetation, but it was always easy to pick up the trace again.

"The Incas' roads," Robert Vauguyon observed, "lose nothing by comparison with the celebrated Roman roads that created the power of the Latin Empire; they're still practicable after four centuries of neglect. Thanks to them, the Incas were able to transport themselves from one end of their empire to the other with a disconcerting rapidity and maintain surveillance on all its provinces."

The three friends had been marching for several hours, and the sun, suspended at the zenith, was darting ardent rays at the ground, when the route, after a bend, came to an abrupt end on the edge of a ravine. The cliffs framing the abyss were only seven or eight meters apart at that point. The rock was overhanging, and down below, at a depth of a hundred meters, the white foam of a torrent was detectable in places beneath a luxuriant vegetation. Its monotonous roar filled the gorge.

The explorers stopped and considered the impassable gorge, perplexed.

Were they about to be stopped when they were so close to the goal?

They could certainly have attempted to go around the obstacle, descending into the gorge and scaling the other slope, but God alone knew where such an enterprise might take them. They might need to cover several kilometers in almost impracticable terrain before finding a place enabling the decent, and once at the bottom, there was no guarantee of succeeding in the ascent of the opposite cliff.

"This time," said Pierre, "with the best will in the world, we're forced to admit that we're beaten."

"Not yet," said Jacques. "If I'm not mistaken, there was a bridge of *maguez* here, like those the Incas constructed and the indigenes still know how to contrive today."

Leaning over the edge, he pointed to a suspended mass resembling tangled creepers, which was attached at its extremities to large spikes encased in the rock to either side of the abruptly-interrupted route. They were the remained of a suspended bridge made with the solid fibers of a kind of Peruvian osier known as the maguez.[27]

It was easy, given that, to deduce what had happened. The suspended bridge had still been in place that morning, and the Indians who had deserted the mission had made use of it to cross the precipice, but once on the other side they had detached the extremities to prevent the archeologists from following them.

"The fellows have cut off their own retreat," Robert observed. "The fact is that they risked being badly received if they returned to Cuzco without us."

---

[27] *Agave americana*, usually spelled maguey in English, is actually a flowering plant rather than a tree, as the comparison with an osier seems to imply.

"That's definitely the debris of a bridge," said Pierre, "but I don't see how it helps us get across."

"Let's try to figure out what the people who constructed the first bridge here did," said Jacques.

"I imagine that some of them went down to the bottom of the gorge and climbed up the other side, and then the builders threw ropes from one side to the other."

"I think I've found a simpler means, or at least quicker, and if you like, we can try it."

"I'd be curious to know…."

"We have nearly thirty meters of cord, thin but solid enough to support a man of my weight. I count on using it to get to the other side."

"How are you going to do that?"

"On the other side of the precipice, as on this one, there are two solid spikes to either side of the route, which serve as attachments for the principal cables of the suspended bridge. If we can fix the extremity of our cord to those spikes, the rest will be child's play."

"Indeed! But it's a matter of fixing the cord first, without moving from here, sand as we don't know how to throw a lasso…."

"A demonstration will be better than an explanation," Jacques declared.

He took the cord, made out of all the pieces that he had taken from the tents and assembled with knots, attached to the extremity of one of the iron pegs that he had also brought, and then made a series of loops along the cord about fifty centimeters apart. That formed a kind of rudimentary rope-ladder, prolonged by some fifteen meters of thread.

Jacques gripped the peg, fixed crosswise at the end of the cord, the other end of which he had confided to his companions, and launched it over the precipice. His first attempt having failed, he pulled the peg back, and threw it a second time. After several attempts, he succeeded in throwing it in such a way that the cord was caught between two of the spikes fixed in the ground on the other side of the gulf. It was sufficient for him to pull it toward him slightly to fix it definitively, thanks to the crosspiece of the peg to which it was attached, which was wedged behind the spikes.

A light, fragile bridge was now extended between the edges.

"Now," said Jacques, "it's a matter of making a solid cable, with the aid of which I can draw the suspended bridge toward me.

The explorers began by hoisting on to the edge the tangled maguez that was hanging down into the abyss. They observed that the light construction had retained its ingenious design; two strong cables sustained, by means of a series of threads as thick as a finger, a kind of floor made of interwoven woody fibers. It was reminiscent of a broad V-shaped gutter, at the bottom of which humans and animals could pass in Indian file.

Jacques and his companions were able, without seriously damaging the ensemble, to detach a certain number of threads, which they assembled into a solid cable.

When that task was concluded, Jacques put his foot into the final loop of the cord that was attached to the other side of the ravine, put his arm in the second loop, and had the thread that his friends were holding attached around his waist. Then he let himself slide into the gulf, suspended on the one hand by the mooring-rope, which Robert and Pierre paid out slowly, and the other by the cord furnished with loops, which united the two sides of the abyss.

He could not help shivering when he found himself suspended a hundred meters above the bottom of the gorge, like a spider at the end of a thread, and his friends shivered at the thought that the cord might break.

As they let him down carefully, Jacques gradually drew away from the edge he had just abandoned and drew closer to the opposite wall.

In the end, the bold pioneer made contact with the wall. He had no more to do than climb up the ten meters of his improvised rope ladder to reach the ledge on the far side of the ravine.

"Bravo!" cried Pierre, enthusiastically. "You're a marvelous fellow, Jacques! The mission owes you a unanimous vote of congratulation."

"Patience! My task isn't finished."

"Bah! The rest's nothing. Forgive me for having doubted your ingenuity momentarily."

Robert had attached the fibrous cable to the end of the cord. Jacques pulled it toward him and made use of it to weave the extremity of the maguez bridge.

That was the most difficult part, because, in spite of the lightness of the materials that had served for its construction, the bridge was nevertheless quite heavy, and the strength of one man was scarcely adequate to lift it. Jacques had to start again several times, being careful to moor the cable to the spikes fixed in the ground.

Finally, he was able to grasp the extremity of the bridge and attach it solidly.

The passage was reestablished!

Jacques rejoined his companions.

"With a fellow like you, we'll never be stuck, even in the most difficult circumstances, and I no longer doubt our success.

The reestablishment of the bridge had required considerable time; the explorers calculated, by means of the position of the sun, that it was at least two o'clock in the afternoon. They were fatigued by the heat and the efforts they had made, and were beginning to suffer, above all, from hunger, for the tunas thy had eaten in the morning did not constitute very substantial nourishment.

They decided to open a tin of corned beef

"Too bad if it diminishes our reserves," said Pierre. "I'm as hungry as an ogre."

"Me too," said Jacques.

"And me," agreed Robert.

"After this, my dear Jacques," Pierre went on, "we're counting on you to restock the larder. Another opportunity to distinguish yourself!"

III

When they set forth again, after two hours of well-earned rest, having crossed over the precipice on the bridge so audaciously reconstructed, the voyagers, still following the ancient Inca road, went into a valley in which they did not enjoy the magnificent view that they had had while moving alongside the ravine. A few trickles of water running along the edge of the road, however, maintained a rich vegetation dotted with brightly-colored flowers. There were sunflowers there, red begonias, daturas, the entire spectrum of poisonous Solanaceae and abundant specimens of the carmine-tinted cornflowers that the Indians call *chihuahuas*.[28] Among the Incas, the chihuahua was a sacred flower from which crowns were woven for adolescents promoted to the rank of warriors.

Frightened birds with brilliant plumage flew away from the bosom of flowering bushes as the men approached.

The archeologists found a spring from which they refilled their flasks and drank with delight.

A little further on, they dug up a few tubers of a wild species of potato.

"These could take the place of bread for us," said Jacques. "It's a pity that we don't have a few kilos of them."

"It would be necessary to cook them," said Robert, "and we don't have anything with which to make a fire."

The Indians had, in fact, stolen the explorers' lighters as well as their watches. Further maledictions were pronounced with regard to the deserters, but Jacques smiled.

"I'll wager that you have a trick for lighting a fire," said Pierre. "Perhaps you know how to produce a flame by rubbing two sticks together, as the Redskins do."

---

[28] *Graptopetalum bellum*.

"No," said Jacques, "I haven't yet readapted well enough to the savage life, but I remember the way the Incas lit the sacred fire in the Temple of the Sun."

"They made use of a concave mirror," said Robert, "with which they concentrated the sun's rays on a small tuft of cotton."

"We don't have a concave mirror, but, by way of compensation I have a magnifying glass, of which we occasionally made use for map-reading. Fortunately, it was in my knapsack and escaped the cupidity of our thieves."

"Perfect!" said Pierre. "But if it's the sun that's going to give us fire, we need to hurry to take advantage of its rays. In an hour, it'll be too low to set fire to a fragment of tinder through a lens."

The attention of Pierre and Jacques was deflected by an exclamation from Robert: "Ruins!"

The leader of the mission extended his hand toward a ruddy mass projecting from the verdure: the vestiges of a brick wall that must once have been part of a large building.

The friends ran in that direction.

The ruins rose from rocky ground in which the brushwood had hardly been able to take root, so they were sufficiently disengaged to be easy to explore. The friends discovered the traces of four sections of wall, comprising a huge rectangular enclosure.

"A *tambo*!" said Robert.

Tambos were the hostelries that the Incas had taken care to build along the routes in order to lodge there with their retinues when traveling

"I propose that we establish ourselves here for the night. We've had a good deal of trouble today, and we ought not to abuse our strength. Let's stop and set up camp. These sections of wall will shield us from the cold wind that blows from the mountains by night and will serve as a rampart if necessary, if brigands take it into their heads to seek to harm us.

Robert's proposal having been approved, Jacques left his two friends to proceed with setting up camp while he collected dry grass and set about lighting a fire by focusing the sun's rays on it with his magnifying glass. Soon, the flame rose up. As soon as a little ash had formed, Jacques buried the potatoes in it. A few twigs thrown on top stimulated the fire. Twenty minutes later, the tubers were cooked and ready to eat. The explorers combined them with the remainder of the corned beef they had opened earlier in the day, and had a true feast.

When they had finished their meal, the sun was almost touching the horizon. They hastened to complete their preparations for the night, for twilight is brief in the tropics.

With bricks and stones they constructed a little wall in a corner of the tambo, in such a way as to fashion a redoubt, which they covered with a roof of foliage. It formed a kind of cabin well sheltered from the wind and the dew.

It was agreed that the three men would take turns on watch, revolver in hand, because, since their misadventure, they were afraid of what the Indians might do. If the latter had abandoned them specifically in order to prevent them reaching the holy city, they might well be spying on them. They would have seen them persevere in their expedition, reconstruct the bridge and cross over the gorge; perhaps they were meditating setting an ambush for those they regarded as profaners.

It would therefore be prudent to remain on their guard.

Jacques took advantage of the last rays of the sun to effect to make a brief patrol in the vicinity of the tambo and to make sure that no immediate danger was threatening the little company.

That brief reconnaissance permitted him to discover, a hundred meters from the ancient Inca hostelry, the ruins of a small stone edifice that a curtain of trees and bushes had previously hidden from view.

The four walls were quite well-preserved but the roof and wooden beams had disappeared. Like the majority of edifices of Inca times, it had no windows; the doorway was narrow and tapered from top to bottom; above it the traces of a sculpted figure could still be made out, surrounded by rays, which suggested that the ruins were those of a small temple to the sun.

Nothing any longer remained inside except a crude idol devoid of arms and legs with a flat forehead and brutal features, mounted in a pedestal. It had an open mouth and, passing through the hole, the end of a stick broken from a bush. Jacques deduced that the statue was hollow.

Is that one of the tricks that the priests employed to make the divinity speak? An oracle hidden in the statue making prophetic words resound?

But the tall stone figure was backed up against the wall, and no apparent passage allowed communication with the outside. Jacques thought that the passage might be subterranean, but must be filled in by now. All the same, when he came out of the temple, however, he was curious enough to make a tour of it, and clicked his tongue in satisfaction when he discovered a cavity invaded by grass behind the wall, at the place where the statue stood.

I'll wager that that hole communicates with the interior of the idol, he said to himself.

He promised himself that he would come back the next day with his companions, in order to study the curious little temple at leisure, but at present, night was falling and it was prudent to return to the camp.

"Nothing suspect," he said to his friends when he rejoined them. "I think we can sleep tranquilly. But I've found a curious ruin, which we can visit tomorrow morning."

"Have you picked up the trail of a vicuna?" asked Pierre. "We need to think seriously about shooting some game. Hunger is lying in wait for us."

"Well, I've been thinking about that," said Jacques, with apparent insouciance. "I'm conscious of my responsibility; it's me who persuaded you to continue our voyage, so I ought to nourish you." Ironically, he added: "Nevertheless, remember that yours is to help me if the opportunity arises."

Jacques was more anxious than he wanted to appear. The hope he had conceived of being able to kill a wild llama was beginning to ebb away. No game had showed itself apart from a few birds that only Buffalo Bill could have brought down with a bullet.

If that continues, Jacques thought, *we'll be reduced to eating worms and insects.*

The setting sun was darkening rapidly. In its last gleams, a star appeared near the horizon. It was the planet Venus, which the Incas called Chasca, the page of the sun, and represented as a young man with long curly hair.

IV

In consideration of the difficult efforts and fatigues he had imposed on himself during the day, Jacques had been allocated the third turn on watch. When Pierre extracted him from his slumber to confide the guard of the camp to him, he was in the middle of a dream about Redskins, Incas and llamas.

Enveloped in his poncho, he initially sat down in front of the redoubt that the explorers had made to shelter them.

The sky was resplendent with all its stars and the full moon, descending in the west, was spreading its silvery light over the earth: the moon, Mama Quilla, the sister and spouse of the sun, whom the priests of the Inca Empire represented by a silver disk with a human face

The view was limited by the ruined wall of the tambo, so Jacques, a lover of logic, immediately looked around or a better observatory.

The first condition of being a good sentry, he thought, *is that of being able to see a long way.*

The damaged wall was riddled with holes, which formed as many footholds. It was not difficult to hoist himself up to the summit of the enclosure, which was about a meter thick. Revolver in hand, Jacques took up a position on the crest of the wall, a veritable terrace, and said down on a spur. From there he could see a vast extent, and distinguish in the moonlight, above the trees and bushes, the ruins of the little temple that he had discovered the previous evening.

The time went by slowly, talking the great circle of the moon and the stars westwards. The shadows lengthened, becoming increasingly opaque as Mama Quilla sank toward the horizon. The silence was only troubled by the gusts of the breeze blowing through the jungle. Once, however, Jacques thought he heard the hoarse cry of a jaguar. That made him hopeful; if the redoubtable feline was prowling in the vicinity, it must have sniffed a herd of vicuna. The country could not be completely devoid of game.

The temperature dropped, the cold becoming increasingly intense—a sign that daybreak was not far away.

Jacques, who felt himself shivering in spite of his poncho, was about to stand up and get down from his observatory in order to move around a little when he saw shadows moving, some distance away, on the Incas' paved road. Immobilizing himself again, he gazed more attentively, and recognized men who were advancing, driving a heard of llamas in front of them. They were coming from the same direction as the explorers. Were they Quichua herdsmen or the deserters of the mission?

If they were herdsmen, it might be possible to obtain their aid, or at least buy a llama from them; but if they were the deserters, it would be as well only to approach them prudently, for there was no way of knowing how far hatred and fear of punishment might push them.

Having observed for a minute, Jacques got down, in order to wake his companions and bring them up to date with what was happening.

"Get up. Indians are coming, with a herd of llamas. We need to take advantage of it to renew our provisions, whatever the cost."

"Let's go offer to buy one of their animals from them," said Pierre. "If they refuse, we'll take it from them by force."

"Let's be cleverer and avoid a fight. Dawn's breaking. Let's follow them, sliding through the brushwood. We'll eventually find an opportunity to take possession of a llama without being seen."

The three men left their luggage in the camp, only taking their weapons, and set out on campaign.

They drew nearer to the road, sneaking through the long grass, and watched the Indians go past. This time, there was no doubt; they were definitely dealing with their deserters. Since these were now behind them, they must have stopped on the road the day before and had hidden when they saw the explorers arriving. They must think, in consequence, that the Frenchmen were still ahead of them. The fact that they had no hesitation in following in their tracks, at the risk of catching up with them and having to quarrel with them did not imply that they were animated by the best intentions.

"I'm going to jump into the midst of those rascals and constrain them to obedience. If one of them resists, I'll blow his brains out."

Jacques intervened to calm his friends.

"Don't risk a battle, I beg you. We're too weak to be sure of victory. Even if the Indians pretend to yield, they won't take long to take their revenge."

The explorers were already discussing whether they ought not to return to the camp and fetch their baggage when the Indians called a halt and started arguing animatedly in their Quichua dialect, which Robert and his friends spoke.

Although they were too far away to hear everything, they gathered that it was a question of Inti—which means "the Lord" and indicates the sun—a llama and a sacrifice.

Then the troop headed toward the little temple that Jacques had discovered the day before.

"I've got it!" said Jacques. "In accordance with the custom of the ancient Quichuas, they're going to sacrifice a llama in order to render the gods propitious in the war of cunning or violence that they're going to undertake against us. Well, let me see—I'll do them a bad turn in my fashion. Stay here and watch, and only come to my aid if I fire a revolver shot."

"What are you going to do?" Robert murmured anxiously. "Don't let them catch you."

"Don't worry. Haven't I recommended you to be prudent? But we need to try something to recover the upper hand. Stay alert, ready to intervene in case of need. As for me, I'm going to talk to these fellows and inspire them with a salutary terror, borrowing the voice of a divinity."

Having pronounced those enigmatic words, Jacques left his companions and, creeping through the jungle, drew away in the direction of the little ruined temple.

"As long as nothing happens to him!" said Robert.

"Bah! He's capable of taking on a band of Redskins. We're here to bring him help in case of danger."

It was already daylight, although the sun was still hidden behind the mountains.

The Indians had gone into the temple and two of them were dragging a black llama to the foot of the crude idol. As if it divined the fate that awaited it, the animal threw itself backwards, curving its long neck back over its spine and turning its head. Its long eyes were full of fear and it was bleating plaintively, but it was pushed on to the slab that formed the pedestal of the statue.

There were a dozen Quichuas assembled in the temple. They were almost all specimens of the pure race, with features of a classical beauty. Their garments consisted of light brown culottes and red ponchos. They were shod in sandals and coiffed in black monteras ornamented with shiny metal plaques. The underside of the brim of their hats was lined with green or red, whose bright shades harmonized with their bronzed complexion. The gaze of their large and shiny eyes had something wild about it.

When the sun appeared over the mountains, they all turned toward the doorway, orientated eastwards, and invoked the Lord, Inti, who spread heat and light over the world.

Then they cut the llama's throat in front of the idol.

"Inti, give us strength and valor, turn away from our sanctuaries the accursed strangers who have profaned and devastated the land of our ancestors."

Jacques knew very well how that scene would finish; he was sufficiently informed of the ancient customs of the Quichuas.

Although the majority of the Indians of modern Peru, who still form the majority of the population, have ostensibly adopted the Catholic religion, they generally maintain their ancient superstitions, and Jacques had heard it said that some of them remained faithful to the religion of the Incas, but he had never had the opportunity to witness a sacrifice in honor of the sun.

Having quit his friends, he had slipped behind the ruins of the temple in order to carry out the bold plan he had conceived. He had succeeded in squirming through the plants in the hole that he had noticed at the base of the wall, which communicated, as he had supposed, with the interior of the statue. Doubtless there had once been a second chamber there where the priests prepared their mysteries.

A man of Jacques' height could easily lodge himself inside the crude idol, but as it had not been used for centuries, it was cluttered with all kinds of detritus brought by animals, spiders' webs and vegetable debris. The archeologist required a certain courage to penetrate into the cavity in spite of the sticky dirt on the walls and the vermin he could sense there swarming all around him.

When he had hoisted himself up to the open mouth of the statue he was, at least, able to see and hear through that narrow window what was happening in the temple.

Now, he said to himself, *the rascals will take the llama away, roast it on a big fire and have a feast in honor of the divinity. But it's a matter of reserving that beautiful item for our table. It will furnish us with a supply of meat that will enable us to envisage without dread a long sojourn far from any civilized center.*

The Indians had begun to chant a kind of hymn to the sun.

"Lord, it is you who warm and illuminate us, you who render or fields and pastures fertile, you who causes our trees to fruit and our herds to increase, you who sends us the rain and fine weather. Lord, you make the tour of the world once a day, to see what each of us might need, and your gaze is present everywhere...."

A voice rose up, cavernous and terrible, crying in Quichua: "Perfidious ones! You have betrayed those that the Lord had taken under his protection, those he was guiding toward your temples and your sacred cities in order to show them the grandeur of your ancient civilization and the sublime beauty of your beliefs. No longer have the audacity to invoke him after that blow! You have prevented the triumph of the truth, delayed the resurrection of our empire and the return of the happy times in which you lived under the clement law of Inti."

At the first severe words that had escaped the lips of the statue, the Redskins had abruptly fallen silent, looking at one another in bewilderment, and as the idol continued to heap reproaches upon them, they were gripped by panic. They ran to the door, fighting to get through it, and disappeared into the brushwood.

One of them, however, less frightened and perhaps incredulous, wanted to load the llama on to his shoulders before fleeing. That was not to Jacques' liking—so the idol with the mysterious voice began roaring even more loudly:

"Leave the llama, son of a dog! Will you have the temerity to take back from the Lord the victim that you have offered to him?"

The man hesitated momentarily, and then, terror-stricken in his turn, ran away to rejoin his companions.

"May Catequil crush you, vagabond!" the state roared.

On hearing the invocation of Catequil, the god of thunder, the Indian increased his pace; he flew, and when he had caught up with his companions he dragged them further away, along with their herd, in a hectic flight.

In the abandoned temple, meanwhile, the idol emitted a loud burst of laughter.

V

The explorers spent the day in the ruins of the tambo in order to butcher the llama so adroitly conquered by Jacques, cooking and curing the best pieces.

For a long time now, they were sheltered from hunger. They could each carry enough meat to last for a week; they would merely have to complete their menu by adding fruits and tubers that they could collect along the route. In addition, they left an abundant reserve of cured meat in the tambo, carefully enveloped in dry grass and put under a heap of stones, safe from the voracity of wild animals. They would find it there on their return, and perhaps draw from it at need.

Robert and Pierre laughed a great deal as they listened to the story of the ruse that Jacques had employed to put the Indians to flight. They were particularly amused by the final episode, when the indignant idol had shouted at the Redskin to leave the sacrificed llama where it was.

"Can you believe," said Jacques, "that the fellow intended to take the animal away? And I would have gone to all that trouble for nothing!"

He had emerged from the statue unrecognizable, his garments soiled, his face and hands the color of soot. Now, after a thorough wash, all the more difficult because water was scarce, he had resumed a human appearance.

His ruse had had a double purpose: to procure the members of the mission the food they lacked and to inspire respect for the archeologists in the Indians by placing them under the protection of the ancient gods of the Incas.

The travelers hoped, therefore, that after that, the deserters would not dare to attack them and would perhaps even be disposed to help them by resuming their functions in their regard.

After a second night spent in the ruins, they set forth again, penetrating deeper into the mountains. They felt sure of themselves now that they had good reserves of food, but there is no advantage that is not paid or with some inconvenience; the burdens they had to bear weighed them down and slowed their pace.

At midday they arrived at a fork in the narrow but clearly marked path that they had been following since the morning. Two rugged gorges converged at the place the explorers had reached. They offered fantastic perspectives to the gaze of abrupt red and gray cliffs clad in hanging vegetation, heaps of rocks from which clumps of verdure sprang forth here and there, and summits that seemed to be trying to climb, step by step, to the heavens.

"Let's eat," said Robert. "While eating we can reflect, and try to decide which way it would be better for us to head first."

For a temporary camp, the three friends chose a small natural platform that overlooked the path and as shadowed by a crag.

"While you set the table," Jacques said to his companions, "I'll try to pick up the tracks of the troop of Indians that preceded us. I think, in fact, that we have every chance of reaching our goal if we choose the path they've taken."

"All right," said Robert. "You can even visit both branches of the path—you go one way and Pierre the other. But don't go too far, and beat a retreat at the slightest appearance of danger. It would be very clumsy of us to let ourselves get separated and to be unable to help one another. Take a revolver each, and I'll keep the rifle. If one of us fires, the others will hasten to rejoin him—and even if all goes well, be back here within an hour at the latest, no matter what."

So, while Robert made the preparations for lunch, Pierre and Jacques set out to reconnoiter the issues of the two narrow gorges that opened into the canyon.

Jacques had only kept his revolver, his water-flask, slung over his shoulder, which he hoped to have an opportunity to refill with fresh spring-water and, wound around his waist, the cord of which he had made such ingenious use to reestablish the bridge cut by the Indians. He had taken of his poncho in order to render himself more agile.

He walked a few hundred meters along the path at the bottom of the narrow gorge into which he had moved, seeking traces of the passage of the Redskins, but without ceasing to keep a careful eye on his surroundings, in order that he would not be surprised by any ambush.

It was obvious that men and llamas had recently passed along the path, but there was no firm evidence that it had been the previous day or the day before, and Jacques wanted to find more conclusive indications, so the archeologist walked for half an hour with the most extreme precaution, and then thought about returning. He calculated that he had covered some two kilometers, and that was already more than prudence recommended.

He therefore turned round and was about to retrace his steps when he noticed, some distance away, a man climbing the flank of the rock by means of a kind of natural stairway formed by projections and fissures in the stone.

So far as Jacques could judge from where he was standing, the individual in question, with his poncho and his broad flat hat, had to be a Quichua herdsman.

The explorer had taken cover behind a clump of aloes and watched, revolver in hand. He was intent on not losing sight of the man, who was hoisting himself up the cliff face, and whom the brushwood partly hid at times.

There was undoubtedly a secret passage up there.

Suddenly, Jacques uttered a cry, immediately stifled; a piece of fabric had fallen over his head, while his revolver was snatched from his hand before he had time to make use of it.

In the blink of an eye he was rolled up in a poncho, lifted up and carried away.

He attempted to struggle, but in vain. Vigorous hands paralyzed his resistance, and he was incapable of making a cry heard; his voice scarcely emerged in feeble groans.

Rapidly recognizing that he would not achieve anything by force, Jacques constrained himself to keep calm and think.

In such circumstances it was necessary above all to take account of the direction in which he was being taken.

The poncho in which he had been rolled was tightly wound, but it did not prevent him from breathing. His abductors were holding him firmly, but without brutalizing him. He therefore retained all his mental lucidity.

He was being carried at a rapid and regular pace, which it would not have been possible to sustain over uneven ground. Jacques concluded in consequence that the band by which he had been surprised, doubtless composed of the men in whom he had been able to inspire such fear two days before by making the idol speak, were continuing to follow the path traced along the floor of the gorge. The man that Jacques had seen climbing the cliff could not have been part of the same company, unless his climb was a ruse devised in order to distract his attention and give the others the opportunity to jump him.

He was certain, at any rate, that the abductors were taking their prisoner into the depths of the gorge and not toward the issue where Robert was waiting.

The leader of the mission and Pierre would not take long to set out in search of their vanished companion. As long as the band remained on the path, the trail should not be difficult to pick up.

It was difficult for Jacques to measure the passage of time, which his critical situation caused to seem particularly long. He estimated that he band must have been marching for between three and four hours when his porters finally halted, set him on his feet and removed the poncho in which he was wrapped.

Dazzled and dazed, Jacques stood there unsteadily for a moment or two, blinking.

He had been set free, but he could see that he was surrounded by a dozen men, and was not insensate enough to try to fight or escape them. He was unarmed, and could not compare with the Indians in the matter of agility.

As he gradually recovered the use of his faculties, he was better able to make out the physiognomy of the bandits, and recognized among them some of those who had been attached to the service of the mission and had abandoned it. He scanned them with a haughty gaze.

"It was you," he said, "in whom we put our confidence, and who behind in our regard like bandits. Not content with having deserted the mission, you've attacked me by surprise and carried me away I know not where. What do you want with me, then?"

While speaking he had observed a small house with a thatched roof behind some guava-trees. The men who surrounded him did not reply to his criticism, but another emerged from the house and advanced toward the explorer. He was better dressed than his companions, with a veritable elegance. He wore a costume of red cloth ornamented with fringes, and his montera was ornamented with gilded plaques and lined under the rim in red. He had aristocratic and regular features and a proud gait.

It was in correct Spanish that he addressed Jacques,

"Forgive us, Señor, for having employed slightly rude means in your regard, but it is your own fault; you were wrong to want to penetrate no matter what into a region that is forbidden to foreigners."

"Forbidden!" exclaimed Jacques. "By whom? I have an official authorization from the Peruvian government, and I'm not aware that I've crossed the frontier of the State."

"No, but there are reserved territories that are not dependent on Lima or Cuzco, in which your authorization has no value."

"We'll see about that. I shall appeal to the French consul."

The Indian smiled disdainfully. "The intervention of the French consul won't give you the right to penetrate into private property. One can only reach here by a single road, by traversing a bridge that care had been taken to sever in order to prevent access. Who gave you permission to reestablish that bridge?"

"I think it's always praiseworthy to rebuild a bridge destroyed by bandits."

"The master of a domain has the right to dispose of it as he sees fit, and those who obey him on his own land cannot be regarded as bandits."

"Are you the master of his domain, then?" Jacques demanded, ironically. "Do you claim to be the legitimate owner of such a vast territory?"

The Indian frowned. Anger caused his shining pupils to vacillate, but serenity reappeared immediately in his face, and it was in a calm voice that he replied:

"What is the point of arguing, Señor? We will gain nothing by saying disagreeable things to one another. You cannot have the pretention to oppose me, surrounded as I am, and I invite you instead to accept the hospitality that I am ready to offer you. My name is José Alvarez. I assume that you must be hungry and that you would be glad to share my meal."

Already convinced that he would achieve nothing by violence, Jacques considered the Peruvian with perplexity. He resolved to imitate him, to contain his indignation and to employ cunning.

Intelligence has been given to humans to substitute for strength, he told himself. *This is the moment to remember that.*

He suddenly changed his expression, adopting a smile, inclined slightly, and said aloud, in a good-humored tone: "Although my sentiments might seem to you to be devoid of spontaneity, it's not without pleasure, believe me, that I accept your hospitality. You're right to say that I'm very hungry, and I'm ready to do honor to your menu. Permit me, however, to ask you one question regarding your intentions toward my traveling companions?"

The Indian made an evasive gesture. "If they are obstinate in following you, they will not find anything ahead of them except the wilderness, unless…."

"Unless what?"

The Indian turned away abruptly.

"Let us go eat, Señor Lasserre."

VI

"You won't be surprised, Señor Alvarez, if I tell you that your attitude in my regard appears to me to be quite enigmatic."

The Indian smiled, without making any reply. He was sitting opposite his guest, and invited him with a gesture to serve himself from a dish of *humitas* that a young Indian woman had just brought.

Jacques looked curiously at the curious foodstuff, which hunger caused him to find appetizing.

"It is a mixture of maize flour with fat and shredded meat that is divided up into pellets, enveloped in maize leaves and cooked in boiling water," Alvarez explained. "My cook has a particular talent for the confection of that national dish. You will also taste crepes irrigated with melted caramel shortly, of which you must tell me your opinion."

Jacques did honor to the *humitas* and the *chicha*, a kind of maize beer the color of amber, sharp to the taste.

He was annoyed, however, at being unable to obtain any response to his questions.

Where was this José Alvarez trying to get to? What did this mixture of violence and affability signify? If the Indian had had the intention of having Jacques and his friends murdered, nothing would have prevented him from carrying out his crime without further ado. It would have been easy for him to make the bodies of the explorers disappear. The Indian auxiliaries of the mission would be suspected, but it would be impossible to set a hand on them.

Jacques thought, therefore, that he could assume that his life was not in danger, in the absence of any unexpected complication.

But why had Alvarez, who had boasted of being able to set emptiness before Robert and Pierre, in order to lead them astray, not done the same with Jacques? Why had he encumbered himself with a prisoner who could only, one way or another, create difficulties for him?

"Señor Alvarez, don't you think I have a right to know what you propose to do with me?"

"Why are you so intent on knowing? You are a man, if I am not mistaken, who likes adventure and the unexpected."

"Does that mean that you have a surprise in store for me?"

"Perhaps."

"Good or bad?"

"That will depend on you."

"I don't understand."

"I cannot explain myself any more clearly."

Leaning over the hot dish in which the Indian cook had just served a gilded crepe, Jacques declared:

"I imagine, Señor Alvarez, that you're a fervent admirer of the ancient civilization of the Incas, that you have a reverence for the vestiges of that great epoch, for the relics of the power of the Son of the Sun and that, knowing our intention to discover and visit the as-yet-unknown ruins of a holy city, you wanted to prevent us from committing what you regard as a profanation."

Alvarez seemed slightly disconcerted by that direct attack.

"It is not good," he said, shaking his head, "to trouble the slumber of the dead and the meditation of the gods."

"But does the man trouble the gods and the dead who comes to officiate at their altars or pray over their tombs?"

The Indian smiled disdainfully.

"What do you know," he said, "about our ancient kings?"

"I will tell you if you wish," said Jacques, "how the empire of the Incas was founded nine hundred years ago. The men of those times lived like beasts and had no religion. They were ignorant of the art of building houses, did not know either how to cultivate the earth or to spin wool or cotton. Caverns served as their refuges and dwellings. They nourished themselves on wild fruits, herbs and roots, and also sometimes ate human flesh.

"The Sun, touched by compassion, decided to send two of his children from the heavens, a son and a daughter, to teach human beings knowledge, to give them laws, to teach them to build houses and cities, to labor the earth, to grow crops, to raise herds. Thus, humans would no longer be savages, but reasonable and civilized beings.

The Sun deposited, on the shore of Lake Titicaca, his son Manco-Capac and his daughter Mama-Ocllo. 'Act,' he said to them, 'at the behest of your inspiration. Take this golden plowshare, it will serve to prove the earth; where you can embed it at a single stroke, establish yourselves and form your court. When you have submitted the people to your obedience, take care to maintain them by law and reason, in piety, clemency and equity, doing for them everything that a good father is accustomed to do for his children. You will be following my example, since you know that I never cease to do good to all mortals. I am the one who gives them life; I am the one who nourishes them. I want your empire to extend over all the people that you instruct by your good actions.'

"When the Sun had spoken to them thus, Manco-Capac and Mama-Ocllo set about exploring the earth, attempting, at each new step, to prove it with the golden plowshare that their father had given to them; but the earth would not allow itself to be pierced anywhere. They wandered thus for a long time before arriving in the valley of Cuzco, where they saw nothing but mountains and precipices. Then, at the first stroke they delivered, the plowshare dug deeply into the soil. The children of the Sun recognized the will of their father and resolved to settle in that valley. They presented themselves to the savages of the surrounding area and announced to them that they would be their benefactors.

"Surprised to see the two strangers clad in the brilliant costumes that the Sun had given them, the savages worshiped them and recognized their power. They gathered in great numbers, and thus was founded the empire of the Incas."

When Jacques fell silent, Alvarez inclined his head slowly and murmured, thoughtfully: "Yes, Señor, you recount the history of the origin of our empire very well. Perhaps the souls of our ancestors would not regard you with anger."

"They could only be propitious to a man who admires the grandeur of your race. I don't believe that the Empire of the Sun has disappeared forever. Is Peru not populated primarily by the descendants of the Incas' subjects? How could that nation not be faithful to its origins and not return to them, sooner or later, doubtless evolved and metamorphosed, but always animated by the same interior fire? Others might be deceived, Señor Alvarez, but I have perceived strange glimmers in the eyes of the men and women of your country, and I have divined the secret with which their minds are incessantly occupied. That is why I merit not being treated as a profane individual, but as an initiate."

"You can do nothing for our cause; you would betray it in trying to serve it. You are not of our race and yours has shed our blood."

Jacques made a gesture of denial. "I am not descended from those who ruined the Empire of the Sun. Remember too, Señor Alvarez, that the Incas, of whom you are perhaps distant offspring, initially prepared their misfortune themselves. If they had not been divided by a merciless civil war, Francisco Pizarro would not have been capable, with three hundred adventurers, of putting an empire of several million inhabitants to fire and the sword."

"Our ancestors, I agree, were subjected to the punishment of their own sins," said Alvarez, with a somber expression, "and the time of expiation is not yet finished. Ours will be fortunate if they can maintain, until the distant day of our renaissance, the flame that you mentioned just now. That is why it is important for us to guard it, why we must watch over it jealously, driving away without weakness everything that threatens it. Too many of our hearths, once dazzling, have been extinguished by sacrilegious hands.

"I know who you are, you and your companions, Señor Lasserre; there are no scholars more disinterested, endowed with a broader and more welcoming intelligence. I would like to be your friend. I am, insofar as I am a Peruvian, and a member of the society of this century, but I cannot be insofar as I am the son of an ancient race, the heir of its thought, the guardian of its secrets and its faith. For, noble of heart as you might be, everything that a miracle of our gods has saved through the ages from the cataclysm of our ruin would be put up for sale, dispersed or odiously profaned on the day when you revealed your discovery to your brethren."

"How can you suspect us of being so barbaric?"

"It's not you I suspect; but you would be proud of your discovery, you would talk about it; your very enthusiasm would betray you. And do you not know that a horde of curiosity-seekers would follow in your tracks? Curiosity-seekers, I tell you, perhaps less bloodthirsty than Pizarro's brigands, but no less deadly. No, Señor Lasserre, I will not surrender to you the key to the sanctuary over which I have the mission to keep watch."

"You have just pronounced moving words, Señor Alvarez, and I respect your reasons, which are great. But what if I were to swear on oath, for myself and my friends, never to betray your secret?"

"You want me, as the price of that oath, to serve as your guide and initiator?"

"Why not?"

"Do you believe me disposed, then, to compromise an immense interest with the sole objective of giving you pleasure? If your child were playing in the middle of the road, would you permit a galloping horse to pass over his body, on the pretext that the rider had sworn to you to jump over him without wounding him?"

"Who can tell whether I might not have been sent by your gods to aid your recognition?"

Alvarez considered his interlocutor silently for a moment, as if he had just heard his own thought expressed, and replied, slowly: "Well, that might be the case. That is why the idea occurred to me to have you brought here and to treat you with respect. But I do not want to make any decision lightly, and I am counting on you to submit to the proofs that will enlighten me as to the will of my gods."

Brave as he was, Jacques could not suppress a shudder.

"Proofs?" he said. "And if I don't triumph therein?"

"Then you would have been wrong to persist in this adventure when the first obstacles raised in our path should have warned you that it would be prudent to renounce it."

"You're inviting me, I see, to a redoubtable game."

"You are the one who began it."

"Would you hold me in esteem if I were afraid?"

"No, undoubtedly—but temerity is no longer bravery. Listen: I am offering you one last chance; you can still take back your stake. I am ready to set you free if you desire to return to our friends and beat a retreat with them." The Indian added, with a smile: "I think, moreover, that they are no longer far away, for they must have set out to search for you."

"Well, they'll rejoin me, and they'll submit, like me, to the proofs to which you have the intention of subjecting me."

"No: I do not want to expose myself to a triple hazard; one is already too many. If you decide to stay with me, I will make sure that your companions cannot rejoin you. Come on: there is still time; you can recover your liberty."

"My choice is made. I prefer the adventure."

VII

Leaving Jacques alone in the little house where he had shared his supper, Alvarez had gone out to confer with the other Indians and give them his orders.

The explorer no longer had any reason to flee, since he had agreed to accompany the band, in the hope of being initiated into the secret of the Incas, so his host had not taken the trouble to have him watched.

"Please wait for me here, Señor; I have to instruct my men to make arrangements for the departure."

Jacques was meditating in a room with bare clay walls, equipped with rudimentary furniture.

The house was merely a temporary abode, a refuge for the rare travelers who risked traversing that wilderness, but Robert and Pierre would not fail to notice it and investigate it. They would certainly have set out in search of their companion when they had not seen him return. As Alvarez had observed, they ought not to be very far away, although the band had obtained a long start on them before halting. If the departure had been delayed even by an hour, they would have arrived in the Indians' midst—but Alvarez had apparent decided to travel by night in order to give them the slip completely.

Jacques would have liked to leave a message for Robert and Pierre, but he dared not scribble a letter and leave it in evidence in the room, Alvarez having naturally refused him that authorization. It was all too evident that an imprudence might cost him his life and also suspend a threat over the heads of his friends.

When he had sat down at the table with Alvarez, he had deposited his water-flask against the wall, with the cord that he had previously kept wound around his waist, and which his abductors had not removed. As his gaze paused on those objects, it occurred to him that if he left them there, his friends would doubtless find them and draw deductions therefrom.

He began pacing back and forth, still pensive.

The Indians, when they took him away, would doubtless abandon the traced path that they had been following thus far and head into the wilderness, where their trail would be almost impossible to pick up for men like Robert and Pierre, who had not been trained since childhood to notice the slightest indications of the passage of an animal or a human.

If I could only imitate Petit Poucet, the explorer thought, *and drop white pebbles along my route.*

He had advanced mechanically to the threshold of a communicating door. Is gaze plunged into another room, which, to judge by the objects with which it was cluttered, served for domestic tasks. It was from there that the Indian woman had emerged to bring the dishes to Alvarez and Jacques at table.

For the moment, there was no one in the room. The oven-fire had gone out; an alpaca cloth, dyed red, was drying on a line above a tub, where the remains of a scarlet decoction of campeachy wood was still stagnating.

The rays of the low sun were penetrating through the unglazed window and reflecting ruddily from the bottom of the tub.

An idea passed through Jacques' brain like a flash of light.

That decoction of campeachy wood, if it were possible to take it away, might be capable of replacing Petit Poucet's white pebbles. It would be sufficient to let drops fall along the way. Many would doubtless be lost, soaked up by soft ground, but some would cling to stones and grass, and an attentive observer would be bound to spot them.

Jacques thought that Alvarez' cook might come back at any moment, and that in such circumstances, rapidity of decision is the first condition of success. Without further reflection, he went swiftly to pick up his flask, emptied its contents into a hole that served as a drain, and, arming himself with a ladle picked up from a table, replenished it from the tub of dye. The flask, which contained more than two liters, was soon full.

Jacques returned to the other room and made a small notch in the cork of the flask with his penknife, in such a way that when it was inverted, the liquid could trickle out, one drop at a time.

Having completed that task, he slung the flask over his shoulder.

I hope they'll leave me enough liberty, he thought, *that tonight, during the march, I'll be able to distribute red spots without anyone noticing.*

And, continuing to meditate, he said to himself: *Very good, but in order for Robert and Pierre to have the idea of searching for red splashes, they need to be alerted. How can I tip them off? Why don't I send them a quipus—the kind of message composed of colored cords and marked with knots that the Quichuas once used for communication, in accordance with a system of agreed signals?*

His eyes fell upon the cord that he had dropped on the ground against the wall, and he remained perplexed for a few moments, seeking a practical means of realizing the plan that had just come to mind.

Why not? Two adjacent knots could make a dash, an isolated not a dot; that way, one could compose a message in Morse code. Robert and Pierre, who read Morse fluently, will certainly be struck by it and will understand, if they find the cord. Let's try. As long as I have time before Alvarez comes back!

Having picked up the cord, Jacques hastily set to work composing his message. First of all, three dashes separated by two dots composed the call signal to mark the beginning of the message; then, continuing to represent the dots and dashes with knots, the explorers formed the words: *Prisoner. Walking to holy city. Follow red dots. Jac....*

He had only composed the first three letters of his signature when he heard the sound of footsteps. Quickly rolling up the cord, he threw it in a corner.

He was just in time. Alvarez came in.

"We are leaving, Señor," the Peruvian said. "Follow me."

At the same time the Indian cook went into the next room to collect the objects she intended to take away.

"I can have you carried on a litter, if you wish," said Alvarez, as he emerged from the house with the explorer.

"No, I prefer to walk," said Jacques, who needed to have freedom of movement to put his plan into execution.

Provided, he thought, *that Robert and Pierre find the cord and understand my quipus!*

The sun had just disappeared at the extremity of the gorge, in the gap in the mountains with grandiose perspectives. A few minutes more, and everything would be drowned in the shadows of the night.

The herdsmen of the band drove the llamas forward. The animals only walked reluctantly; it was not their habit to travel by night, they preferred to lie down when the sun set. An old male was at the head; its fleece was gray with dust but its haughty head was decorate with red feathers; its gait was grave and arrogant; it resembled a patriarch guiding his tribe.

Alvarez walked alongside Jacques and the rest of the band, some twenty men and women with bronzed skin and gleaming, shrewd eyes, brought up the rear.

The troop continued to follow the ancient Inca road. Night had fallen completely. Discreetly, Jacques tilted his flask and caused a few drops to leak out.

After an hour of rapid marching, one of the llama conductors, who was in the lead, uttered a guttural cry and drove his herd off the road, into the bushes and the rocks. There was a moment of disorder. The men had to part the bushes and jump from stone to stone in order to get through.

Jacques thought it as well not to spare the red droplets that were replacing Petit Poucet's white pebbles, because his friends might have difficulty finding the place where the troop had quit the road.

The march continued with difficulty for ten minutes through a chaos of rocks, and then the band moved into a narrow fissure that opened like a kind of portal in the seemingly-inaccessible wall of the cliff. There, Jacques could economize with the red liquid with which he had filled his flask, the provision of which was beginning to run low, because, once engaged in the defile, it was no longer possible to go astray.

The moon was shining, but its light scarcely penetrated the rocky corridor. The men, who had to grope their way forward at times, were careful to call out from time to time in order to guide one another.

We'd never have discovered this passage on our own, Jacques thought.

The floor of the defile rose up in a stiff slope, and here and there, when the inclination became too steep, large steps were hollowed out, the regularity of which indicated the intervention of human hands. Jacques no longer doubted that he was on the secret path to the holy city of the Incas. The defile with the smoothed floor and the rustic stairways were part of the as-yet-unknown vestiges of the brilliant civilization of the Emperors of the Sun.

Jacques suddenly perceived the sky in front of him, between the abruptly-terminated rocky walls, fully ornamented with lunar splendor. The defile seemed to be opening out into the void. The Indians marching at the head of the troop projected their silhouettes one by one in the bright cutting, and disappeared, as if swallowed up.

When Jacques, still walking alongside Alvarez, arrived at the extremity of the defile, he exclaimed in admiration.

Alvarez, who had not pronounced a word since the departure, stopped in order to show his companion the vast crater whose rim the troop had reached, the slopes of which plunged vertiginously into depths carpeted with an abundant vegetation.

"My country is beautiful," said the Indian. "Know, Señor, that no white man has ever set foot in it. You are the first of your race to cross this threshold. But remember my words. We are about to descend to the bottom of the crater; you will never get out again if you are unworthy of the favor I am granting you."

"Take my hand, Señor Alvarez, and tell me whether it is trembling," Jacques replied. "I want you to have in my regard no more evil inventions than I have formed against you. Need I quote to you the celebrated maxim of your prophet-king Pachacutec? 'He who is envious of honest men will find in them the substance of his ruin, as we see the spider extracting poison from the most beautiful flowers.' Pachacutec's comparison lacks exactitude in the eyes of modern zoologists, but we both understand the meaning of it well enough to profit from it."

"May Inti's protection be upon the man who possesses the science of our ancestors!" replied Alvarez, gravely.

And he resumed his march.

The troop was now descending through a maze of rocks, in which Jacques did not observe any appearance of a traced path.

The explorer had resumed distributing droplets of red dye, but he soon perceived, with irritation, that his flask was empty. Even supposing that his friends would succeed in following his trail this far, they would not have anything to guide them further but the uncertain traces left by human and animal feet.

The band took nearly two hours to reach the bottom of the crater. Having reached open ground appropriate for the installation of a camp, Alvarez signaled a halt. They had been walking for about six hours.

The Indians hastened to construct shelters with branches, and Alvarez offered one to his guest.

"Rest, Señor Lasserre. You must be tired after yesterday's excitements and that difficult march. Recover your strength; you will have great need of it in order to see this adventure through to the end."

He had a poncho given to Jacques, who lay down on a bed of dry grass and, genuinely exhausted, did not take long to fall into a profound sleep.

VIII

Brushing the crest of the ridges that formed the rim of the crater, the sun darted its rays over the shelter of foliage in which Jacques was still asleep. Penetrating through the interstices, they fell upon his eyelids.

The explorer woke up, his limbs still weary, stretched, and made an effort to recover consciousness of reality, which dreams had transfigured. He sat up beneath the roof of foliage.

No sound resonated in the morning. Jacques was astonished not to hear the bleating of the llamas that ordinarily salutes the appearance of the sun, nor the voices and footfalls of the Indians. Was everyone still asleep?

The impression that he had experienced a few days before, when he has perceived on awakening the desertion of the mission's Indians, suddenly returned to Jacques' memory. Gripped by suspicions, he threw himself outside.

No one! Not a single living being! Alvarez, the Indians and the llamas had all disappeared.

What did it mean? If the Peruvian had had the intention from the start of abandoning the archeologist in the heart of the wilderness, why had he taken the trouble to take him prisoner and bring him this far? After having decided to guide him to the holy city, had he suddenly changed his mind? But nothing seemed to justify such an about-turn.

Hardly able to believe his senses, Jacques wandered this way and that for a while, seeking in the vicinity of the camp for traces of his vanished companions. Meanwhile, he reflected, and recalled certain words charged with enigmatic menace that Alvarez had pronounced during the nocturnal march.

We are about to descend to the bottom of the crater; you will never get out again if you are not worthy of the protection of our gods.

Yes, everything became clear now to Jacques. Had Alvarez, that mysterious individual, not declared that he would submit his prisoner to redoubtable proofs? He had let it be understood that he was a descendant of the Incas, and that he reigned as such over a domain into which white men had never penetrated.

So the fellow is amusing himself losing me in a labyrinth and saying to me: 'Now get yourself out of it. If you can, it's because Inti's protection extends over you....' Has the animal at least left me something to eat?

On that matter, Jacques was soon reassured. He found a bag beside his shelter containing a maize broth mingled with shredded meat, and a leather bottle of chicha.

That will suffice for a day or two...but they've taken my revolver, so I no longer have a weapon. If I find myself face to face with a jaguar, I'll only have the magnetic force of my gaze with which to defend myself. Apart from that, however, the situation isn't so tragic. Don't I have the resource of going back, toward Robert and Pierre, who are certainly searching for me and perhaps already on my track?

As he was thinking about that solution, his gaze searched mechanically for the path by which the troop had descended into the crater, and observed with anxiety that it would not be so easy for him to find the passage again. The rocks that formed the rim of the crater were all alike. Even by orientating himself in accordance with the memory he had of the position of the moon at the moment when he had crossed the threshold of the defile, Jacques could not pinpoint the location of that issue. In every direction the slopes were formed by gigantic aggregations of rocks, in the midst of which the archeologist might wander for days, making a thousand perilous ascents, before finding the way back.

"Damn!" muttered the archeologist. "Now is the time to invoke the protection of Inti. Señor Alvarez, the great-grandson of that powerful divinity, has played a nasty trick on me, it seems. I'll be lucky if I don't leave my bones at the bottom of this accursed hole...."

Let's see! If Robert and Pierre have found my quipus in the little house and have deciphered its meaning, they only had to set out en route again this morning at daybreak. In the best hypothesis, they won't be here for seven or eight hours. I therefore have time to explore the crater. But I need to leave them a signal to guide them if, by good luck, they reach the issue of the defile....

Jacques broke off a long branch, stripped it of its leaves, and planted it in the ground in the middle of the bare space in which the band had camped, after having hooked his jacket to the extremity. A stick passed horizontally through the sleeves gave the improvised signal the appearance of one of the crude scarecrows that peasants often set up in their fields.

Having done that, the archeologist decided that it would be wise to equip himself with a weapon. He had soon improvised one by carving a solid spear, sharpened with his knife.

Undoubtedly, if I'm attacked by a jaguar, I'll have difficulty putting an end to it with this primitive weapon, but all the same, it's better than nothing. Prehistoric men were only a little better equipped when they battled cave-bears. I could also make myself a stone ax, not to mention a bow and arrows, but that would take too long; let's wait until it becomes absolutely necessary.

Jacques then undertook a reconnaissance in order to try to find the path by which he had arrived. He was careful to design little crosses with pebbles at intervals, in order not to risk going astray when he retraced his steps. He explored the labyrinth of rocks in that fashion for some time but, as he had feared, could not discover the exit from the defile. Everywhere, the rocky heights were terminated by sheer walls that offered not the slightest passage. It was as if the cliff had reclosed behind Alvarez and his troop.

Sufficiently discouraged, Jacques returned to the camp.

I've decidedly got myself into a sticky situation. If my friends don't find me, I'm well and truly stuffed...unless I adopt the other solution, which is to penetrate the heart of the holy city. Then Alvarez, the descendant of the Incas, will regard me as a sacred individual, sent by the gods themselves, and will take me under his aegis. Except that the difficulty is precisely that of reaching the holy city. If the route is as secret as the way back, I'll have time to die in this wilderness, which is also a prison.

Jacques also thought, bitterly, that even if his friends succeeded in catching up with him, he would not be saved in consequence; Robert and Pierre would simply be sharing his predicament.

He ate, reluctantly, a little of the broth that the Indians had left him. He had not taken the trouble to light a fire in order to heat up the dish in question, which, when it was cold, was not at all appetizing.

In spite of his bravery and his appetite for adventure, Jacques felt his heart sink. He was not very optimistic about his prospects of getting out of the dire situation into which he had allowed himself to be drawn.

After his summary breakfast he set about exploring the vicinity of the camp for the traces that the band must have left as they drew away, but, either because he was insufficiently skilled in that kind of investigation, or because the Indians had taken great precautions to efface their trail, the archeologist searched in vain.

Discouraged, he was returning to the camp, above which his jacket was still floating in the guise of a flag, when he heard a kind of brief snort, followed by a loud rustling of branches and foliage, which revealed the presence of a large animal, probably a jaguar.

It was coming from a thicket that Jacques was going past in order to return to his shelter.

The explorer leapt backwards, and waited, the point of his spear directed toward the suspect location.

A stick to fight a jaguar! Jacques was under no illusion regarding the efficacy of such a weapon. In order to escape death, he could only count on his sang-froid, and the fear that he might be able to inspire in the beast—but a jaguar is only slightly less redoubtable than a tiger, and is not easy to intimidate.

Jacques held himself still, his gaze fixed on the thicket, which he saw agitating at the passage of the animal. Suddenly, it appeared, with its tawny spotted skin, its flat face, short ears and broad muzzle.

The jaguar stopped on perceiving the man, and considered him fixedly, as if to measure the adversary with which hazard had unexpectedly confronted it. For a few seconds, the man and the animal tested one another with the force of their gaze.

It was the wild beast that gave the first sign of lassitude. It turned its head away slightly, blinking, with one paw raised, its muzzle contracted with rage, and uttered a dull growl, which translated both fear and the desire to frighten its adversary.

The animal hesitated; it was not yet beaten. It was tempted to flee, but it knew that retreat is not always the best means of escaping danger, and wondered whether it might not be better to switch to attack. The man's immobility, which had initially intimidated it, began to reassure it. Its neck extended, its head at ground level, it brought its gaze back to Jacques, sniffing noisily, its claws laboring the ground. It curved its spine, arching its back, and gathered itself, ready to pounce.

Jacques gripped his spear more tightly, resolved not to perish without a fight, even though he sensed that the struggle would be an unequal one.

The jaguar uttered a roar that was angrier and more menacing, and….

A gunshot rang out.

The beast turned a somersault, fell, rolled over, got up, and, taking flight, disappeared into the densest part of the thicket.

At the same moment, Robert and Pierre launched themselves into the open space in which the drama had just been played out.

"Bravo!" cried Jacques, delighted. "You're just in time, my friends. But for you, I was lost!"

Robert, carbine in hand, was watching the bushes through which the jaguar had frayed a path. He was ready to finish the animal off if he found an opportunity to take aim.

Jacques placed a hand on his arm.

"Leave it. It's no longer dangerous. No need to waste a second cartridge; our ammunition is too precious. And then, I've thought of something. Let's go back to the camp; we can rest for a few minutes and confer. I assume you found my knotted-string message back there, and were guided this far by my jacket hoisted on its pole."

Indeed, Robert and Pierre, not seeing their comrade return, having set off in search of him, had explored Alvarez' little house, deciphered Jacques' quipus and, having set out at first light, had been fortunate enough to find the trail marked by the droplets of red dye.

When the friends had brought one another up to date with their adventures, Jacques observed: "You're doubtless not yet aware that we're at the bottom of a veritable oubliette here. You've reached me thanks to the signal I exposed to your sight, but I defy you to find the breach by means of which you penetrated into the crater.

As the friends protested, Jacques told them about his vain efforts to retrace his steps.

"I'm not saying that we wouldn't end up finding the issue again after days of research, but for the moment, I think we have better things to do, if you're determined, as I am, to reach the sanctuary of the Incas. I've got an idea: a wounded animal, when it isn't mortally afflicted, tries to put the greatest possible distance between itself and the hunter. Our jaguar won't fail to follow that rule. If we follow its trail, therefore, we have some chance of finding a way out of the crater. We might, of course, come across its cadaver a few hundred meters away, but if it still has the strength, it might perhaps guide us all the way to the heart of the unknown land we've dreamed of visiting."

The three friends fell into agreement. Jacques' plan was adopted, and after having hastily absorbed a little nourishment, the little troop set forth once again.

The jaguar's trail was not difficult to find, thanks to broken or warped branches, trampled grass, imprints of its paws in the soil and the bloodstains that the wounded animal had left in its wake. But as it was going through dense thickets or chaotic terrain, the archeologists had to employ exhausting gymnastics to follow it.

They were, at least, recompensed for their troubles, for after hours of marching and numerous detours, they found themselves at the opening of a narrow canyon, in the depths of which a thin stream of water was flowing.

There, the traces of the animal became indistinct on the smooth rocky ground, but that was no longer of any importance; the explorers felt sure that they were on the right path.

IX

The moon had not yet risen, and dense shadow reigned in the depths of the canyon. Exhausted by a long and effortful day, the archeologists had called a halt at dusk at the entrance to a little cavern, which offered them a natural shelter. They had restored themselves with a few pieces of cured llama. Now they were exchanging their reflections in low voices before going to sleep, while keeping their ears pricked for noises from outside.

"Can you hear that kind of hoarse plaint?" said Jacques, suddenly.

They could, in fact, occasionally perceive a faint gasp, which also sounded akin to a mewl.

"That's our wounded jaguar," Jacques added, "dying somewhere nearby."

"That shouldn't prevent us from sleeping," said Pierre. "We have nothing more to fear from that direction."

In conformity with the rule of prudence that they were accustomed to observing, the explorers decided to take turns on sentry duty. Jacques, who was the least fatigued, took the first watch.

He saw the moon rise in the cleft of the canyon, which was suddenly bathed in soft light, which was nevertheless bright enough to reveal all the details of the landscape.

Armed with the carbine, which Robert had passed to him, Jacques remained crouched at the entrance to the grotto for some time, observing the rocks that extended toward the sky like walls or immense columns, and listening to the angry plaints that the jaguar uttered from time to time.

Then he stood up, took a few strides along the canyon, in the bottom of which the stream was silvered by reflected moonlight. He expected to perceive the recumbent body of the wounded animal.

As he supported himself against the cliff in order to clamber over a landslide he felt a block of stone vacillate under his hand.

He stopped, intrigued, and applied a more vigorous pressure. The block swung, uncovering an opening, a kind of doorway in the rock. Beyond that doorway, which seemed natural, Jacques perceived the first steps of a stairway open to the sky, over which a little moonlight descended, reflected from an overhanging cliff.

Having studied it momentarily, he returned to the cavern and woke Robert.

"Take over the sentry duty for me. I've found a passage that might lead to the Incas' holy city.

At first, Robert did not want to let his companion investigate the route he had discovered on his own.

"You'll only fall into the power of the Indians again," he said.

"In that case, Alvarez will probably consider that I've triumphed in the proofs to which he subjected me; but I'll remain on my guard, and I think it will be easier for me to pass unperceived by night than by day."

"Let's all go, then."

"No; experience has taught us that it's better not to risk all of us being captured at the same time."

Robert continued protesting for a little longer, but allowed himself be persuaded, and Jacques, having exchanged the carbine for a revolver, set off along what seemed to him to be a secret path dating from the time of the Incas.

He climbed a stairway of a hundred steps, carved in the rock, with occasional landings, and went through three doorways, which would have been easy to close and defend. He advanced cautiously, always afraid that an enemy might suddenly surge forth. There were, however, no unfortunate encounters, and, when he arrived at the top of the staircase, after having come through one last doorway, he suddenly discovered an astonishing spectacle.

He was in a vast enclosure formed by a natural rampart of cliffs, or perhaps constructed by human hands, which surrounded buildings grouped or isolated.

The holy city! Jacques said to himself. *I've discovered the secret of the Incas!*

The moonlight was bright enough to reveal to him the general character of an architecture that was quite familiar to a scientist like him: broad straight stairways, rigorous lines, windowless walls, doorways narrower at the top than the bottom.

Although there were a few sections of collapsed wall here and there, the ensemble was well conserved. This city, whose existence had remained unknown, had not been subjected, like the other vestiges of a vanished civilization, to the depredations of the conquistadors; the stones had not been taken away one by one to construct modern buildings.

What drew Jacques gaze most of all was, in the center of the city, an edifice larger than the rest—the only one that possessed a roof. That roof must have been reconstructed, or perhaps maintained, in the course of the ages, for the beams and thatch of which the Quichuas made use would not have resisted the erosions of time. The building in question was taller and slimmer than the neighboring edifices; a broad terrace formed a kind of pedestal for it, to which access was gained via a staircase occupying the entire width of the construction. And what struck the gaze first was a fire burning in the middle of the terrace, launching a high and vivid flame toward the sky. Colossal idols framed it, and to one side, Jacques thought he could see shadows, human silhouettes.

Thus, in this ruined city in the heart of a mountainous wilderness, there were mysterious inhabitants, or at least temporary residents.

Jacques had no doubt that Alvarez was here, with his band, perhaps in the process of presiding over some ancient ceremony.

He had seen enough for the moment.

I'll go back down to the grotto, he thought. *We're within reach of the goal, and it's not the time to get caught. Finally, our efforts will be recompensed, and I'll be able to demonstrate to Alvarez that I enjoy the protection of the gods.*

He started to go back down the steps to the bottom of the strange corridor hollowed out through the rock like a trench. He felt anxious, because he was, in effect, caught in a veritable mousetrap. If any Indians had been coming up at that moment, there would have been no way to escape them.

However, he was able to rejoin his friends without difficulty.

"We've found the holy city," he told Robert. "We're next door to a kind of secret entrance, and up there, the last depositaries of the religion of the Incas are apparently making preparations for a great ceremony."

"I've been thinking about that," Robert exclaimed. "We're in the vicinity of the June solstice, which, in this latitude, corresponds with the start of winter. Doesn't that tell you anything, Jacques?"

"Yes, you're right; that's the date of the great Festival of the Sun, Hatoun Raymi, which the Incas once celebrated every year, and which gave rise to grandiose manifestations." Jacques added: "Let's get a little rest anyway. Tomorrow will be a great day for us, and we need to be ready to profit fully from our victory."

Robert rolled himself up in his poncho again and went back to sleep.

Two hours later, relieved by his comrade, Jacques immediately fell into a deep sleep.

His brain, overexcited by the extraordinary adventures of the preceding days, evoked in his dream images of the ancient Empire of the Sun. Jacques found himself suddenly transported five hundred years back in time, into the great city of the Incas, Cuzco, their political and religious capital.

He penetrated into the Temple of the Sun, where a thousand virgins, consecrated to the divinity, had the mission to maintain the sacred fire night and day. The walls of the temple disappeared under ornaments of gold and silver. The paths that led to the sanctuary were paved with precious metal. The chalices, the ewers, the amphorae, vessels of every sort, and the least of utensils, were made of gold or silver.

Here comes the Inca, the omnipotent sovereign, a god on earth, who arrives in the temple followed by the aristocracy of his empire. He has descended from a golden litter at the door of the temple; his garment, woven from the finest vicuna wool, is dyed in rich colors and ornamented with a profusion of gold and precious stones. He coiffed in a *lantu*, a kind of turban decorated with a red fringe and two feathers from a coroquenque, a rare bird with rich plumage similar to a bird of paradise.[29] His eldest son, the legitimate heir, is walking beside him, wearing a lantu fringed with yellow.

Behind him, the princes of the empire who belong to the Inca's family make an imposing cortege for the sovereign. Nothing can be seen but crimson or saffron robes, scintillating gems, gold or silver necklaces, girdles and bracelets.

A crowd of worshipers is gathered on the parvis, and its members prostrate themselves as the man-god pass by. A choir of numerous voices chants a monotonous hymn, supported by an orchestra of drums and conches, five-note flutes and trumpets; and every time a verse ends, all the singers, as a sign of exaltation, clamor at the same time the word *hailly*, which means triumph.

In the temple, the Virgins of the Sun, with their robes women in golden cloth, appear in a splendid double row in the gold-paved pathway that the Inca will travel in order to reach the altar.

There, the priests of the Inca's family are standing; they have prepared, on a golden table, a pile of dried herbs and twigs, to which the Son of the Sun must set fire, as he does every year, marking by that action the grandeur of his mission on earth.

---

[29] *Trogon viridis*, the green-backed trogon..

To either side of the altar, strange individuals are sitting, ten men on one side and ten women on the other, clad in princely costumes, their tunics dyed red, their headgear ornamented with the royal insignia. They are motionless on their golden seats, their heads bowed, their arms crossed over their breasts. Their features are emaciated, their cheeks like parchment, their eyes closed. They are present at the ceremony but they are no longer of this world. They are the dead Incas and their legitimate spouses, whose embalmed bodies are deposited in the great Temple of the Sun.

The *villa vmu*, the high priest, has bowed before the emperor and handed him a silver mirror. The mirror is concave. Striking a hieratic pose, the Inca presents it to the sun, which is pouring its rays through a gap in the roof. He concentrates the light and heat of the star, directing them at a tuft of tinder, which smokes and bursts into flame, communicating the fire to the little pyre prepared by the priests.

Then, from all mouths, rises the hymn of gratitude to the god who illuminates and warms, who fertilizes the fields and the pastures, who makes the trees bear fruit and the herds increase. The Virgins of the Sun sway their heads coiffed with golden diadems; the priests sacrifice a llama at the foot of the altar. A young knight, his head crowned with chihuahua flowers, raises the standard of the Incas, on which the rainbow is deployed, the symbol of the race. Trumpets resonate, drums roll, and outside, throughout the city, where the criers are hastening to announce the miracle, the exultant people raise clamors.

X

"It's necessary," said Pierre, "that we find a means of making a sensational entrance to the city, in order to strike the imagination of the Indians; then they'll really take us for envoys of the gods."

Still under the influence of the marvelous dream he had just had, Jacques was pensive.

In the silence of the canyon, into which the rising sun was insinuating its light, the angry plaint of the wounded jaguar rose up again momentarily.

"That beast has a stubborn life," Robert murmured. "I hit it full in the body, and my bullet must have gone all the way through."

"It's like the cats that have to be killed nine times, according to the English proverb, in order to be sure that they're dead," Pierre observed.

After a silence, Jacques suddenly exclaimed: "Hey! I have an idea!"

"Naturally," said Pierre, admiring and amused. "You're a machine for fabricating ideas. Speak—we're listening with all the deference due to genius."

"If you mock me, I won't say a word."

"I'm sincere—word of honor! Come on, don't sulk. Tell us your idea."

"What if we made a triumphal entrance into the holy city escorted by a jaguar? That, I think, would be sensational."

"I agree—but I don't see…"

"Wait. I'll explain the plan."

Pierre raised his hand. Permit me to sit down comfortably, for I want to be all ears in order to lose none of the pleasure of listening to you."

"The jaguar is doubtless grievously wounded; otherwise it would have fled further way when it scented our presence. Nevertheless, I wouldn't be surprised if it still had enough strength to drag itself for a certain distance, and perhaps even defend itself if it sees itself threatened."

"Certainly," said Pierre. "I'd look twice before going to tease it in its lair."

"That's what we're going to do, though," said Jacques, "if you adopt my plan."

"What?"

"I propose to frighten the animal in order to drive it into the secret passage that leads to the sanctuary of the Incas, and chase it before us all the way to the city, where we'll arrive in the middle of the ceremony, guided like gods by the prince of the jungle."

"Not bad," said Robert. "It remains to be seen whether the jaguar still has enough life to accomplish the exploit, or whether it has too much left to obey us with docility. Suppose it turns against us."

"Then we'll be obliged to kill it, naturally. I can't promise you that my plan will succeed, but we can still try, because, if it does succeed, our triumph will be splendid."

"All right—let's try, then."

"You, Robert, go place yourself at the entrance to the secret stairway, across the canyon, to prevent the jaguar going back down to the crater we came from. Take the carbine. Only fire as a last resort, though, for if we sacrifice or lead actor, we won't be able to perform the play. Pierre and I will go higher up the canyon, striving initially not to disturb the wounded beast, and we'll go past it in order to block the passage upstream. Pierre will hold the revolver, ready to intervene in case of present danger. I'll have my spear, and I'll take charge of driving the animal to the entrance to the secret passage."

"Approved!" said Pierre. Turning to Robert, he asked: "What does the leader of the mission think?"

"The leader approves too, and feels obliged to express his congratulations to our friend once again."

"Don't compliment me until we've succeeded," said Jacques, modestly.

The archeologists immediately set about executing the plan that would permit them to appear so advantageously in the holy city of the Incas. Cautiously, Jacques and Pierre went up the canyon hollowed out like a corridor in the rocky massif.

A few meters above the point where the secret passage to the city ended, they perceived the jaguar lying in a cleft. The animal was extended on its side, its feet extended, its head supported on the rock. When the explorers went past it, it raised its head abruptly, uttered a brief roar of anger, and gathered itself, tucking its feet beneath its body.

"There's still life in it," said Pierre.

"So we have a chance of triumphing," Jacques replied. "Where there's life, there's hope! Listen—I'll drive the beast out of its hole by prodding it with my spear. Keep close to me, revolver in hand, but don't shoot unless I shout 'Fire!'"

The jaguar was surrounded. Robert was barring the way downstream and Pierre was menacing it from upstream.

Jacques, pointing his spear, advanced toward the animal, which, seeing him coming, raised itself up on its front paws and roared, opening an enormous maw armed with formidable fangs; then it dragged itself backwards, at the price of painful efforts, its rear end half-paralyzed. It was evidently incapable of pouncing, and Jacques sensed that he was the master of the situation.

With a thrust of the point, the explorer dislodged the beast from its refuge. Furious but impotent, the jaguar continued retreating before its enemy, making as if to leap at times, but falling back limply on to the rock.

In the end, the beast half-turned, and crawled as fast as its wound would permit in order to try to get away from Jacques' tormenting.

Robert saw it coming, and started shouting and waving his arms in order to frighten it.

Cut off, the jaguar hesitated, not knowing which way to go, sometimes turning toward Robert and sometimes toward Jacques, mouth agape and growling.

Jacques pricked it in order to drive it toward the secret stairway

With a desperate effort, the beast lifted itself up, lashing out with its claws. Jacques only just had time to leap backwards. He took his revenge by landing a heavy low with his stick on the jaguar's head; the latter recommenced beating the retreat and went into the secret stairway to the city, as the explorers wanted it to do, while continuing to exhale its rage in frightful roars.

"Hurrah! Victory is ours!" cried Pierre.

They had no more to do than follow the beast, which fled, crawling a certain distance when it perceived its enemies, then stopped, exhausted, and waited to be threatened again in order to drag itself further.

Preceded by that strange advance guard, the little troop reached the top of the stairway, and the jaguar, finding an open space, plunged on ahead.

Robert, Jacques and Pierre stopped side by side, observing the ruined city that extended before their eyes.

The temple that Jacques had remarked during the night was surrounded by a crowd of several hundred Indians, some clad in brown cloth or enveloped in ponchos, others adorned with red or yellow tunics, coiffed in feathered turbans, charged with girdles, necklaces or bracelets of precious metal.

On the parvis, the fire that Jacques had perceived was still lit between the stone colossi. Two men were standing in the center of the crowd, face to face, with their partisans behind them, and seemed to be trading insults. They were both richly adorned, as the Incas had been in the time of their power.

Scarcely had Jacques and his friends had time to glimpse the scene, however, than the appearance of the jaguar provoked a sudden metamorphosis.

The Indians had turned round and were gazing, with a stupefaction mingled with terror, at the beast that was crawling and roaring in front of the three white men. Intimidated, no longer knowing which way to beat a retreat, the animal had stopped, and contented itself with roaring, making supreme efforts to stand up on its buckling legs. It was exhausted, the sounds only emerging from its maw in gasps. At times it fell back. It was on the point of death.

A few more twitches, one last grunt, and it remained inert.

Then, proudly embracing the bewildered crowd with his gaze, Jacques advanced, followed by his companions, and the Indians stood aside respectfully to let him pass.

Robert and Pierre sensed all the audacity of the attitude that their friend had adopted. Only of the Indian chiefs only had to give a signal for the members of the meager little archeological expedition to be immediately massacred, and there would never be any further word of them, no one being capable of discovering what had become of them. They understood however, that Jacques' boldness was their only chance of success, and did not hesitate to take the great gamble along with him.

In one of the two men richly adorned and emplumed who were standing in the middle of the parvis, seemingly in confrontation, Jacques recognized José Alvarez.

The latter had turned toward him and was watching him come with an astonishment mingled with admiration and mystical dread.

Resolved to extract all possible advantage from the situation, Jacques shouted in Quichua, loud enough to be heard by the entire crowd, but addressing himself to Alvarez:

"I am here under the protection of Inti. The jaguar sent by him has guided my companions and me. We bring peace, not war. Let the sovereigns be good and clement to their people; let the sovereigns be reconciled; let humans unite in universal love, to render thanks to the gods!"

"Salutations to you, emissary of the omnipotent!" cried the Peruvian. "You have triumphed in the proof, and that is the sign of your divine mission. How can it be doubted that you have been sent by Inti himself, when your intervention has occurred at the precise moment that we have need of it?

"Approach and judge. Beneath the mask of José Alvarez, Peruvian of this century, I am the last of the Incas, descendent of Huascar, who was the victim of the conquistadors, and of his brother Atahualpa. Our oppressed race is not extinct, and the Sons of the Sun have succeeded one another, accomplishing here in the secret of the wilderness the rites of their religion.

"Thus, for four centuries, they have continued to reign over thousands of faithful subjects, unknown to the official government of Peru. They are waiting patiently for the moment to proclaim the resurrection of their murdered fatherland. Then their empire will be reborn and the astonished world will see, resplendent again, the great civilization of the Sons of the Sun.

"Fifteen of my ancestors and their spouses are there in the temple, sitting on golden seats, adorned by their royal vestments, sleeping their eternal sleep. Our priests have embalmed them and transported them to this mysterious sanctuary in order that they would not share the fate of the ancient emperors, who were despoiled, profaned and cast into the dust by the conquerors. I am their heir, and like my unfortunate ancestor, my name is Huascar…."

He was speaking thus when the individual confronting him, clad with the same richness and maintaining the same majestic attitude, interrupted him, crying:

"You are Huascar, descendant of Huascar, as I am Atahualpa, descendant of Atahualpa, and we both have, as a common ancestor, Huayma Capac, who was the last to reign before the coming of the Spaniards. In the same way that Huascar and Atahualpa had equal rights to reign over the empire four hundred years ago, today, we, Huascar and Atahualpa are equally well-founded in claiming the throne of the Incas."

"Atahualpa was not the son of a princess of the divine race. He could not, therefore, claim, as Huascar could, the heritage of the Empire."

"The mother of my ancestor was the Queen of Quito; her origin was no less divine than that of the Incas. And I ask who had more entitlement to exercise power: Atahualpa, who was capable of command and combat; or Huascar, who lived in softness and idleness, thinking of nothing but seeking pleasure?"

But the new Huascar cried, indignantly: "Have you, then, forgotten the treason of Atahualpa, who, to satisfy his ambition, delivered his empire to the adventurers without scruple?"

"Atahualpa was betrayed himself when he sought to save the empire from ruin."

The man that Jacques had known first under the name of Alvarez turned to the explorer.

"If it is in reality our father the Sun who has guided you and your companions here, decide between us. Here are our people, divided by our rivalry. Our partisans are threatening one another, ready to come to blows, and the vivid flame of memory that we have maintained piously for four hundred years might perhaps be extinguished by the wind of a new disaster. Then all hope will be banished from our hearts; we shall have to curb our heads and submit to the fatality that has changed the face of the world for us.

Atahualpa wanted to speak in his turn, but Jacques raised his hand in a gesture of appeasement, and said, solemnly:

"It is an evil day when sons quarrel over the heritage of their forebears. Are you not ashamed, when your people are in a state of ruination, mourning their treasures, their power, their lost religion, when they are reduced to searching their fatherland with anguish or the almost-vanished traces of its ancient civilization, to be disputing the right to save the memory of your ancestors? Do you not know that the law that presides over life, over happiness, over everything that is noble and great, is love? Love one another, and all hope will be permissible to you, but if hatred sterilizes your aspirations and your efforts, you will be swallowed up by oblivion."

Those words, to which Jacques had deliberately given a certain grandiloquence, made an impression not only on the two rivals but also on the several hundred Indians assembled around the temple, A murmur of approval rose up, and Jacques, sensing that he was understood and encouraged, continued:

"You are descended from the same ancestor and you were ready to take up arms against one another. Are you still astonished that men of different races cannot live in peace? If you want your empire to rise again one day from its ashes, it is necessary that you first learn the law of love, that you forgive one another your offenses and forget your rivalries."

Huascar, the Inca who was also the Peruvian Alvarez, extended his hand toward his rival, who was listening with his head bowed, his brow furrowed harshly.

"My brother," he said, "let us unite for the wellbeing of our people. Inti's envoy has pronounced words of wisdom. We are menaced by grave dangers from every direction; let us not add to them the more terrible one of hatred."

But Atahualpa, raising his head with an expression full of arrogance, proclaimed: "I cannot renounce a right that is the very basis of our empire. Rather war than abdication!"

Jacques extended a menacing hand toward the rebel.

"In the name of Inti, I pronounce judgment against you, who has not wanted to hear the divine words. There is only one Inca here whom everyone ought to obey, and here he is."

As he concluded that assertion, Jacques had turned to Huascar.

Atahualpa laughed, and said: "The judgment without value of an impotent judge!"

At the same moment he drew a blade that he was wearing at his side, and plunged toward the surprised Huascar.

The latter's partisans leapt forward, protecting their sovereign with a living wall.

Atahualpa, hesitantly, turned to dart a glance at his friends; he was awaiting their aid.

The Indians, however, were looking at Jacques. The presence of the envoy of the Sun intimidated them. How could they rise up against the order of the divinity?

Atahualpa saw that he had been abandoned.

Then, exasperated against the stranger who had intervened in such an untimely manner to ruin his prestige, he wanted to sacrifice him to his vengeance; he leapt forward, blade in hand, to slake his rage by sinking it between his ribs.

Pierre and Robert had advanced to stand beside Jacques, framing him, ready to help him at the first sign of danger. Their weapons thundered in unison.

Atahualpa collapsed, struck dead at the feet of Inti's envoy, without his partisans, completely subjugated, making the slightest move to attempt to avenge him.

In that circumstance, moreover, Huascar gave proof of his presence of mind.

"Glory to Inti!" he cried, prostrating himself before the trio of explorers. "He has signified his will to our people by striking our unfortunate brother, who listened to the inspirations of the evil spirit. I weep for Atahualpa, led astray by pride, and I order that honors be rendered to his remains. But hear the voice of the Lord, who wants you to be united under my power. Through me, you shall know renewal; through me, your fatherland and religion will be returned to you."

While Atahualpa's body was carried away, at a sign from the priests, Huascar turned toward the altar, where the sacred flame was burning, and extended his arms in a gesture of prayer.

"Glory to Inti, who illuminates and warms us! Glory to Inti, who makes our trees bear fruit and our herds increase!"

And the crowd repeated, ecstatically, in a single voice: "Glory to Inti!"

XI

An hour later, the archeologists were conducted solemnly into an immense hall, into which the light of day only penetrated through three doorways with oblique uprights. The walls were ornamented with plates of gold. The tables and chairs with which the room was furnished were also made of gold.

"They're worth millions," said Pierre, admiringly. "It's a pity we can't take home a few of those trinkets hanging on the walls."

"We aren't conquistadors," said Robert. "Their work of discovery would have been great without their cupidity, which debased everything."

"So," said Jacques, pensively, "not all the secrets of the Incas have been profaned. At least one city remains on which our modern civilization has not put its imprint, and in that city there's a temple that has retained its riches. I understand why Huascar/Alvarez was so hesitant to admit strangers into his sanctuary, why he raised so many obstacles before us and subjected us to such rude proofs. One indiscretion would be sufficient to attract a host of pillagers to this place, and the last treasure of the Incas would soon have disappeared forever."

Precious metals finely sculpted, imitated plants and animals. There were cornstalks with silver leaves and golden ears. There were figures representing the Sun and the Moon, Viracocha, the gods of the waters, Pachacamac, the god of fire, the divine serpents, and the condor, the messenger of the Sun.

Left alone in the room, the explorers were admiring it when Husacar rejoined them.

But he was Alvarez again, for he had abandoned his tunic and turban, and the Inca' adornments in order to resume his costume of red cloth and his flat hat—and he no longer spoke in Quichua, but in Spanish.

"I owe you, Señor Lasserre, as well as your friends, an infinite gratitude," he said to them, gravely. "Without you, it would have been all over for the last sanctuary of the Incas; civil wars would have annihilated that which the incursions of strangers has not yet destroyed. You were right to say that our gods were favorable to you, and I have no doubt that they did indeed guide you here, as you proclaimed before the assembled crowd. I therefore consider you henceforth as the benefactors of my subjects, and mine, not only as my guests but as dear friends, brothers who can demand anything from their brothers. Visit the city at your leisure, with its palaces and its temples; your hands, I know, will not profane them."

The Indian interrupted himself in order to collect himself momentarily, and then resumed in a more emotional voice:

"Nevertheless, I have one plea to address to you, and I remind you, Señor Lasserre, in that regard, of what you declared yourself ready to promise me, in order to obtain the right to visit our sanctuary. I implore you not to reveal the location, or even the existence of this city. The laws of the Peruvian State would soon be used to dispossess me, and the last heritage of the Incas would increase the profane wealth of our oppressors."

The archeologists looked at one another, hesitantly. Had they taken so much trouble then, and deployed so much ingenuity, to renounce taking advantage of the victory that they had finally won?

"Señor Alvarez," said Jacques, "can we appear to return from our expedition empty-handed?"

"Don't let that hold you back! I'll take you on a voyage such as no archeologist before you has ever boasted on accomplishing. Guided by me, you'll visit ruins that only initiates have known until now, grandiose vestiges of our past, whose discovery will make you famous, and which I'm ready to abandon to the curiosity of scientists and tourists, provided that this city remains inviolate."

The offer was tempting, and he three friends had not spent long years studying the civilization of the Incas without experiencing admiration and respect for it. They shared Alvarez' sentiments, when the latter feared that the holy city would be profaned and that its discovery would lead to its destruction.

They consulted one another with glances, and Robert, in his capacity as leader of the mission, declared: "So be it! We accept your proposition, Señor Alvarez, and we give you our word of honor not to betray your secret, the secret of the Incas."

That pact concluded, the explorers received a truly royal hospitality in the holy city. They stayed for a week in order to witness the festivals of Hatoun Raymi, and during that time, they forgot that they were Frenchmen in order to believe that they had been transported four hundred years back in time to the resuscitated empire of the Incas.

They went through the staircase streets, taking their curiosity from palace to palace, circulating in the citadel with square towers and the subterranean passages. The granite edifices had, for the most part, retained their imposing architecture. It would have been sufficient to reconstitute the roofs of wood and thatch to return them to their original appearance. Within the walls, enormous riches were still accumulated, for pillagers had not come to steal the gold and silver ornaments and utensils.

Finally, Huascar, the last of the Incas, set forth with his guests and an imposing cortege. Under his guidance, the mission made magnificent archeological discoveries, which repaid Jacques and his friends handsomely for their respect for the secret of the holy city.

They returned to Cuzco two months after their departure, accompanied by numerous porters laden with archeological specimens, and a businessman from Lima named José Alvarez, whose acquaintance they had made in the course of their travels.

A few weeks later, when they embarked for France, Alvarez accompanied them as far as the deck of the boat.

"I hope," he said to them as they separated, "that it won't be long before you come back. You will always be welcome in the house of Alvarez in Lima and the palace of Huascar in Tampu-Tocco, the holy city."[30]

---

[30] Hiram Bingham, who discovered Machu Picchu in 1911, thought that it must be the legendary Inca holy city of Tampu-Tocco, but that was pure speculation; however, the city's legend is associated with a different origin myth than the one earlier quoted by Jacques, which Alvarez endorsed, so there might be a hint of dissonance there.

SF & FANTASY

Adolphe Alhaiza. *Cybele*
Alphonse Allais. *The Adventures of Captain Cap*
Henri Allorge. *The Great Cataclysm*
Guy d'Armen. *Doc Ardan: The City of Gold and Lepers*
G.-J. Arnaud. *The Ice Company*
André Arnyvelde. *The Ark; The Mutilated Bacchus*
Charles Asselineau. *The Double Life*
Henri Austruy. *The Eupantophone; The Olotelepan; The Petitpaon Era*
Barillet-Lagargousse. *The Final War*
Cyprien Bérard. *The Vampire Lord Ruthwen*
S. Henry Berthoud. *Martyrs of Science*
Aloysius Bertrand. *Gaspard de la Nuit*
Richard Bessière. *The Gardens of the Apocalypse; The Masters of Silence*
Chevalier de Béthune. *The World of Mercury*
Albert Bleunard. *Ever Smaller*
Félix Bodin. *The Novel of the Future*
Louis Boussenard. *Monsieur Synthesis*
Alphonse Brown. *City of Glass; The Conquest of the Air*
Émile Calvet. *In a Thousand Years*
André Caroff. *The Terror of Madame Atomos; Miss Atomos; The Return of Madame Atomos; The Mistake of Madame Atomos; The Monsters of Madame Atomos; The Revenge of Madame Atomos; The Resurrection of Madame Atomos; The Mark of Madame Atomos; The Spheres of Madame Atomos; The Wrath of Madame Atomos* (w/M. & Sylvie Stéphan)
Félicien Champsaur. *Homo-Deus; The Human Arrow; Nora, The Ape-Woman; Ouha, King of the Apes; Pharaoh's Wife*
Didier de Chousy. *Ignis*
Jules Clarétie. *Obsession*
Michel Corday. *The Eternal Flame*
André Couvreur. *Caresco, Superman; The Exploits of Professor Tornada* (3 vols.); *The Necessary Evil*
Camille Debans. *The Misfortunes of John Bull*
Captain Danrit. *Undersea Odyssey*
C. I. Defontenay. *Star (Psi Cassiopeia)*
Charles Derennes. *The People of the Pole*

Georges Dodds (anthologist). *The Missing Link*
Charles Dodeman. *The Silent Bomb*
Harry Dickson. *The Heir of Dracula; Harry Dickson vs. The Spider*
Jules Dornay. *Lord Ruthven Begins*
Alfred Driou. *The Adventures of a Parisian Aeronaut*
Sâr Dubnotal *vs. Jack the Ripper; The Astral Trail*
Odette Dulac. *The War of the Sexes*
Alexandre Dumas. *The Return of Lord Ruthven*
Renée Dunan. *Baal; The Ultimate Pleasure*
J.-C. Dunyach. *The Night Orchid; The Thieves of Silence*
Henri Duvernois. *The Man Who Found Himself*
Achille Eyraud. *Voyage to Venus*
Henri Falk. *The Age of Lead*
Paul Féval. *Anne of the Isles; Knightshade; Revenants; Vampire City; The Vampire Countess; The Wandering Jew's Daughter*
Paul Féval, *fils. Felifax, the Tiger-Man*
Charles de Fieux. *Lamékis*
Fernand Fleuret. *Jim Click*
Louis Forest. *Someone is Stealing Children in Paris*
Arnould Galopin. *Doctor Omega; Doctor Omega and the Shadowmen* (anthology)
Judith Gautier. *Isoline and the Serpent-Flower*
H. Gayar. *The Marvelous Adventures of Serge Myrandhal on Mars*
G.L. Gick. *Harry Dickson and the Werewolf of Rutherford Grange*
Delphine de Girardin. *Balzac's Cane*
Léon Gozlan. *The Vampire of the Val-de-Grâce*
Jules Gros. *The Fossil Man*
Edmond Haraucourt. *Daah, the First Human; Illusions of Immortality*
Nathalie Henneberg. *The Green Gods*
Eugène Hennebert. *The Enchanted City*
Jules Hoche. *The Maker of Men and His Formula*
V. Hugo, P. Foucher & P. Meurice. *The Hunchback of Notre-Dame*
Romain d'Huissier. *Hexagon: Dark Matter*
Jules Janin. *The Magnetized Corpse*
Michel Jeury. *Chronolysis*
Gustave Kahn. *The Tale of Gold and Silence*
Gérard Klein. *The Mote in Time's Eye*
Fernand Kolney. *Love in 5000 Years*
Paul Lacroix. *Danse Macabre*
Louis-Guillaume de La Follie. *The Unpretentious Philosopher*

Jean de La Hire. *The Fiery Wheel; Enter the Nyctalope; The Nyctalope on Mars; The Nyctalope vs. Lucifer; The Nyctalope Steps In; Night of the Nyctalope; Return of the Nyctalope*
Etienne-Léon de Lamothe-Langon. *The Virgin Vampire*
André Laurie. *Spiridon*
Gabriel de Lautrec. *The Vengeance of the Oval Portrait*
Alain le Drimeur. *The Future City*
Georges Le Faure & Henri de Graffigny. *The Extraordinary Adventures of a Russian Scientist Across the Solar System* (2 vols.)
Gustave Le Rouge. *The Dominion of the World* (w/Gustave Guitton) (4 vols.); *The Mysterious Doctor Cornelius* (3 vols.); *The Vampires of Mars*
Jules Lermina. *The Battle of Strasbourg; Mysteryville; Panic in Paris; The Secret of Zippelius; To-Ho and the Gold Destroyers*
André Lichtenberger. *The Centaurs; The Children of the Crab*
Maurice Limat. *Mephista*
Listonai. *The Philosophical Voyager*
Jean-Marc & Randy Lofficier. *Edgar Allan Poe on Mars; The Katrina Protocol; Pacifica; Robonocchio; Return of the Nyctalope;* (anthologists) *Tales of the Shadowmen 1-12; The Vampire Almanac* (2 vols.)
Ch. Lomon & P.-B. Gheuzi. *The Last Days of Atlantis*
Xavier Mauméjean. *The League of Heroes*
Joseph Méry. *The Tower of Destiny*
Hippolyte Mettais. *Paris Before the Deluge; The Year 5865*
Louise Michel. *The Human Microbes; The New World*
Tony Moilin. *Paris in the Year 2000*
José Moselli. *Illa's End*
John-Antoine Nau. *Enemy Force*
Marie Nizet. *Captain Vampire*
Charles Nodier. *Trilby and The Crumb Fairy*
C. Nodier, A. Beraud & Toussaint-Merle. *Frankenstein*
Henri de Parville. *An Inhabitant of the Planet Mars*
Gaston de Pawlowski. *Journey to the Land of the 4th Dimension*
Georges Pellerin. *The World in 2000 Years*
Ernest Pérochon. *The Frenetic People*
Pierre Pelot. *The Child Who Walked on the Sky*
J. Polidori, C. Nodier, E. Scribe. *Lord Ruthven the Vampire*
P.-A. Ponson du Terrail. *The Immortal Woman; The Vampire and the Devil's Son*
Georges Price. *The Missing Men of the* Sirius

Edgar Quinet. *Ahasuerus; The Enchanter Merlin*
Henri de Régnier. *A Surfeit of Mirrors*
Maurice Renard. *The Blue Peril; Doctor Lerne; The Doctored Man; A Man Among the Microbes; The Master of Light*
Jean Richepin. *The Crazy Corner; The Wing*
Albert Robida. *The Adventures of Saturnin Farandoul; Chalet in the Sky; The Clock of the Centuries; The Electric Life; The Engineer Von Satanas*
J.-H. Rosny Aîné. *Helgvor of the Blue River; The Givreuse Enigma; The Mysterious Force; The Navigators of Space; Vamireh; The World of the Variants; The Young Vampire*
Marcel Rouff. *Journey to the Inverted World*
Marie-Anne de Roumier-Robert. *The Voyage of Lord Seaton to the Seven Planets*
Léonie Rouzade. *The World Turned Upside Down*
Han Ryner. *The Human Ant; The Superhumans*
Frank Schildiner. *The Quest of Frankenstein*
Pierre de Selenes: *An Unknown World*
Angelo de Sorr. *The Vampires of London*
Brian Stableford. *The Empire of the Necromancers (1. The Shadow of Frankenstein; 2. Frankenstein and the Vampire Countess; 3. Frankenstein in London); Eurydice's Lament; The New Faust at the Tragicomique; Sherlock Holmes and The Vampires of Eternity; The Stones of Camelot; The Wayward Muse.* (anthologist) *News from the Moon; The Germans on Venus; The Supreme Progress; The World Above the World; Nemoville; Investigations of the Future; The Conqueror of Death; The Revolt of the Machines; The Man With the Blue Face; The Aerial Valley; The New Moon*
Jacques Spitz. *The Eye of Purgatory*
Kurt Steiner. *Ortog*
Eugène Thébault. *Radio-Terror*
C.-F. Tiphaigne de La Roche. *Amilec*
Simon Tyssot de Patot. *The Strange Voyages of Jacques Massé and Pierre de Mésange*
Louis Ulbach. *Prince Bonifacio*
Théo Varlet. *The Castaways of Eros; The Golden Rock.; The Martian Epic* (w/Octave Joncquel); *Timeslip Troopers* (w/André Blandin); *The Xenobiotic Invasion*
Pierre Véron. *The Merchants of Health*
Paul Vibert. *The Mysterious Fluid*
Villiers de l'Isle-Adam. *The Scaffold; The Vampire Soul*

Gaston de Wailly. *The Murderer of the World*
Philippe Ward. *Artahe ; Manhattan Ghost* (w/Mickael Laguerre); *The Song of Montségur* (w/Sylvie Miller)

MYSTERIES & THRILLERS

M. Allain & P. Souvestre. *The Daughter of Fantômas*
A. Anicet-Bourgeois & Lucien Dabril. *Rocambole*
A. Bernède. *Belphegor*; *Judex* (w/Louis Feuillade); *The Return of Judex* (w/Louis Feuillade); *The Shadow of Judex* (anthology)
A. Bisson & G. Livet. *Nick Carter vs. Fantômas*
V. Darlay & H. de Gorsse. *Arsène Lupin vs. Sherlock Holmes: The Stage Play*
Séamas Duffy. *Sherlock Holmes in Paris*
Paul Féval. *The Black Coats (The Parisian Jungle; Heart of Steel; The Sword-Swallower; 'Salem Street; The Invisible Weapon; The Companions of the Treasure; The Cadet Gang); Gentlemen of the Night; John Devil*
Émile Gaboriau. *Monsieur Lecoq*
Goron & Émile Gautier. *Spawn of the Penitentiary*
Paul d'Ivoi. *Around the World on Five Sous* (w/Henri Chabrillat)
Rick Lai. *Shadows of the Opera: Retribution in Blood; Sisters of the Shadows: The Curse of Cagliostro*
Steve Leadley. *Sherlock Holmes: The Circle of Blood*
Maurice Leblanc. *Arsène Lupin vs. Countess Cagliostro; Arsène Lupin vs. Sherlock Holmes (1. The Blonde Phantom; 2. The Hollow Needle); The Island of the Thirty Coffin; 813; The Many Faces of Arsène Lupin* (anthology)
Gaston Leroux. *Chéri-Bibi; The Phantom of the Opera; Rouletabille & the Mystery of the Yellow Room; Rouletabille at Krupp's*
Richard Marsh. *The Complete Adventures of Judith Lee*
William Patrick Maynard. *The Terror of Fu Manchu; The Destiny of Fu Manchu*
Frank J. Morlok. *Sherlock Holmes: The Grand Horizontals; Sherlock Holmes vs Jack the Ripper*
Jean Petithuguenin. *The Adventures of Ethel King*
Antonin Reschal. *The Adventures of Miss Boston*
P. de Wattyne & Y. Walter. *Sherlock Holmes vs. Fantômas*
David White. *Fantômas in America*
Pierre Yrondy. *The Adventures of Thérèse Arnaud*

www.ingramcontent.com/pod-product-compliance
Ingram Content Group UK Ltd.
Pitfield, Milton Keynes, MK11 3LW, UK
UKHW041409180426
11947UKWH00007B/31